C000003969

PARADIGM

S A CARMODY

KMCS Publishing

Copyright 2021 © by S A Carmody

www.kmcspublishing.com

www.sacarmody.com

Publishers note: This is a work of fiction. Names, characters, places, places and incidents are a product of the author's imagination. Locales and public names are sometimes used for atmospheric purposes. Any resemblance to actual people, living or dead is completely coincidental.

Cover and Layout Design by Richell Balansag

Paradigm/SACarmody. – printed 2021.

ISBN 978-1-7398387-0-6 Paperback

To my wife and soulmate Beryl, whose love,

encouragement, kindness and sheer brilliance lights up my every

day.

She came into my world and showed me how to let it

'SHINE'

AND

To a pertinacious superhero whose patience, skill, humour

and suggestions…

Are constantly teaching me how to 'Fill my little world

right up.'

CONTENTS

CHAPTER ONE

It was a damp, early autumn evening; the last of the daylight was beginning to fade, and the fog was slowly descending on the stumpy brown hair of the skinny, bedraggled child. Oblivious to the elements, she remained sitting on the wet pavement, leaning against the wall of the shop car park.

There was a constant flow of people entering and leaving the shop. Many deliberately avoided eye contact with the scruffy, beaten teenager. Others tentatively approached her, only to swerve away at the last second, afraid that even speaking to her would leave them open to accusations of wrong-doing. Others, a gang of three men in their twenties, approached her and invited her to their house for "a drink." Meg was fourteen, but looked much younger. After everything that had happened to her, she knew exactly what they wanted, and it was much more than a drink.

The nearby church bell chimed to signal seven p.m. Meg realised she had been sitting in the same place for six hours. She groggily considered options where to sleep that night. A small, local railway station was nearby. But the indoor waiting rooms were firmly locked on an evening, directly after the last train had made its stop; something she discovered the night before when she searched for eternal darkness, not shelter.

Staring at her torn shoes, feeling physically and emotionally battered, she suddenly jumped in fright as her name was spoken.

'Meg?' A familiar-sounding voice made her look up cautiously. She saw a tall, medium-built woman with short blonde hair, wearing a business suit and carrying a container of milk hovering above her.

'Jo?' Meg whispered so quietly her voice was not audible over the passing cars on the main road behind her.

'What on earth are you doing sitting here?' Jo demanded. 'You must be freezing! Come on. Get into the car, and I'll take you home.'

Meg shook her head. 'I would rather die than go back there.' She spoke louder, her voice hoarse after almost twenty-four hours of not talking or drinking.

It was then the woman noticed the bruising on Meg's face and the dark bruising around both wrists just visible in the remaining light.

The woman spoke with greater urgency. 'Will you come and sit in my car? Just to warm up?'

Meg was unsure; she did know the woman and felt reasonably safe with her, but even the most well-meaning adults always thought they knew best. 'Do you promise not to drive off and take me back to the home?'

'Yes, I promise, but I will turn the engine on to make the car warm as you're shivering. Come on.' She held out her hand. Meg looked at it for a while, then hesitantly took it and stood up with a groan, her body aching from sitting for so long.

'If you start to drive, I'll jump out!' Meg stated.

'No driving unless you agree. I promise. Please get into the car.'

Jo ushered Meg into the passenger seat before getting in and turning on the engine, then putting the heating to its highest setting. Meg shivered violently. Her teeth chattered, and her damp clothes began to make the car windows steam up as the hot air hit them.

Then, a heavy silence fell in the car; Meg was not bombarded by questions. Her body began to warm, but her fear left a chill deep inside her. Meg's aching muscles remained tense and alert, ready to run as soon as they sensed danger.

Meg was with one of the few people in the world she didn't feel completely unsafe with. Joanne McGloughlin, the head of the City's Youth Service department. Jo had overseen and spent many evenings at a new youth centre, for which she had fought to gain funding. Her job was to train the new manager and staff and encourage young people, mainly in the care system, to come along.

Meg was in one of the first groups to attend with some children from her kids' home. None of them wanted to go, but the staff at the home threatened them with a loss of pocket money if they didn't attend at least one.

Meg, who had an intrinsic distrust of adults, was surprised when she and Jo hit it off. As Meg slowly thawed with Jo, they spent a lot of time talking, playing pool, and Jo taught her to play chess, much to the disgust of the other kids from her home, who called her a creep.

Jo's visits became less frequent as the centre began to take shape, as did Meg's, due to events in her life dictating her attendance. When the centre was fully set up and running, Jo returned to her nine-five office job. Meg was angry at being abandoned again and slightly relieved as the shame became somewhat more bearable when she could disappear into the shadows once again.

But now, there she was, sitting in Jo's car, on a Friday night, well out of work hours. 'Do you want to tell me what happened?' Jo asked so kindly that Meg wanted to cry.

Silence fell once again. Meg couldn't bring herself to meet Jo's eyes, never mind describe the latest in a long line of terrors she had been subjected to.

'The bruises on your wrists.' Jo turned on the light inside the car. 'They appear to be fairly new; they look like fingermarks. Were you grabbed? Or held down? You don't need to talk. Please nod if I'm right.'

Seconds went by; Meg took a deep breath, attempting to inhale some courage from the hot car, and hesitantly nodded.

'Did this happen today?'

Meg shook her head.

'Last night?'

The trembling child nodded.

'Have you run away from the children's home?'

Meg nodded again and began to sink into the memories of the night before.

'Do you think you can look at me a little, so we can talk?' asked Jo, bringing Meg back to the present.

Meg hesitated and started shivering again, more from fear than cold.

'Take your time,' Jo said calmly. 'We can stay here for as long as you need.'

Meg watched the minutes tick by on the dashboard clock.

'I don't know what to say,' she eventually blurted out. 'Or how to say it.'

'Can I be blunt?' asked Jo.

Meg looked away and shrugged.

'Were you raped?'

Meg's stomach churned and bile rose into her mouth. Jo slowly reached for Meg's hands and separated them. Meg noticed the blood marks from where she'd been unknowingly pressing her fingernails into her other hand.

She gave Jo a darting gaze and then held her head in her hands, eyes scrunched shut. 'Yes,' she answered tonelessly.

'I'm so sorry, Meg.' Jo was desperate to hug the girl but afraid that she would run away. 'Was it by someone who you know?'

Meg nodded, her head still in her hands.

'Was it another young person at the home?'

'No. They're all away on a half-term holiday except for me.'

'A member of staff?'

Meg winced at Jo's words and her hand jerked towards the door handle in terror. 'Please don't go, Meg,' pleaded Jo. 'I'm on your side and here for you.'

Meg's shaking hand released the handle. She cleared her throat. 'Yes. A member of staff.'

'You don't need to go into detail, but can you tell me when and where, and how you ended up sitting in the shop car park?'

'It was last night. He was the only one working. I stayed in my room reading, and he came in and...'

'You're doing great,' Jo assured the trembling child. 'Can you tell me what happened next?'

'He attacked me and walked out. He didn't say anything. The fire escape is in my room; the alarm on it broke ages ago, so I quickly left straight away in case he came back. I couldn't stand it all anymore. I tried to fight him off. I didn't let him!' said Meg, her voice getting louder. 'I went to the train station, but it was locked. So, I walked around all night, I think. I don't really remember. I spent a few hours trying to sleep on the floor of a garage in the garden of an abandoned house, but I heard footsteps and ran away. Afterwards, I stuck to park benches and then came and sat here hours ago as I couldn't walk any further.'

'I'm so sorry,' said Jo, trying to disguise her emotions from coming out in her words. She opened the milk container she had just purchased from the shop. 'Drink this. You need to hydrate.'

Meg gratefully took the carton and gulped the milk desperately; she was so thirsty, and the cold drink felt like the best thing she'd ever tasted.

'Thanks.' Meg gasped in relief when she had finished. 'Sorry I drank so much.'

'Keep hold of it. Drink as much as you like, and then, will you let me take you to the police station?'

'*No*!' shouted Meg. 'They won't believe me!'

'They will. You're covered in bruises. Are you still wearing the same clothes as when... as when it happened?'

Meg nodded.

'Please let me take you to the police station. It's the only way to do something, and maybe your only chance. It's basic procedure to report a child missing. If the police find you, they might not listen to you and return you to the home. You will have been reported missing by the care worker. He'll be worried you'll talk, but it would make him appear more guilty if he hadn't reported that you'd absconded. This is your chance to tell your story. Maybe your only chance.'

Meg didn't speak and began to shake again. She looked at Jo, her eyes showing pain and conflict.

'I don't like the police. They won't believe me.'

'They will! You have evidence, and I will demand they listen and take you seriously. I will stay with you all night if I need to and ensure they do not send you back to that home. Please... trust me.'

Meg was tearful and couldn't answer. Trust was one ability that had left her many years ago. She swore to herself not to trust anyone ever again. It was too dangerous.

'Can we go?' Jo persisted.

'They'll tell you horrible things about me, and then you'll leave!'

'I don't think they will, Meg, and on the off-chance they do, I will not leave. They *will* listen to you!'

'And you'll definitely stay, no matter what?'

'I promise.'

'Why?' Meg's eyes narrowed as she looked suspiciously at the woman.

'To make sure you're listened to and to be there for you, nothing else. The monster who attacked you needs to be locked up. You have the power to do that. It won't be easy, but I promise I will stay,' Jo said with total sincerity.

'All right,' Meg whispered, still not fully trusting that Jo would stay, but she realised her only other option was the police finding her on the streets and taking her back to the home. To him.

The police station was cold and impersonal. Meg sat down on a hard, plastic chair which was bolted to the floor, while Jo went to the desk to speak to someone before joining her. Ten minutes later, a woman in a smart suit appeared.

'Megan Walsh?' she enquired. Jo nodded on Meg's behalf.

'Would you both come this way, please?'

Meg and Jo followed the woman to a less formal room that had a sofa and armchairs.

'I'm Detective Sergeant Murray,' the woman said. 'I work with children who are victims of sexual assault. I did a quick check on your name before coming down to meet you. There is a report to say you have absconded from Crookshaws Children's Home, is that correct?'

Meg nodded.

'Can you tell me what happened?'

Meg remained quiet, staring at the floor.

'Can I explain who I am and tell her what you told me?' asked Jo.

Meg didn't respond; her muscles twitched as her panic grew into the urge to run.

'I'm the head of youth services for the city,' said Jo, firmly taking hold of Meg's hand. 'We set up an evening and weekend youth centre, mainly aimed at children in the care system to keep them from hanging around the streets. I built up a good rapport with Meg while overseeing the setup, and we talked a lot. She came to every session in the early days. Then, both of our visits became more erratic. On the increasingly rare occasions when we were there simultaneously, Meg appeared to be on edge and would occasionally have facial injuries. Meg said they were a result of fights at the home. I contacted the home and spoke to a couple of staff members about this. They confirmed it.'

'Yeah, bet I can guess who you talked to!' Meg snorted.

'Who?' asked the police officer.

Meg looked away and refused to answer. It was pointless; they wouldn't believe her.

Jo went on to explain everything that had occurred in the shop car park.

'Can I ask why you didn't go on holiday?' asked the police officer.

'The staff organise a half-term holiday every October. But you're only allowed to go if your school attendance is three weeks or more and you haven't got into trouble. I did the three weeks, stayed out of trouble, but then I lost my homework. My teacher said I was lying, but I wasn't! Anyway, I swore at her and got suspended, and that was the end of the holiday. He hid it because he was on the duty rota to stay behind with any naughty kids!'

'Who is he, and for what reason?' DS Murray asked.

'Javeed! They wanted to get me alone.'

'They?'

'Sorry, I meant hhhim,' croaked Meg.

'I spoke to the home when I raised concerns about your injuries,' Jo said. 'Javeed on one occasion, and Peter on another.'

'I know!' Meg glared at Jo. 'They would have told you I'd constantly been fighting. Check the incident reports at the home; there won't be any of me fighting. They lied to you, and you believed them!'

'Right!' said DS Murray assertively, moving the conversation away from Meg and Jo. 'This all needs to be recorded. Firstly, we will send some officers out to arrest this Javeed, and we'll talk more later. Right now, we need to do some examinations and keep your clothes for testing. Will you let us do this?'

'Where will you send me after? I can't go back to Crookshaws!'

'One thing at a time, Meg,' said Jo gently. 'Please will you have the examinations? They will be difficult, but the police need the evidence to lock this creep up.'

'Will you stay with me?' Meg asked begrudgingly, feeling conflicted. She was angry that she needed Jo, and yet she didn't want her to leave.

Jo glanced at the officer, who nodded. 'Yes, of course. Every step of the way.'

Meg went into a changing room and entered a cubicle alone, while Jo took a seat on the other side of the curtain. Meg took off her clothes and put them in the bag she was given, then a woman came in and photographed her bruises. Meg was given a hospital-type gown to wear; she reluctantly put it on and opened the curtain to find Jo waiting.

'Was that part, okay?' Jo asked quietly.

Meg didn't reply as a doctor entered the room and gently asked her to lie down on a trolley. She gently explained to Meg what she was going to do and did her utmost to put the trembling girl at ease.

Swabs were taken; she lay terrified and in pain, but Jo held her hand and whispered calmingly to her, telling her it would be over soon. When it was finally over, the police gave her a white jumpsuit and showed her the shower room where she could wash away the shame and disgust which imbued every pore of her being. Meg stayed there for twenty minutes, scrubbing her skin until it was red and painful.

Tentatively drying herself, she put on the thin, uncomfortable, scratchy jumpsuit and stepped out of the shower room.

'Sorry about the suits,' DS Murray said, who was waiting with Jo. 'They're not great. Are you ready for the interview?'

'Ccccan Jo stay?' Meg asked, frustrated at her stammer returning.

'Not in the interview room; it can only be you, a social worker, and me,' the DS replied. 'Jo will be able to view everything. You won't be able to see her through the double-sided glass, but she will only be a couple of metres away. The interview will be recorded, and we'll be in the lounge where you sat earlier. You are so brave, Meg. One last bit to go, then you can rest.'

'Where? I'm not going back to the children's home.'

'The duty social worker is coming down, and we'll find you somewhere for the night, so don't worry.'

'Not a kids' home or foster home. They know all the locations, and they'll find me.'

'They?' asked the DS.

'I meant hhhhim...' said Meg, her eyes exuding terror.

'Meg, is there more than Javeed and Peter involved in this?'

Meg looked away, refusing to answer as Jo and DS Murray exchanged concerned looks.

'Come on, Meg. I'll show you to the interview room, and I'll join you shortly. Jo, would you mind waiting here a minute?'

Jo nodded and added to Meg, 'You won't be able to see me, but I'll be close by, and I promise I won't leave.'

Meg nodded as she was led away to the interview room, where another, younger police officer was waiting. 'Hi, I'm Liz,' said the woman. 'I'm going to wait with you until the interview begins.'

DS Murray left the room and met Jo. 'The social worker has arrived,' she said. 'I think we need to talk to my Inspector before the interview, don't you?'

'Yes,' said Jo firmly. 'Obviously much more is going on than Meg is able to say. I began to suspect something wasn't quite right towards the end of my time at the youth centre. She became less chatty and withdrawn as the weeks went by. But both of our visits became infrequent. I was hoping to wrangle some time alone with her to talk, but I was only there to set up the project and train the new manager. Then I was back in the office. I didn't see her at all for the last two weeks of my placement. I was informed that she appeared a couple of weeks ago, asking if I was around and abruptly left when the staff said I wouldn't be coming back. I gave my mobile number to them, just in case Meg returned, but she left so quickly they didn't have the chance to give it to her.'

Steph Myers, the on-call social worker, was shown in to the Inspector's office to meet with DS Christine Murray, Jo, and Inspector Gina Phillips.

'Have we met before?' Jo asked Steph after the introductions. 'You look familiar.'

'I don't think so,' Steph replied, 'but I meet so many people every day, and my memory for faces is shocking!'

'Moving on.' DS Murray addressed her Inspector. 'Ma'am, we have a fourteen-year-old who alleges that she was raped by her care home worker. However, at times, she's referred to them, or they. She has said another care home worker is also in collusion, but I believe there is reason to suspect that more than two individuals are involved in this sexual abuse.'

'Do you mean an OCG? An organised crime gang,' the Inspector clarified for Jo, who was looking confused.

'I think so. We will arrest the care home workers, but I want to search their home premises and the children's home. We can keep them locked up for the weekend, so I want a thorough, slow, and careful search for evidence.'

'Fine,' said the Inspector. 'I'll organise a warrant. What about the victim? If a gang is involved, she'll need to be somewhere safe, unregistered. Any ideas?' She looked at the social worker.

'If an organised gang is involved,' Steph began in a considered voice, 'they'll be aware of every home and foster place in the city. They'll be able to find her no matter where she is. My advice is that she's kept in protective custody, in a secure unit, until we can find somewhere suitable. I can see no other solution.'

'You mean lock her up?' spat Jo. 'Do you have any idea what this girl has been through? She already blames herself! She'll think being locked away is a punishment. She needs care and looking after.'

'I'm aware!' said Steph, rubbing the back of her neck. 'But other than arranging to send her to the other end of the country, what else can we do? If it is a gang, they *will* find her at any registered home. They will have knowledge of them all, and the kids they're already grooming will talk.'

'She can stay at my house,' said Jo impulsively. 'I can show you my full police check and my husband's, so getting it approved won't be difficult.'

'Excuse me,' said Steph. 'Procedure does not allow a child to go to someone's house on a whim. They need vetting or, at the very least, it needs to be approved by someone higher up.'

'That won't be a problem,' said Jo calmly.

'Well, I'm afraid it is.' Steph snapped, her face turning red.

'I'll ring the Director of Child Services now.' Jo pulled out her phone.

'That's not possible. He is definitely not at work as my office is next to his, and I saw him leave hours ago.'

'I didn't realise you knew each other,' Jo said, and Steph looked puzzled. 'Also, you are correct. The Director of Child Services is not at work. He'll be at home wondering where the hell I am, considering I rang him on my way home from work to say I was stopping at the shop to pick up milk.'

'What?' demanded Steph, turning even redder.

'Sean McGloughlin is my husband, and Director of Child Services.' Jo looked at the Inspector.

Jo went outside to explain the situation to her husband and returned a short time later, passing the phone to Steph. The social worker said many 'yeses' and 'of courses' before ending the call, appearing to be unsettled by the turn of events.

'All approved,' snapped Steph to the Inspector. 'Meg can go home with Jo if she agrees.'

Everyone focussed on the Inspector. 'Fine,' she said. 'Ensure the paperwork is in order.

The child's location stays in this room only. DS Murray, can you delegate paperwork immediately and keep it strictly confidential?'

'Of course, Ma'am.'

'Also, the FME, the police doctor, has reported that Meg needs an x-ray, as she suspects some broken ribs judging by the bruising. However, another complication has emerged in respect of having an x-ray.'

'Why?' asked Jo. 'I can take her for an x-ray.'

The Inspector hesitated and picked up the medical report on her desk.

'We undertook a urine test during the examination... Meg is pregnant. Obviously, it won't be from the most recent attack as it'll be too early to tell, but it proves this is not the first time she has been assumedly raped. She'll need an ultrasound to discover how many weeks she is. It will help with evidence, but she'll also need to make some decisions about the situation.'

'Does she know?'

'No, not yet. I suggest we do the interview first and obtain as much information as possible, and I'll inform Meg afterwards.'

'Can we wait?' asked Jo. 'I'll tell her and take her for an ultrasound, but only when she's ready.'

'It needs to be soon,' urged the Inspector. 'We have to find out how many weeks or months pregnant she is, as things become more complicated the longer we leave it.'

'I'm aware. I'll tell her soon and give her time to talk and think. We'll ensure the scan is done by next Friday. A few more days won't make much difference.'

'I agree,' added DS Murray. 'Let's get the interview done so Meg can go and rest. Giving the statement will be hard enough. I'm keen to progress before she changes her mind.'

'Fine,' said the Inspector. 'Focus the interview on what happened last night. Ask about other involvement afterwards, but don't push it. We need the evidence to lock up the care home worker who she said raped her and have him remanded in prison. As soon as you arrest him, seal his home and the kids' home. Search for mobile phones, computers, find out if he rents any flats, storage units, or uses any separate sheds or garages. Also, find this Peter and question him. I suggest we all meet on Monday, without Meg, to discuss it further and form an action plan. Go and interview Meg,' the Inspector said to DS Murray. 'And ensure this hideous man is kept in a cage!'

'Ma'am,' Murray nodded as they all stood to leave.

'I need to ring home again,' said Jo. 'I'll meet you in the observation room.'

'Please tell me the second she is ready for the scan,' said the Inspector. 'I'll book it as part of a police investigation and ensure she's in and out with no waiting rooms or questions.'

'Surely I should handle this,' the social worker interjected. 'Meg is only staying with the McGloughlin's for the night, so...'

'I suggest she stays with us for at least the weekend and Monday until after the meeting where we can discuss this properly,' Jo said.

'Agreed,' Inspector Phillips ordered. 'Inform me of what is said in the interview asap.'

The DS and social worker nodded and headed towards the room to interview the terrified child.

The interview room had soft, almost homely seating, Meg thought. They'd tried to make it comfortable. Still, the large black wall which was one side of the double-sided mirror removed the illusion of homeliness, as did the video camera and equipment.

DS Murray and the social worker entered, both with deep frowns on their faces. The junior officer was dismissed.

'This is Steph Myers, the duty social worker,' said DS Murray. 'My name is Christine,' she added. 'I am only DS Murray for the purpose of the tape. Call me Christine. Call me nothing if you like. Your choice. Before we begin, I want to tell you that I believe you completely, but I will need to ask some difficult questions. Please remember that I am on your side. You are so brave to have done so much this evening. I can only imagine how exhausted you are, but this is the final part for today, then you can go to bed.'

'Where?' asked Meg quickly.

'If you want to, you can go and stay with Jo and her husband. Would you like that?'

'I think it might be okay to stay with Jo,' Meg said hesitantly. 'But I'm not sure about staying with a strange man.'

'Meet him first, and if there are any worries, ring me, but I can assure you that you will be safe. They are good people. Are you ready?'

Meg stared at the black window. She couldn't see anyone, and she desperately hoped Jo hadn't suddenly changed her mind and gone. She then heard a throat clearing, and Meg knew it was Jo sending a message to say she was near.

Meg took a deep breath and looked up. 'Yes, I'm ready.'

CHAPTER TWO

Meg found the journey to Jo's house difficult. She didn't think Jo would hurt her, but this man, the husband, being trapped in a building with an unknown man, terrified her.

'I'm not… err, sure about this,' Meg said hesitantly.

'About what?' Jo asked.

'Your house and that man.'

'My husband, do you mean?'

'Yes. I don't want to sound ungrateful, but it might be better if you let me out here, and I'll sort myself out.'

'No, sorry. You're in my care, and whether that be for one night or a few days, I won't allow you to wander around the streets alone at night, or during the day, for that matter. You have the number for DS Murray. If you feel scared, you can ring her, and she will arrange somewhere else for you. I know you don't totally trust me, or anyone, but please believe me that neither Sean nor I will ever hurt you.'

'Sean?'

'My husband. He's worked with children since leaving university. He isn't violent or inappropriate, I promise. I know you're scared of men, and rightly so, but Sean isn't scary. He's the most caring man I've ever met. Hey, I married him, didn't I? Would I marry someone awful and unkind?'

Before Meg could question Jo further, they pulled into the drive of a pleasant-looking house. It was two a.m., and they were both exhausted. 'Sean is waiting up for us,' explained Jo.

'Wwwhy?' Meg stammered, her breath speeding up as her chest tightened with fear.

'Because he's concerned and angry about what happened to you, and he wants to meet you and also make sure that I'm okay.'

Meg stared at her feet again.

'Come on. You need a hot drink, a snack, and bed.'

Meg reluctantly got out of the car, her legs shaking. Jo opened the door, and they walked into a lovely, warm, cosy house.

Meg noted that the front door had a latch, but also a lock that needed a key. This caused anxiety, as it limited her escape route. The door was around two metres from the foot of the stairs. The laminate flooring in the hallway led to the kitchen directly ahead. There were two doors to the left of the corridor before reaching the kitchen.

'You are safe here,' Jo said, noting Meg's assessment of the building. 'If you want to leave at any point, please don't run away. Tell me, and we will call DS Murray.'

A large man appeared in the kitchen doorway; he was at least six foot five inches, very broad and muscular, with stubbly brown hair. The sheer size of him terrified Meg.

'You must be Meg.' He spoke in a low, deep voice before moving to give his wife a quick kiss. 'I'm getting hot chocolate and crumpets ready. Would you like butter and honey on them?'

'Yes... pplease,' Meg whispered with difficulty.

'Great,' said Jo. 'While they're cooking, I'll show you where you're sleeping.'

'I'll bring them up,' Sean said to Jo and Meg, who were making their way up the stairs. 'Just call when you're ready.'

Jo showed Meg into a comfortable attic bedroom with a single bed made up with what appeared to be new sheets. She saw pyjamas and a dressing gown on the bed.

'Do you want to put your pyjamas on?' You can't be warm in that... suit.'

'My pyjamas. What do you mean?'

'I rang Sean earlier when we decided at the police station that you were coming to my house. I asked him to go to a 24-hour supermarket and pick some things up for you. Just something to sleep in and some things to wear for a few days.'

Meg scowled at the clothes in front of her.

'What is it?' Jo asked.

'I'm not a charity case!'

'I know, but you can't access the children's home, so some emergency shopping was rather essential. Would you like me to leave the room so you can change?'

Meg glanced at Jo, who saw the fear in Meg's eyes.

'I know, I'll turn around. Tell me when you have your pyjamas on,' Jo said reassuringly.

'What if… what if... that man comes in?'

'Sean won't come anywhere near until I shout for him.'

Jo turned around, and Meg uneasily put on the pyjamas, which felt so comfortable after the prickly all-in-one white police suit.

'I'm done.'

Jo turned to face Meg, surprised to find tears welling up in her eyes as she saw how young and small Meg looked in her slightly oversized pyjamas.

'Is it okay if I shout Sean to come up with our drinks and crumpets?'

'Will you stay?'

'Of course.'

'Sure,' uttered Meg faintly.

Two minutes later, Sean appeared with two steaming mugs of hot chocolate and buttery crumpets oozing with honey. The smell made Meg's stomach rumble; she had barely eaten in days.

'Here you go!' Sean proudly produced a tray of food and drink and placed it on the bedside table.

'Meg, I've put a bolt on your side of the door. I want you to feel safe. You are, but you need to know it and be in control of it.'

'You've been busy,' said Jo, smiling at him.

'Well, I'll leave you to it.' He returned his wife's smile, then, looking at Meg, he added, 'Goodnight. It'll be nice to chat tomorrow. I hear you're a football fan. We'll definitely need to talk about that team of yours.' He headed to the door, grinning.

Meg mustered up a weak smile. 'Thank you for the food and hot chocolate,' she muttered, relieved the man was leaving. His size made the room feel tiny, and Meg realised her hands were shaking.

'Come on,' Jo said. 'Get into bed. I'll sit in the chair next to it, and we'll eat. Can I suggest we don't talk any more about the past few days? I want you to eat and sleep for now.'

'How did he know what football team I support?' Meg snapped.

'That's down to me. I would talk about you from time to time. I missed you when you disappeared, and I was worried.'

'I'm sorry.'

'There's nothing to be sorry for.' Jo insisted, and firmly changed the subject. She began to tell Meg about her work and where she was from, and just general chat until they'd finished eating.

'Why don't you lie down and get under the duvet? You still seem to be cold.'

Meg did as she was told, and it felt amazing to put her head on a soft, clean pillowcase.

'Do you want me to leave now?'

Meg felt conflicted. She wanted Jo to go, but she also wanted her to stay. 'No,' she said eventually. 'Bbbut only if you want to stay. You don't need to...'

'I want to stay,' Jo answered reassuringly. 'Can I sit on the side of the bed and hold your hand?'

Meg shrugged and then nodded. Her teeth were still chattering, and she felt like ice.

'I'm going to lie on top of the duvet and put my arm around you. I'm worried about how cold you are. Is that okay?'

Meg nodded.

Jo lay down, and despite her mind telling her to keep away, Meg snuggled closer to her until she found herself encompassed in a huge, desperately needed, hug.

'You've been so brave, Meg,' said Jo, stroking Meg's head. 'I'm so proud of you, and I'll make sure you're safe.' Jo's gentle voice carried on until she noticed Meg was fast asleep. She lay there watching the sleeping child, feeling sickened and devastated by the horrors that had been inflicted on her.

Finally, she got up, quietly, said goodnight to the tiny-looking child, and silently left the room.

Meg woke the following day and was hit by the silence. She was used to waking up to shouting, sounds of fighting, windows being smashed, police sirens, and fire alarms blaring.

All she could hear were birds tweeting outside the window and the occasional car passing on the street below. Realising she was desperate for the toilet, she wasn't sure what to do and was too scared to go wandering about the house.

Half an hour passed, and she couldn't hold it anymore. She crept out of bed and opened the door. Apprehensively, she popped her head out onto the landing. There was only a staircase ahead, and no other rooms, so she had no choice but to go down the creaky stairs to the next floor.

There were lots of doors, all closed, and she stood there almost in tears. Her urge to wee was nearly beyond control. Sean suddenly sprang out from one of the rooms, whistling away to himself. He jumped as he saw Meg standing on the landing, and she also jumped.

'Are you okay?' he asked and silently berated himself, realising what a stupid question it was. 'I mean, do you need something? We wanted you to sleep as long as possible, so we tried not to disturb you.'

'Bathroom,' whispered Meg.

'Door in front of you. I know you won't have had time to explore, but there's an en-suite in your room.'

'Thanks,' said Meg, making a run for the door ahead of her, wondering what an en-suite was.

She sat down and gave a huge sigh of relief as her bladder emptied. Tentatively leaving the bathroom, feeling sick to her stomach with fear about being in a strange house, she was immensely relieved to see Jo sitting on the bottom step opposite the bathroom.

'Morning!' She smiled. 'I'm so sorry. I forgot to tell you there's a small bathroom in your bedroom.'

'Is that what an en-suite is?'

'Yes. Come on. I'll show you.'

They went back up the creaky stairs to the attic. 'These stairs have come in very handy over the years.'

'Why?'

'Well, before we had the extension, one of the kids had a bedroom up here. The creaky stairs were convenient for when they were sneaking into or out of the house late. The stairs always gave them away.'

'What did you do to them?'

'They'd normally end up being grounded or given a long, boring job to do, or worse, a very long conversation with Sean and me. We have never hit any of our children if that's what you are thinking. Still, they invented some amazing ways to try to get down these steps without touching them. It never worked, but their ingenuity was impressive.'

Considering this information, Meg continued up the stairs and into the bedroom. Jo came in and walked over to a door that Meg hadn't noticed and opened it. 'Here you go. Basic en- suite. A shower, and a toilet. Saves you having to go downstairs if you need the loo in the night.'

'Does anyone else use it?'

'No. It's just for this room and whoever sleeps in it. Now, can I suggest you look in the wardrobe, pick out some clothes, then have a shower and get dressed? They might not be perfect, but they'll do for now. The police doctor said you had a lot of bruising on your back and ribs. Do you mind if I have a look? It'll be good to keep an eye on them over the next few days.'

Meg stared at Jo angrily, but seeing the care in her deep blue eyes, she turned away and hesitantly lifted the bottom half of her pyjama top.

Jo's eyes widened in shock as they focussed on the black bruising all over Meg's back. 'Can you turn around so I can see your stomach and ribs?' she asked gently.

Meg turned around and displayed a mass of both new and older, more yellow bruising all over her stomach and ribs.

'Are you able to walk without them hurting?'

'They still hurt, but it's worse when I'm in bed or sat down.'

Jo silently cursed herself for not offering Meg painkillers the night before. 'Why don't you have some breakfast, some paracetamol, and we'll wrap up and go for a walk. Would that be okay?'

'Where to?' Meg demanded, looking scared.

'I know some lovely places about a half-hour drive away from here. Would you like that?'

Meg stepped back, crossing her arms tightly around her chest and staring unblinkingly at Jo.

'What is it?'

'Where will you take me after the walk? Will you take me to somewhere I know? Iiii…' Meg punched her forehead with both fists, as though to dislodge the stuck word.

'Meg.' Jo took a step towards the girl. 'It's just a walk. We will go in my car and then come back to this house, in the same car. I promise I won't leave you.'

Meg saw the sincerity in Jo's eyes and, once again, felt her stomach spin and acid rise as the prospect of trusting someone brought on the usual fear.

'Okay,' she muttered, looking away from Jo.

Jo smiled and Meg watched carefully as she left the room. Locking the door, Meg went to the wardrobe and found lots of comfy clothes, all roughly her size. Feeling mortified that Sean had bought her knickers, she snatched a pair and headed off for a shower.

Meg went downstairs; her wet, short hair was still dripping. Jo passed her a towel. 'Here, dry your hair. You'll be freezing outside.'

'I always let it just dry on its own.'

'Not today. Just rub it dry. Your breakfast is just there on the side. We'll go as soon as you've finished.'

Meg made a feeble effort of rubbing bits of her hair with the towel, feeling a bit confused.

She was not the only one.

'Meg, do you know how to dry your hair?' Jo asked.

'I'm doing it!' she snapped, immediately regretting her tone. 'I'm sorry I didn't mean to...'

'Don't worry. Now give me the towel.' Jo reached for it and then proceeded to rub Meg's hair vigorously.

Sean walked in and grinned. 'Oh, no! Our kids used to run a mile when Jo tried to towel dry their hair. One even

33

accused her of trying to make him bald! He was a bit dramatic. Still is, though,' he added thoughtfully. 'I'm sure you'll be fine!'

'Shut up, Sean,' said Jo light-heartedly. 'There, done. Do you want a comb to tidy it up?' Meg didn't answer and just gave Jo a withering glare.

'I'll take that as a no, then!' she grinned at the irritated child.

After a breakfast of scrambled eggs and toast, which Meg wolfed down, Jo appeared with a worn-looking waterproof, lined coat.

'One of my old ones. It's too big, but it'll keep you dry and warm. Are you ready?'
Meg shrugged, so Jo gave her the coat and told her to put it on and led her to the car.

They travelled for around fifteen minutes, Jo navigating her way through the busy roads. Then they hit the countryside and narrower lanes. Meg was taken aback at how peaceful the view of expansive fields and trees felt.

She observed farmers' fields full of cows and sheep that were happily grazing on the almost bare pastures. But it was the silence that struck Meg, who realised that she hadn't been around true silence in a long time.

Parking near a massive reservoir, Jo got out of the car and waited for Meg to follow.

'Do I have to wear this coat?' she asked, disgruntled, flapping her arms to show that the sleeves were a good ten centimetres longer than her arms.

'Yes,' said Jo, rolling up Meg's sleeves. 'You're what? Five foot two? And barely over five stones, I imagine. I'm five foot ten, so yes, the coat is huge on you, but it'll keep you warm and dry. You certainly need to eat a lot of pies!'

'Pies?' exclaimed Meg, startled. 'Why have I got to eat pies? I don't think I even like pies...'

'It's just an expression.' Jo cut her off, laughing at Meg's outburst. 'I just meant that you need to have a lot of good meals and put some weight on.'

Jo then set off briskly; Meg had to almost run to keep up with her. Remembering Meg's injuries, Jo fell back to a slower pace. They did an entire lap of the vast body of water without speaking.

'How are you?' Jo asked as they began the second lap.

Meg frowned and kicked a nearby stone into the water.

'I'm not going to try to make you talk to me, Meg, but I will listen.'

Another five minutes passed without a word until Meg said, almost in a whisper, 'Scared.'

'What are you scared about?'

'Those... I mean that man in the kids' home.'

'But there isn't just one man in a kids' home, is there, Meg? Other people are involved in this, aren't they?'

Meg nodded.

'Do you want to tell me?' Meg shook her head.

'I've got something tough to tell you,' Jo said gravely.

'I know you're chucking me out when we get back. It's okay. I knew it was temporary.'

'Absolutely not!' said Jo. 'You are going nowhere until the police have more information. What I have to say is a lot harder.'

For the first time during the walk, Meg glanced up at Jo's face and noted uncertainty in her normally sparkling eyes.

'What is it?'

'You're pregnant, Meg. It showed in your urine test yesterday.'

Meg stopped walking; her face turned so white that Jo thought the girl was about to faint. Suddenly, Meg ran over to the nearest tree, leant against it, and vomited. Jo came over, making soothing noises and rubbing Meg's back until there was nothing left to come up, and she was dry-heaving.

'Stand up straight, Meg, and take a deep breath.' Meg did as she was told. 'And another breath.' Meg inhaled. 'Brilliant, and another. Now have a drink of water,' Jo said, passing a bottle to her.

'I need to sit down.' Meg gasped. 'I feel dizzy.'

Jo guided Meg to a nearby bench, and Meg sat hunched over, with her head facing the ground.

'Keep taking deep breaths,' said Jo softly. 'It will help you feel less dizzy.'

Meg shivered in the autumn sunshine. Jo moved closer and put her arm around her.

'You're in shock. I'm so sorry this happened. We will get through it, I promise.'

'We?'

'Yes, we! When the police interviewed you, you only said it was the man in the home that had attacked you, but a few times you said "they". Who are they?

'It takes two weeks minimum for a pregnancy to show up on a urine test,' Jo continued as Meg remained silent.

'So, it wouldn't have happened on Friday night, which leads me to think one of two things. Either the same man attacked you several times, or there are more people involved. I'm not saying you have to tell me now, but for your safety and the safety of the others, we need to find out.'

'How long am I staying at your house?'

'I don't know. Sean and I are going to a meeting with the police and social care on Monday.'

'With me?'

'No. They requested that you didn't attend as they've searched the care worker's houses and the children's home. If they've found any evidence, then there may be certain things they can't tell you about yet as it may jeopardise your case.'

'*It's a meeting about me!*' shouted Meg, making an elderly couple passing by walking their dog jump and glare at Meg. '*What are you staring at?*' she demanded, glaring as they hurried off.

'Come on,' said Jo. 'Let's walk some more.'

'No! Not unless you make them let me go to the meeting.'

'It's not going to happen! On your feet. You need to move.'

Meg glared at Jo, who didn't break eye contact, and then slowly dragged herself up to stomp after her.

They did another lap of the reservoir in silence, Jo's pace getting brisker as they moved.

Meg did start to feel a little better for moving but didn't want to admit it.

Breaking the silence, Meg suddenly tried to talk, but the words struggled to come out. 'Hhhhh.... Hhhhhow llllllong...' she managed to say before punching a tree in frustration.

'I don't know how far along you are. What I do know is that we need to find out soon.

'You need a scan at the hospital sometime this week.'

'Why?'

'To check the age of the foetus.'

Meg looked at Jo in confusion.

'I'm not going to call it a baby, Meg. What you have is the potential of life inside you. We need to find out the age of it, so we can talk about your options and also get a clearer idea of when this happened.'

'I want to go now!'

'Now? Are you sure?' You're still in shock. Wouldn't it be better to wait a few days?'

'Please, Jo!' begged Meg. 'I need to know.'

Jo considered the child in front of her for a while. 'Okay, it's your choice, but I'm not sure. I'll ring the Inspector. She'll book us into a private room so you won't have to wait around.'

Jo walked away and made a phone call. She finished speaking and stood motionless, looking over the water. Her phone rang two minutes later. Meg couldn't hear what she was saying, but Jo, probably for the first time since she'd met her, appeared unsure.

She walked back to Meg. 'If you're still sure, we can go now. The Inspector has spoken to the hospital. You can still change your mind, though.'

'I want to go,' said Meg, sounding determined.

Jo attempted a reassuring smile that was more of a strained grimace. 'Come on, then.'

They made their way back to the car and took a silent forty-five-minute drive to the hospital.

Upon arrival, Jo gave Meg's information, and they were ushered into a private waiting room. Minutes later, a woman entered.

'Meg?'

Meg and Jo nodded.

'The room is next door. Will you follow me?' Her voice was friendly and reassuring to Meg, who was terrified, but she was certain the woman would consider her to be a dirty and disgusting person.

Meg and Jo stood and entered a small, dark room that contained a hospital bed, screens, and various other complicated-looking equipment.

'Would you mind pulling your trousers and underwear down slightly and tucking this in?' asked the woman, handing Meg a large piece of what felt like scratchy kitchen roll.

Jo helped Meg tuck it in properly, and then she was asked to lie on the trolley. She cast a nervous glance at Jo, who quickly took Meg's hand and guided her to the trolley. She sat down, feeling extremely vulnerable.

'You're doing great, Meg,' whispered Jo, while still holding her hand. 'And you are safe.'

'Would you mind lying down fully?' asked the sonographer. Meg glanced at Jo for reassurance and complied.

'Now, I'm going to squeeze some gel onto your stomach. Don't worry, it's not cold. Then I'm going to run what's called a transducer around your lower- stomach area then look at the screen and take some photos. Are you ready?'

Meg nodded and lay nervously while a ball-like implement was rolled up and down her stomach. 'Okay, I just need to turn the volume up.'

The woman turned a knob on the machine, and Meg heard a beating noise.

'I want to see the screen!' Meg demanded.

'Meg, I don't think...' began Jo.

'I want to see!'

The woman turned the screen to face Meg and Jo; they saw what appeared to be a reasonably small sack with something moving inside it.

'What's moving?' Meg asked, her eyes narrowing in confusion.

'The heart. If you listen, the movements correspond to the sounds. It's a tiny heart beating.'

'How pregnant am I?'

'Approximately nine weeks.'

'Can you tell me what date you think it'll be born? Does your computer know?'

'*No*!' said Jo loudly. 'Don't push me on this, Meg. The answer is no, and that's final.'

'Tell me!' Meg pleaded with the sonographer.

She glanced at Jo, who firmly shook her head.

'I'm sorry. The police have asked me to find out how far gone you are. That's the only information I can give.'

'This is bullshit! I've got a right to know.'

'It won't help,' said Jo gently. 'We'll talk about it when we get home. Are we finished?' The sonographer nodded.

Meg refused Jo's help to get off the trolley. She got down alone and wiped the gel aggressively from her stomach. Angrily she threw the tissue paper in the bin and stormed out of the room.

'Thank you,' said Jo to the sonographer and rushed out to catch up with Meg.

Jo finally found her leaving the front door of the hospital.

'Meg! Wait for me!'

'No! I'm going.'

'Going where?'

'Anywhere away from people. I want to be on my own.'

'I can't let you do that. It's dangerous. Something is going on, and I've got a fair idea what. I'm not letting you go off on your own. You're staying with me so no one can find you. You are not safe out there alone!'

'*You've no idea what's going on*!' screamed Meg as she continued marching out of the hospital grounds.

Jo grabbed her arm to stop her. 'I do know what's going on! Or at least, I think I do. Do you want me to tell you?'

Meg slumped, all of her anger turning into sheer exhaustion. She shook her head.

'Come on. Let's get you something to eat and back to bed. You're exhausted.'

Jo gently guided Meg to her car, and within half an hour, was back in Jo's house, in her pyjamas, and tucked up in bed with Jo sitting next to her. Meg snuggled in and fell asleep almost instantly.

CHAPTER THREE

Meg glanced at the clock when she woke, shocked to see she had slept for eighteen hours. She thirstily gulped down a glass of water that had been placed on her bedside table at some point, then went to the en-suite, thankful she didn't need to go downstairs.

Unsure what to do next and feeling self-conscious about being in someone else's home, she sat and stared out of the window. It was a beautiful autumn day again. The sun reflected on the newly brown and golden leaves; she watched as they fell off the trees and lazily floated to the ground.

Meg's mind drifted to the past six months of hell, during which she was constantly on guard and hurt, abused, bullied, and terrified. No matter how many times she washed, she couldn't remove the dirty, disgusting essence of shame and self-disgust. She blamed herself for every single thing that had happened to her. And now, a pregnancy; it was too much to process.

Meg recalled the night she ran away. She knew they would find her unless there was nothing left of her to find. She recalled why she'd headed to the train station. She knew, without hesitation, that she was prepared to step in front of the next train and end it for good. That sensation of having control over her own life, finally, felt strangely empowering. She got to decide how to end it, not those ruthless, evil monsters who had killed before and would do it again. She was determined not to die by their command.

The numbness of her body spread to her brain. Meg felt as though she were floating out of her body, watching herself move as she entered the en-suite and searched the small cabinet above the sink. Not finding what she so desperately desired, she opened the bedroom door and heard faint noises from the kitchen. Feeling safe, she crept down to the bathroom on the floor below and found precisely what she needed.

Creeping upstairs again, not entirely avoiding all the creaking steps, she made it to her room and bolted the door behind her. Taking the packet of razors out of her pocket, she easily released the blades from their safety cases, as she had done many times before. Holding one of the blades firmly, she began with her forearm. Digging the edge of the sharp metal into her skin, she applied pressure and ran it quickly up her arm. Watching the skin separate and the blood seep out, Meg sensed some of the tension leave her body. She then dropped her arm and observed in fascination, the blood travelling towards her hand in swirling lines. *Almost like a creek*, she thought, her mind now entirely dissociated from the present.

She sliced her arm again, this time in a different place and applying more pressure, and then repeated it over and over.

Deciding the time was right to proceed with her plan, she looked away from the blood covering her forearms, clothes, and dripping onto the carpet, reached for a fresh blade, and turned her arm around. Meg inserted the corner of her blade deeply into her wrist and prepared to force it up her arm, through her skin, veins and arteries, and ultimately obtain the oblivion she craved.

Taking what she hoped would be a final, deep breath, she focussed her mind on the result, not the pain that was about to come.

She forced the blade deeper, and her adrenaline surged. She was ready to end it. Meg moved the blade a fraction and jumped as there was a massive bang, and the door literally flew off its hinges and landed halfway across the room.

Sean charged in and yanked the razor blade from Meg's hand, and Jo followed, immediately grabbing a towel and bound Meg's wrist with it. Sean grabbed another towel and wrapped her arm. They held it with an unyieldingly firm grip and hoisted her arm into the air, not releasing their tight hold for a second.

'*Get off me!*' shouted Meg, trying to escape.

Jo and Sean put Meg into a sitting position on the bedroom chair so she couldn't move.

They both kept their insanely tight grip on her elevated wrist and arm.

It took at least five minutes for the towel to stop showing more blood. Jo cautiously moved the towel away from Meg's wrist and had a look.

'You didn't hit an artery.' She gasped, wiping away the mixture of sweat and tears that were rolling down her face.

Sean removed the other towel from her arm. There was still some slight bleeding from a particularly deep cut, but it was little more than the odd drop.

'Come on,' demanded Jo, marching Meg firmly by the uninjured arm out of the room, followed by Sean, and they went to the middle floor bathroom. Sean wrapped another towel around the cut that was still bleeding and applied tight pressure, and held it in the air again while Jo got out the first aid box.

'I'm not going to hospital!'

'I'll be the judge of that!' Jo said firmly, getting out antiseptic wipes and steristrips. She cleaned the cuts, which were still bleeding a little, and examined the hole in Meg's wrist where she stuck in the edge of the razor blade. Jo moved methodically, almost professionally, dabbing bits here and cleaning bits there and ordered Meg to keep her arm up in the air. When the last drop of blood had finally stopped, she painstakingly attached the strips across the cuts.

'Can I put my arm down now?'

'No!' said Jo and Sean in unison. They observed Meg's arm and wrist for another five minutes until satisfied that there was no more bleeding, and that the cuts remained powerfully bound. Jo then wrapped a bandage securely around the damaged arm.

'Luckily, I bought a new pack of razors and went for a shave when I did,' Sean said gravely.

'Also, lucky that those creaking stairs can be heard from the kitchen!' Jo added.

'Can I go back upstairs now?' asked Meg, staring at her shuffling feet.

'No. You're staying where one of us can see you today,' Jo answered. 'And I think we need to talk, don't you?'

'No!'

'I do, Meg. Come on, downstairs."

'I'll go clean up the bedroom,' Sean announced after Jo looked at him in a way that let him know she wanted some time alone with Meg.

In the kitchen, Meg waited as Jo made two cups of hot chocolate in grim silence.

'Come on,' she said to Meg and carried two cups into the lounge. 'Take a seat.'

Meg sat down as far away from Jo as possible, so Jo moved a chair and sat directly opposite Meg.

'Drink!' ordered Jo. 'You need something warm and sweet.'

'How does your arm feel?' asked Jo after a few minutes of silence.

'I can't feel it.' Mumbled Meg.

'You will do later. It will sting and itch. You mustn't scratch it. I'll check the dressings tonight.

'Did you intend to kill yourself?'

'Yes!'

'Why the cuts on your forearm then?'

'Getting my technique right,' came the flat reply. 'And I was about to when...'

'When the door came flying across the room,' Jo replied dryly. 'As soon as Sean came down to look for his razors, and we realised we'd heard the stairs creaking only ten minutes before, I just knew. If it had been ten seconds later, you probably would have died. Is that what you really want?'

Meg nodded and stared at a spot on the carpet. 'I'm sorry,' she mumbled. 'I shouldn't have done it in your house.'

'It's not about where! It's about why. Have you tried to... have you attempted this before today? I noticed the scars on your arms. Older ones.'

'I've cut myself a lot in the past,' Meg said, embarrassed. 'It makes me feel better. The night I ran away from Crookshaws, the night before you found me, I was going to walk in front of a train. But the trains had finished for the day as it was so late. I was going to do it the next day, but I was confused and so tired, I just sat down in that car park; I couldn't move anymore.' The desperation in her eyes made Jo shudder. Noting this, Meg quickly turned her head towards the window.

'I'm so sorry,' Jo began. 'Will you come and sit on the sofa with me? Please?'

Meg shuffled to the sofa, head down, feeling ashamed. Jo sat close to the child and held her hand gently. 'Do you think you would be able to tell me if you were thinking about hurting yourself again?'

'I'm not doing it for attention!' Meg barked. 'When I cut myself, I feel less angry, less dirty, and like... I don't know, kind of like I'm in charge of my body.'

'I understand,' Jo replied. 'I really do. I certainly do not believe anyone would hurt themselves for attention. I know it's not about that.'

'Some people think it is, like the staff at the kids' homes.'

'Well, they need some training then!' Jo retorted angrily and put her arm protectively around Meg, who snuggled closer.

'Are you angry with me?' Meg suddenly blurted out.

'I'm not angry,' Jo said softly. 'I'm worried about you. You tried to kill yourself. I'm devastated for you and want to help. I really didn't want you to go for the scan yesterday; it was too soon.'

Meg sniffed and angrily wiped away the tears that were rolling down her face. 'I needed to do it! I've seen it now. I thought it would have arms and legs.'

'Not at this stage. It's too early. But what else did you think? When you saw that screen, I mean.'

'I don't know. I want to think and sort it out in my head, on my own!'

'Meg, please let me in, just a little more,' pleaded Jo. 'You've been so brave in telling me what you have, and I want to help you with this. You can't do it alone, and you don't have to.'

'Yes, I can. I've done nearly everything on my own. And I did let you in a little, and then you dumped me!' Meg snapped. 'You got me to trust you and then left me, like they all do!'

'I was setting up the centre, and I enjoyed talking to you and spending time with you, but you knew I wouldn't be there forever. I did begin to wonder if other things were happening. You became more withdrawn and anxious, and I had planned to talk to you about them, but you disappeared. But I didn't "leave you." I did what I was there to do. For the record, I missed you afterwards and thought about you a lot, and yes, we grew close. I wanted to talk to you about our relationship and maybe us meeting up occasionally.

'My official work came to an end. If I had anything more than a feeling you were being abused in care, I'd have acted on it. I even talked to the safeguarding team, but, and this is no fault of yours, they said they couldn't proceed just because I felt something wrong. Was the abuse happening when I was working with you?'

'It started a couple of weeks after I started coming to the centre.'

'And it has carried on for the past six months?'

'Yes.'

'I'm so sorry. Can you tell me who was involved?'

'I told you already.'

'You're not telling me the full story, Meg.'

'What does it matter to you? You're seeing those social workers tomorrow, deciding on where to dump me, and I'll never see you again.'

'It's not the only reason for the meeting, but yes, your longer-term living arrangements will be a factor. And I am going to insist that some urgent therapy is arranged for you…'

'No way am I seeing some therapist. I've been dragged to two different ones, the first one said she felt really upset and wanted to cry for me, she was pathetic.'

'And the second one?'

'He tried to get me to play with a load of baby toys that were in his office. I told him what to do with them and walked out.'

'The therapists, did you see them before the sexual abuse started?'

'Yeah. Some social worker sent me because he said I had anger issues and said I needed to talk about my parents. The therapists gave me more anger issues instead of taking them away!'

Jo stifled a grin at Meg's account of the therapists. 'You will need to see one, a specialist therapist who can help you get through this.'

'Not going to happen! Can I go now?'

'Where to?

'Upstairs.'

'No. Sean is still cleaning up and putting the door back on, and I'm not letting you out of my sight today.'

'But you are tomorrow, so I can do what I want.'

'Actually, no, you can't. I believe you'll be at risk if left alone, so I'm going to ask the Inspector to send a police officer to come and sit with you.'

'I'm not spending the day with some copper!' Meg shouted. She jumped off the sofa and made to leave the room.

'Don't you dare leave this room!' ordered Jo, her tone of voice sounding very different.

Meg halted in her tracks and glared at Jo with a whole load of insults on the tip of her tongue, but she couldn't say them. Not to Jo. Not after what she had just put her through.

'Please sit down again,' said Jo in a softer voice, attempting to de-escalate the situation. 'I won't try to make you talk any more or discuss therapy. Not today, anyway.' They continued staring at each other. 'Please...'

Meg backed down, nodded, and sat on the sofa. Jo grabbed the remote control.

'Shall we watch something easy and switch our brains off for a while?'

'Sure,' came Meg's shaky reply.

'What do you fancy?'

'I don't know. Will you choose?'

Jo nodded and began to scroll through the options when Sean entered. 'Time for a film, I see! But, please, no romantic clap-trap!'

Meg was surprised to hear a slight laugh come out of her mouth. It wasn't what he said, it was how he said it that made her laugh.

'Ever seen *The Quiet Man*, Meg?' he asked, and Jo groaned. Meg shook her head.

'Perfect Sunday afternoon film! But you'll need to vote with me, or Jo won't let me watch it.'

'I'll give it a go,' Meg answered hesitantly.

'Hmmm,' said Jo. 'I feel rather ganged up on here! Okay, *The Quiet Man* it is, for the thousandth time!'

As the opening credits rolled onto the screen, Jo put a cushion onto her knee. 'Come lie down, Meg.' She patted the cushion. 'You'll need to watching this film!'

Meg hesitated and then put her head onto the cushion on Jo's knee and curled up, still shivering slightly from the shock of earlier. Jo reached for a throw from the top of the sofa and put it over the child.

'Is it okay if I put my arm around you?' Jo asked.

Meg nodded and allowed the blissful calmness, warmth, and safety to wash over her as scenes from the old Irish fields flashed before her eyes. She was asleep within minutes, as was Sean. Jo turned the volume down and closed her own eyes. Exhaustion from the past few days, and that morning, hit them all, and the three-hour film ran without anyone seeing it.

'Glad you all enjoyed the film!' Sean said, and Jo and Meg immediately woke, startled. Meg saw the closing credits of the film rolling.

'I think you'll find you were the one to fall asleep first,' said Jo. 'Your marvellous film selection sent us all to sleep. I'll choose next time! Your own choices obviously bore you.'

'Huh,' he said, switching channels to the news and a politician speaking enthusiastically about why his party cared about the poor.

'Yeah, right,' said Meg out loud. 'The cost of living has gone up since this lot took power. Wages have barely risen, especially for the working class, and nurses and teachers. He's talking rubbish.'

Sean looked at her in surprise. 'How do you know that?'

'I'm not stupid!'

'I don't think you are. But I don't know many fourteen-year-olds who could reel those figures off.'

'I try to read newspapers when I find them on benches, and in the library, they had books there too, about politics. I was never allowed to take them out, I wasn't a member and the staff wouldn't help me join. But I've always loved reading and I hate liars.

'A couple of million unemployed, and food banks are being used for people who work a forty-hour week, never mind the homeless. They also voted against tougher regulations on landlords. And most of them own at least one extra rental home. They make me sick.'

'Me too,' said Jo.

'And me,' added Sean. 'Have you always been interested in politics?'

'Yeah. I prefer American politics, it's weird that someone can get the most votes and not become president as it's down to the Electoral College.'

'Think you'll need to give me a lesson on that over dinner. I've never quite understood how their elections are won and lost. But before that, is there anything you would like to watch?'

Meg glanced at the clock and nodded shyly.

'What is it?'

'Can we have the football on? It's Man United vs Arsenal.'

'Fantastic choice!' Sean burst out, looking excited.

'Oh, no!' Jo put her head into her hands.

'What?' asked Meg quickly.

'Sean is a massive Arsenal fan, I don't think I can stand being in the room while the pair of you are shouting for different teams. I need calm! I think I'll go to the shop and get something for dinner. It'll be ready at full-time.'

But she was barely heard as Sean changed the channel and turned the volume up, and the roar of the crowd began blasting through the speakers. Jo slid out of the room and put her coat on. Heading out, she paused at the lounge door and listened with a slight grin, happy that Meg felt comfortable to be left with Sean for a little while.

Meg watched the match with Sean. It was a tense affair, and she tried her best not to swear. It was strange as she didn't feel scared of Sean, but she was worried he might get angry if she swore at the TV.

After an ill-tempered match with three penalties, two sending offs, half a dozen yellow cards, and a 2-2 draw, Jo popped her head around the door.

'Come on. Dinner's ready.'

Meg and Sean trudged to the dining room and sat down to an excellent-looking roast dinner.

'It looks lovely,' remarked Meg, astonished that, not only could someone produce such a fantastic-looking meal, but she was allowed to eat it.

'Thank you!'

'You're welcome. Now tuck in.'

They ate in thoughtful silence for a few minutes before Sean said, 'No way was that a sending off or a penalty!'

'Rubbish! It was a dirty tackle. Typical of your lot when you go down by a goal.'

'Well, yours was offside to start with. The ref is biased, and no way was that a penalty!'

'Stop!' ordered Jo firmly. 'No talking football at the table, Sean, as you know! We banned football talk at the table years ago,' explained Jo to Meg. 'Our now grown-up kids all support different teams. So, after many arguments and one of my sons throwing a plateful of food at the other, we banned any football talk when eating as it drove me mad!'

Meg grinned. 'Do you have all boys?'

'No. Two boys and two girls, three of them football crazy, rugby crazy, basically sport crazy in general. Our youngest is the only one who doesn't like sport.

'They're all at university. Tom, the oldest, has recently begun a medical degree. He took a few years out to travel the world so, even though he's the oldest, he's only just beginning his studies.'

'Meaning he has yet to leave a classroom and see what a Saturday night in A&E is like!' Sean added, the concern in his voice obvious.

'The others,' Jo continued, 'are in their first, second, and third years. They were not interested in travelling, though I hoped Kayleigh would. It may have helped her impulsive nature somewhat!'

'Wow, you had them close together,' Meg said.

'Yes. We didn't want the age difference to be too far apart; that's why we had the extension. Everyone moaned about the attic room being too small or too hot, even though it's bigger than a couple of their actual rooms.

'They would rotate rooms every six months to make it fair.' began Sean. 'Well, that's what they said. In the end, we got fed up with the arguing and had an extension built. I needed a home office as I work from home a couple of days a week. We got to have a guest bedroom in the attic, and the kids all got a smaller room each on the middle floor, which was funny as it meant they were all closer to our bedroom, so we could hear what the lot of them were getting up to.'

'We gave them space to develop their own personalities and opinions, but they knew the rules and boundaries too.' Jo added. 'We wanted a big family, and being brought up with love and care and being interested in them is what every child deserves. Every single child, not just ours. It's what you deserved, and I'm so sorry you didn't get that.'

Meg sat, staring at her plate, unresponsive to Jo's words.

'I agree,' added Sean. 'I'm sorry too. By no means are we the perfect parents. We made our mistakes, but the kids were our priority, even when they were little buggers.' He grinned, breaking the tension slightly.

Jo rolled her eyes. 'Right, you two. I cooked, so you can both fill the dishwasher and clean the kitchen. I'm going to go watch something non-football related, and when you're finished, Meg, I suggest you have a bath and an early night.'

'I'm not tired.'

'You will be after a warm soak, and it'll help the pain on your bruises. I'll get you some paracetamol before bed, so it hurts less.'

'Come on, Meg.' Sean started picking plates up. 'Let's sort the kitchen.'

'Tell me when you've finished. I'll run you a bath with some tea tree oils in it, but I need to check your cuts first and change your dressings afterwards.'

Meg nodded, her cheeks reddening with embarrassment. She stood and began collecting plates.

Later, Jo gently unwrapped Meg's bandages and had a look at the home stitches she'd put on. 'They're looking fine. Keep that arm out of the bath. It's not fully scabbed yet, and I'm worried it'll bleed. I think you need to leave the bandage on for a couple of days, more to protect you from knocking the stitching off, and then fresh air will be the best healer.'

'I'm sorry,' whispered Meg.

Jo stood forward, wrapped the girl in her arms, and gave her a tight hug. 'Please, will you tell me if you think of doing it again?'

'It doesn't matter. I'll probably be sent off somewhere miles away tomorrow after the meeting that I can't come to, even though it's about me, and...'

'Ssshh,' said Jo. 'Don't start getting angry again. I promise I'll tell you everything that is said.'

'Everything?'

'Everything!'

'Thanks, and just in case you don't get a chance to tell me tomorrow, thank you for promising. And if I don't get a chance to say goodbye, I just want to say thank you for this weekend.'

'Why won't you have a chance to say goodbye?'

'There'll be a copper here, won't there? They might just radio him or her and tell them where to take me.'

'I won't let that happen,' Jo promised.

'You don't know them like I do.'

'Do you trust me?'

Meg suddenly looked tearful, and she turned away. 'Can I have a bath now?'

'Of course.' Jo turned to leave the room. 'I'll come up and sit with you when I hear you going up to bed.'

'No, it's okay, but thanks,' Meg murmured, continuing to look away to hide her tears, 'I need to start doing stuff on my own again. Goodnight.'

Jo paused, about to say something, but changed her mind. 'Goodnight,' she said eventually. 'Sleep well.'

Meg had a quick bath and then got into bed. She cried and cried until she finally fell asleep.

Jo sat on the bottom of the stairs, holding her head in her hands, making no attempt to wipe away her own tears of devastation.

Chapter Four

At eight a.m. the following morning, Jo knocked on Meg's bedroom door, but despite several knocks, there was no reply.

Tentatively, she opened the door and peered into the room. Jo was shocked to see the state of Meg, who appeared to be in the midst of a horrendous nightmare. She was writhing around the bed, her clothes soaked with sweat, and she was making some of the most devastating sounds Jo had ever heard.

Unsure what to do, she approached the bed and cleared her throat loudly several times after banging the door shut, but Meg was so entrenched in the dream that no sound roused her.

Jo called Meg's name several times, each time getting progressively louder and louder. It didn't work. Taking a deep breath, Jo shook Meg gently and then a little more vigorously until, eventually, Meg's eyes flew open. Terrified, she dived out of bed and ran until she smacked into the wardrobe and fell in a heap on the floor. She lay there, dazed and confused, trying to remember where she was. Jo rushed towards her and helped Meg sit up, telling her to take deep breaths.

'What's going on?' Meg demanded. She remembered where she was, but couldn't work out why she was sitting on the floor.

'You were having an awful nightmare, and I had to wake you. I'm sorry if I scared you.

'Are you hurt from falling?'

Meg stood and rubbed her head, which hurt from hitting the wardrobe. She noticed her pyjamas clinging to her skin and her hair dripping with sweat. She glanced at the bed, that was also soaked. 'I'm sorry,' she mumbled. 'I'll take the covers off now.' She staggered towards it.

'Meg, sit in the chair!' Jo ordered. 'You're wobbling. You're going to fall. Drink some water.'

Meg downed the glass of water in one gulp and tugged at the clothes that were plastered to her body.

'Do you want to talk about what was happening in the dream?'

Meg shook her head.

'Are you okay to stand now?'

Meg looked around the room; her mind was still half in the dream and half in reality. She felt shaken and scared, but stood up with a slight wobble. 'I'm fine,' she muttered.

'The police officer has arrived. She's downstairs. Go and jump in the shower and put some clothes on. I'll wait here and take you down to meet her.'

Meg headed off to the en-suite while Jo stripped the soaking bed, picked some clothes for Meg, and put them near the bathroom. She sat with her back to the door and waited, lost in thought.

'Can I have the clothes I had on when you found me the other night?' came Meg's voice, making Jo jump.

'No, sorry. The police took them for forensic examination. Why do you want them?'

'I don't want to take anything that isn't mine.'

'These clothes are yours. Sean wouldn't be able to fit his big toe into one of your socks,' quipped Jo, smiling, trying to lighten the atmosphere. 'And you're making a lot of assumptions about being whisked off immediately.'

'I know the system,' Meg stated flatly.

'Come on. Sean and I need to leave soon.'

Meg scooped up the clothes and reappeared from the bathroom two minutes later; her hair was still dripping.

'Do you want me to dry your hair?'

Meg shook her head and took a step away from Jo. She couldn't bear any more physical contact with her. She was angry with herself for lowering her protective barrier and allowing herself to feel close to Jo. The weekend had given her a small taste of family life, and Meg was furious that she allowed herself to be sucked in by it. She forced herself to switch back to her familiar self-protective mode, which included no affection or closeness from anyone, especially Jo.

Jo recognised this and didn't push it, and reluctantly led the girl downstairs and introduced her to the PC, who sat at the table, having a cup of tea and chatting to Sean.

'Morning,' Sean said, attempting to sound cheerful as Meg walked in.

'Morning,' Meg said quietly, refusing to look at the uniformed woman.

'Hi, I'm Liz,' she said. 'You may remember me from the police station. I sat with you before your interview. I'll just be around while Jo and Sean are out, so do as you please. Indoors only, okay?'

Meg nodded, went to the lounge, put the TV on, and sat, not looking at the screen.

'We're going now, Meg,' said Jo, popping her head around the door. 'I'll see you afterwards.'

Meg gave a sarcastic laugh and shrugged.

'I will see you after the meeting,' Jo asserted.

Meg ignored her and stared at the TV; Jo had no option but to leave.

Thankfully, Liz sat in the kitchen throughout. She also had a good view of the house's entrances, but made no attempt to engage Meg in conversation, much to the girl's relief.

Meg had no idea of the time or how long had passed since Jo and Sean had left. She felt numb and just sat on the sofa without moving. Her brain was too overloaded to think about anything.

Eventually, she heard cars pulling up on the driveway. Meg, glancing at the clock which showed one p.m., stood apprehensively.

Jo entered first, looking solemn and angry, followed by Sean, who appeared worn out, but most striking was the flustered social worker who entered last. Steph's perfect yet old- fashioned hairstyle, which was never out of place, was now ruffled.

'Are we going?' Meg asked Steph, her voice hoarse.

'Sit down, Meg, please,' said Jo. 'Have you eaten or had a drink since we left?' Meg shook her head, still standing.

'Sean...' Jo glanced at her husband, who went off to make drinks for them all. 'Meg, I asked you to sit down.'

'I don't do goodbyes. Can we go to wherever I'm being sent?'

'Sit down and listen, please,' said Jo, with an edge to her voice.

Noting Jo's eyes, which held an unrecognisable expression, she sat down anxiously. Jo took a seat next to her just as Sean came back with a jug of water and four glasses.

'Have a drink,' pestered Jo, giving Meg some water. 'We need to discuss some things and I'm so sorry. It's not going to be easy.'

'Save your breath. I'm going. Wouldn't it be best to leave now instead of dragging it out?'

Jo ignored Meg and nodded to Steph, asking her to begin.

'Meg,' said Steph, 'as you are aware, the police arrested the children's home worker who attacked you on Friday night. He has been locked up all weekend and was charged with rape this morning. He'll be held in prison on remand until the trial.

'A thorough search was undertaken. This included the children's home, Javeed's own home, his computer, his mobile phone, and some others hidden beneath a floorboard.

'A lot of evidence was found, not only against him but others, who still need to be identified. Digital recordings showing other men and children were played. Some children were from your home, some from different homes, and others we have no idea about where they have come from or who they are. By some children, I mean a lot of them. They were filmed in a large, industrial-type building and also at rather grand houses where parties appeared to be taking place.

'Can you remember what may be on those videos?'

Meg's face went so white that Jo grabbed hold of her because she thought the girl would pass out.

'A senior police team, which covers child sexual exploitation, attended, along with Inspector Gina Phillips, Sean, who happens to be my ultimate boss, and Jo, of course. The meeting was smaller than it would typically be due to confidentiality concerns. We had to watch those films to assist with identifying other girls and further the investigation. The horrendous images showed you and other girls being attacked sexually and physically by several men. We haven't identified where these attacks happened yet, but the sooner we find the locations, the better. We need all the help we can to lock these men up. Do you know where the attacks took place?'

Meg shook her head, deeply ashamed that Jo and Sean had seen what had happened to her.

'It wasn't in the kids' home or Jav...' began Steph.

'*Stop saying his name!*' shouted Meg.

'I'm sorry. The videos were not made inside that man's house. However, he has two young daughters, and they've been taken to a place of safety for the time being. His wife said she knew nothing about it, but we saw her in one of the videos. She was, and I'm sorry to say this, but she was one of the people holding you down while you were being...' the social worker stopped, seemingly unable to say the word.

'Raped,' Jo spoke weakly.

'Can you tell me anything about her?' Steph persisted.

Meg didn't speak and stared at her feet, head spinning.

'Meg, I cannot begin to comprehend what has happened to you,' came Jo's gentle voice. 'I'm so sorry this happened. But if you can remember anything, it would help.'

'What about Peter, the other care worker?'

'He was also arrested and questioned but released on police bail for the time being, as there wasn't the evidence to charge him. Not yet anyway.'

At that moment, Liz returned to the room. 'I've been asked to take any notes that may be useful if you've finished telling Meg about the conference.'

'Tell me where you're placing me!' Meg demanded. 'If you're sending me back to Crookshaws or somewhere near, they'll find me and kill me before it gets to court.'

'I don't think murder is their thing,' said Steph condescendingly, her cheeks flushed as she received a glare from Sean.

'Ha!' spat Meg. 'Did you ever find Jenny Evans? Bet she was on a video! She threatened to talk, and they killed her! I saw it. They cut her throat in front of us. He said it was a warning.'

Everyone appeared to freeze; a stunned silence chilled the room.

'I need to call my Inspector,' said Liz, taking a deep breath. 'Please don't talk about this anymore until she gives further instructions.'

'No way am I giving a statement! They'll be after me. I'm not making it any worse. They'll give up Jjjj... the kids' home bloke. He will not talk because he knows they'll kill his family. I'm saying nothing else official. They have a list of all the homes and foster places They'll find me.'

'I know one place your whereabouts would be unknown,' said Jo.

Liz came back in again, and everyone fell silent. 'I've been ordered back to the station.

'My Inspector asked if you will come later today and give a statement about Jenny Evans?' Everyone stared at Meg.

'No! They'll kill me if I talk.'

'We will keep you safe, I promise. We'll talk about protection when you come down later.'

Meg ignored her and returned to staring out of the window, but all she could see were images of Jenny and her last moments.

'Meg, stay with us and turn your head towards my face,' said Jo.

Meg startled and her eyes refocussed on the people in the room, momentarily confused about where she was.

'These people are rapists and murderers,' said Jo. 'While they are roaming the streets, you and a lot of other children are at risk. I will support whatever decision you make. But you do have the power to stop these people. You possess an enormous amount of courage. You can do it. Will you?'

Meg nodded blankly.

'Thank you, Meg,' the Constable said. 'Jo is right. This is a courageous thing to do. I'll tell the Inspector to expect you at, say... five p.m.?'

Jo nodded, and Sean got up to let the PC out.

'Do you want me to stay?' asked Steph, addressing Sean as he returned.

'No. We'll talk to Meg. I want you to collect all the information we hold on Jenny Evans and ensure it is in Inspector Phillips's hands only by five p.m., along with details of anyone else she was friends with. Remember, this stays strictly confidential!'

Steph stood and hurried out of the room. Meg watched her in distaste; she really did not like social workers. She relaxed slightly now she was with only Jo and Sean in the room. Jo still had her arm protectively around her.

'Will you please tell me what's happening?' Meg pleaded.

'You've been through unimaginable horrors,' said Jo. 'I'm so, so sorry.'

Meg shrugged. 'You didn't do it.'

'Meg?' Sean asked. 'Would you like a foster placement with Jo and me until this is all over? It'll be safe. Well, safer, as those people are not aware of this address. It will be kept confidential. Our home is not like a kids' home with loads of people in and out, everyone fighting and shouting. Well, not until the kids come back for Christmas, then it's carnage,' he added with a grin.

'I can't! If I do, you will be in danger too. I can't do that to you both. These people will do anything to stop me from giving evidence, and if you two happen to be in the way, they will hurt you as well.'

Jo grasped Meg's hand. 'Looking after Sean and me is not your problem. We are the adults, and it's our job to take care of you. You have fought to survive alone all of your life; you need time to be a child and hopefully experience a proper childhood when this is all over. But, in the meantime, you don't need to live day-by-day, not knowing where you will be sleeping each night. We will give you consistency and safety until after the trial. Also, police protection will be arranged. We will make sure of it.'

'You'll get fed up with me and throw me out.'

'No, we won't!' said Jo truthfully. 'Please come and stay with us.'

'Why?'

'Because I...'

'We,' interrupted Sean.

'Sorry, we. Because of everything I've just told you, and we care about you.'

'I'm scared of men,' Meg whispered, refusing to look at Sean. 'All the men I've known have hurt me in different ways.'

'Of course you're scared of men,' Sean replied. 'And you have every right to be. Every one of them has been a complete and utter bastard.'

'Sean!' Jo exclaimed.

'He's right,' Meg burst out. 'But how do you know?'

'Your social care file was read at the meeting. You don't need to talk about the past until you want to. A lot of information appears to be missing. The paperwork was a mess and what had been put on to the computer was barely readable. Still, we were able to decipher the basics. Due to an oversight, which is being investigated, when your previous social worker went on maternity leave, you were not appointed another one. Steph has kindly offered to be your main social worker until after the trial at least.'

'Why kindly? Isn't that her job?' Meg asked.

'No. Not anymore. Steph is based in my department. She works on the compliance side now. She visits foster and children's homes and makes sure that their policies and paperwork are all in order, and also ensures all the files in social care offices are kept up to standard.'

'It sounds like she didn't do a very good job with mine if it's a mess.'

'That is being dealt with,' Sean replied, sounding agitated. 'Anyway, Steph volunteered to do the on-call rota on the night you were found. We are understaffed, and the person covering your patch called in sick. Steph certainly didn't need to volunteer. She is under no obligation to take on any cases, but she was concerned for you. She didn't want you to have to start again with a new social worker, especially as they all have multiple caseloads.'

'I will never get bored of being just a caseload.' Meg sighed sarcastically.

'I agree; the language is terrible. The system has let you down. Everyone has let you down. But please, give me a chance. We'll take it day-by-day. I'll never come to your bedroom unless I'm worried that you're going to hurt yourself. I won't hug you or initiate any physical contact unless you do. I won't even tell you off until we develop a positive relationship, one in which you trust me,' he finished, glancing at his wife.

'Great,' she huffed, but with a smile. 'Make me the bad guy! Do you want to give it a go?' Meg stared at her shoes on the floor, a vast array of emotions swirling around her head.

She knew it wasn't safe to stay with these people, but not in the way they imagined. She knew the longer she stayed the more she would care about them. She already did with Jo, and then it would be time to leave and she'd be abandoned and devastated again. But she didn't want to say no. The cuddles, the food, the safety was something she'd never had.

'Okay,' she said quickly, going against her better instincts.

'Thank you for trusting us,' said Jo. 'This whole process of finding these evil people has only just begun. I'm sorry, but there will be more statements, interviews, and probably a court case. However, we need to discuss one incredibly urgent thing, and that is your pregnancy.'

Meg's facial expression turned utterly blank. All sounds around her faded into the background, and she disappeared into her own mind.

The next thing she knew, Jo was on the floor in front of her, repeating her name continuously. Finally, Meg turned and made eye-contact with Jo. 'Take a deep breath,' begged Jo. 'And breathe out for six seconds.'

Meg complied and did it again and again.

'Can you wriggle your toes on the carpet and feel the sensation?' Meg pressed them down and nodded.

'Look around the room. Name five blue things.' Meg did as she was told, then Jo told her to name four yellow things, three orange things, two red things and one green thing. 'Tell me what you can smell.'

'You, or your perfume,' rasped Meg.

'Describe it.'

'Safe,' she blurted out, surprised she felt that way.

'What can you hear?'

'The birds outside, err, a car going past... that's it.'

'Good. You're drenched in sweat. Did you notice?'

'No, but I'm cold.'

'That'll be it drying. Can you manage a wash and a change of clothes?'

'Will you sit in the bedroom?' Meg asked reluctantly, annoyed about her dependence on this woman.

Jo nodded and put her arm around the girl.

'Should I do some food while you're doing that?' asked Sean uncertainly.

'Please,' Jo answered gratefully.

'I'm okay,' said Meg, 'but thank you.'

'You are eating!' Jo replied. 'You need to eat and drink plenty before we go to the police station. Come on!'

Later that afternoon, Jo and Meg arrived at the police station yet again. Sean went to his office to meet with Steph and search through the paper files of all the children Meg and Jenny Evans were associated with. He intended to make a list of suspected victims and establish how many children were missing or had absconded frequently.

Meg and Jo entered a different, more formal interview room. Gina greeted them and gestured to an extremely serious-looking man.

He stood and shook their hands. 'I'm DCI Leek from the Murder Investigation Team; thank you for coming in. Please, take a seat.' He gestured to two screwed down plastic chairs on the opposite side of the table from where he and Inspector Gina Phillips sat, and set up the audio recording device and then the video camera.

He stated his name again, as did the Inspector, and began. 'Will you please tell me what you disclosed about Jenny Evans earlier today.'

Meg told the story of Jenny's death again. She described the man who had killed Jenny the best she could and tried to give details of the building she was taken to most frequently, and its whereabouts. 'It was like a huge warehouse. Chains with massive hooks hung from the high, metal ceiling. The floor was concrete and cold. An aeroplane went over once or twice, but I don't remember hearing any cars. An odour was floating around constantly. I can't remember what it was.'

'How many other children were present during the murder?' pressed the DCI.

'About twenty. They made us sit in the corner and watch. If we turned away, they would punch us and grab our heads and force us to watch. But most were too afraid to look away in case they decided to kill more of us.'

'What did the man say before he killed Jenny?'

'He said that she'd threatened to talk and tried to run away. He said that no one speaks and no one gets away, and this is what would happen to the rest of us if we tried the same, and then he... he...'

'I'm sorry, Meg, but you need to say it.'

Jo grabbed hold of Meg's hand and squeezed it tightly.

'And tttthen he...' Meg took a deep breath, 'cut her throat in a quick movement. Jenny collapsed onto the floor. Blood was spurting out of her neck. So much blood. She had her eyes open and looked so frightened and was shivering, and then she just stopped. Her eyes were still open, but we knew she was dead, and the blood kept flowing across the floor and down into a grid.'

'You are doing brilliantly, Meg,' said the DCI. 'What happened next?'

'The men and a couple of women all made us put our blindfolds back on.'

'Blindfolds?'

'They make us wear them when we're travelling. Someone was always next to me in the back, and if the mask slipped, then a punch to the head would follow.'

'How many adults do you recall being present? A rough number will do.'

'Loads. Probably about forty.'

The DCI gave the Inspector a startled look. 'And what happened next?'

'When my eyes were covered again, two people dragged me across the ground, then the sound of heavy doors being lifted up.

'It sounded like a chain was lifting them. Next, I felt fresh air briefly and was pushed into a car. Lots of car doors were being opened and shut, and engines were starting. Our engine started, and we moved.'

'Do you remember anything about the car? Was the radio on? Do you remember what the material on the seats felt like? No detail is too small.'

'Music was on the radio, but the DJ spoke in a different language; I didn't recognise what it was. It wasn't German, as I did that at school in my first year. The car smelled of cigarette smoke and sweat from the men.'

'Anything else?'

'The seats were leather, and I kept sliding on them. They always felt like they'd just been polished. But that's it.'

'Approximately how long did you travel for? Did they take you back to the home? What speed were you travelling at? Where there lots of stops and starts?'

'We drove very fast at first, and I didn't hear any traffic. That was for, I don't know, about fifteen minutes. Then we slowed, and I think we stopped at traffic lights. I knew this because the beep-beep noise they make when someone presses the button to cross the road started pinging. Then, a couple of minutes later, it went dark. They told me to leave the car and count to 100 before I took my blindfold off. I counted, and the car skidded away. When I took my blindfold off, I was in the arches under the railway station in the city centre.'

'Thank you. One last question. Can you tell me the names of the other children that were in that building?'

'No!' snapped Meg

'Is that because you don't know them or because you're afraid?'

'Some girls see it as a laugh and go along on their own and are not blindfolded, and they're treated better. The men give them cigarettes, drugs, and alcohol, and don't beat them up. Well, not much. If I give you their names, they'll tell the men.'

'How about we make two lists? Those who are forced to go and another one of the girls who believe that they're going willingly. But please, let me emphasise, they are not willing; they have been groomed and exploited just like you. Do you know what Stockholm syndrome is?'

Meg shook her head.

'In a nutshell, Stockholm syndrome is a condition in which hostages develop a psychological bond with their captors during captivity. Emotional bonds can be formed between captors and captives during intimate time together. Still, these are generally considered irrational in light of the danger or risk endured by the victims. It is pure survival. By behaving and doing as they are instructed by these men, they are, therefore, treated better, or so they think. Still, they are no less a victim.'

Meg remained silent.

'I need you to trust me on this,' the DCI urged. 'This is a mammoth case, and a massive gang, one on the scale I have never seen, is at large. We need to stop them. The girls who believe this is their decision will be put under surveillance. The others will be taken from their placements and interviewed, and a secure place found for them. Still, it won't happen overnight, as, if we move them all at once, the gang will become suspicious.

'We will invent plausible reasons for each one. We will prioritise locating where they meet and try to catch as many as possible in one go. We will provide you and the place you live with police protection. Your safety is paramount, but we need to save the others too.'

Three hours after the interview had begun, an exhausted Meg was finally told the questions were over for now.

But the DCI had one final question. 'Before you leave, would you be able to look through some photos on our database? We have images of known sex offenders. It would be helpful to the investigation.'

'No!' said Jo firmly. 'Not today. Meg is exhausted. It's just gone eight p.m. I'm taking her home, she's having supper and going to bed. If you want us to come back tomorrow, then we shall, but no more today.'

The DCI opened his mouth to argue.

'That's fine,' said Gina. 'Why don't you come back on a day to be arranged? You have provided many details for us to work on. Thank you. Your courage is outstanding, and don't forget that!'

Meg looked down at the floor, embarrassed at the compliment.

'Thank you,' said Jo to the Inspector. 'Come on, Meg. Home.'

CHAPTER FIVE

Meg was exhausted. She barely uttered a word in the car on the way home and later couldn't eat, despite Jo's encouragement. She lay in bed that night tossing and turning, fighting to remove the image of the life leaving Jenny's eyes from her brain.

She got up and paced the room and looked out of the window to see if she could spot the police officers who were watching the house, only to be surprised to see that the ground was thick with snow and there was a blizzard. Meg paced more and began to feel as though the walls were closing in on her. She needed to get out of the room. Nervously, she sneaked downstairs as quietly as possible and went into the lounge. Leaving the lights off, she put on the TV. She scrolled through the channels, disinterested. Still, the noise, even with the volume low, provided a welcome distraction.

Just as she settled on some old romcom film, she screamed as she saw a shadow in the doorway.

'It's only me,' said Sean, snapping the light on. 'It's okay. What are you doing?'

'I'm sorry,' Meg said, trembling slightly. 'I couldn't sleep and needed to leave the bedroom. I'll go back now. I'm sorry.'

'Don't worry. Stay where you are. Do you fancy a cup of Horlicks? Or something else?'

Meg didn't say anything and just sat there nervously.

'Horlicks it is then,' said Sean. 'And you can turn the TV up. Jo is a deep sleeper, or should I say a selective sleeper. She seemed to have a sixth sense and would always wake when the kids were up to no good. Anyway, I'll get you a drink.'

Meg turned the TV up slightly, and Sean returned five minutes later with two cups of Horlicks.

'Do you mind if I join you? I can't sleep either, and I've not seen this film in years!'

'Okay,' said Meg hesitantly and thanked Sean for the drink, observing him as he chose a chair as far away from her as possible.

'Jo wants me to go to a therapist,' Meg blurted out after a few minutes of silence.

'I know.'

'What do you think?'

'I make a point of never arguing with my wife when she's right. To be honest, I try not to argue with my wife when she isn't right! But I agree with her about the therapist.'

'I wouldn't know where to start.'

'Yes, but that's not your job. It's the therapist's. Jo is so keen for you to talk to someone and have treatment because she doesn't want what's happened to you to haunt you for the rest of your life. These things have a habit of affecting you, not only psychologically, but physically too.

'Apart from the past six months, I know very little about your life, but I guess it hasn't been the happiest considering that you were put into care when you were nine years old. I've seen things in social workers' notes; your file was sketchy, to say the least. There's an awful lot not in there that should be. I received more information about you during the meeting on Monday in my capacity as your potential foster parent rather than professionally.'

'Why was my file so messed up?'

'I don't know. As I said, we've started an investigation. Maybe some of it got mixed up when it was computerised. I read what I could find. But, and only if you want to, I'm happy to listen to anything you tell me. Not just to fill in the blanks, but it may help you to talk, but only when you're ready.'

'It feels too big to talk to anyone at all about, and seeing someone professional and telling them all about my life is scary. I'm scccaar...'

'Scared?' Meg nodded.

'Don't blame you. I saw a therapist years ago. I was having a tough time; work was stressful, then I was coming home to four young kids every day. It was hard. I love the buggers to death, but I just felt like I'd lost myself. Became a bit depressed, to be honest.'

'Did it cure you?'

'There is no cure, but there are ways to manage things differently. So, yes, eventually. It took me a while to warm up and talk properly. I'm from a family were talking about feelings, especially if you're a man, is considered weak. The men in my family would go to work, go to the pub, neck ten pints, go home, pass out, and start again the next day. None of them talked about feelings and stuff. I wasn't very good at that until I met Jo, and I did not want my kids to follow in the footsteps of my dad, grandad, and all the others. She made me look at myself, learn to talk, and break that cycle. And when I did become depressed, she even came to the first therapy session with me. Felt like a bit of a fool, a grown man needing his wife to hold his hand, but she was supporting me. That's what real couples do; when one is down, the other steps up. So, I don't blame you for being scared. I'm scared for you. I'm scared about how you'll be after the sessions. I'm scared you'll try to hurt yourself. But I do know if you find the right person, you'll get there. It may take years of work, but you can do it.'

'I'd rather have a fight and race around in a nicked car like we used to do in the kids' homes!'

'Ha, not a chance, and I wouldn't want to be in your shoes if Jo caught you,' he added, grinning. 'Are you tired?'

'No. My mind is mad. It's spinning and won't stop.' 'Get dressed,' said Sean. 'Lots of warm clothes.'

'Why?'

'Just get dressed. I'll do the same. Meet back here in five, and be quiet!'

Meg did as she was told, though confused and wary. She wrapped up and even put on the gloves and new coat that had been bought for her. She met Sean downstairs; he was also wrapped up.

'You need a hat,' he said, taking his off and handing it to her.

'No way am I wearing an Arsenal hat!' she said in disgust.

He laughed. 'Come on. Let's find one of Jo's.'

'What are we doing?'

'You'll see,' he said, passing her a bobble hat. 'Now. *Do you want to build a snowman?*'

Meg yelped and jumped behind the kitchen door. She waited nervously and then poked her head around and looked at Sean.

'*Do you want to build a snowman?*'

'Why are you doing a weird thing with your voice?' Meg asked, still looking unsure.

'I'm singing!' said Sean indignantly.

'Singing? Singing what?'

'*Do you wanna...*'

'Please, stop,' said Meg, coming out from behind the door. 'It's awful.'

'Yes, but it's from *Frozen*.'

'Frozen what?'

'The film. Have you never seen it?'

'Never heard of it. Who's in it?'

'Well, they are kind of animated characters.'

'You watch cartoons and are singing songs from them?'

'It's not a cartoon, it's... never mind. Let's go outside.'

'No singing?'

'No singing!' said Sean, sighing. 'But we are watching *Frozen* soon.'

'I'm too old for cartoons.'

'It's not a... just come on.' He opened the back door. They crept into the back garden, aware that the police protection officers were probably wondering what the hell was going on.

Meg looked at the snow, amazed at how clean and fresh it was, and how quiet and peaceful it felt in the garden. Then, *whack.*

'*Oy*,' she shouted at Sean as the snowball bounced off her head.

'Oy what?' He grinned.

'Right!' said Meg, determined, rolling up some snow and pelting Sean in the middle of the chest.

They spent the next fifteen minutes in a fierce battle, each finding hiding places and showing no mercy in the pounding of the snowballs.

Meg saw Sean hide behind the garage and grinned. 'Got you,' she whispered.

She grabbed a shovel and approached the side of the garage, reached up to the roof, and started pushing.

By then, a good half a metre had settled onto the roof. With a sudden surge, Meg pushed the shovel as hard as she could and ran round to watch the avalanche fall on top of Sean, knocking him over onto his back. When he was down, she started to pound him with snowballs.

'*Stop*!' he shouted, trying to find cover.

'*No mercy*!' Meg cried to Sean, who managed to get to his feet and run to the side of the garage. Meg followed but fell over, landing flat on her face. Sean grinned as he spotted his wheelbarrow filled with snow, grabbed the handles, and tipped it over Meg's head and returned to his hiding place, pummelling Meg with snowballs.

'*Ha, no mer....*'

'*What on earth is going on here*?' came a voice, though it sounded slightly muffled to Meg, who was buried underneath a wheelbarrow full of snow.

Sean popped his head from around the garage and sheepishly peeped at Jo, and Meg cleared her eyes and did the same.

'In! Now! Both of you! It's three a.m.,' said Jo.

In the kitchen Jo grabbed a towel and began to scrub Meg's hair dry without pausing for breath. 'I've had a phone call from the police to ask if the "disturbance" in the garden was an organised event! What are you doing, rolling around in the snow? Sean, you nearly buried Meg. What are you playing at?'

'I buried him first,' said Meg, grinning.

But Jo didn't hear, and the hair scrubbing got more vigorous. 'Now go and put dry clothes on. Both of you!' she demanded, looking menacing. 'I'll make some hot drinks. Go on, move!'

She watched as they shuffled out of the kitchen, and she put the kettle on.

'The fire is on in the lounge,' she announced when they both reappeared wearing pyjamas. 'Go and sit in there!'

'I think we're in trouble,' whispered Sean to Meg, seeming relaxed. 'Come on.' Jo joined them in the lounge with hot drinks.

'I think my eyebrows are melting,' said Sean, whose eyebrows were indeed dripping.

'Mine too,' said Meg, and they both shook their heads as water dripped from their now defrosting eyebrows.

'Would anyone like to tell me why you were trying to bury each other in the snow?' asked Jo.

'Sean started it!' Meg said.

'Grass,' hissed Sean, which earned him a dirty look from his wife.

'He kept making weird noises about snowmen.'

'I was singing!'

'Didn't sound like it.'

'From *Frozen*.'

'Can't believe you watch cartoons at your age.'

'Oy!' he said. 'And it's not a cartoon. I'm putting it on now, and you can watch it.'

'No one is watching any cartoons at this time,' said Jo, bewildered.

'It's not a cartoon!' said Sean loudly.

'Sounds a bit weird to me,' Meg retaliated.

'Right. Bed!' said Jo, as Sean turned to continue his defence of the film.

'Both of you! Meg, come on. I'll tuck you in. Sean, can you make it to our bedroom without causing chaos?' she asked dryly, and left with Meg without waiting for an answer.

'I'm not tired,' said Meg as Jo ushered her into bed.

'You will be when you warm up,' said Jo. 'Your cheeks are all rosy. You look like you've had fun.'

'Am I in trouble?'

'Of course not. However, that husband of mine...' she trailed off, grinning.

Meg grinned too. 'It was fun.'

'Good. Now lie down and warm up.' Jo got in next to her, sat up, and put her arm around Meg, who snuggled in and hugged her until she fell asleep.

Meg appeared in the kitchen at lunchtime the next day, and by the looks of him, Sean hadn't arrived long before her either, as he was desperately ferreting around for coffee.

'Good sleep?' he asked.

'Yeah,' said Meg, sounding surprised. 'I was out for the count. No dreams or anything.'

'Probably concussion from my superior snowball throwing.'

'Don't start again!' said Jo, coming in behind Meg, giving her an absent-minded kiss on the head. 'I am so pleased you slept through. I thought we could go for a walk when you've eaten, the snow has thawed a fair bit.'

'Sure,' said Meg. Something about Jo's tone sounded hesitant, and even a bit nervous.

Meg and Jo went to a different lake from their last walk, which was again around a half-hour drive away, but in a different direction. Unlike the previous walk, Jo initiated a conversation immediately.

'Meg, what are your thoughts on the pregnancy?' Meg shrugged.

'Sorry, no shrugging today. We need to work this out, or start to at least, and you need to talk. I do have to push you on this. It's the last thing I want to do, and I'm so sorry. The foetus is growing every day. It may not survive full-term. There are a lot of unknowns with pregnancies, and there can be dangers when the person giving birth is as young as you'.

'Why do you call it a foetus and not a baby?'

'It's not a baby yet. It has the potential to become a baby, but currently, it's a lot of cells all joining together.'

'But it has a heart.'

'Meg, people have life-support machines switched off, even when there is a heartbeat.

'But they are still counted as clinically dead as there is no brain activity.'

'What are the options?' asked Meg after digesting Jo's words.

'I can think of three. One, go through with the pregnancy, make a baby, and keep it. Two, have the baby and give it up for adoption, and three, have a termination.'

'Kill it?'

'You are not killing anything. You are stopping it from progressing into a baby.'

'What do you think?'

'I think you need all the facts and then you can make an informed decision.'

'So, you've no opinion at all?'

'I didn't say that, but this has to be your decision, and I will support you with your choice.'

'Do you think abortion is murder?' Meg asked, her voice trembling. The scan had felt like a dream, and the memory of it was blurry. All Meg could see was a fully-formed baby, not a bunch of cells joining together and growing. She wondered if it would look like her, or if would look like… Meg's knees buckled, and she was on the ground before Jo could get to her.

Despite the cold, Meg was drenched in sweat once again, her eyes unfocused, her brain in that room. The same pain was recalled by her muscles. She let out an agonising moan that shook Jo deeply. The woman sat Meg up and cradled her, there on the ground, repeating her name over and over. She reached into her bag for her perfume and sprayed some under Meg's nose. Meg's stiff body loosened slightly, so Jo sprayed and sprayed until Meg began to blink and her eyes focussed. Jo made Meg take sips of water and continued taking to her gently.

Eventually sitting up, Meg wiped the sweat from her face, her body trembling. The sensation of being out of her own body was still present, though not as severe. She stared at the water and drank more water.

'Iii…

'Take your time,' Jo soothed.

'Tell me! Is it… is it murder?'

'Absolutely not! Even if you were older and had a consensual one-night-stand and got pregnant, I'd still think the same as I do now. That it's your choice and your right to choose. Also, though you'll probably appear by video link, those awful videos that Sean and I witnessed at the meeting will still play in court. The last one we viewed was dated nine weeks ago. I don't know if anything on that scale has happened since, but you likely got pregnant then. But no more for now, I want to get you home.'

'I don't want to go home; I want to know what to do and I need to decide quickly! Please, Jo! Please tell me more about all this baby stuff. You've had four of them. Please…'

Jo thought back to the joy when she discovered that she was pregnant with each of her children. The excitement, celebration and anticipation that she and Sean had was magical as was seeing each child for the first ever time.

Looking at the desperate child in front of her, Jo was desperate to fix it all and tell Meg what to do, what would be best for her long-term. As heart-wrenching as it was, she knew she couldn't. The decision had to be Meg's but Jo's inner fury burned fiercely at the injustice of Meg being forced to decide on what to about a pregnancy that was caused by rape devastated her.

'Oh Meg, nothing we do will make this easy and I'm so sorry. I hate that a decision has to be made so quickly. You need respite, not rushing decisions.

'If you do go down the abortion route, the sooner you do it, the safer it will be for you. Having a baby at your age will be so difficult. I struggled. I'm an adult with a supportive partner, and having children was something we tried for, together. This situation for you is heart breaking, and you are to blame for nothing. Please keep telling yourself that.

'The other option is to have the baby and give it up for adoption. Again, a decision an adult would find agonising. Giving a child away is also permanent. I'm sorry, Meg.' Jo sighed, tears glistening in her eyes. 'I'm so sorry I can't do more to help you with this.'

'You are helping,' Meg answered. 'There is no right answer. I don't know what to do.' Jo put her arm around the girl as they walked in thoughtful silence.

'Would it hurt?'

'A termination?' Meg nodded.

'We can have a look at what it involves when we get home.'

Jo and Meg headed back to the car; Meg was exhausted again.

'I think you need some food and a nap,' said Jo, noticing how pale the child looked.

'You said... you ssssaid we could... you know, look at...'

'Are you sure you still want to do that today?' Meg nodded.

'You promised!'

'Okay.'

They headed home with Jo chatting in general about the scenery, the winter sun, and anything to distract Meg.

Sean was just finishing packing his car when they arrived back. 'I don't know how the kids are going to fit in,' he said, puzzled, while looking at the sheer number of items in the car. 'By the time they've got their stuff in, one, if not two of them, will be riding on the roof!'

Meg looked confused.

'Fishing,' he said to Meg. 'I'm taking the brood to Ireland for the week.'

'Where very little fishing and a lot of drinking will be done,' interjected Jo.

'Well, a few drinks after a long day at sea won't do any harm,' Sean said with a grin.

'Right, I think I've got everything. I'll see you both on Sunday.' He moved to hug his wife.

'Give my love to the kids.' said Jo. 'And tell them they are all back for Christmas, no excuses!'

'I don't think they'd dare not to.'

'See you Sunday, Meg. I hope this week is okay. I'll be thinking of you.'

'Have a nice time,' Meg mumbled.

Sean got into his massive seven-seater car and set off down the road, beeping his horn.

'How come you're not going?' Meg asked. 'Is it because of me? I don't want...'

'No, it's not because of you. I hate fishing. Sean has always had a fishing week with them, ever since they were old enough to not fall out of a boat. Well, sort of. But I've never gone along. I go on a camping trip with them in early spring when it's slightly warmer. We try to have a proper holiday all together during the summer. But the older they get, the more they want to do their own thing, which is how it should be, I know. But I still miss them. To me, they are those babies whose first steps I watched and whose first words I heard. But they're all happy, so I couldn't wish for more. Anyway, soup and bread, okay?'

'I'm not that hungry.'

'Soup and bread it is then.' Jo opened the door. 'Go sit down. I'll shout you when it's ready.'

Meg sat at the dining table, feeling slightly resentful. She wasn't used to being told what to do, unless being told to keep out of the way counted. Her so-called birth family had never cared, and eventually had got rid of her. Kids' and foster homes were overcrowded and so understaffed that no one really cared where you were or if you ate.

Now, she had something she'd always desperately yearned for and was struggling with it. It may have been easier to try to accept it if she knew this would be her life from now on, but going back to kids' homes after the trial would be hard.

Meg had experienced many adults in her life, some she became close to, but they left to do other jobs. Others remained distant, and her affection was not reciprocated by the people paid to be her carers. There came a point in her young life when she decided to keep away from adults who had good intentions, as they always let her down. Meg grew lonelier and lonelier, but it was better than feeling resentful when the people she became attached to treated her like a caseload, which, in reality, was exactly what she was to them.

Jo appeared with lunch and placed Meg's down in front of her.

'Thank you,' she mumbled.

'Strange question, given the circumstances,' said Jo. 'But what's on your mind?'

'You. Being here. Wondering why. For how long after the trial? What's your plan?'

'No plan, apart from getting you through everything you're going through, getting the trial out of the way, making sure you are taken care of.'

'Why?'

'During my training, many, many years ago at university,' Jo began with a twinkle in her eye, 'we were taught about boundaries and keeping our distance, emotionally, from clients. You were the one that got away. Even when I saw you professionally, I broke my golden rule. I cared about you. Thought about you. I just wanted to take home that kind, curious girl in front of me and give her what she craved. A home, safety, and an education. I don't know what the pull was, but it was strong. I missed you enormously after my work at the youth centre was complete; it felt a bit like grief.'

'Me too,' said Meg angrily, glaring at Jo. 'I swore I'd never trust anyone because they'd hurt me, and I was right.'

'I'm sorry,' said Jo. 'But I was hoping we could see each other on a more informal basis afterwards. Maybe meet up

103

occasionally and go to the cinema or for walks, just hang out together.'

'That would have been worse,' Meg said sadly. 'I would have felt like a burden. I guess you would have seen me when you decided you had time and always on your terms, but sometimes a little bit of something is worse than not having it at all.'

'Can you explain?' Jo asked carefully.

'I've seen it before; other kids have had visitors. I don't mean those nasty men. But people who were kind and would take them out and do nice things, and then they would go home. It's more upsetting. These people think they're doing a nice thing by showing people like me a small part of a normal life, but they're not. They're showing us what we will never have full-time. It's cruel, not kind. It doesn't do us any favours. It just gives a small glance at a life that we could have had but never will. You and me, here now, it's not real. It's not forever, and it's hard. I hate that I want to be with you and that I trust you because it will all come to an end.'

'I'm sorry,' Jo said. 'I *am* sorry. I know people who act as befrienders, and it's difficult for them also. But yes, they go away, back to their homes and families and leave you with an emotional void, and you don't know if they genuinely care about you or not. I don't know what the solution is. I understand that you want all or nothing. It's human nature to want your feelings to be returned.

'Can I ask, and you don't need to answer... if you trusted me, and I'm not blaming you, why didn't you tell me about what was happening to you?'

'Because I was and am scared, ashamed, and embarrassed, and we didn't have much time left. I knew you were going, so what was the point?'

'I'd have done something.'

'Yeah, something professional, by the book, that would have got me killed.'

'I'm sorry,' Jo said again, her shoulders drooping and eyes reddening, 'And I'm also sorry for being yet another person who let you down. I could sense you felt close to me, and yes, I let that develop because I felt the same. If I knew how much it would upset and confuse you, I would have... well, I don't know what I would have done, to be totally honest. I wouldn't have ignored you or pushed you away, but I guess I didn't realise that a little of a nice thing made your everyday life harder.'

'It's done now,' Meg said bluntly. 'What's next?'

'You will have to see someone for some in-depth trauma therapy.'

'No, I won't.'

'You will. You watched a child be murdered. You were attacked...'

'Stop!' said Meg. 'I know what happened! I don't mean that, I mean this, here! I don't know how to do it.'

'Do what?'

'Be in a family.'

'You were in a family,' Jo said, instantly wishing she could take her words back.

'How can you of all people say that? I told you what it was like! I don't understand this!' She gestured around the room. 'Photos of your kids everywhere, saving their bedrooms, taking them on fishing trips, doing stuff with them. And I don't want to go back to school. I'm too far behind. I'll look like an idiot.'

'School can wait for now. You're not emotionally ready for it, and it's not safe. But as for the rest, there's nothing unusual about us spending time with our kids. You had the bad end of the deal. A stack of different step-fathers and getting tossed aside every time a new one came along until, and I'm sorry to be so blunt, but from what you told me, you just were not wanted at all. I don't know how any mother can do that. It's incomprehensible to me and is to any decent parent, and not just mothers, but fathers too. Not all men are abusers or bad fathers. Sean and I were always a team when bringing the kids up, and we loved them more than anything. They knew it then and still do.'

'Why didn't she want me?'

'Your mother?'

Meg nodded.

'Your mother was discussed at the meeting, and some of the paperwork from when you first went into care had survived. What you need to believe is that it wasn't about you. It was about her. It sounds like she has some serious issues. She lies. She's a narcissist and only wants people around her to give her utter devotion and worship the ground she walks on, and that is without her drug and alcohol problems. From everything you've told me and from getting to know you, it's obvious that you have always been you.

'Even from being very little, you always had a sense of yourself. That should have been celebrated, not belittled and met with disinterest. And you are clever, so you certainly need to go back to school eventually. Still, I think you'll need to restart a year or two below as you've had many gaps in your education.'

'*No way*! Everyone will call me an idiot.'

'Well, you'll have to prove them wrong, then. But you can't go back yet anyway. There's going to be many more police interviews, and a trial. But, most importantly, you are going to have to decide what to do about the pregnancy. Eat a little more, and we'll go and look on the computer and research the options and get all the information you need. Whatever decision you make, I'll support you.'

'What if I keep it? Will you throw me out if it comes before the trial?'

'Whatever happens, you're staying here until you are safe.'

'If I had a baby, would I stay and look after it instead of going to school?'

'No, as well as going to school. There are childminders and nurseries, but you will be sharing a room with a baby, getting up in the night to feed it, change nappies, trying to settle it. Babies sleep when they feel like it.'

'Can you tell me honestly what you think I should do?'

'No. It has to be your choice. But I care about you, and I think you need to be prioritised for the first time in your life. You need time to get over everything and talk about what you've been through. You need nutrition, exercise, safety, love. I think whatever is decided, it has to be what is best for you.'

Meg pushed her plate away. 'Can we go and look now?'

Jo sighed. 'Okay then. Come on.'

CHAPTER SIX

Jo took cautious charge of navigating the internet pages. Abortion, being a highly emotive and much written-about topic, made Jo nervous. She went online, and she turned the screen away from Meg's view while she searched. Finally, she found and loaded only factual medical and practical unopinionated pages, so Meg didn't view a ton of opinions or horrendous images.

'From what I know and what it also states here,' Jo began, 'if you decide to proceed with the pregnancy, then you would need to have a pre-birth assessment by social care. They will assess if you have the capacity to take care of a baby, but, as you are a "looked after child", they will consider how you will be able to live with the child and bring it up. You are fourteen. Well, you will then be just fifteen if you give birth.

'Also, there are serious risks involved for pregnant teenagers. They have a higher risk for pregnancy-related high blood pressure, which is called pre-eclampsia, which has all kinds of dangerous complications. But there are also risks for the baby of a very young mother, which include premature birth and low birth weight. Pre-eclampsia can also harm the kidneys or even be fatal for you and a baby. You are underweight, have suffered a huge amount of physical and emotional distress, and giving birth could put you both in danger.'

Meg absorbed the information silently, giving Jo no indication of what she was thinking. They moved on to looking into giving a baby up for adoption, and finally into the facts around a termination.

'Will you please just tell me what to do?' Meg pleaded yet again, slowly trying to digest the information.

'No,' Jo repeated. 'I'm sorry, but I can't. This has to be your choice, and I'll support you, but you have to make this decision. I can't decide for you. All I can do is give you the facts. But I'll be with you every step of the way.'

'How long have I got before I decide?'

'Not long, I'm afraid. I'd say by the end of the week. I'm sorry, but if you choose a termination, earlier is better.'

'Can I tell you by Friday?'

Jo nodded. 'The next few months will be hard, and I'm sorry. Will you please talk to a therapist? I'll find a good one.'

'No!'

'Meg, you need support during this from outside of this house. From someone who isn't as emotionally involved as I now am. Please...'

Meg looked at Jo and saw the stress and sadness on her face and immediately felt guilty. If it weren't for her, then Jo wouldn't be going through all of this. She would be having a pleasant time with her family, or be at work, or simply getting on with her life. Meg's stomach churned as the familiar sensation of acidic bile burned her gut, and the adrenaline activated by guilt and shame began to course through her veins.

'There's also something other things I need to discuss with you. Well, not discuss, but talk and work with you on. During the meeting, your arrest record was raised.'

Meg turned red with anger.

'After everything we've been talking about, you're going to have a go at me for getting arrested before I even met you!'

'I'm not judging you or having a go at you!' Jo stated firmly. 'I know you had to literally fight to survive or join in. But you do not need to do that while you're here. So, under no circumstances are you to meet up with anyone you were in care with, even the people who were not involved in the horrendous trap you were lured into.'

'Hang on. That's not fair! Some of them are my friends... we hung out together and had fun.'

'Fun? Riding in stolen cars? Being chased by the police? That is not fun, that is breaking the law and putting yourself in danger. Shoplifting is not fun. Neither is smashing windows. Have you ever taken drugs?'

Meg glared at Jo. 'No!' she seethed. 'Not willingly anyway.'

'Willingly? What do you mean?' Jo asked, puzzled.

'Those men...' Meg began and stopped.

'I'm not a drug addict. If you think that, then you can f...!'

'*Stop*!' Jo ordered. 'I'm not accusing, I am asking. If you did use drugs, I would help you to stop. I'm not attacking you, and I'm not trying to catch you out. I want to help in any way I can. But I stand by what I said. No meeting anyone from your past. It's not safe, and your location is a secret.'

'Anything else?' Meg asked sarcastically.

Jo reached into her pocket and put something else on the table. 'My mobile phone!' Meg exclaimed. 'I thought the police had it?'

'They've copied the data from it and are remotely monitoring the network. Any calls or texts go to a police computer and not the phone. I've got you a new phone and an iPad,' said Jo, putting them on the table. 'They've been set up with a new email address for you. I know you like writing, so you can write on the iPad if you like. Maybe try to write about how you feel?' Jo said hopefully.

'Thank you,' said Meg, overwhelmed to receive such expensive gifts. 'I can just back up my old phone and transfer it onto the new one.'

'I'm afraid that won't be possible.'

'Why?'

'Firstly, it doesn't work. As I said, the police have diverted all calls and messages to their computers. They gave it to me temporarily so we can find any specific numbers or email addresses you want to keep. Meg, the people you used to hang around with, in the homes and other places, need no way to contact you, and you can't see them until after the trial, and maybe not even then. I don't want you hanging around with them, or visiting the homes. Your old life has to end. You're in danger. More so if people know how to contact you.'

'But not everyone was involved in... Well, you know. Some are friends.'

'It's not negotiable. You are starting a new life. A safe life. I also don't want you to have any social media accounts. You need to disappear from that life and have no contact with any of those people.'

'No! You can't stop me from seeing my friends.'

'Are they your friends? People who led you into danger?'

'Well, you either follow or get your head kicked in. What did you want me to do?' Meg retorted.

'Nothing other than what you did, as you had to survive in that environment. But you are not in that now, and you are not to associate with anyone you met in care. Meg, I'm not asking you,' Jo said firmly. 'I am telling you!'

'You can't tell me what to do!' Meg said mutinously.

'I just have done,' Jo replied calmly. 'Now, pick up your new phone. I'll go through the contacts on your old phone and ask who they are, and I will decide if you can keep their number, okay?'

Meg shrugged.

'Right, let's start then...'

An hour later, and after lots of arguing, Meg's new phone list consisted of Jo, Sean, the social worker, Inspector Phillips, and DS Murray. The same applied to her email address book. Meg stared at it despairingly. 'Can I not just change my name on my online accounts and delete a few people?'

'No social media. We are keeping you safe. You need to understand that and work with us.'

Meg didn't answer and just stared at the floor.

'I'm going to go and take this to the police station,' said Jo, nodding at Meg's old phone. 'Do you want to come?'

'Do I have to?'

'No, you can stay here, but I want you to promise that you will not leave the house.' Meg nodded.

'Meg,' said Jo softly. 'I need to hear you say it.'

'Fine! I won't leave the house!' she snapped.

'Okay. I'll back in an hour.'

Jo left, and Meg sat looking at her new phone despondently. She tried to get into the app store and realised it was blocked. Her new email address would not access the apps, and she didn't know the password. Meg had a suspicion Jo may have been linked the app store to her own email address, so she could stop her downloading anything without her permission. She went to the internet home screen and tried to log into Facebook. 'Email address or password incorrect' was displayed on the screen. Meg was given the option to change her password, but again, she suspected Jo had also linked this to her own email address and didn't dare try.

Sighing, she threw the phone across the room, watching it land on the sofa and silently cursing herself for not memorising any phone numbers. Fuelled by anger, frustration, and having no control, Meg stormed into the family bathroom, allowing the urge to hurt herself to grow stronger. All the razor blades had gone. Returning downstairs, she rummaged in the kitchen, and the sharp knives were missing.

She went to her room, punching the pillow in anger, sobbing with rage until she finally fell asleep.

Meg woke up and was surprised to see daylight. She glanced at the clock, and it was nine a.m. Her shoes were gone, and a duvet had been thrown over her. She counted back and realised she had slept for seventeen hours. She gratefully downed the pint of water that Jo must have left for her, along with a chocolate brioche roll, which she greedily unwrapped and ate in two mouthfuls.

When she had properly woken up, she was surprised her brain was clearer and space to think had been somehow created. Meg cautiously placed her hand on her stomach, thinking of what was inside. Nothing appeared to be different, but memories of how it had got inside her came flooding back. She wasn't even aware which one of *them* had made it happen. Her mind started to disappear. Meg wasn't remembering the scene; she was in it.

Being held down, her mouth covered. The awful stench of the sweaty men eroded her nostrils; she physically re-lived the pain inside her, the never-ending pounding agony, the screaming and shouting of other girls. Then being sat up and held. Forced to watch Jenny, the knife, the smell of blood, her body falling...

'*Meg!*'

Meg jumped and saw a different room.

'Breathe in deeply, now breathe out,' came the voice.

She became aware of the sweat that covered her soaking wet body. The trousers she had slept in were now particularly wet, and she realised she'd wet herself.

'It's Jo. You're safe and in your room.'

Jo held the girl's hand tightly. Meg's brain slowly refocused, and she came back into the room slightly, still disoriented and afraid.

'Press your feet onto the carpet and move your toes,' said Jo. 'Now rub your hands on the bed. Notice the texture of the sheets. Now, look at me.'

Meg slowly lifted her head, visibly disoriented and dizzy.

'Cast your eyes around the room. Find five blue things and tell me what they are,' Jo requested.

Stuttering badly, Meg obliged.

'Good, you're doing brilliantly,' Jo said softly. 'Now find four yellow things and tell me what they are.'

Meg obeyed.

'Can you tell me three things that you can hear? 'Now two things you can feel...

'Now, one thing you can smell...

'Well done,' said Jo, still holding her hand. 'Can you tell me what was happening?' Meg shook her head.

'That's fine. Are you feeling fully present in this room now? Can you hear my voice clearly?'

Meg looked around, still a bit dizzy and confused, but she was back in the room.

'I've w- w-wet myself,' Meg whispered, tearful and ashamed.

'That's what showers and washing machines are for.'

'I don't want to have a baby.'

'Okay,' said Jo. 'We will talk later. Drink some more water,' she added, producing a bottle of ice-cold water. Meg obliged.

'Can you feel the coldness of the water going down your throat and hitting your stomach?'

Meg nodded.

'Good. Can you stand up and walk across the room? I want to see how shaky you are before you have a shower.'

Meg staggered a little but regained her balance and walked across the room.

'Why does my head keep doing weird things?' Meg asked, scared and confused. 'One minute I'm in my bedroom, and the next I'm completely in... Other places.'

'Other places where you were hurt or witnessed horrendous events?' Jo asked.

'Yes. It happens and quickly. The smells are the same, and I'm watching the things I saw, kind of like being in a film. I'm sorry, I can't explain this properly.' Meg hit her head in frustration.

'I understand,' Jo began. 'When you have a flashback, you don't remember traumatic events, you re-live them. They are a lot like a nightmare, but you have them while you're awake, and all the vivid sensory experiences such as smell, taste, and touch become real. Your mind takes you there and is unable to tell you that you're safe now, as the events are still live for you. That's why I tell you to look around the room and name things that are various colours, or to listen for sounds, or even feel the texture of the carpet or your bed. It's to try to ground you in the present moment and bring you back to safety.'

'How will I ever make it stop?' Meg asked, beginning to shiver.

'A good therapist will help you process those events and turn them into memories. They will always be horrible memories, but you will learn how to stop disappearing into them and re-living them. I suspect you have Post Traumatic Stress Disorder, or PTSD as it's commonly known. When bad things have happened, your brain almost becomes hijacked. None of this is your fault, and you will be able to manage the flashbacks and learn to prevent them, in time, with work.'

'I am not seeing a therapist. My mother always said there was something wrong with me and I needed to see someone! Anyway, you can make them stop, so can't you just teach me?'

'Meg, it's not all about making them stop. Therapy will help you understand why the flashbacks are happening and teach you to eventually stop them before they start. I've done a short course on childhood trauma. Still, I'm only aware of the basics, such as how to recognise a flashback or dissociation and help someone during one.'

'What's dissociation?'

'Have you ever found yourself sitting there and suddenly hours have flown by in what feels like a minute?'

'Yes!'

'That's one form of dissociation. But that is something for you to cover with a professional in therapy.'

Meg sighed. She didn't want to discuss therapy again, and she certainly wasn't going to go.

'I need a shower. I stink,' she said evasively.

'Fine. Go into the en-suite and throw your clothes out. Do you want to shout me when you're dressed, or are you okay to come downstairs alone?'

'I'll be fine.' Meg headed towards the bathroom. 'I can put my clothes into the washing machine. They are sweaty and have wwww....'

Meg stopped as she couldn't the word out.

'Just throw them outside; I'll deal with them,' said Jo firmly.

Meg peeled off the soaking clothes slowly and reluctantly passed them out of the bathroom door. She stepped into the shower, placing the dial onto the coldest, most powerful setting, and stood there, allowing the flowing water to strike her so hard that it felt like sharp needles penetrating her skin.

Meg thought about her sudden decision to have a termination. She hated the word just as much as 'abortion'. Everything she had ever been taught in her life about how evil and awful it was to murder an unborn child came back to her. She remembered the nuns at primary school saying it was a 'sin against God'. Though she didn't really believe in, or even understand the Bible passages she had been forced to recite. That guilt, the Catholic guilt, played on her conscience and taunted and bullied her.

'Is an abortion murder?' she asked Jo, yet again, when she went downstairs.

'No. It's your body, and you have a right to choose what happens. You didn't choose for this to happen, but you do have the choice to decide how to proceed. One day, in years to come, I hope you'll meet someone amazing, who deserves you, and, if you choose, you can make a baby out of love and the need to have one, and that baby will be so loved and lucky.'

'I don't want to, you know, have an ab... but I don't want this inside me anymore. It feels like what they did is still there, and is growing in my belly.'

'I understand,' said Jo. 'Are you 100 percent sure before I make some phone calls? It was a bit of a snap decision.'

'Yes,' she said eventually, '100 percent, but I feel like a murderer and a monster.'

'You are not!' said Jo firmly. 'You are making a choice that is best for you, and I'm relieved for you that you've made a decision. Once I make the phone call, it'll probably happen quickly. Is that okay?'

'Wwwwwill you come?' asked Meg, stammering.

'I'll be there every step of the way. Do you believe me?'

Meg nodded. Her eyes started to fill up, and she let out an unwitting sob. The sadness, shame, guilt, fear, and horror of the last few months erupted out of her, and she cried and sobbed as she'd never done in her life.

Jo embraced her tightly. 'Let it all out,' she whispered, trying to hide her own tears as the broken child in her arms sobbed uncontrollably. 'We'll get through it. I will take care of you.'

'I'm sorry,' said Meg in a sob.

'Don't you dare apologise. You are doing nothing wrong.'

'I'm going to be sick,' said Meg and ran off, getting to the bathroom just in time. Downstairs, Jo sat at the kitchen counter, head in hands, allowing her own tears to flow as she heard the sound of retching from the child upstairs.

Jo wondered if she was getting out of her depth. She wanted Meg to have a termination and then try to have some sort of childhood, but she couldn't tell her that; this had to be Meg's choice, as hard as it was for her. Jo desperately wished that Sean was home and not out at sea with no phone signal, as it wasn't only Meg who needed guidance and support. Despite all of her training and many years of working with teenagers, and even bringing up her own, Jo seriously began to doubt if she was the best person for Meg, who had been so damaged by many, many adults. She certainly did not want her own judgment and guidance to be wrong and hurt the girl further.

Chapter Seven

The hospital abortion ward reminded Meg of scenes of cattle farms she had seen on television. Women of all ages were walking around in gowns and no shoes, some laughing and joking and bumping into people they knew. Others sat silently, nervously, waiting for their name to be shouted so they could be herded into a cubicle.

Meg's name was called from down the corridor by a nurse who gestured for her and Jo to enter cubicle number five.

'I'm going to give you these tablets,' the nurse said, not looking at Meg. 'It will start the process of the termination before you go into theatre. Once you've taken these, there's no going back. Do you understand?'

Meg nodded silently and took the tablets, swallowing them with lukewarm water from a plastic cup.

'Now, sit in the corridor, and we'll shout you when it's your turn.'

'Does she have to sit in a line in a corridor?' asked Jo.

'There's nowhere else,' said the nurse briskly. 'We need the room for the next one.'

They went outside and sat in the corner on the hard, plastic chairs in a corridor full of women, Meg holding Jo's hand tightly.

'I don't want to stay here. Can we go?' pleaded Meg.

'No. I'm so sorry. It's horrendous, but the procedure has already begun. That hideous nurse said so.'

'Why does she work here if she hates it... well, hates people like me so much?'

'I doubt she hates you. She obviously missed the training about bedside manners.' Jo put a protective arm around Meg.

Both of them were lost in their own thoughts and had no idea how much time had passed until Meg's name was shouted once again.

They both jumped and then slowly stood and set off down the corridor to the doors where the voice was coming from.

'Sorry,' a nurse said to Jo. 'Only patients past this point. You can wait for her in recovery.'

'But...'

'It's either that or we can't do it,' said the nurse briskly.

'I'll be fine,' said Meg.

Jo kissed her gently on the head.

'I'll be here Meg.'

'Thank you.'

Meg was ushered into an operating theatre and told to lie on a trolley. Two men in scrubs appeared, ignoring Meg and continuing a conversation about golf with each other. They inserted needles, a cannula, and put a heart monitor on her body.

'We're going to put you under soon,' one of them said, still not making eye contact but hovering above her.

'What are you going to do to stop this happening in future?' demanded the surgeon. Meg felt vulnerable and terrified. He stared at her, awaiting an answer.

'Not let men near me,' she said finally.

'Huh,' he said with a nasty laugh. 'That's what they all say!'

'Count down from ten,' said the anaesthetist.

Meg got to six, and the next thing she knew, she was in a room with five other people on trolleys, some crying, some reading magazines, and others fast asleep.

Jo sat next to her bed, holding her hand firmly.

'Water,' said Jo, passing her a bottle, which Meg gladly accepted.

'Is it... has it... is it done?'

Jo nodded and was just about to reply when a nurse walked past the end of the bed and slapped one of Meg's feet off the other as she lay with her ankles crossed.

'You'll get blood clots,' she snapped and walked away.

'Are you okay here for a few minutes?' asked Jo, looking furious. 'I just need a chat with the nurse.'

Meg nodded, and Jo marched off towards the nurses' station. Meg only heard snippets of the conversation. Still, she saw the nurse going redder and redder in the face as Jo appeared to verbally annihilate her.

'I'm sorry about her behaviour,' said Jo as she returned. 'It was disgusting.'

'It was as bad as in the theatre,' Meg said and proceeded to tell Jo what the surgeon and anaesthetist had said.

If Jo looked furious before, she now was completely incandescent with rage.

'Do you mind if I leave you again for a short while? I'm going to raise this now and then take it further and ensure those appalling men do not work on this ward any longer.'

'Okay,' said Meg, surprised at Jo's anger. She wasn't used to people sticking up for her like this. It felt strange, but oddly safe.

Jo was gone for half an hour this time, and returned looking grim.

'Sorted,', she said. 'Luckily, there is CCTV in all operating theatres in this hospital. I spoke to the hospital administrator, who looked and listened to the footage. Those two men will be fortunate to have a job shortly, and I've submitted a formal complaint. How dare they behave like that! Anyway, it's my job to deal with that. Let's concentrate on you now. How do you feel physically?'

'A bit drugged, but okay. I just want to get out of here.'

'Stand up and take a few steps. If you can walk, we're going.' Meg stood. She took a few wobbly steps and then was fine.

Jo closed the curtains around the cubicle. 'Get dressed. We're out of here.'

Jo stood outside the cubicle and heard the same nurse who slapped Meg's feet ask Jo what was happening.

'She's going home,' said Jo firmly. 'Her stats have been checked, and she's fit to leave. She's not staying here while you mess around with paperwork.'

'But that's not our procedure,' said the nurse. 'The doctor has to sign the form.'

'I really don't care about your procedures; he gave a verbal okay, so I suggest you stick your forms in the most uncomfortable place possible. Today, the staff have been disgraceful and treated a child who has been through unimaginable horrors with contempt and cruelty. Would it actually kill you to show compassion?'

The nurse reddened. 'It's nothing personal. We work long hours and see a lot of distress. It becomes the norm, eventually.'

'Well, maybe it's time you transferred to a different department. One in which you do not have to communicate with patients. I would suggest the mortuary, but even the dead would not rest in peace with someone like you around!

'*Meg*,' called Jo. 'Ready?'

Meg had been listening to the conversation from inside the cubicle and had been shocked to hear Jo lose her cool. Shocked, and again, surprised that someone, an adult, was fighting for her. She came out of the cubicle dressed and ready; she glared at the nurse and then looked at Jo and nodded.

'Good,' said Jo. 'Let's get you out of here.' She walked past the nurse without giving her a second glance.

Jo tucked Meg into bed when they got home. She brought her a steaming mug of hot chocolate and sat next to her.

'You'll probably bleed for a few days,' Jo explained. 'Much like a heavy period.' Meg half nodded, trying to absorb the information.

'What do you need right now?'

'I don't know. My head is a mess. My body doesn't feel real. Those men in the operating theatre, it reminded me of...'

'I'm sorry,' said Jo. 'I'm sorry about the disgraceful experience you went through at the hospital. I'm sorry it's all so sad. You need to rest and let me look after you properly without complaining while you're recovering.'

'What does that involve?' Meg asked, sounding fearful.

'Sleep, rest, nutrition, walks when you're up to it, time to talk about it when you want to, and believe that I am on your side.'

'You really tore a strip off that nurse today,' Meg said with a slight grin. 'And what you said about the mortuary. I wish I'd seen her face.'

'She certainly didn't look very comfortable! I'm sorry you got bad people on a horrific day. I have met healthcare staff who work on termination wards. Many are professional and compassionate people and understand that what you did today is a terrifying experience. It's probably one of the most difficult decisions an adult ever makes, never mind a child. I have a list of people I shall be emailing this evening. I will not let the hopefully small minority of staff you met today continue to treat people in that manner.'

'Where will it be now?' Meg asked.

'Where will what be?'

'You know, the erm, baby, or the other word that you called it.'

'Foetus?'

'Yes.'

'I don't know,' said Jo, lying to Meg for the first time ever. She knew the police had requested a DNA extraction from the foetus, but she certainly didn't want to tell Meg what would happen after that. It would cause her more distress and guilt, and Jo decided that the girl certainly did not need any more of that.

'What you need to concentrate on is getting better, making your body strong again, and allowing me to help you do that.'

'I'm drained,' Meg said.

'Do you want me to go, so you can go to sleep?'

Meg glanced at Jo who saw the fear in the girl's eyes.

'You're safe here,' said Jo. 'No one will hurt you. I'll give you a stack of rules you'll hate, yes,' she added, grinning, 'but you are safe. Do you want me to stay while you close your eyes, and I'll read to you?'

Meg nodded and snuggled down. Jo picked up a book and began reading the story softly until Meg's eyes stayed shut.

Jo watched the girl sadly, feeling so angry about what she'd been put through in the hospital. She knew that this day would play on Meg's mind for a long time, possibly forever.

Sleep and rest turned out to be a week in bed for Meg, with plenty of nutritious food and vegetables that she hated. She protested loudly, but Jo persisted and even resorted to watching Meg eat after discovering a

large piece of broccoli in the toilet bowl that obviously had been too large to flush.

Jo was infuriatingly stubborn, Meg thought as she ate the stupid green things. However, she warned Jo that they would make her vomit.

'That's fine,' Jo answered calmly, but with a hint of a smile. 'I'll just make you some more if they project across the room, or even if they happen to land under your pillow. Vomit can land anywhere.'

Sighing, Meg pulled a handful of carrots from under her pillow, violently threw them all into her mouth, and began to chew viciously, glaring at Jo, who said nothing. Instead, she calmly returned to reading carefully chosen articles from the newspaper to Meg.

Sean returned from his fishing trip with an array of stories so surreal that Meg was sure he was making them up. Jo, however, was not surprised at any of his elaborate tales, and just shook her head in disapproval.

'Were any of you sober for even a day?' she asked.

'Cora certainly was!' Sean said. 'She was a pain in the backside. Kayleigh threatened to throw her overboard and would have done if I hadn't got between them.'

'Well, they'd better behave at Christmas!' added Jo in a mock menacing tone. 'I wish those two would not revert to small children every time they get together!'

Sean set up several TV channels on Meg's iPad so she could watch the football and anything else she wanted. However, she was annoyed that he and Jo had put a block on films over the age of PG.

'That's not fair,' she muttered to Jo. 'I've watched loads of over 18 films.'

'No more for a while. Easy viewing is what you need. I'm not keen on screens in the bedroom, but I'll make an exception, for now.'

'What will happen next with... you know, everything?'

The police had taken a written and recorded statement of Meg's version of events regarding Jenny Evans. However, she knew she still had to do another video interview at the police station.

'Nothing for a couple of weeks at least,' said Jo. 'The police are investigating and searching for Jenny's... well, they are looking for her.'

'And then?'

'And then you'll probably need to try to identify some of the people responsible for her killing and those in the grooming gang. It was helpful that you gave names of other children you knew who were being assaulted. They've gradually been removed from care and been placed in separate locations around the country. Hopefully, they will provide statements and give evidence too, and the police can catch all involved. You've been so brave, you know. I'm truly in awe of everything you've done.'

Meg looked away, her cheeks reddening, unable to take a compliment. 'When will the trial be?'

'We don't know yet. The evidence is still being gathered. What you need to do is keep safe and well. I'd like to arrange for a therapist quite soon.'

Meg looked away again, feeling angry.

'You need someone to work on this with. I've explained before. It's so important.'

'I'm dealing with it fine. I don't need some therapist! It's too much. It's too big to start the whole story. I don't want to tell anyone about it. They'll know it's my fault.'

'Do you think this is all your fault?'
Meg shrugged and refused to answer.

'Nothing that has happened is your fault at all, and a good therapist will help you understand that.'

Meg didn't reply.

'Shove up,' said Jo, getting on the bed. 'Let's find a film to watch on your iPad.'

'A PG one!' said Meg with disdain.

'There are a lot of good PG ones. Are you going to choose, or am I?'

'You do it. I've no idea.'

Jo got under the duvet with Meg, selected a film, and put her arm around the girl who snuggled in and put her arm around Jo's waist. Meg then realised that she didn't care what she was watching. To be hugged, loved, and to feel safe was the best feeling in the world, and she wished she could stay there cuddled up forever.

The week in bed flew by. Meg watched a film a day with Jo, and Sean came upstairs one evening while Jo sat in the room reading. He sat on a chair near enough to Meg to see the screen and watch a football match together. She enjoyed it but still needed Jo present. Though she was starting to become less wary of Sean, she wouldn't let her guard completely down around him. Meg doubted she'd trust any man ever again.

The second week, she started taking some short walks with Jo, who insisted it would help her regain her strength. She also insisted on afternoon naps and lots of food with vegetables and vitamin supplements. Meg quickly learnt that it was tough to get around Jo. When Meg said no, Jo had a hundred reasons why the answer was yes. She was a kind, loving woman, but refused to take no for an answer. She would patiently listen to Meg and then explain, in great detail, the workings of the body and why she needed to eat well and drink plenty of water. Every time Meg finished a glass, another one would appear. Meg knew Jo was looking after her, but she'd never been 'looked after' properly, so it was difficult, and at times, a fractious adjustment.

Meg became used to her routine of daily walks but then Jo had to return to work. Meg stuck to her promise of staying in the house when alone during the day. It was sometimes dull, but Meg enjoyed the silence, comfort, and safety. She read books, watched TV, and even tried to cook dinner for Jo and Sean one Friday night, which resulted in them returning home in panic as all the smoke alarms were going off. Meg was standing in the kitchen, looking despairingly at a broken Pyrex dish and its burnt contents scattered everywhere.

'I'm sssorry,' she stammered, terrified, mistaking their looks of worry for anger.

'It's fine,' said Sean, getting a brush and opening the windows. 'I quite fancied a takeaway tonight.'

'Thank you for trying to make us dinner,' said Jo, hugging the girl. 'It was very thoughtful.

I'll teach you how to cook if you want to learn.'

'Only if you have time,' Meg said, feeling that eternal guilt of being in the way rise up again.

'I'd enjoy it,' replied Jo. 'Though I must warn you, my cooking skills are not amazing.' She ignored a snort from Sean. 'But I can show you the basics.'

Meg nodded, and they choose dinner from a local takeaway menu.

'Can I go to bed?' Meg asked after dinner.

Jo and Sean looked meaningfully at each other.

'What have I done?' asked Meg, feeling panic well up inside her. Neither Jo nor Sean spoke; the silence became deafening.

'Will you please just tell me!' demanded Meg, who was beginning to sweat with anxiety.

'The police contacted us on Tuesday,' said Sean. 'They found Jenny's body. Her injuries fit with your version of events, and they found a great deal of DNA from the crime scene and on Jenny. It will help them track more people down if their DNA is on their database.'

'*Tuesday*!' shouted Meg. 'Why didn't you tell me then?'

'I've taken extended leave from today,' said Jo. 'More of a sabbatical. Given the circumstances, my manager was very supportive. We wanted to tell you at the point when someone would be around you to look after you and support you in the build-up to the trial and ensure you're not alone. The police will probably need to see you a few more times in light of the new evidence. Hopefully, you'll be able to ID some of the other people involved.'

'What does that mean?'

'Looking at photos they have of any known people who match any DNA, and also, they want you to look through photos of children who are either missing or who abscond a lot. They need your help to find out more about this gang and where their base is. The care home worker won't talk unless he and his wife get immunity.'

'What's immunity?'

'A witness protection scheme. New life, new identity. Basically, he'll go free, and so will his wife.'

'That's bullshit!' Meg said, her face going red with anger.

'That's why they need your help,' said Sean. 'If other girls are identified and come forward with stories just like your own, not only is there safety in numbers, but the evidence is more significant. Let's get these animals locked in a cage where they belong. What do you say?'

Meg looked at him for a while. He looked fierce, but she didn't feel scared. She felt protected.

'Okay,' said Meg, sounding more determined. 'Let's get them.'

'You are one of the bravest people I've ever met.' Sean sounded proud and spontaneously gave the girl a hug, which she returned without a second thought.

'Do you fancy a hot chocolate with all the trimmings?' asked Jo in a slightly croaky voice. Meg and Sean nodded.

'Fancy watching the news before bed?' he asked.

'Yes, that'll be great.' She flopped down next to him on the sofa, feeling totally natural and safe.

Chapter Eight

Christmas was almost upon them, and Meg felt nervous at the thought of finally meeting Sean and Jo's children. *What if they hate me? Or what if they think I'm taking their mum and dad away?* Her anxiety and insecurity grew, and she became quieter and more withdrawn each day.

Though she wasn't banned from seeing her birth mother, she didn't want to be around her, but she didn't want to be a burden at Jo and Sean's at Christmas and spoil their family gathering.

As Jo was on leave, she ensured they both went for a long walk every day, regardless of the weather, insisting that Meg wore gloves, a scarf and, much to her disgust, a bobble hat.

'I'm not a toddler!' she moaned, putting the hat on.

'Yes, I'm aware,' said Jo. 'Ready?'

'Would it matter if I wasn't?' Meg mumbled under her breath.

'What was that?'

'Yep, I'm ready,' Meg replied.

The journey to their walk seemed longer than usual this time.

'Where are we going?' asked Meg.

'Wait and see.' Jo grinned.

Meg looked out of the window at the enormous landscape that was so remote and isolated; there wasn't a single person in sight.

'It's creepy round here. I hope we don't break down. It's well scary.'

'See that building over there,' said Jo.

Meg looked and saw a huge, ugly, almost triangle-shaped tall building that had just appeared out of nowhere. It looked formidable and uninviting. As they passed the entrance, a sign proclaimed:

"Trespassers are at risk of being shot."

'Nice!' said Meg. 'What is it.'

'A military spy base, I think, though no one knows for sure. Most people say it's a listening base where they monitor communications over mobile networks.'

'It's a bit obvious for a spy base.'

'I know. Imagine being a soldier and being based here. There's not a lot to do except look at fields.'

'I always wanted to join the army.'

'Why?' asked Jo stiffly.

'Don't know. I've thought about it ever since I was little.'

'Was it so you could escape home, or because it's something that feels right for you?'

'Bit of both, I suppose. And you get to travel and have a gun, and then no one can hurt you.'

'Yes, but other people have guns too, so you are just as likely to be shot. Or be blown up by a land mine before you get a chance to point your gun at someone.'

'I might try to get a paper round or a Saturday job when, you know, when everything is over, and save up and buy an air rifle.'

'You most certainly will not!'

'What? Why?'

'Guns are dangerous! I hate them! And there will not be one in the house!'

'But I'm only staying with you until the trial is over, then I'm going back to a kids' home.'

'Who told you that?'

'You did!'

Jo said nothing and continued to look at the road ahead.

'I was thinking,' continued Meg, 'that I'd go to her. I mean, my, err, mum's house for Christmas.'

'Do you want to do that?' Jo asked cautiously.

'I don't want to be in the way when your kids come home. I don't want to spoil your Christmas with them. You don't see them a lot, and I know you miss them, and you don't want me there getting in the way. I don't want to be somewhere I'm not wanted.'

'You don't half get some wild ideas in your head sometimes, you know.'

'It's not wild. I'm just being realistic.'

'Well, it's not realistic. Your so-called mother has no rights over you. Legally, you are a ward of social care. As your foster mum, I have a responsibility towards you, and there is no way on Earth I will allow you to go anywhere for Christmas, understand?'

'But....'

'No!' said Jo firmly. 'No buts. It's not up for negotiation. Besides, all the kids know about you and are looking forward to meeting you.'

'Well, it's all a waste of time and cruel!' said Meg angrily, thinking of the Christmases before she went into care and getting excited, only to come down on Christmas morning to discover there were no presents, and often, no mother because she hadn't returned from going out the night before. Or the Christmases when a new man would be on the scene and make it clear she was in the way, so Meg would spend the day alone in her bedroom, listening to them getting drunker. Christmas had always been so painful and would be again when she was back in care, where the staff did make something that resembled an effort but it was hard for a lot

143

of the other kids who would either stay in their rooms or be angry and looking for a fight to hide their loneliness or memories of their families.

'What is?'

'You, this, Christmas, Sean, meeting your kids, trying to make me feel like I'm part of your family. I'll be in a kids' home after the trial and never see any of you again. It really is cruel. I don't want to see what a real family Christmas is like and be sad forever when I'm back in a crappy kids' home.'

'You're making a lot of assumptions.'

'No, I'm going on what was said! *So don't lie to me!*'

Jo pulled the car over and parked at the side of the desolate country road, high up in the moors.

'Why have you stopped?' demanded Meg.

'So we can talk! Besides, I can't concentrate on the road while you're angry and shouting.'

'*You only stopped because I said it was scary here!* Well, fine. I'll go.' And with that, Meg marched off, sidestepping bogs and heather as she went.

Jo jumped out of the car and chased after the furious child.

'Meg, stop, please! I told you I stopped because you were getting angry, and I was driving and couldn't talk properly.'

Jo caught up with her.

'I'm so sorry I scared you. Will you please stop walking!' she said as Meg continued marching into the unknown and forbidding land.

Meg swung around to face Jo. '*Why? Why should I stop walking? Why do I have to stop being angry? Why should I do anything you say? You are worse than the rest of them, my mother included. At least she made no secret about not wanting me, and the other foster parents didn't care! They just filled their house with kids so they'd get more money, and the kids' home staff didn't give a crap and didn't pretend to, and I don't want to wear this hat!*' She snatched it off and threw it to the ground.

'Just come back to the car, please. It's freezing. We can talk there.'

'I don't want to talk,' said Meg stubbornly, her teeth chattering with the cold.

'Okay, we won't talk yet. But we are going back to the car,' said Jo sternly, picking up the hat and putting it firmly onto Meg's head. Taking her arm, she marched her back to the car, totally ignoring Meg's protests. She opened the door and half pushed the child into the car and then got in herself, turned on the engine, and started driving again.

They travelled for another thirty-five minutes. Meg stared out of the passenger window, refusing to look at Jo, and Jo made no attempt to speak.

Eventually, they arrived at what seemed to be an ancient village. The buildings were made mainly from old stone, and there were lots of giant birds flying around that Meg didn't recognise.

Jo parked, got out of the car, and opened Meg's door. Meg begrudgingly got out. They walked down a street that was full of arcades, chip shops, and gift shops. They approached a steep slope, and Meg stopped in fright.

'What's that!' she said, forgetting she wasn't talking to Jo.

'The sea. Come on.'

'I'm not going in there!' said Meg, her eyes widening in terror at the endless, ferocious- looking water.

'Well, of course you're not. We're going for a walk along the beach.'

Meg followed Jo, who marched down the slope onto the sand. Jo walked very fast, and Meg was half running to keep up with her.

'Maybe I should have told you more about my children earlier,' began Jo, 'but so much has been happening and you've had so much to think about, I was reluctant to fill your brain with more information.

'Anyway, Tom is twenty-two, and, as you know, he's just begun a degree in medicine and hopes to be a doctor. Tom is the spitting image of his dad when he was the same age, and they are so unbelievably alike. They have a lot of banter now. It wasn't so easy when he was a teenager. Very clever, but easily bored. Sean and Tom clashed a lot. He's at university in London and lives with his boyfriend, Wes, who is also in his first year of a medicine degree.

'Kayleigh is twenty; she's doing an English degree at St Andrew's in Scotland. She's not sure what she wants to do with it or what to do when she graduates, but that's fine.

'She works hard, gets good grades, and I suspect, parties hard too. Kayleigh is more like me in terms of looks. She was a crazy toddler and always the kid at school who was raising petitions to change things. Kayleigh and I had a tough time during her teens. She's definitely a daddy's girl. She certainly knows how to press my buttons, and I'm afraid she's inherited my temper. But she's not yet learnt to control it quite as well as I have.

'Kayleigh is kind, outrageous, generous, fierce, and utterly unpredictable. You never know what's going to come out of her mouth! She's still a campaigner at university and nearly got kicked out in her first year after organising a peaceful protest on the campus grounds. There had been some attacks on female students, and the university didn't seem to be very proactive. They had no objections to the protest. However, they took objection to 200 female students sitting there, naked, holding placards that said:

147

"Still not asking for it!"

The university went ballistic as it ended up in the press. I've never been prouder of her than I was when I picked up the newspaper that day. I was a bit shocked to see my daughter naked on the front page, holding a megaphone and leading a chant. But also, extremely proud and very pleased that certain areas of her body had been blurred from the photograph!

'Jack is nineteen, and at Loughborough University. He is an amazing athlete; there's not a sport he doesn't excel at. He's probably looking at going into teaching or being a professional trainer. Still, he has a few ambitions himself; one is to win an Olympic medal. His strongest area is running; anything from the 100 metres to a marathon he is great at. He's a quiet man. He was always a quiet boy, not exuberant like his big brother and big sister. But he is content, has a great passion for what he does, and is a very gentle, sweet, and kind person. He has a girlfriend, Gemma, but we've not met her yet. He'll invite us to meet her when he's ready. Jack considers everything carefully; the others call him a "mummy's boy" as we talk a lot and always have done. He flew through his teens and would always talk about anything that bothered him. He may appear to be reserved at first, or even standoffish. He isn't. He's warm and welcoming, he just doesn't dive into situations like the older two.

'Cora is eighteen. She started university in September and is studying history. I think we've had two phone calls and one returned text message from her since she started. I told Sean to have words with her about that on the fishing trip!

'Though she's the youngest, she's the most independent of them all. Even as a little girl, she would insist on making her own packed lunches for school and would iron her own clothes. She likes things her way and has very set ideas about the strangest of things. Her teenage years were a struggle for both Sean and me, as we never knew what she was thinking.

'It is hard to admit, but I don't feel as though I know Cora very well. I try, Sean tries, but there's a distance there, and I wish I could fix it. Cora is also not keen on Kayleigh's 'excesses,' as she calls them. So, they do argue a fair bit, but it doesn't end up in Sean and I having to separate them now like it did when they were kids. Well, not often.

'Cora always struggled with being the youngest child. Everything she achieved was not a novelty, as her siblings had been there and done that. Also, Cora is the only one who struggled academically, and she hates the fact that the others sail through work and exams with seemingly little effort. She will find herself one day, I hope, but the jealousy of her brothers and sister does eat her up.

'They are all very different people, but love each other dearly, even though they would never admit it. I've told them that we've fostered you.

'They don't know why, and they don't know what's happened to you. They know your name and age, that's it. I don't think you've anything to be afraid of, and it may even be good for Cora to no longer be the youngest. Most of them are secure in my and Sean's love for them. They are curious about you, obviously. Kayleigh especially keeps asking questions about you, but only because I think if she finds out you've been wronged in some way, she'll want to help.

'And I'm sorry, but you can't tell them anything. Not with a court case looming. I'm not saying they would tell people deliberately. Still, one accidental word from any of them when drunk or a slip of the tongue could spread, and we don't know how far this net reaches.'

Jo carried on marching, with Meg hurriedly following until they reached a cove with a small chip shop.

'Table for two, please,' said Jo as she strode through the doors.

They were seated and given a menu and gave their drinks orders, then sat in silence. Jo looked at the menu, and Meg stared out to the sea.

'What would you like?' asked the waitress, returning.

'Fish, chips, and peas, please,' said Jo.

The waitress looked at Meg expectantly. 'I'm fine.' She tossed the menu down.

'Please make it fish, chips, and peas twice,' said Jo to the waitress, who gave a slight smirk at what looked like a typical mother/daughter argument.

The food arrived, and Meg still hadn't spoken. She folded her arms and returned to look out of the window. She realised she was starving, and the food in front of her looked and smelt amazing, but she was too stubborn to eat.

Jo ate for five minutes, completely ignoring Meg and concentrating on her food. Meg found this more and more annoying.

Eventually, she looked at Jo. 'I know my mother has no legal rights over me, but when I was officially put into care, they recommended some visits.'

'If it's in your best interests. Why do you think it's in your best interests after so long? And eat! Now!'

Unable to resist any longer, Meg picked up her knife and fork and started to wolf the food down.

'It'll be Christmas. She might want to see me at Christmas, and I'm not going to be at your house for Christmas. I don't want to. I've never had a proper Christmas, so why would I want just one, and then that be it? It's better not to know what it's like than to have just one and then be sad forever.'

'Will it be a nice Christmas if she and whatever boyfriend she has agrees? Will you be taken care of? What if you have a flashback? Will she know what to do?'

'I can deal with them myself,' Meg snapped.

Jo looked around the almost empty café and then pulled out her phone and sent a text. A reply came through a few minutes later.

Jo looked around the café again. The lunchtime crowd had left, and no one was in earshot of them.

'Ring her and ask her then,' said Jo. 'My only condition is that you do it on speakerphone.

'I won't talk unless she agrees, and then arrangements can be made. Okay?'

'Sure.' Meg's voice quivered slightly.

Jo dialled the number and put the phone in the middle of the table with the speaker on. After several rings, a voice on the other end barked, 'Hello! Who is it?'

Jo looked at Meg, who seemed shocked to hear her mother's voice. 'HELLO?' barked the voice again, getting angry.

'Mmmmm, it's me, Meg.'

'Oh. Still talking in that stupid way, then?'

'Hhhow aare yyyou?' replied Meg, her stammer getting worse and sweat pouring down her face.

'Fine. What do you want?'

'I, I wwwas...'

'Just spit it out, will you? I haven't got all day.'

'Was wondering if I could come to stay with you for Christmas?' Meg said as fast as she could, holding her hands together to stop them from shaking.

Meg heard laughing coming out of the phone speaker. 'Stay with me? For Christmas? Don't be stupid. Why?'

'Thhhought iiittt wwwwould bbbee nn....'

'Oh, shut up with that stupid talking. You sound just like your father, another waste of space. Like father, like daughter, eh? No wonder he scuttled off back to Ireland to sit in a field, looking at sheep. It is all he's good for.'

Meg suddenly heard urgent whispering in the background.

'Hang on,' said her mother. 'I signed you over to the state, and they pay foster parents a ton of money, so if you came to me, they'd have to pay me, right? I could put up with you if you kept out of my and Jeff's way. There's only a sofa, no spare room.

'*Jeff, pass me another beer*,' shouted Meg's mother. 'I'll find out how much I can get and let you know; how about that?'

Meg tried to talk, but the words wouldn't come out. Suddenly, Jo snatched the phone, took it off the speaker, and began a tirade so full of anger that Meg was shocked.

'I am Meg's foster mother,' she began, 'and you are the most disgusting excuse for a human being, never mind a mother, that I've ever heard in my life. Meg is not coming for Christmas. She is not coming to see you, and she most certainly isn't a nice little payday for you. You are a foul creature, you utterly disgust me, and I hope we do not speak again!'

Jo ended the call and looked up at Meg, who was back to staring at the sea. 'Meg,' said Jo, making the girl jump. 'Come on. Time to leave.'

Meg stood up and wobbled a bit; she noticed that her skin felt numb, and then she felt her brain begin to feel eerily detached from her consciousness. She robotically followed Jo as they made the return walk to the car. Meg was surprised when they arrived home so quickly. She couldn't remember the journey at all. She remembered getting into the car, and Jo putting some music on, and that was it.

'Can I go upstairs and be on my own?' she asked Jo. 'And can I miss dinner? I'm not hungry.'

'Sure,' Jo answered hesitantly, but she could see Meg needed time alone. She watched as the devastated child slowly walked through the hall and up the stairs, and all they could both hear was the voice of Meg's mother and her disgusting suggestion.

That night, Meg ran away.

CHAPTER NINE

Meg went upstairs and looked on the internet on her iPad. Once she found what she was searching for, she put on as many layers of clothes as she could and waited until Sean's car pulled up on the drive as he got home from work. Meg then opened the bedroom window, slithered through, and shimmied down the drainpipe.

She had about £5 on her, which she knew wouldn't get her very far. She got the bus into the city centre and then headed towards the motorway entrance. Rush hour was over, and there were fewer cars on the road. She stuck her thumb out and waited, getting colder and colder.

Meg began to think it would take hours to get a lift, but was pleasantly surprised that a car pulled up in less than five minutes. The driver pulled down his window.

'Where are you going?' he asked.

'Holyhead in Wales.'

'I can take you as far as Manchester. Any good?'

Meg hesitated. She desperately hoped a woman would stop. She looked around. There were very few cars around, and she knew the police would pick her up if they saw her.

'Are you getting in or not?' asked the man. 'I need to get moving.'

'Yeah, thanks,' said Meg, nervously getting into the warm car.

'I'm Ewan,' said the driver. 'And you are?'

'Err, Janine,' said Meg, saying the first name that came into her head.

'Well, err Janine, what are you doing out in the dark hitchhiking at your age? How old are you?'

'Sixteen,' she lied. 'Lost my purse and trying to get home.'

'Is home in Holyhead?'

'No, Ireland, but I can get a ferry from Holyhead.'

'You don't sound Irish.'

'My father is, and he lives there.'

They drove for another thirty minutes without speaking and listened to Christmas songs on repeat on the radio.

'Shit,' Ewan exclaimed. 'I'm running out of petrol. There's a service station coming up. I'm going to have to fill up.'

'Okay,' said Meg.

'They have food halls inside. Are you hungry? We could grab a bite to eat.'

'Err, I'm in a bit of a rush.'

'Well, I'm starving. Come on, I'm giving you a lift and offering to buy you dinner. Don't be so ungrateful.'

'Sure. Sorry,' said Meg, feeling bad. 'Food would be good, thank you.'

Ewan filled up with petrol and moved the car over to one of the many parking spaces in front of the food hall.

'Hang on,' he said. 'I'm just going to get my jacket from the boot. Wait there so you don't get cold.'

Meg waited, wondering what was taking the man so long to get a jacket. She looked through the rear-view mirror and saw him bending down. He stood up and caught her watching.

'Dropped my wallet,' he muttered as he walked round to her door and opened it. 'Come on.'

Meanwhile, many miles away, Jo and Sean sat down to dinner, and Jo told her husband about the day's events and the horrendous phone call with Meg's mother.

'Wow, she sounds like a right piece of work,' said Sean. 'But I don't get it. Why did she want to ring her? And how did you get her number?'

'I texted Steph, and she had it on file.'

'*What*!' shouted Sean. 'And she gave it to you? She had no right to do that. I'll be having words with her! And I don't understand why you let her call that woman.'

'What choice did I have?' asked Jo. 'Meg's gone into full rejection mode. She's terrified that the kids are coming home for Christmas. I suspect she's afraid they'll think she's taking their place, or that they'll be jealous.'

'But that's ridiculous. They would never...'

'I worry Cora may might be, but the others certainly won't be,' interrupted Jo. 'But Meg doesn't believe she's wanted here.

'All of her life, she's had her head messed about by her mother, getting affection one minute and then being tossed aside every time a new man came along. The last one said it was a choice between Meg or him. So, Meg was the one to go. Well, that was until the boyfriend saw pound signs and worked out that he could probably get money for letting her go back there. They are both drunks and drug users; going there would be catastrophic for Meg after all she's been through.'

'Well, it's not happening.' Sean stated firmly. 'More than that, it's not her choice. She won't be allowed to stay in a place with people who are drinking and using drugs.'

'I know. The other problem is that Meg has started to pull away from me emotionally. I'm aware she's protecting herself, but she's said several times that she'll be back in a kids' home when the court case is over as we said, we'd foster her while she got through this.'

Sean didn't respond, and they both sat there, eating their dinner in thoughtful silence. 'Should we go and talk to her?' asked Sean when they'd finished eating.

'And say what?' asked Jo. 'There's nothing new to say. We did say we'd foster her until after the court case. We never said we'd offer more.'

'But what if we do? How would you feel?'

'Make it permanent, you mean? It was you that was against it. You know what my feelings are.'

'Well, maybe my feelings have changed.'

'Maybe, or definitely? We can't mess about with this. We either commit for life or don't do anything other than what we promised. It's not fair.'

'I must admit, the thought of bringing another kid up, another teenager, after our four, fills me with dread. She has some complex issues, so it's going to difficult, but... arrrggh. I just don't know.'

'Difficult!' Jo declared. 'It's also difficult for her!'

'Don't have a go at me! I don't mean the investigation or even the trial. But what about the longer-term effects? Not just psychological, but practical. She hasn't been to school for a considerable length of time. Settling her into school will be hard for her and us. She's in shock at present. What about when that manifests into her behaviour? Will she start to run away again every time she's told off? Or skip school? Or even be violent?'

'Sean, that was pack mentality. She lived with fifteen other troubled teenagers and in complete chaos. It will take time for her to settle down. An adult would struggle to pick their life up after that, never mind a child. So yes, she will struggle. That's why it is an enormous decision.'

Sean tapped his fingers on the table. 'I don't know, Jo. I think the world of her, but that feeling I have for our kids, that unconditional love, the urge to do anything to protect them, which hit me the second I first laid eyes on them when they were born… I can't just transfer it to another kid that easily.

'You're a natural, but she also deserves a father who can do all of those things naturally. Also, I really don't know if I can do it all again. We've only just got the last one off to uni, and you've got to admit, we both gave a sigh of relief as Cora wasn't the easiest teenager, and that was without Meg's problems.'

'Think about it,' said Jo. 'She deserves people who love her and want her. If I do and you don't, she'll know and never agree to it anyway.'

'That's a bit harsh!'

'It's the truth.' Jo stood up and picked up the empty plates. She went into the kitchen, washed up, made a light snack and a drink for Meg, and headed upstairs.

She knocked on the door, but there was no answer. Knocking louder, there was still no reply. Jo noticed a cold breeze coming out from under the door. Filled with an awful sense of terror, she dropped the plate and screamed for Sean.

'What is it?' he said, breathless from running up to the top of the house.

'I can't bring myself to open the door,' said Jo, near to tears. 'I've knocked, and there's no answer, and there's a freezing draught coming from under the door. What if she's done it and k...'

'Move out of the way,' said Sean, 'and out of view of the room.' If Meg had fatally hurt herself, he didn't want Jo to see it.

He tried the handle, surprised to find the door unlocked, and walked into the room. Jo waited fearfully outside while Sean looked around the room and the en-suite.

He returned to the doorway; his face ashen. 'The window is open. She's gone.'

He ran downstairs and outside to the police officers who were meant to be keeping watch. He found them both asleep in the car. Sean yanked the door open and pulled the man in the driver's seat out of the vehicle.

'You lazy imbecile!' he shouted. 'We've got a missing child, and you are meant to be protecting her. Did you see her leave?'

'Errrrm, no. She never goes out when it's dark.'

Sean threw him against the car and pinned him to it by the throat.

'*Sean*!' shouted Jo as Sean raised his arm to punch the police officer. '*Stop*!' Sean let go of the man's throat.

'I should arrest you for that,' he said, stumbling over his words.

'You won't have a job after this, you idiot,' Sean snarled.

Jo got out her mobile phone and rang the Inspector.

'Has she got her mobile phone with her?' the Inspector asked.

'I think so,' said Jo. 'I called it. It was ringing, but I couldn't hear or see it anywhere.'

'We'll get a trace on it. Can you pass the phone to one of my officers, please?'

Jo passed the phone to the man who was rubbing his throat after being thrown against the car.

No one knew what the Inspector said, but the officer replied with a great deal of "yes, Ma'ams" and "no, Ma'ams" before ending the call.

'We are to stay here in case we get a trace, then we'll be able to blue light it to her location.'

'I'm coming too,' said Sean.

'I'm afraid that won't be possible. It's against...'

'Oh, shut up, you fool,' growled Sean. 'Do you want me to get your Inspector on the line again?'

'Fine,' he muttered.

'What do we do now?' asked Jo.

'Wait,' said the police officer, swaying slightly.

Meg sat down on a plastic chair and leant against a plastic table in an anonymous service station. She ignored the silent, vibrating phone in her pocket. Ewan ordered, then came and sat down.

'Shouldn't be long,' he said. 'I'm starving. How about you? When did you last eat?'

Meg thought about the fish and chips earlier that day and felt a sudden pang of regret and sadness at leaving. She shook the feelings out of her head, remembering Jo and Sean were not her family and didn't want to keep her. They had just got stuck with her due to a chance meeting in a car park.

'Errr, not since lunchtime,' she said.

'Is your dad expecting you? Might he be worried? Do you want to use my phone to give him a call?'

'No,' Meg said. 'It was kind of a surprise visit. He's not expecting me.'

She looked up as the server arrived at the table, just missing the gleam in Ewan's eyes.

'Cheeseburger and fries?' she asked.

'That's me,' said Meg.

'Great,' said the woman happily. 'And here's the double cheeseburger for your dad. Enjoy your meal.'

She walked away just as Meg was about to correct the woman.

Ewan made inane conversation, talking about his job as a travelling salesman and how it got boring and lonely being on the road so much. He started talking about the cleaning materials he sold to different companies. Meg was bored with the conversation. Under the service station's bright fluorescent lights, she saw Ewan looked a lot older than in the car's darkness. His suit was rumpled and worn, and his blonde hair was dirty and greasy.

'Finished?' he asked.

Meg jumped out of her daydream. 'Yes, thanks. That was good.'

'Great, come on. Let's get to Manchester.'

They walked down the steps out of the service station, and Meg realised how bitterly cold it had become. Snow had begun to fall, and she thought wistfully of the bobble-hat Jo had made her wear.

Meg walked to the car's boot with Ewan while he took off his jacket again and slid it inside without opening it fully.

'Oh, shit!' he snarled.

'What?' asked Meg, scared. 'Look at the bloody tyre!'

Meg looked at the back left tyre; it was completely ripped to shreds.

'Someone has done that on purpose. Look at it!'

Meg looked helplessly at the tyre.

'What do we do now?'

'Go and sit in the car, and I'll call the AA out to come and sort it. I don't have a spare tyre.'

Meg sat in the passenger seat and watched in the mirror as Ewan marched around outside in the snow that was now settling. He was gesturing angrily to whoever he was talking to. Eventually, he ended the call and approached the passenger door.

'They're going to be at least three hours,' he said, opening the door. 'Or longer if the snow gets worse. Come on. We can't sit here for hours, we'll freeze. I told them we'll wait in that small hotel over there.' He pointed to a basic service station hotel. 'They'll ring me when they get here.'

'Maybe I'll try and get a lift with someone else,' said Meg, unsure.

'Like who?' asked Ewan, looking around. The car park was empty, and the snow was getting deeper. 'Best to wait for the AA,' he said. 'You'll freeze to death standing out here asking strangers for a lift. Come on.'

He grabbed his jacket and a bag from his boot.

'What's the bag for?' asked Meg.

'I'm a travelling salesman. I always keep a bag of essentials in the car for situations just like this.'

They walked into the hotel, which felt blissfully warm after being outside for so long. 'Go sit over there,' said Ewan. 'I'll go talk to them at the desk and see if we can hang out here for a few hours.'

Ten minutes later, Ewan came back. 'Good news and bad news, I'm afraid. The bad news is that they won't let us hang about in the lobby for free, but the good news is that I can rent the last room in the building while we wait. Come on. It's on the third floor.'

Ewan picked up his bag and walked towards the lift. Turning back, he saw Meg still sitting down. 'Get a move on,' he said. 'Or they'll chuck you out.'

Meg looked out of the window at the snowy blizzard and reluctantly got up and followed Ewan. Her instincts were screaming at her to run. She was scared, but Ewan had been so kind to her and didn't seem like he'd do anything wrong, and she felt mean just running off. She stepped into the lift and watched the doors close, wishing nothing more than that she was at Jo's house, snuggled up in bed and having a huge, safe cuddle.

Jo, Sean, and the two exhausted-looking police officers sat in the house, drinking coffee. Sean was glaring at them. Jo was quiet and worried. The silence in the air was deafening, then Jo's phone rang, the police radio sprang into life, and there was a banging at the door. Everyone jumped. Sean ran to the door, Jo answered her phone, and the police got on the radio.

The Inspector entered the house. 'We've traced her mobile. Did she have any money on her?'

'No, I don't think so,' said Jo.

'Then we need to move. Jo, you come with me. Sean, you go with Tweedledum and Tweedledee here.' She nodded at the officers fiercely. 'Do not mess this up!'

'Yes, Ma'am,' they said in unison and moved slowly to the door with Sean hot on their heels. They were off with sirens blazing in seconds.

'Come on, Jo,' said the Inspector. 'I'll explain on the way.'

'Put the TV on if you like,' said Ewan. 'I'm going to have a quick shower. Been on the road all day and need to freshen up.' He picked up his bag and headed to the bathroom. 'And help yourself to whatever is in the mini-bar; it's all on expenses!'

Meg looked out of the window at the snow and the motorway ahead of her, and farther, just countryside. She couldn't see any houses; they really were in the middle of nowhere.

Meg put the TV on and sat in an uncomfortable chair, avoiding the bed. Ewan was taking ages in the shower. Her feeling that something was very wrong increased, and she felt increasingly unsure about being trapped in a hotel room. Deciding to leave, she stood up just as Ewan came out of the bathroom with a towel wrapped around his waist.

'Damn cheap hotels. They don't even provide a dressing gown,' he barked, shutting the bathroom door. 'Oh, don't go in there. The toilet is blocked. I've called down, and they'll send someone up to fix it.'

He walked over to the mini-bar, reached for a small whisky, and downed it in one before getting another. 'Do you want a drink?' he asked Meg. 'There's vodka, red wine, white wine, gin.'

'I'm fine, thanks.'

'Oh, have a drink,' Ewan insisted and poured some wine in a glass. He put it on the table in front of her.

'So, how old are you really?'

'I told you, sixteen.'

'Bullshit,' he said aggressively. 'The problem with women is they tell lies, and now even the girls are doing it. What is it? Are you all pulled out of class at a young age and taught how to lie to men and ridicule them and told that we're all stupid?'

'I think I'll go now,' said Meg, standing up.

'*Sit down*!' he screamed, and Meg sat down, shaking with fear. 'My ex-wife was like that.' He got another whisky and knocked it back. 'Manipulative, cunning, sly. *A liar*! Are you like that?' He slapped his hand down on the table, making Meg almost jump out of her skin.

'Nnnnnooo.'

'Nnnnnnoooo,' Ewan repeated, laughing. 'Do you stammer when you lie?' Meg didn't respond and looked around the room towards the door.

'Don't even think about it. It's locked, and I'd take you down in seconds. I used to do martial arts in the army. Was quite good at it. Fast. They never saw it coming.'

Meg found herself on her back on the floor in agony. Ewan had punched her right in the face, and she hadn't seen it coming at all.

'See, told you I was good,' he said, getting another whisky. 'Get up and sit down.'

Meg straightened the chair and grabbed a tissue from the table to hold to her bleeding nose. Tears from the blow streamed down her eyes.

'If you cry, I'll punch you again,' Ewan said, and then looked out of the window. 'Snow's getting pretty bad. It looks like we may have to spend the night here. But that's not such a bad thing, is it? We can have some fun.' He stood up, closed the curtains, and grabbed another drink. 'Some friends of mine are in trouble.' He took a gulp of whisky. 'It seems a naughty little girl has been telling lies about them, saying they had sex with her when she didn't want it. And *Meg*, yes, I do know your real name. It seems like you are the ringleader in these lies when we all know it was your fault. You were asking for it. Begging for the attention. Loving every minute. You're to blame for this, aren't you?'

Meg didn't answer and was sent spinning off the chair again as she received a backhanded slap from Ewan.

'*Do not ignore me, ever!*'

'No, I am not to blame,' said Meg quietly, refusing to cry despite the pain and terror.

'Oh, yes you are,' said Ewan, moving closer. He reached out and touched Meg's face. 'Tut tut, aren't you accident-prone. Do you think it was a coincidence that I picked you up tonight? We've been watching you in your secret hiding place. We have people everywhere. In the police, social services, children's homes. You've chosen the wrong side here. I followed your bus, waited until you got to the motorway junction, and there you were, like a lamb to the slaughter.' He laughed manically. 'Did you think you were special? We've got hundreds of girls just like you. Kids' homes are easy pickings. Sad, lonely girls who no one loves. It's just so easy. Supply and demand, you see. Our supply has gone down thanks to you, and our customers have been complaining! But we always get more. We've got a storage container on a boat right now, bringing another couple of hundred girls like you. All unwanted kids who won't be missed. They'll arrive at Dover on Christmas Eve, just in time for our important clients who have, well, let's say, some Christmas gatherings with a difference planned. Hedonistic, fun parties, in the type of houses that you attended!'

'I was dragged to them!' spat Meg. 'And drugged!'

'It's pretty funny, really,' he went on, appearing not to hear Meg. 'Their parents think they're coming for a wonderful life in a children's home, where they'll go to school. We even made brochures and said we're a church organisation that would sponsor them. Idiots, the lot of them. Now, be a good girl and go lie on the bed.'

'No!' said Meg. 'You are a sad old man who everyone hates, so you hang around, trying to pick up teenage girls. You are disgusting.'

Sean was growing more and more furious in the back of the police car as they blue lighted up the motorway over the Pennines.

'Have you been drinking?' he demanded of the driver.

'No, sir,' said the officer, who was now slurring his words.

'Pull over, I'm driving!' Sean ordered as the officer took a dangerous swerve, just missing an articulated lorry.

'That's not allowed, I'm afraid. Only a police officer...'

'Pull over now, you drunken idiot, before you get us all killed, or I swear to God I'll jump in the front and throw you out.'

The car skidded to a stop on the hard shoulder. Sean got out and opened the driver's door.

He noticed the officer in the passenger seat was fast asleep.

'I don't believe this!' Sean said, seething with rage.

'You, *out*!' he said to the driver, who hesitated and slowly got out, staggering towards the moving cars. For the second time that evening, Sean grabbed him by the scruff of the neck and then threw him into the back seat. He took the driver's seat and set off at full speed, causing other cars to swerve to avoid a collision. He put on the blue lights and raced through the snow, hoping he wasn't too late.

Meg knew another punch would come, but this time she was ready. She ducked, grabbed the big lamp at the side of the bed, and smashed Ewan over the head with it. He reeled back in shock, and Meg charged forward and kicked him between the legs. He made for an easy target as his towel had fallen down. He doubled over in pain, and she picked up the chair and started beating him over the head with it. She lost her grip, and the momentum of swinging the chair sent it flying towards the curtains and straight through the window. The noise was horrendous, but Meg only saw that as an advantage. She looked around for something else to hit the man with but made a mistake by taking her eyes off him. Then he was standing, pushing her against the wall and putting his hands around her throat.

'Well, that wasn't very nice, was it?' he said, blood dripping down his face. He picked up a large ceramic vase and whacked Meg hard over the head with it. She reeled back, feeling dizzy. In excruciating pain, she saw him approaching her, but her legs had turned to jelly. He had her against the wall and grabbed her again by the throat. He squeezed tighter and tighter; Meg's vision became blurry.

'I'm afraid it's time for you to leave,' Ewan said, smiling. 'Any last words before the final squeeze? Oh, I forgot. You can't talk, can you? Such a shame.'

The Inspector radioed the station while speeding down the motorway; she was doing 100mph, despite the horrendous weather.

'Have any units arrived at the hotel? Over.'

'Negative, Ma'am,' came a voice that was barely audible over the static. 'The weather is bad and impeding progress. Greater Manchester Police are en route but are stuck on the moors. The snowploughs are on their way. Over.'

'Where's the helicopter? Over.'

'Negative, Ma'am. Visibility is poor. We can't get an NPAS unit in the air. What's your ETA? Over.'

'Five minutes if we don't get stuck. Over.'

'Roger that. I've lost main set and PR contact with Victor Charlie 72.'

'Find them! Out.'

'What was that about?' asked Jo.

'They can't contact the personal radios or the main radio in the car that Sean is in.' The Inspector applied more pressure to the accelerator. 'It's probably snow-related. Don't worry too much.'

Sean skidded to a stop outside the hotel. Reaching into the unconscious officer's pocket, he pulled out his warrant card and grabbed his hat and a high-vis police jacket. He raced to the hotel reception and flashed the police badge. 'Do you have this girl here?' Sean showed the receptionist a photograph that was on his phone.

'Yes,' she replied. 'She arrived with her father earlier this evening.'

'Where are they?' Sean demanded.

The receptionist hesitated.

'I swear to God that if you do not give me the room number, I'll have you locked up for aiding a kidnapping.'

'Room 304!' she replied fearfully.

Sean ran before she could give him a spare key card.

Minutes after Sean arrived, Gina and Jo swerved to a stop outside the hotel, as did an ambulance.

Gina examined the car Sean had arrived in and found two of her officers sound asleep inside and looking up to a broken window.

'We should wait for armed backup,' Gina told Jo.

'No way. Sean and Meg are in there. I'm going with or without you.' She headed towards the doors, and Gina ran after her and gestured for the paramedics to follow.

Meg began to lose consciousness and started to fall. She heard a crash and assumed it was her own body hitting the floor, then the squeezing stopped. She saw a man who looked like Sean grab Ewan and start beating him to a pulp. Meg knew it wasn't real. It was her imagination, or maybe it was even death. Two more people came into the room. One grabbed Meg, forced her into an upright position, and held her tightly. Then a blurry image of people in bright yellow jackets started feeling her body and shining lights into her eyes.

More and more blurred images of people in yellow jackets entered the room. A lot of shouting reverberated around Meg's eardrums, none of it making sense.

'That's enough, Sean!' she thought she heard a woman say, and Ewan slumped next to her on the floor, his face covered in even more blood. Meg's eyes finally closed, her body flopped down, and the noises stopped.

Meg could smell Jo. She knew her nose was broken, so it wasn't an actual smell. Maybe it was just her mind finding the happiest smell it could before she died.

And then there was nothing.

CHAPTER TEN

Five days later

Sean looked in the mirror, straightening his black tie, and grimly noted the remaining scabs on his knuckles from beating that animal half to death in the hotel room. Ewan had even filed assault charges against Sean, but it was his word against a police inspector who said she had been with Sean the entire time and witnessed no assault.

Sean had never been a violent man and never would have believed himself capable of what he did to Ewan. He really thought he would have killed him if the Inspector and Jo had arrived just a couple of minutes later. He was surprised yet grateful that the Inspector lied on his behalf when that animal tried to press charges against him.

His mind wandered to the scene in the bathroom, which consisted of giant bolt cutters, plastic sheeting all around the floor, and a giant vat of acid. That image, which had made him throw up, would be etched into his brain forever. He stared at himself grimly in the mirror, searching his soul, thinking about what he could have done to stop such a horror from occurring.

Feeling dizzy, he sat on the bed, remembering his and Meg's snowball fight and Jo going mad at them both. Arguing about football. Meg accusing him of watching cartoons.

'Still not a cartoon,' he muttered to himself as tears began to fall down his face faster and faster until he was sobbing uncontrollably.

After that grim day, news emerged that Ewan, who was being held in custody, had been charged with the murder of his ex-wife and her new boyfriend. He was also being questioned about another ten female hitchhikers who had gone missing. By the third day, he confessed to the murder of all of them, insisting they all deserved it. Ewan had shown no remorse.

Furthermore, he was another link in the chain. His DNA matched some of the DNA that was found on the body of Jenny Evans.

He was questioned endlessly about how he knew Meg's location, and who else was involved, but he just grinned. Every pore of him exuded pure evil.

Sean stood up, wiped his face, and left the house, dredging as much strength as he could muster. The cold, empty building didn't feel like home anymore, and he drove off with a knot of dread in his stomach.

He approached the expansive old building and slowly made his way up the steep steps. Not noticing people looking worried or those in tears, he just kept his eyes straight ahead, knowing he had to be there for Meg.

He entered the courtroom, passing the two armed guards outside, just as Ewan, whose actual name was Leon Hughes, was entering the dock. He made eye contact with Sean and grinned; Sean stared back, wishing he'd had just five more minutes alone with that animal.

The courtroom was sealed, which meant no reporters, only the judge, court reporter, two barristers, and Sean. The proceedings were surprisingly short. Ewan, as he continued to be referred to for security reasons, pleaded guilty to the murder of twelve people. However, he pleaded not guilty to being involved in child sexual exploitation. He was given twelve life sentences without parole. At the same time, his suspected role in the grooming gang and Jenny's murder was to be investigated.

He was being sent to a prison on the Isle of Wright, as far away as possible. He would be kept in solitary confinement so he was unable to get messages to any other gang members. Ewan looked furious, shouting at the judge, and attempted to escape from the dock. He was face down, handcuffed, and had guns pointing at him in less than a second. He turned his head and glared at Sean.

'This isn't over!' he shouted menacingly. Sean smirked at him in return and left the court, feeling slightly happier.

He arrived at the hospital an hour later. Meg was in a private room guarded by an armed police officer. They nodded to each other, and Sean walked in to see his wife sitting on a chair with her head on Meg's bed, fast asleep.

Meg was heavily sedated; there were many internal injuries, an internal bleed, a head injury, and trouble breathing. She'd been seconds away from dying, the doctors had said. They were concerned about possible brain damage. A scan also showed significant swelling on the brain. She wasn't out of the woods yet; she was still classed as 'critical', and Jo had refused to leave Meg's side for the past five days and nights.

He went and got some coffee, returned and gently shook his wife. She sat up and gratefully took the steaming cup.

'How did it go?' she asked.

'Twelve life sentences for murder and remanded in custody. Just a formality while they investigate his role in the child sexual exploitation gang and Jenny's... well, you know.'

'How did he find her?' Jo asked, sounding distraught and nodding at Meg.

'I've no idea; maybe she will have some answers if... when she wakes up. Now, I've ordered a taxi, and you are going home to eat and sleep.'

'No, I'm staying here.'

'What if they decide to try to wake Meg tonight or tomorrow? She'll need you at your best, not like this. You haven't slept properly in days. I'm going to stay right here, and I promise I will ring if anything at all happens, but please, for all of our sakes, go home.' Sean moved over and wrapped his arms around his wife. 'I love you so much, and you need to sleep. Please go home, will you?'

She looked into her husband's eyes, feeling such love for him, and she saw the worry there. It had been an awful time for them all, and she agreed to go, just to give him one less thing to worry about.

'Okay,' she said, 'but I'll be back tonight.'

'Just eat, have a shower, go to bed, and come back when you're awake and more rested. I promise I will ring if anything changes.'

Jo nodded and kissed her husband. She then went over, kissed Meg on the head, whispered something to her that Sean didn't hear, and then left with tears in her eyes.

Sean took Jo's seat and looked at the child in front of him; he couldn't see anywhere that wasn't bruised.

Returning to his earlier thoughts and now looking at Meg, he was confident he would have killed Ewan or Leon, or whoever he was, with his own bare hands if given a chance again.

There was a knock at the door, and Sean jumped, relieved to see the consultant enter.

'Hello,' he said. 'Is your wife here still?'

'No, I've sent her home to sleep. She's exhausted.'

'Well, I'm glad she finally listened to someone. We've been trying to send her home for days for the sake of her own health.

'Anyway, there's no easy way to say this, but the next twenty-four hours are crucial. The results from the brain scan are in. It shows that the brain swelling has not improved, which is unusual after five days. It has actually got worse, and we need to do something about it.'

'What?'

'We're not at the point where she needs surgery yet, but we are going to have to control the intracranial pressure.'

'How?'

'We use something called hypertonic saline to try to control pressure in the brain. If we're lucky, it will work by drawing the extra water out of the brain cells into the blood and let the kidneys filter it out.'

'So why are the next twenty-four hours crucial?'

'We're starting the treatment now. If there is increased swelling tomorrow, it means the saline isn't working. If that is the case, we will need to operate or, more specifically, do a craniotomy.'

'What does that involve?'

'I think it's best to discuss that if we need to do it tomorrow. It's two p.m. now. We will know more within twenty-four hours. I suggest you leave your wife to sleep, but she'll need to be here tomorrow afternoon as you both need to give consent if we do have to operate. It's a last resort, but if it comes to it, she won't survive without the surgery. She may not survive the actual surgery.'

Sean nodded grimly. 'Start the saline course then; she'll get through it. I've never met such a fighter in my life.'

The consultant nodded. 'Would you mind stepping out for half an hour while we do what we need to do?'

Sean nodded, looked at Meg, kissed her on the forehead, and left just as his wife had done.

He returned half an hour later to the second, just as a medical team was leaving.

'What now?' he asked the consultant.

'We wait, keep her sedated, and hope. I'm sorry.'

'Can she hear me if I talk to her?'

'I doubt it.'

'Doubt?'

'We've no idea what state her brain is in, or even if it recovers, she may not understand language anymore. We've no idea what her cognitive function is.'

'Doubt, though,' said Sean. 'You don't know for sure.'

'No, but don't get your hopes up.'

Sean went back into the room. Nothing about Meg had changed; she just looked   asleep.

Battered and bruised, but still asleep.

He removed his iPad from his bag. 'Right, you,' he said to her firmly. '*Frozen* is not a cartoon! I'm downloading it. I know you can't see it, but I hope you can hear it.'

He pressed play, put the iPad on Meg's bed, and watched the film.

'See,' he said at the end. 'It is a film and has some decent songs like, *Do You Want to Build a Snowman*,' he sang, causing the armed officer to look through the window. Sean gave him a sheepish wave.

'Next,' he said, 'and I can't believe I'm doing this, is Man United's Champion's League cup final from 1999. I know you've watched it about 1000 times. I've seen the downloads on our TV. I remember watching it live, way before you were born. But spare me the first half. It's so boring. Let's skip to the good bit.' He played the last ten minutes of the game and turned up the volume just before Sheringham, and the super-sub Solskjaer, scored. He then explained what was happening. 'Now Schmeichel and Fergie are lifting the trophy. That always looks weird, Schmeichel is about 6'7; Fergie was lucky not to be thrown in the air with the cup!

'I've downloaded a selection of books, political fiction. This one is good but is by Jeffery Archer, so don't tell Jo; she's not a fan. It's called *First Amongst Equals*. Four men. Sorry it's all men, but it's an old book. It tells the story from their first day becoming MPs to each trying to become prime minister.' He settled back and started reading; his voice grew hoarse, but he read and read throughout the night and finished the book at three a.m. 'Hope you liked it,' he said.

'I'm going to snooze for a couple of hours, let your brain have a rest, and then I'll read the morning newspaper to you. Goodnight, sweetheart.' He kissed her on the forehead again before settling down under his jacket.

At five a.m., Sean woke, went downstairs and got a newspaper, along with a much-needed coffee. Yawning loudly, he took the stairs back up to try to wake himself up a little.

'Good morning,' he said to the unresponsive Meg. 'I've got you a *Guardian* and a *Daily Mirror* for the sport, as they only seem to talk about that team of yours!'

He read *The Guardian* from cover to cover and even asked Meg the answers to the crossword. He then started on the *Daily Mirror* and was reading a match analysis when Jo suddenly walked in, still looking tired, but more rested.

'Hello,' he said, looking at his wife and giving her a smile.

'Morning. How was the night?'

'We need to talk, I'm afraid. Do you want to go somewhere else?'

'Why?'

'I know it sounds daft, but I don't want her to hear it again.' He nodded at Meg. 'I don't know if she can hear or not, but I've spent all night watching a film and football matches and reading to her. I don't know what she can hear, but I want to keep it positive.'

'Come on then.'

They entered the empty visitors' room.

'There was a kind of, er, development after you left yesterday.' Sean began.

'What development? And why didn't you tell me, as agreed?'

'Because the consultant said that today is going to be tough and you needed sleep. We need you to be able to process the information, and you can't do that when you're sleep deprived.'

'What development?' barked Jo, glaring at her husband.

Sean sat down and explained about the brain swelling and how the treatment they provided yesterday would basically give Meg a twenty-four-hour window to recover. If not, they'd need to do very invasive brain surgery today.

'What's the prognosis for the surgery?'

Sean shrugged helplessly. 'She has severe injuries as well as the brain injury. It would be a 50/50 prognosis if someone just had a brain injury, but in her current condition, the odds are slightly against her.'

'Well, she's not having it then!' said Jo.

'You have to listen to me,' said Sean, standing up and holding his wife's shoulders. 'If the scan this afternoon shows no improvement, and they don't operate, she will die. If they do operate, she might live.'

'I told you to tell me if anything changed, and not stay up with her all night playing films and football matches and reading books and newspapers. Her brain needs rest.'

'I disagree! Her brain needs stimulation! She needs to remember all the things she loves and be reminded why she has to fight for that chance to survive. Meg is a fighter, Jo. You know it too. And, after everything she's been through, I wanted to remind her of all that she has to fight for.

'Most people would have given up by now. She nearly did so herself when she first came to stay with us. Meg couldn't see a life worth living. The hurt was too big, but that began to change. I know I didn't tell you, but what would you have done? Come back here, that's what. It's going to be a long, hard day. We both need you not nearly fainting with exhaustion!'

'You still should have told me!'

'Can we leave it for now, please? The consultant will be doing his morning rounds soon, so can you leave off accusing me of being the world's biggest git until after that?'

'This isn't over,' said Jo, approaching the door.

'Yep, thought so,' mumbled Sean.

They reached Meg's room to find the consultant inside. 'Ahh, there you are,' he said, looking carefully at a chart.

'Is everything okay?' asked Jo quickly, as the consultant frowned over Meg's chart as his eyes moved down the page.

'Strange,' he muttered absent-mindedly.

'What is?' demanded Jo.

The consultant looked up. 'Meg's heart and brain activity were unusual last night. Very unusual.'

'In what way? Can you be specific?' asked Jo, glaring at Sean.

'Look at this,' he said, showing them the charts. 'There were significant spikes in brain activity during the night that directly correspond with spikes in her heart rate. Sean, you were with her last night. Do you mind if I ask what you did?'

Sean reluctantly told the consultant everything he had done the night before and was asked to get out his iPad and note when and what he was playing. Then he was asked to record the times he was reading to Meg.

The consultant made a quick graph of these and then held them next to Meg's charts; the times matched precisely to the spikes.

'What does it mean, though?' asked Jo curtly.

The doctor smiled. 'It means she was listening. I'm going to get her down for a brain scan now instead of waiting. We can always do another one later if we don't see anything different.'

The consultant left the room momentarily and returned with two porters, who began to move Meg's bed and machinery.

'Can I come?' asked Jo.

'Afraid not. But we won't be long, and the results will be seen immediately.'

Sean and Jo returned to the uncomfortable chairs they'd both spent many hours in. They sat in silence; Sean knew Jo was still angry, and it was pointless to broach the subject again, even though his actions may have helped Meg.

After an hour, Sean left the room and began pacing the corridor outside, getting in people's way and earning tuts and sighs from patients and staff alike.

Then the consultant returned alone and ushered Sean back into the room.

'Where's Meg?' demanded Jo. 'We've not consented to surgery, so you'd better not have...'

The consultant held his hand up to stop Jo.

'She's not in surgery. It appears that the almost fatal brain swelling has reduced by 50% overnight. We've upped her dose of the medication and are keeping her near the MRI room so we won't need to keep moving her to do checks. I don't know how you did it, Sean, but you kickstarted her system. She was closing down, slowly but surely. She'd stopped fighting. But now, it feels like, and this isn't a medical term, she's found her fight again. Meg is battling with her body to survive. The medication helped, but we rarely see such rapid results. If she continues to improve, we may be able to look at lowering or even stopping the sedation.'

'So, she'll be, okay?' asked Sean hesitantly.

'It's still a brain injury, and there are no certainties, but I'm cautiously optimistic. Why don't you both get out of here, together? Go and have breakfast, have a walk, go home. There won't be any more news until late afternoon, and I'm afraid you're not allowed in the MRI suite. But I will ring you if there's any news, or if we plan to bring her out of sedation.

We won't do it until you're both here. Please, just go. Have some time alone.'

They both nodded somewhat reluctantly and left the building.

'Home?' asked Sean.

'Home.'

They were both in different cars and set off in opposite directions to their vehicles. Once home with a hot drink and food, they sat in the lounge, feeling slightly more relaxed.

'Sean,' said Jo.

'Hmmmm?'

'I'm sorry. I was wrong. It looks like your mad ideas may have saved Meg's life.'

'So close to the perfect apology,' Sean said, grinning. 'You could have left the "mad" out.'

'I know. I'm sorry, I really am.' Jo looked tearful. 'You said you were scared you wouldn't feel as protective of Meg as our other kids if we adopted her.'

'And your point is?'

'You nearly beat a man half to death to protect Meg. I have never seen you so angry, ever!'

'Point taken,' Sean said, and moved to the sofa to hug Jo. They lay down, and he held his wife in his arms.

'I love you,' he whispered, but Jo was already asleep, and in seconds, he was too. They woke suddenly several hours later to the sound of the phone ringing.

'It's five p.m.! Why did you let me sleep for so long?' Jo demanded unreasonably from Sean, who had also just woken.

Ignoring his wife, he answered the phone.

'On our way.' He turned to Jo. 'Hospital. We need to go now.'

Jo went white. 'They say that when someone is about to die!' she said desperately.

'Come on, we need to move.' Sean left the house and approached the police car. 'We need to get to the hospital, blue lights.'

The officers, who were different from the previous ones and now armed, nodded. Sean got in, and Jo ran to the car and jumped into the back seat.

They arrived in less than ten minutes and charged up to the third floor. The consultant and a team of medics were standing outside Meg's door, talking urgently, and issuing instructions.

'What's happening?' demanded Sean.

'That was quick!' exclaimed the consultant. '*What is going on?*'

'It's good news,' the consultant said quickly. 'Did they not tell you that?'

'Obviously not,' said Jo dryly.

'The swelling has decreased dramatically. I don't believe in miracles, but this... well, I'm stumped. Meg's brain is showing what you'd see in a mild concussion, so we're going to wake her up and thought you'd want to be here. But I have to warn you, Meg suffered from a lack of oxygen when being strangled and has had a severe head injury. She'll be confused when she wakes up, but we simply do not know if her cognitive function has been impaired.'

'Brain damage?' asked Sean.

'Possibly. We have no way of knowing. Do not dive in asking questions. Just be where she can see you. When people wake up from sedation to this extent, they often get agitated and try to pull wires and tubes out. We may have to hold her arms to stop this. We will be as gentle as we can, but you need to trust us and not jump in, understood?'

Jo and Sean nodded.

'Right, let's do this.' The consultant marched into Meg's room, followed by his entourage.

Jo and Sean stood at the foot of the bed, close enough to be seen, but not in the way of the hospital staff.

The medical team began their work and then finally removed one of the tubes.

'Meg,' said a nurse. 'Meg, come on. Time to wake up.'

Meg groaned slightly, and her closed eyes began to flutter. The nurse swabbed her dry mouth with water. 'Meg,' she repeated louder. 'Come on. Time to wake up.'

Meg's eyes fluttered faster and faster, and then, ever so slowly, she opened them. Her eyes came into focus, and immediately, as predicted, she violently started thrashing about and trying to pull off her oxygen mask and reach for the tubes.

The medics grabbed her arms and legs and held her firmly. Sean took a step forward as if to stop them, but Jo put her arm in front of him and shook her head. Distressed, he stepped back again.

The thrashing continued, and the consultant glanced at his colleague 'We might have to sedate her again,' he said, looking at the clock.

'Wait!' said Jo. 'Let me come and talk to her.'

He looked at Jo for several seconds and nodded.

Jo went to the head of Meg's bed. 'Meg, it's Jo. You're safe in a hospital. Sean is here too.

'No one is going to hurt you. They're making you better.'

'Is it safe to touch her head?' she asked, looking at the doctors.

'Yes. Gently, obviously.'

Jo began to stroke Meg's hair as she used to when she hugged her at bedtime. 'You're going to get better. We're not leaving you. Everything is safe.'

Jo repeated her mantra several times over, and Meg's body relaxed. The medics moved back so Sean could join Jo. He held her hand gently.

'You are really safe. There's even a policeman outside with a gun!'

Jo looked at him and rolled her eyes, but at the same time, something that looked like a smile showed on Meg's face.

'She's breathing independently,' said another doctor. 'I'm going to remove the oxygen mask. Raise the top of the bed into a semi-upright position. Remember the broken ribs,' she said to a nurse, and he reached for the bed control pad.

'Okay, give her sips of water. Small sips; her throat is still damaged, so it may hurt.'

Meg swallowed the water, grimacing each time. Her eyes then focussed on Jo and Sean.

She stared at them blankly for a minute, and then her eyes filled with tears.

Jo leant down and kissed her on the head. 'We're here for you. We're not going anywhere. You're safe.'

Sean squeezed her hand gently, and she looked at him and squeezed it back.

'Excellent,' said the consultant. 'Her stats are good considering what she's been through; if they change, an alarm will go off, but don't panic. We will leave you alone for a while, but we'll be doing fifteen-minute obs. If anything changes, get us immediately.'

They both nodded, lost for words, but were relieved to see the medical team leave. Meg looked around the room, seeming confused and disorientated.

'You're in hospital. You are safe,' repeated Jo. 'No one can hurt you. No one will hurt you.'

Meg rubbed her throat, and Sean got more water and helped Meg to take small sips. She cleared her throat slightly, which obviously hurt.

'Don't try to talk yet,' said Jo. 'Your throat is swollen and very sore, but it'll be okay. You just need some time for it to recover.'

She looked at the water, and Sean helped her drink more. She felt so thirsty and just couldn't stop her mouth from drying up.

The doctor came in to check Meg's obs. 'Is it okay to give her ice chips?' asked Sean. 'She keeps asking for water.'

'Sure, but only one at a time. I'll have some brought in. Her obs are unchanged, which is good. See you in fifteen,' he said, and smiled. A nurse appeared shortly after with a cup of ice chips, and Sean put one in Meg's mouth.

She smiled at him, a genuine smile. The coldness of the ice felt terrific. She nodded to the cup to ask for more, and Sean willingly obliged.

Eventually, Meg's eyes began to droop, and within seconds, she was asleep.

Sean left and got the doctor. 'It's fine,' he said. 'She's on a morphine drip and has a great deal of sedative in her system. She'll be doing this for a few days. Don't worry. It's a good sign.'

Turning to go back to the room, Sean saw Inspector Phillips and then DS Murray, who'd first interviewed Meg. Also, the PC whose name he couldn't remember, the one who stayed in the house with Meg while he and Jo attended the first social care meeting.

'You are not interviewing her!' Sean said, skipping the pleasantries. 'She literally cannot speak yet. Her throat is too damaged, thanks to your crap coppers who fell asleep when they were meant to be watching the bloody house!'

'It wasn't their fault,' said the Inspector.

'Seriously? Don't give me that crap. You lot look after your own. They were drunk! I'll have them sacked.'

'They returned to the station after the hotel. Well, after I woke them up!' began the Inspector. 'I was ready to sack them myself, but they were acting... odd. Their words were jumbled, and they appeared unsteady on their feet. I sent them to the FME. She took one look at their pupils and did a blood test. They had both been drugged. A slow-acting sedative. We normally send a snack bag to officers on obs. We searched the car, and one of the sandwiches was unfinished. We tested it and found the sedative in it. Which means...'

'*Which means you've got a leak*!' shouted Sean.

'Sean,' said Jo quietly. He spun round to see her standing in the doorway. She had heard it all. 'Listen and stay calm, please. This won't help.'

'I'm sorry, but do I know you?' said Jo, looking at the PC.

'Liz,' she replied. 'Well, PC Everett. I stayed at your house with Meg when you went to a meeting.'

'Of course. A lot has happened since then, Inspector, you were saying?'

'Oh, please just call me Gina, will you?'

'Okay. Gina, I know you need to talk to Meg. She's still drugged up and is asleep again. She can't speak yet as her throat is too swollen. I'm aware of the urgency, but you'll need to wait at least a few days. Also, no more police stations. You either interview her here or when she returns home. Are we clear?'

'Crystal.'

'Can the three of us talk privately?' Jo said to Gina, and the three of them moved away from Liz and DS Murray.

'So, do you think you have a leak?'

'Off the record?' Gina asked. Jo nodded. 'Yes, and we have no idea who it could be. We believe we're dealing with a paedophile ring of massive proportions. I'm hoping Meg can tell us more when she wakes. The courtroom was sealed. I interviewed Leon with DS Murray. We've decided to keep referring to him as Ewan, so only the four of us and those in the courtroom know his real name. You can tell Meg, of course, but she has to stick with Ewan when discussing him in the interview or with anyone whatsoever.'

'Why?'

'We don't know who the leak is. If we refer to him as Ewan, then whoever is spying on us will tell the gang we don't know who he is. It may make them drop their guard.'

'But what about in prison?'

'It's okay. He's been booked in as Ewan and is staying in solitary. He's likely to know people there who will tip the gang off. He's not the ringleader, but he's undoubtedly in the upper echelons, so keep it to yourselves.'

They both nodded.

'We'll go,' said Gina, 'but we do have to talk to her. It could save many lives.'

'When she's ready,' said Jo firmly.

The Inspector nodded and left, and Sean and Jo headed back to Meg's room. She was awake again and smiled when she saw them enter.

Meg tried to talk, but it hurt too much, and she just made a strange, groaning sound. 'Save your voice,' said Jo. 'It'll take a while for the swelling to reduce.'

She moved her hand as though writing, and Sean reached for a pad and pen from his bag.

He helped put the pen in Meg's hand and held the pad.

Meg took a long time, shakily trying to write a few words, but persevered, and eventually pushed the pad back to Sean.

He read the note and burst out laughing. 'More than anything in the world,' he said, with tears in his eyes. 'And we bloody well will do!'

He passed the pad to his wife, and tears came into her eyes at the words that simply read: "Do you want to build a snowman?"

CHAPTER ELEVEN

Meg's voice gradually improved, and five days later, Jo allowed the police to interview her.

'I'm afraid you or Sean can't be present,' said Inspector Phillips. 'You've both given statements about what you witnessed that evening. We can't risk accusations of either of you prompting Meg. I'm sorry.'

'But she needs someone with her,' Jo pleaded, feeling helpless.

'Steph, the social worker, has agreed to step in. It's not ideal to do it in a hospital room. I desperately need the facts. I wish we could wait and give Meg more time to recover. But it has to be sooner rather than later, I'm afraid. Memories fade quickly.'

'I only wish that was the case,' Jo replied wistfully, watching as the video cameras and microphones were set up.

Jo pleaded with Steph to keep Meg safe and to end the interview if the girl showed signs of being overwhelmed. The social worker promised Jo she would and entered the room, leaving Jo to pace up and down anxiously.

The interview lasted for over three hours; Meg remembered almost everything Ewan had said to her. The police were particularly interested to hear that a container full of girls would be arriving soon. However, it only confirmed their fears that this was an enormous and highly dangerous, well-organised crime gang they were dealing with. One whose tentacles reached far and wide.

Armed with new information and satisfied Meg had given as much detail as possible, they left with a lot of work to do.

'She was brilliant,' said Inspector Phillips to Jo. 'She's provided us with a considerable amount of evidence. Also, as Ewan thought he had nothing to lose as he intended to kill Meg, he told her far more than his bosses would have liked. This is bigger than we thought; there also appears to be a worldwide trafficking...'

'Can I help you?' said the Inspector sharply to Liz, the PC, who was hovering.

'I was wondering if you'd like me to go sit with Meg while you two talk?' she asked, smiling.

'No thanks,' said Jo. 'I'm going back in now. I'll call you later,' she said to the Inspector. Meg looked harassed when Jo entered the room and was sweating profusely.

'I'm sorry you had to go through that,' said Jo, sitting next to the girl and giving her a hug. 'It was a courageous thing to do, and I have huge admiration for your bravery.'

Meg looked down, embarrassed, refusing to believe the compliment. 'They are shipping a load of girls, children, over here to, to... hurt. I told the police, so I hope they catch them. The gang, those men... well, they go to poor countries and tell parents of young girls they are a church group and will bring them to England to look after them and give them an education. They shove loads of the kids into shipping containers, and...'

'Enough,' Jo said gently. 'You don't need to discuss it again. Hopefully, your bravery will save many lives.'

'It's my fault! I should have escaped sooner and told someone what was happening. I was a coward.'

'No, you were surviving. You were lured into a trap by evil, despicable people. It was very deliberate and methodically planned. They are experts at this. You are fourteen years old. You didn't stand a chance. Leave it to the police now and concentrate on getting better so we can get you home for Christmas.'

Meg looked at Jo and opened her mouth to speak. Jo held her hand up. 'No more talking.

'You need to rest your throat. Lie back and rest your eyes,' she said firmly. Meg sighed and lay back onto the pillows. She was asleep in seconds.

It was ten days before Christmas when Meg was finally allowed to leave the hospital. Her injuries were still there, and her facial bruising was a mixture of green and yellow. Jo and Sean appeared, along with Meg's social worker.

'You are allowed to leave, thankfully,' said the social worker. 'I'm so sorry about what happened regarding this Ewan character. You're in safe hands now.'

Meg nodded glumly. 'Where am I going? I heard Crookshaws had been shut down.'

'What do you mean?' she asked, confused. 'You're not going to a children's home. And, yes, Crookshaws has been shut down for now. There is a tremendous amount of work going on behind the scenes. We are going to get justice for you.'

'Where am I going?' Meg asked again, her voice hoarser.

'Home,' said Jo. 'Home with us. To your home, your bedroom, where you are safe.'

'And no climbing out of windows,' said Sean firmly, earning himself a dirty look from his wife.

'So, why are you here?' Meg asked the social worker, who glanced at Sean and Jo.

'We were wondering, well, hoping, if you'd like us not to foster you anymore...'

'Yeah, thought so. You...'

'Stop and let me finish!' said Jo firmly. 'As I was saying, we were wondering if, and only if you want to, we will still foster you. If you don't, but well, the thing is, we were hoping...'

'Oh, for God's sake,' said Sean impatiently. 'We want to adopt you. Do you want that?'

'I was getting to it,' said Jo indignantly.

'She'd have been too old to be adopted by the time you'd finished!'

'I was going for the subtle approach!'

'Any subtler, you'd have bored her into a coma again.'

'She wasn't in a coma; she was sedated!'

'Don't be so pedantic!'

Meg watched them arguing; it was like watching a verbal tennis match. Jo was on one side of her bed and Sean on the other. The argument was getting ridiculous, and Meg started laughing, which led to a spluttering, painful cough.

'Look what you've done!' Jo and Sean said to each other at the same time, and both laughed.

'Meg,' said the social worker. 'You can take as long as you want to think about it; there's no rush, okay?'

Meg nodded. 'Can I talk to Jo and Sean when I get… err… hhhome?' she replied, struggling to get the word out.

'Of course. Let me know when you're ready, and I'll set the wheels in motion if you decide to go ahead. I'll have to interview you alone to make sure you're happy with everything.'

'Thanks.'

'Well, I'll let you three finally go home,' Steph said, leaving, while Jo and Sean helped Meg out of bed, holding her arms as she hobbled to the car.

'Home at last,' Sean announced as they pulled up onto the drive.

'Why the copper with the gun still?' Meg asked Jo when spotting the armed police officer standing at the front door.

'The gang obviously know Ewan has disappeared, and they will either assume he has gone into hiding, or he is in prison. Regardless, they'll know you're still alive. So, we're under armed guard until they've rounded up those monsters.

'It's nothing to worry about, and I doubt they'll try anything again, but we need to keep you safe,' said Jo gently. 'But please, don't worry. That's our job. You need to get better physically and emotionally. Leave the worrying to us.'

'You weren't the one who nearly died! How can I not worry?'

'Fair point,' said Jo. 'Come on, let's get in the house. Your bed is all made up.'

Walking into the only house that had ever smelt like home to Meg was terrific; it made her feel warm and happy. 'Can I not go to bed? Please?' she begged. 'I've been in bed for weeks.'

'Okay,' said Jo. 'We do need a chat with you anyway.' As they both sat down on the sofa, the atmosphere suddenly felt a little cooler to Meg.

Sitting down in an armchair, Sean began. 'We need to discuss your running away.' Meg looked down at her feet in embarrassment.

'We know why,' continued Sean, 'but there's no excuse for it. You almost died.'

'Yes, I know!' Meg snapped. 'I was there, remember?'

'I do remember. I remember things that I won't forget until my dying day. We don't want to scare you more, but you have to take this seriously. Jumping out of a window because you thought you were in the way was reckless.'

'I know!' Meg croaked, staring out of the window.

'Do you?' asked Jo.

'Yes.'

'Look at me. We need to tell you something shocking. We don't want to, but if it means you won't run away again, then we have to.'

'Tell me what?' asked Meg, looking at Jo and Sean.

'I can't....' said Sean to his wife.

'There's a leak. That monster and his gang knew you were here. The police officers guarding the house had been drugged. Their food was laced with a sedative, which makes me believe the leak is from the police station as the sedative was in the sandwiches they picked up from their canteen before doing the night watch.'

Meg went paler than she already was.

'There's more,' said Jo, her voice strained. 'Leon, or Ewan, as we have to keep referring him, was watching the house the night you climbed out of the window...'

'But how did he know I'd climb out of the window that night?'

'He didn't. We assume he would have broken in at some point during the night and got you. It was pure luck on his part.'

'I'm sorry,' said Meg, her voice breaking. 'But it was better I did run away, otherwise, you and Sean might have got hurt if he broke in.'

'It certainly was not better you ran away!' said Sean in a tone Meg had never heard before.

'But...'

'No buts,' said Jo firmly. 'I'm with Sean on this. At least if he tried to break in, we'd have got him.'

'How do you know that if they've got a leak? He could have tried to kill you two as well as me!'

'I would have liked to see him try!' Sean growled.

'Your bedroom window is alarmed now, as are all the upstairs ones. Only Jo and I know the keypad code to open them. There are panic buttons in all the rooms, and the police have upped our protection.'

'Okay, I'm sorry!' snapped Meg.

Jo and Sean looked at each other meaningfully. Sean nodded.

'Meg,' began Jo. 'In the hotel bathroom, the police and Sean saw plastic sheeting all over the floor, huge bolt cutters, a bag of tools, and a vat of acid.'

'Why did he...?' Meg stopped, realising precisely what it was for.

'We didn't want to tell you, but you have to take this seriously. He was going to kill you and...'

'Dispose of your body right there in the bathroom,' finished Sean, looking like he was going to be sick again.

'Do you understand now?' asked Jo. 'You witnessed one child being killed. These people are ruthless, and evil, and will stop at nothing. You have to accept that until they are all locked up, your life is in constant danger. Therefore, you are never, and I mean never, to leave the house alone, even to go to the garden. You are not to answer the door, the phone, or open any mail. I'm not asking you; I'm telling you!'

Meg startled slightly, more from Jo's tone than anything else. 'Okay' she said quietly.

Jo moved over and hugged her. 'This is not your fault, but you have got to take it seriously. Will you?'

Meg nodded.

'Say it.'

'I promise I'll take it seriously.'

'Room for another?' asked Sean, looking at Meg.

She hesitated and nodded, and Sean sat on the other side of Meg and put his arm around her and Jo. Then, much to everyone's surprise, including her own, Meg leaned towards Sean and put her arm around his chest and hugged him tightly. There they remained, enjoying a moment of calmness together.

The peaceful scene was abruptly shattered several minutes later as the sound of someone shouting and swearing could be heard from directly outside the house.

'Ma'am, I have told you to leave the premises immediately.'

They all heard the armed officer shouting and radioing for backup. Before anyone in the house could respond, they heard sirens, and two police cars pulled up, and more armed officers jumped out.

'Put your arms up to where we can see them and get down on your knees, NOW!'

'Go to hell, you fascist pig.'

'Oh, shit!' said Sean and ran outside.

'What's going on?' asked Meg, scared. 'Are they back?'

'No,' said Jo calmly. 'I believe my eldest daughter is home and, as usual, she's brought a whole new level of crazy. Come on.' Jo stood up, trying to hide a slight grin. 'Best not let them shoot her.'

Outside was a scene of chaos; five police officers had guns pointed at Kayleigh and were screaming at her to get onto the floor. In turn, she was hurling insults back at them, and Sean was standing in front of his daughter, acting as a human shield, also shouting. No one could hear what anyone was saying.

'*Stop*!' shouted Jo from the doorway. Everyone paused and looked at her. 'Gentleman, this is my and Sean's daughter, Kayleigh, who is due home for Christmas in three days, which is why she is not on the list. Kayleigh, these are armed police officers, so please stop abusing them before you get shot.'

Guns were immediately lowered.

'I do apologise,' said the senior officer. 'She refused to tell us who she was.'

'Yes, I can imagine,' said Jo dryly. 'No apology needed. Kayleigh, get your bags and come in.'

'Mum! What do you mean, no apology needed? They almost shot me!'

'I can assure you we were not about to shoot you,' said the senior officer stiffly. 'But some cooperation would have been helpful.'

'Yes, it would,' said Jo. 'In, now!'

Kayleigh grabbed her bags and stomped into the house, muttering furiously about police states and fascists, and something about small penises.

Meg watched her in fascination. Kayleigh was like a whirlwind and so brave; she'd just fronted up to five coppers with guns.

Sean and Jo continued to talk to the police and smooth things over, while Meg stood in the hall, watching Kayleigh.

'Anyone told you it's rude to stare?' said Kayleigh.

'Anyone told you it's rude to tell a bunch of coppers they've got small penises?' retaliated Meg with spirit.

Kayleigh laughed. 'I think you and I are going to get on. Come on. Help me upstairs with these bags and tell me why you look like you've done ten rounds with Nicola Adams.'

'Who?'

'Boxer. Olympic gold medal winner. Lives down the road.'

'Sorry, don't know her.'

Meg followed the sighing Kayleigh upstairs to her bedroom. 'Arrrggh!' she exclaimed, throwing her bags, making Meg jump.

'Mum has tidied my room again! I tell her to leave it. I know where everything is when it's on the floor, and she goes on about getting mice. That was once, and I was twelve, for God's sake!' Kayleigh threw everything from her bags and onto the floor.

'Come sit down and tell me what's happened to your face,' she said, eventually gesturing to the bed.

Meg sat down. 'Well, I'm not meant to say, but...'

'No buts,' came Jo's voice from the doorway. 'You are not to tell. That's final! Now,' she continued, looking at Kayleigh. 'Do I get a "Hello, Mum" or a hug?'

'Sorry.' Kayleigh jumped up and grabbed her mum, squeezing her tight. 'Have you missed me?'

'Not even home for a minute and you have half the bloody police force pointing guns at you!' came Sean's voice as he arrived at the doorway and hugged his daughter. 'I don't know how, but when you're not here, somehow, I tend to forget the utter chaos you cause. Maybe I block it out. This is Meg,' he said, gesturing to the bed.

'Well, obviously,' replied Kayleigh. 'Who has done that to her face? She was about to tell me before Mum came in.'

Sean glared at Kayleigh. 'I told you no questions!' He looked at Meg. 'I told you that you can't discuss anything until after the police have found everyone!'

213

'Police? Everyone? What's going on?' demanded Kayleigh.

'*Sean*!' hissed Jo

'Bugger!' said Sean

'What's going on now?' came a new voice from behind them.

'Tom!' shouted everyone, apart from Meg.

'Looks like another normal day at the McGloughlin household,' said yet another voice.

'Wes!' said Jo, giving both men a hug. 'I didn't think you could make it.'

'Change of plan.' He grinned. 'Good job too. Armed police, manhunts....'

'And don't forget the mice, fascists, and small penises.' interrupted Meg, looking amused. The two men looked at her curiously.

'I need a drink.' Sean sighed.

'Excellent idea, Father dear,' said Kayleigh. 'Come on, Meg.' She ordered. 'Let's hit the bar.'

'No bars!' said Jo weakly, but everyone had made their way downstairs. Jo shook her head in despair as she followed her family downstairs.

Everyone sat at the table, all talking over each other, apart from Meg, who was taking it all in.

Jo cleared her throat. 'Meg, this, as you now know, is my eldest daughter Kayleigh, who I've seen in many situations, but never held at gunpoint by five police officers.'

'You did wh...' started Tom.

'Wait!' said Jo, holding her hand up.

'This is Tom, the oldest of our kids, and this is Wes, his boyfriend. Everyone, this is Meg, whom you are aware we're fostering.'

They all grinned at each other.

'Did you say something about a drink, Dad?' asked Kayleigh. 'I could kill for a beer or something stronger.'

'I think I need one too,' said Meg. 'And I hate alcohol!'

'Nope,' said Jo.

'Aww, come on, Mum. She's fourteen. I was drinking at fourteen.'

'What! Where?' demanded Sean.

'Yes, I know,' said Jo at the same time.

'You knew?' said Sean to his wife.

'You didn't?'

'Nice to meet you, Meg,' said Tom. 'How are you coping in the madhouse?'

'It wasn't mad until you lot got here,' said Sean.

'Really?' said Kayleigh sarcastically. 'So having armed fascists on the doorstep is normal?'

'They are not fascists!' said Jo. 'They've been incredible.'

215

'What with?'

'Minding their own business,' said Sean, looking at his watch. 'Right, I need to get to the train station and collect the two of our children who actually did announce their arrival for today.'

'Okay, you lot,' said Jo, looking at Kayleigh, Tom, and Wes. 'Go and unpack. I'm popping out for an hour with Meg. Afterwards, we'll go out for dinner.'

'Excellent,' said Tom, standing up and leaving the room, with Wes closely following. 'Where are you going?' asked Kayleigh.

'We have to do something; we won't be long. Now, go sort your room out. I'm not spending the next few weeks with all of your stuff thrown all over the floor. Go on, move!'

Kayleigh sighed and stomped out. Jo shook her head and told Meg to put her coat on. 'Short walk to catch your breath, I thought. Come on.'

Meg followed Jo, and they got into the car and set off. Meg noticed that an unmarked police car followed them; she wasn't sure if their presence made her feel safer or in more danger, knowing there was a leak.

They stopped at a nearby lake, and Meg accepted the hat, scarf, and gloves Jo passed to her without argument, as she realised there was no point in arguing with Jo on some things.

'Quite a homecoming you've had,' said Jo. 'Sorry it was so crazy! Kayleigh is a whirlwind of chaos. Brilliant, capable, intelligent, but chaotic.'

'It's fine,' Meg replied. 'If you want to talk about me running away, I won't run away again. I'm sorry for all the trouble I caused.'

'You didn't cause the trouble, Meg; it was out there waiting for you. But no, I don't want to talk about that.'

'What then?'

'I want to talk about adopting you.'

'You don't want to adopt me, you just feel sorry for me. That'll wear off, and then you'll be fed-up of me and throw me out.'

'Why?'

'Why what?'

'Why would Sean and I offer to become your parents if we didn't mean it? We will not throw you out ever.'

'What if I did something like, I don't know... get arrested?'

'Your feet wouldn't touch the ground! Yes, I'd be furious, and I'd certainly make it clear, make no mistake, but you wouldn't be thrown out.'

'What about your children?'

'What about them? It seems to have gone fine so far, and Kayleigh has certainly taken a shine to you. I'm not sure if that makes me happy or worried.' Jo frowned.

'But if you want me to be in your and Sean's family, then would I be in their family?'

'Of course.'

'Well, I don't want to tell lies.'

'Lies about what?'

'They've come home for Christmas, had guns pointed at them. There's a copper on the doorstep holding a gun. I want them to know why. All of it. I'm not going to go into this with lies. If you want me, and Sean does, and they do, I want them to know what's happening. They can't even open their bedroom windows! I want to trust them, but I don't want them to feel cut out of their family because of my secrets.'

They walked for a while, Jo considering what Meg had said. 'Okay, we'll tell them, but only if Inspector Phillips gives permission, okay?'

'Okay.'

'But, aside from that, can I ask you why you would like us to adopt you?'

'I never asked you to adopt me,' snapped Meg. 'See, you're trying to wriggle out of it already! You're all talk, just like the rest of them. Full of crap!'

Jo went white with anger, and Meg knew she'd crossed a line.

'Don't you dare speak to me like that,' Jo said in such a firm, controlled manner that Meg felt her knees shake. 'And that is the last time you will ever hurl insults or accuse me of manipulating you. Is that clear?'

'Yes,' Meg whispered. 'I'm sorry. I know how much you've done for me. I'm sorry, honestly.'

Jo nodded and carried on walking. They did another lap of the lake in silence. Meg rightly suspected that Jo was calming down from the way she'd been spoken to.

'I want to adopt you, Meg,' Jo said suddenly. 'So does Sean. But this isn't only about us. It's about you and what you want. Do you even want to be adopted, and if you do, do you want us to be the ones to do it? Or, after the trial, and there will be a trial, I hope, would you prefer to go back to a kids' home where there are no rules, no one nagging you to put a hat on, or to eat properly, or to make you go to school? I'd understand if you did. I know it can be hard to make the transition from a kids' home to a family. A lot of children can't do it.'

'Why do you want to adopt me?' asked Meg. 'I don't want anyone to feel sorry for me.

'I'm not a victim!'

'No, you're not. You are incredibly strong and brave.'

'You've not answered my question!'

Jo took a step towards Meg and looked straight into her eyes. 'I want to adopt you because I love you. Is that good enough for you?'

Meg looked away, tears in her eyes. She didn't know if she wanted to run away or hug Jo. Sensing this, Jo pulled Meg close into a hug and held the child, who let out an unwitting sob.

CHAPTER TWELVE

When they arrived home, Jo threw her arms around two new people who had arrived while they had been on their walk and turned to make the introductions.

'Jack, Cora, this is Meg.'

'Hiya.' Jack greeted Meg easily. 'I hear you like football. We'll have to get down to the park and test those skills if you fancy it one day?'

'Yeah, that'll be good. Thanks.' She looked at the tall, blond-haired athletic man who was bouncing with energy, just as Jo had described him.

'No worries. I'm off to find Tom. Not seen him yet.'

'Hi, Meg,' Cora muttered, then appeared unsure what to say. Meg nodded, also momentarily speechless as she assessed Cora, who had darker hair like her dad. She also had deep, heavy bags under her eyes. Luckily, Sean eased the strange tension between the pair by coming in and breaking the silence.

'We did it!' he gloated. 'All under one roof!'

'Why are there armed police everywhere?' Cora challenged, biting her lip, and swapping from one foot to the other, giving the impression that she was swaying.

'We'll talk soon.' Jo gave her daughter a reassuring smile. 'I just need some time with your dad, alone. Would you mind taking Meg to the living room? I think that's where the shouting is coming from.'

'What's going on?' Sean looked at Jo as Meg and Cora left.

Jo explained what had happened during her and Meg's walk, including the part where she told Meg she loved her.

'But she won't go for adoption until the kids know? Does she want us to tell them everything?'

Jo nodded.

'Well, let's ring the Inspector then.'

It was a long conversation with Gina, but finally, she agreed. But, only on the condition that none of the family discussed it away from the house, or with anyone outside the family.

Sean shouted Meg into the kitchen and told her. She nodded. 'When do you want us to tell them?'

'Now? Please? The sooner the better, then I don't have to lie.'

'Right, come on then.'

'Can I not be there, please?' she asked, staring at the floor.

'Of course,' said Jo. 'Go to your room. Have a nap or read. We're all going out for dinner later, so I'll come and talk to you before that. Does that work for you?'

She nodded. 'Will you tell them you're adopting me and tell me if they don't want you to?'

'Excuse me.' Sean looked at Meg with a twinkle in his eye. 'When were you going to inform me about this?'

'Ssorry,' stuttered Meg. 'I thought Jo had told...'

'I'm only playing, you daft bugger! And I couldn't be happier. I did hear there were hugs, though. I seem to have missed out there.'

Meg laughed and quickly threw her arms around him, and he gave her a tight squeeze.

'Thank you for trusting us, and thank you for trusting me. I won't let you down. Get on your nerves, yes, but I won't let you down. I promise.'

'I know,' said Meg, looking at him fiercely.

'Right, go on upstairs. If you hear banging and shouting, it's because we're wrestling Kayleigh to the floor to stop her going to find those responsible.'

Meg laughed and went upstairs, nervous about how the others would react.

There was a stunned silence downstairs in the lounge; even Kayleigh was momentarily lost for words.

'We know this is a lot of information, but there's more. Your mum and I want to adopt Meg, and she wants it too, but only if we tell all of you what's happened.'

'Why?' asked Cora, her mouth barely moving as her jaw clenched.

'There are armed police everywhere. I assume there's going to be a trial. She doesn't want any secrets from you. She hates secrets and lies, and if she's going to join our family, she wants a clean slate. No secrets. Meg said you all deserve to know why there are police everywhere.'

'That's very thoughtful and incredibly mature, especially considering all she's been through,' said Tom, still digesting the vast amount of information they'd received.

'Are you safe? You and Mum?' Cora asked through gritted teeth.

'As safe as anyone is with police on their doorstep carrying machine guns.'

'Do we pretend we don't know?' Jack asked quietly.

'No,' said Jo. 'It's so hard as she feels like it's her fault, so it's fine to acknowledge that you know, but pick your moment, please. Don't all dive in.'

'*She thinks it's her fault!*' came the inevitable explosion from Kayleigh.

'Kayleigh, please...' Jo pleaded softly.

'Sorry, Mum. I just can't believe... well, it's just ...'

'We know,' Sean finished on Kayleigh's behalf. 'It's unimaginable that people target children in this way.'

'Wow,' said Wes, clutching Tom's hand. 'Just when you thought you'd heard about the extent of evil. This is just on another level.'

Jo looked at her children and their shocked faces, proud of the way they handled such difficult information. 'Does anyone have any questions before I go get Meg?'

No one moved. 'Okay, but can we not have everyone sitting here in silence when she comes down? Will you all start getting ready for dinner? We need to be at the restaurant in exactly one hour. I'll take my car, and Sean can take...'

'A taxi!' he stated.

'Fine,' Jo agreed. 'But if half of you come crawling in at three a.m., keep the noise down!

'Now, move.'

Everyone scattered, making a dive for their bedrooms and bathroom. Jo stood up to go and get Meg.

'Let me take this one,' said Sean. Jo turned, ready to argue.

'Look, we're both her parents now. I need a chance to act like one. That includes talking to her and listening to her and giving her a chance to trust me in her room. I will knock. If she doesn't let me in, we'll swap.'

Jo nodded, her forehead wrinkling as Sean stood and made his way up to the top floor, dodging Tom and Kayleigh, who were both trying to get into the bathroom first.

He tapped on Meg's door. 'Hi, it's Sean. Would you mind opening the door?' Meg slowly opened the door.

'Can I come in and talk?'

Meg stared at him for what seemed like forever.

'Okay.' She moved out of the doorway. Sean sat down on a chair near the window.

'We've spoken to the kids...' he began.

'Do they hate me? Do they want me to leave?' Meg asked tonelessly, her face blank.

'Of course not. They are firmly on your side, like any decent human being would be. They have huge admiration for you and a lot of respect for the fact that you trusted us to tell them and want to join the family with a clean slate, without secrets.'

'Can I stay here? When you all go out for dinner, I mean.'

'No. It's a family meal. No get-outs on this one. And hey, people will think we're famous or royalty. Maybe not royalty, but famous, anyway. Who else will have bodyguards near their table? I'll give Kayleigh an hour before she gets drunk and flirts with one of the men she called a fascist earlier.' He rolled his eyes, grinning. 'It'll be fine. I'm going for a quick shower. Be downstairs in half an hour, okay?'

'Okay.'

'You are doing amazingly,' said Sean. 'I'm so proud of you.' He saw a tear fall onto the carpet from Meg's face. 'Hey, what's made you cry?'

'I'm not used to people saying they're proud of me. Horrible things, yes, but nice things, no.' More tears dropped down.

'Can I give you a hug?' Sean asked, lifting his arms helplessly.

Meg nodded. Sean sat next to her and encased the child in his massive frame, holding her to his chest while she sobbed as though her heart would break.

Worried as they'd been so long, Jo went upstairs and popped her head around Meg's door. She took in the scene and saw the sadness on her husband's face as he tightly held the heartbroken child and quietly left the room without being noticed. *Sean was right*, she thought. As hard as it was, she needed to step back a little now Meg trusted him and let him take his role of being a parent too.

Dinner was crazy. Meg had never been to a real restaurant, so she wasn't sure what to expect. There were huge tables with white tablecloths, music that she'd never heard before playing in the background, and people running around carrying trays with plates of food and drink. It was like something she'd seen on TV, but never in real life. It was lovely and warm, and Christmas decorations filled the place with colour.

They all walked to a counter, and a man greeted them with a beaming smile.

'Buonasera.' He smiled broadly, rushing from around the counter and kissing Sean on both cheeks and giving him a hug before greeting the rest of the family in the same way.

Meg jumped behind Kayleigh to hide. No way was she letting some strange old man touch her.

As he approached Kayleigh, she purposely moved out of the way, taking Meg with her. 'Just going to the loo,' she said and set off in a different direction, clutching Meg's arm.

'Thanks,' said Meg, when they got to the bathroom.

'No problem,' Kayleigh said casually. 'We've been coming here, like, forever, and he's always done that. He means no offence. The opposite, but I wouldn't want a strange old bloke trying to kiss me if I'd been through what you have!'

'You don't hate me? You know, after what your mum and dad said. I was scared you'd all think I was disgusting and horrible.'

'What?' Kayleigh was genuinely shocked and not sure what to say. 'Of course not. It's those sad excuses for men that are disgusting and lured you...'

'Why did Sean get a taxi?' Meg jumped in.

'I imagine he's planning on a drink or twelve,' Kayleigh answered with a grin. 'Then slinking off to the pub afterwards with as many of us that'll go, and come crawling home in the early hours and getting an earful from Mum.'

Meg went pale and began to shake.

'What is it?' Kayleigh asked quickly. 'Sit down on the floor; it's clean. Well, cleaner than the men's toilets, I bet.'

Jo stormed in, not understanding what was taking them so long.

'What's happened?' Jo looked at Kayleigh, who was sitting on the floor next to Meg.

'Don't know. We came here to hide from Franco's kissing, as Meg was a bit freaked by it.

Then I said Dad was probably on the piss and would be dragging whoever he could to the pub after and then crawl in drunk. Then she went all pale and shaky.'

'Ah,' said Jo, also sitting on the floor. 'Not all men hurt people when they drink, you know.' She spoke gently. 'Sean, for example, becomes a bit of an..., well, he's kind of...'

'He just becomes a daft prat!' said Kayleigh bluntly. 'His jokes get worse, but he thinks they are hilarious, and he talks a load of rubbish. He's never aggressive and has certainly never been, well, you know, touchy. He's an idiot when he's drunk, but no pervert!'

'What about everyone else?' Meg asked tentatively.

'Jack would rather run than drink. I've only ever seen him drunk twice. He takes his fitness seriously. Cora gets even more intense,' continued Kayleigh, rolling her eyes, 'and argues about what she considers crucial issues, but basically, she's dull. Tom is like Dad and gets daft, and Wes flirts with every man he sees. The last time we went out, Wes got Dad up on stage with no top on and danced with a drag queen who smeared his chest in baby oil!'

'What? When?' demanded Jo.

Meg laughed just as the door swung open and Cora came in.

'Dad's doing his nut. He sent me to come and get you… Why are you all sitting on the floor?'

'Hiding from Franco's kisses, talking about how boring you are when you're drunk, and how Dad did a half-naked dance on stage with a drag queen,' Kayleigh recited.

'I'm not bo… hang on. Dad did what?'

'Oh, chill out. It was fun. You should try it!'

'Kayleigh!' Jo warned. 'Don't start.'

'Well, at least I don't throw myself at anything in trousers,' came back Cora.

'This sounds like my kind of conversation,' said Wes from the door. 'What are you all doing?'

'Something about Franco's kissing, me being dull, Dad being a tart, and Kayleigh being a man-eater,' said Cora, giving a quick summary.

'Sounds fun.' Wes also sat down on the floor. 'You know Sean is going mad through there, wanting to know what you're all doing.'

'Are you okay to go through?' Jo whispered to Meg, as Kayleigh and Cora continued to argue. 'I will mention this to Sean quietly. Is that okay?'

Meg nodded. 'Okay, and we'd better go, or everyone will end up in here.'

'*Up*!' Jo shouted over the arguing. 'Come on, let's go and sit at the table before Dad's head explodes.'

They piled out of the toilet in single file, much to the surprise of a woman attempting to enter, especially when Wes exited and gave her a wink.

'Finally!' Sean grumbled when his family arrived at the table and sat down.

He opened his mouth to start ranting, but Jo silenced him.

'Would you like to tell me when and why you were dancing half-naked on a stage with a drag queen?'

He stopped, mouth still open, and went red.

'Who grassed?' he asked, looking at Wes and Kayleigh.

They both grinned, and Kayleigh started whistling the tune of *It's Raining Men.*

Giving his daughter a dirty look, he summoned the waiter, who was hovering uncertainly. A man with a gun was standing next to the table. Half of the family had been sitting in the toilets for twenty minutes, and now he'd heard something about the older woman's husband doing something on a stage with no clothes on. It made it difficult to ask if it was a good time to order.

'We're ready,' said Sean firmly.

'I'm not!' said Jo.

'Well, Tom, Jack, and I are, so the rest of you had better decide quickly.'

Meg sat at the very end of the table, facing no one, and was seated next to Kayleigh. Meg had never ordered from a menu in a restaurant before. Not only could she not make her mind up, she definitely didn't want to shout out her order when she finally decided what to eat.

'Is there anything you don't like?' asked Kayleigh.

'Vegetables.'

'Okay, what about a pizza? The Pollo is good; that's the chicken one. I'm getting it, so should I order for us both?'

'Please,' Meg said gratefully. 'And what are you drinking?'

'Errr, Coke?'

'Cool.'

'Two Pollo pizzas and two Cokes, please,' Kayleigh told the waiter when it was her turn, and she gestured to Meg when ordering so the waiter knew she was ordering on behalf of them both.

Jo glanced at her daughter in appreciation. Not only had she helped Meg order, but she had decided not to drink alcohol as well. Kayleigh was usually the first at the bar and the last one out.

Dinner was okay. Meg didn't feel entirely relaxed, but Kayleigh's endless stories kept her amused. Especially the tales about growing up in a big family. She told her about the holidays, the arguments, and the disasters, such as when they all spent five hours in the car going on a camping holiday and arrived to realise that no one had packed the tents.

'Mum and Dad argued for two hours in the middle of a field in the pouring rain about whose job it was to pack the tent while we all stayed in the car. Then Tom got bored and decided he would drive us home to get the tent. He was only seven, and Dad had the keys. So, he sat in the driver's seat and took the handbrake off, and we suddenly started to slide down the hill. Luckily, it wasn't too steep, and Mum and Dad stopped the car by running in front of it and pushing.

Dad was furious. He fell flat on his face and was covered in mud. You couldn't see any of him; he looked like a bog monster.'

Meg laughed and looked at Sean, imagining the scene. He caught her eye and then looked suspiciously at Kayleigh.

The waiter cleared the empty plates, and another round of drinks arrived. Using a spoon, Tom tapped his glass, silencing everyone.

'We have an announcement. Firstly, I know you weren't expecting Wes to come for Christmas...'

'He's more than welcome, though,' said Jo.

'Well, it's a bit complicated... but the good news is that Wes and I are getting married.'

Everyone except Cora, and Meg, who wasn't sure what to do, stood up and hugged Tom and Wes and threw a hundred questions at them: Who asked whom? Demands to describe the proposal. When was the wedding? Where?

'One at a time!' said Tom, laughing. 'We've booked the registry office here, in the city centre, for the 10th of April next year. I want to be married in my home town, and Wes is happy with that.'

'It'll be great to meet your parents, finally,' Jo said to Wes, who darted away from her gaze.

'What is it?' she asked.

'Let me,' Tom said, holding Wes's hand. 'Wes has never been 'out' to his family. They are extremely strict Catholics and it's not like they live nearby. But when I asked Wes to marry me early last month...'

'You've been engaged for, like, seven weeks, and we didn't know!' Kayleigh proclaimed, astounded.

'Hang on,' Tom said to his sister. 'Wes wanted to tell his parents about his sexuality and about us. So, he flew home to Jamaica for a couple of weeks, only to return four days later. The announcement didn't go down well to say the least, and basically, they, err...'

'Said they never wanted to see me again and that I'm no son of theirs anymore. They told me to leave the house and never return.'

There was silence around the table momentarily.

'Oh, I'm so sorry, Wes,' said Jo sadly.

'Me too,' added Sean.

'Seriously?' Kayleigh frowned. 'I don't understand how they could do that. They're your parents.'

'Not according to them,' said Wes sadly.

'Well, they do have a strong belief in God and... Ow!' Cora stopped suddenly after receiving a sharp kick from Jack, who sat opposite her. The usually mild-mannered man glared at his sister in disgust.

235

Tom swung around angrily, ready to rip in to his sister, but was stopped by a small voice from the end of the table.

'Congratulations,' Meg said quietly, her voice shaking a little with nerves. 'You are really lucky to find someone who loves you, and they love you back.'

Her subtle statement took the anger out of most of the people at the table.

'Well said!' Kayleigh grinned at Meg, thrusting her shoulders back proudly. Wes walked around the table and gave Meg a huge hug, and Tom followed.

'Well, who'd have thought that at our age, we'd end up with two more kids,' said Sean, looking at Jo. 'A new daughter and a new son. Bloody hell, that's six of you now. I don't know what we did to deserve that. I'll never be able to retire; they'll eat us out of house and home.' He laughed and joined the group hug at the end of the table.

'Right,' he said, pulling away. 'Who fancies hitting the town?'

'Count us in,' said Tom.

'I'll come too,' Jack announced, much to everyone's surprise. 'It's not every day you hear your brother is getting married.'

'Sorry but not me,' said Jo. 'Or Meg, of course.'

'I'm going home too,' Cora snapped.

Kayleigh glanced at Meg. 'Count me out this time, guys, but seriously, I'm so happy for you and Wes. Meg is right. You're lucky to have found each other. You are amazing. Far too good for Tom, of course!' she added with a grin that earned her a dig in ribs from her big brother. She hugged them all, as Jo did, before leaving.

'Oh, Sean,' she said. 'Try to keep your clothes on this time.' Jo gave her embarrassed husband a peck on the cheek before leaving. 'And don't forget to pay the bill.'

They walked to the car quickly. The temperature had dropped, and the pavements were starting to get icy. Meg noticed the Christmas lights hanging up around the city's sky and pointed them out to Kayleigh.

'They must have been up every year,' she said, 'but I've never noticed them before.'

Kayleigh put an affectionate arm around her. 'You are going to have the best Christmas ever! I'll make sure of that.'

Meg couldn't believe how scared she'd been of meeting Jo and Sean's children; they were great. Cora was a bit weird, she thought, but the rest were fantastic.

Kayleigh and Meg sat in the back seat while Jo drove, with Cora next to her, but even with the heating on full-blast, the car's atmosphere still felt icy.

Worried, Meg leant over and whispered to Kayleigh, 'Have I done something wrong?'

'No, of course not! But the shit is going to hit the fan when we get home. I suggest you and I go and hang out in your room, well out of the way. Mum doesn't lose her temper often, but she's seething with Cora.'

'For what she said to Wes?'

'Yep!'

The rest of the journey was made in silence. Meg occasionally glanced behind her to check the police were still there. They gave her a reassuring wave every time she did, and she shyly waved back.

Entering the warm house was lovely; Meg wondered if she'd ever not notice the comforting smells of safety that she now associated with the place.

'Mum, is it okay if I get some hot chocolate for Meg and me and then go hang out with her in her room?'

'Of course, Kayleigh.' Jo smiled at them both, noticing how eager Meg looked.

'I'm going to bed,' announced Cora, heading towards the kitchen door.

'You certainly are not!' Jo asserted. 'Dining room, now!'

'Why? What have I done? I'm tired, and I'm not in the mood for a lecture. All I did was give a point of view about Wes's parents. I didn't say I agree with them! But you lot are all the same and always have been. Unless I immediately agree, you all dive in and tell me I'm stupid or wrong or, normally, just ignore me! And, no, I don't like Dad going to bars and making an idiot of himself. But I don't care what kind of bar it is, I just think it's pathetic at his age, and so are you, Mum, for finding it funny!'

'Forget the hot chocolate,' said Kayleigh to Meg as soon as Cora called her mother pathetic. She pushed her out of the kitchen and up the stairs. They reached the first floor before they heard what sounded like an eruption.

'Told you Mum was close to losing it,' she said. 'Don't blame her either. Cora's inferiority complex has stuck again!'

'Will Jo hit her?' asked Meg, not knowing what an inferiority complex was.

'What? No. we've never been hit, but Mum won't let this one drop. Anyway, leave them to it.' She spoke louder to make herself heard over the voices downstairs.

Kayleigh flopped down on Meg's bed. 'We all hated this room as teenagers. The creaky stairs always gave us away; I can't believe we never thought of climbing out of the window as you did!'

Meg's face turned pale again and beads of sweat appeared on her forehead.

'Sorry, I've got a big gob. Mum always says that I should take a breath before speaking.

'Are you okay?'

Meg nodded. 'It's fine. I feel crap for doing what I did and putting your mum and dad through so much that night. It was, well, it was just awful.'

Kayleigh looked at her thoughtfully. 'Do you want to tell me your story?'

'What story?'

'Well, kids are generally not born into children's homes, are they? How did you end up there?'

Meg looked at the floor, thinking for a while.

'You don't have to tell me, you know, I'm just...'

'It's fine,' Meg replied. 'I'm just trying to figure out where to start.

'I went into care when I was nine. My dad left when I was about three; he's Irish and went back there. He and my mum drank a lot and got into fights. She hated him for leaving, and I think that's when she started hating me. She never used his name, not since the day he left. Instead, she'd say "him" whenever she spoke about my dad.

'I had a small photo of him by my bed, but she found it and ripped it up and said that he used to beat me up, as well as her. I don't remember that; I remember her hitting me. Anytime I did something she didn't like, she would always say I was just like *him*. One time, she said she hated looking at me because I looked like him. I was never the daughter she wanted; she wanted a pretty little girl who she could dress up and show off so she could get attention. I hated it. I hated dresses, make-up, and all the things she forced me to do so I would be what she wanted. I went my own way. I played football, climbed trees, got dirty, and she'd get angry and say proper girls didn't do stuff like that. After that, she showed no interest in me. She just bounced around from man to man. She couldn't live without a man being around. Some were okay, some were arseholes, but they left me alone. I stayed in my room reading most of the time, and when I was about eight, I joined a karate club. She wouldn't give me the money to go or the bus fare, but there was a woman on our estate who I liked and she kind of looked out for me when she could. She would give me 50p for the karate subs. I'm sure it cost more than that, but it's what they said I had to pay.

'The place was a couple of miles away, so I'd walk there and back every week at night. Scary in the winter as it was a bit rough, but okay. Then when I just turned nine, she met some arsehole called Mike. He got her into drugs big-style, and he'd beat the crap out of her and give me the odd slap if I didn't stay in my room. But he really lost it one night when he brought a load of mate's home. Mum was off her head because she'd nicked his drugs. He went to get his stash, and it was gone.

'Mum blamed me and told him I'd nicked it and sold it at school. I hadn't! And he beat me up, really badly. There was a lot of noise and shouting, and the police came and took me away. Anyway, they put me into care. Mum wasn't bothered, and Mike got sent down. She moved on to a few different blokes, and the one she's with now is just like the others.

'I went to different foster homes and hated them, then a few kids' homes, and finished up in Crookshaws. That's when I met your mum; she was setting up some youth place. I was only going to go once, but I got talking to her and liked her. She made me feel, I don't know, calm, I think, and like I wasn't such a crappy person that I'd always been told I was.

'Then stuff started happening at Crookshaws, and I couldn't face seeing your mum anymore. I didn't want to lie to her about what was going on, and I was too scared to tell, so I stopped going. One night, I went and looked for her, but they said she had left because the place was up and running. Six months later, she found me in the shop car park, and I think you know the rest.'

Kayleigh stared at Meg; she'd been silent throughout the entire story. 'I'm sorry,' she said gently, sounding just like her mum.

Meg shrugged.

'You know none of it was your fault, don't you? Your mother, your father, her boyfriends, these nasty *men* that targeted you at the kids' home.'

242

Meg looked away and didn't speak.

Kayleigh decided to drop it. 'Tell you what, there's a camp bed in the cupboard. How about I sleep in here tonight? I heard Cora slamming her bedroom door when you were talking, so I reckon it's safe to make hot chocolate now. What do you think?'

'That'd be great,' said Meg. 'But I don't want to go downstairs if your mum is angry.'

'She's not angry at you.'

'I know, but...' Meg looked down at her feet again.

'No worries. I'll go make the drinks. You go and pull the bed out of the cupboard.'

'Sure, will do.'

Ten minutes later, Meg was still fighting with the camp bed when Kayleigh appeared with a tray, carrying three cups of hot chocolate.

'I can't do this f...'

Meg stopped speaking suddenly when she looked up and saw Jo behind Kayleigh.

'I've not said anything, I promise.' Kayleigh mentioned quickly. 'Mum wanted to join us.'

'Said anything about what?' Jo asked suspiciously.

'Nothing much,' said Meg. 'I was telling Kayleigh about my life and how I ended up in care and other stuff, and how you found me.'

Jo said nothing but looked concerned and took the camp bed from Meg. She had it set up in a couple of minutes.

Kayleigh jumped into the narrow bed, and Meg got into hers. Jo got in next to her, and the girl snuggled closer.

'Is everything okay now? With Cora, I mean?' Meg queried nervously.

'Don't worry about Cora! Sean and I will deal with her, and that doesn't include you, Kayleigh. Understand?'

Kayleigh sighed. 'Fine, but I don't understand her. Why is she so homophobic?'

'She isn't. Cora was asking a question. A badly phrased one, yes, but there was no intention of homophobia.'

'So what's going on with her?'

Jo didn't reply and took a gulp of her drink. 'Let's just have a nice Christmas, shall we?'

Seeing how stressed and tired her mum looked, Kayleigh relented; she reached over and held her mum's hand. 'It'll be a great one, Mum. Don't worry.'

Jo smiled at her gratefully and placed her and Meg's empty cups on the floor between the beds, then rested her head on the pillow. She put her arm around Meg, who came even closer for a cuddle, and still holding her oldest daughter's hand, she fell asleep.

'Someone should tell Mum it's rude to bust in on someone's sleep-over,' hissed Kayleigh to Meg, but as she looked closer, she saw Meg was fast asleep too.

Grinning, she gently put her mum's arm onto her own bed and rolled over to turn off the lamp. She was also asleep in seconds.

Chapter Thirteen

M orning, sleepyheads!' Kayleigh bellowed. Meg jolted awake, while Jo reluctantly opened her eyes.

'Kayleigh, why do you have to be so cheerful in the morning!' her mother groaned.

'Well, it's definitely not in the genes, but I do have coffee!'

'I take it all back,' said Jo, sitting up and gratefully taking her coffee. 'You are amazing.

'What time is it?'

'Ten a.m.!'

'Oops. Is Dad okay? Was he worried when I wasn't in bed when he got home?'

'Doubt it. Dad, Tom, Wes, and Jack are unconscious in the lounge. It stinks in there; look at this!'

She leaned over and showed her Mum and Meg a photo from her phone of Sean and Wes fast asleep on the sofa, cuddling each other.

Meg burst out laughing, and Jo shook her head.

'Are they still asleep?'

'They were ten minutes ago.'

'Right then, I think we all need to be there for the grand awakening,' Jo said, grinning. 'I wouldn't miss that for the world. Come on.'

The three of them crept downstairs and into the lounge. Jo walked over to her husband, who had Wes encompassed in his arms, and tried to ignore the overwhelming stench of stale curry and beer.

'Sean,' she whispered. Sean groaned slightly.

'Sean,' she repeated louder. 'Time to get up!'

'One more minute,' he muttered and kissed his wife's cheek. Eyes still closed; Sean froze.

He raised his hand tentatively and felt Wes's stubbly chin.

'Tom, give over. I'm not in the mood,' groaned Wes, still half asleep.

'I'm pleased about that,' said Jo loudly.

Both men opened their eyes at the same time, just as Tom shouted.

'Wes, what are you doing to my father!'

Both men gave each other a horrified glare. Still tangled together, they attempted to leap off the sofa at the same time. Inevitably, they landed in a heap on the floor with Sean on top of Wes, whose face was buried in a foil box of half-eaten curry.

'Dad, don't you start. Get off my fiancé!' Tom declared, trying to keep a straight face.

Sean stumbled to his feet, confused. Wes sat up, looking dazed, his eyes stinging from the curry plastered all over his face.

'Anyone want to tell me what's going on?' asked Jo in mock sternness.

'Kayleigh, stop filming and put your phone down!' snapped Sean.

'Hmm, don't think you can play the parent card on this one, Dad, do you?'

'Jo,' Sean said, looking at his wife. 'We, err, had a bit too much to drink and, well, I can't remember the rest.'

'I can only imagine,' Jo replied. 'Now, get this mess...'

'*Meg*!' Kayleigh screamed, dropping her phone and running over to the girl who was sitting on the floor, knees folded and head resting on them. She was shaking violently, shivering and sweating so much that her clothes were visibly soaked.

'Move, Kayleigh,' said Jo, running over to Meg, kneeling next to her. She didn't respond to Jo's voice and continued to shake uncontrollably. To everyone else, it looked as though Meg was somehow having a terrible nightmare while awake, but Jo knew she was having a major flashback.

'Meg, lift your head. It'll help you to breathe,' said Jo calmly.

Meg didn't hear; she was so entrenched in a flashback that she wasn't aware that she was in Jo and Sean's house. She was in that building. She was watching Jenny's throat being slashed; the sound of the knife that ended her life was vivid. Meg watched the blood spurt out of her neck, and she could smell that smell, the one that she couldn't recall at the police station, the odour that had constantly lingered in the air around that building. Stale curry.

Meg's breathing became more erratic; the increased shaking and sweating began to scare Jo.

'Sean, get over here quickly. We have to stand her up.'

They each put their arms under Meg's armpits and dragged her upright; Tom came to help, as Meg wasn't weight-bearing.

'Breathe,' urged Jo over and over. 'Take a deep breath in.'

Meg suddenly gasped inwards and then projectile vomited across the room.

'Shit, Tom. Swap with...' began Sean, but it was too late. His hangover was bad and the smell of vomit sent him over the edge; he suddenly threw up all over the carpet as well. Tom rushed over and replaced his dad, who ran out of the room and tried his best not to be sick himself.

249

It became too much for Wes, who started heaving. He ran out of the room to try to get to the bathroom, but Cora was in the narrow hallway and refused to give way. He attempted to tell her to move, but as soon as he opened his mouth, a belly full of beer and curry covered Cora's body. She screamed dramatically, and the police started banging on the door.

'Open up immediately,' came a fierce voice from outside.

'Kayleigh!' said Jo. 'Open the door before they kick it down, and do not call them fascists!' she shouted as her daughter ran to the door.

The police charged in the second Kayleigh opened the door.

'Hands where we can see them!'

'It's fine,' said Jo to the officers. 'Only the family is here.'

Another officer ran in through the front door and skidded on Wes's vomit in the hallway then propelled feet first into Cora, who landed on top of him.

She began screaming all over again.

'Shut up, Cora!' hissed Kayleigh. 'And get off that police officer before he arrests you for sexual assault.'

Cora and Kayleigh started to argue. The police officer detached himself from the screaming woman and ran outside, also to vomit. Sean reappeared in the lounge, looking green.

'Jo, what do we do?' he asked his wife.

'Tom and I will get Meg upstairs to her room. You can deal with this mess!' she snapped.

They half carried Meg to the top floor. 'Mum, I've never seen anything like this,' Tom said anxiously. 'Do you think we should call an ambulance?'

'I don't know!' said Jo helplessly. 'Let's just get her away from the chaos.'

They half-dragged Meg upstairs and sat her onto her bed. Jo got a damp cloth and wiped Meg's sweaty but cold face, all the time saying her name over and over and telling her she was safe. Meg's eyes were still glazed. With nothing else to do, Jo just put her arms around her and rocked her gently, continuing her mantra.

Meg's body loosened a fraction. She could smell safety again. She blinked several times, took a shuddering breath, and looked around the room before her eyes settled on Jo.

'Thanks, Tom,' Jo said. 'Will you go and help Dad please, and shut Cora and Kayleigh up?'

He nodded grimly and left the room, running downstairs to try to ease the chaos.

'Concentrate on taking some steady breaths,' Jo told Meg. 'I'm getting you into some dry clothes. You're soaked.'

Jo picked a selection of clothing and helped undress the disorientated child, then put her into something warm and dry. She wanted to get Meg a warm, sweet drink, but was too afraid to leave her. Downstairs was a scene of carnage, so she had to make do with water from the en-suite and kept hugging the girl and reassuring her that she was safe.

Thirty minutes later, Kayleigh appeared with hot drinks for them both.

'I'm sorting out downstairs; best not to come down yet. I've got a carpet cleaning company coming in half an hour. I used Dad's credit card and said it was an emergency. It won't be cheap.'

'That doesn't matter. Thank you.' Jo looked at her daughter gratefully.

'And, Mum... I'm sorry for shouting at Cora. It didn't help. I really am sorry.'

'No, it did not help! We are all under a lot of stress, but please, Kayleigh, try to tone it down and give Cora a break. Got that?'

Kayleigh nodded, her face reddening in shame. 'Thank you! Now, what is Dad doing?'

'He keeps being sick. I think he needs to go to bed. And, believe it or not, Jack is still fast asleep in the lounge. He slept through multiple projectile vomiting and an armed raid.'

'Would you mind sitting with Meg for five minutes while I go and see Dad, please? Make sure she has the hot drink and just keep talking gently to her. It doesn't matter what about.'

'Sure,' said Kayleigh as Jo strode purposefully out of the room.

Jo found Sean in the kitchen, drinking pints of water and looking pale. 'What the hell are you playing at, Sean?' Jo asked, glaring at him.

'Nothing! I went out and drank too much. It's not against the law now, is it?'

'Don't be so bloody childish. After everything we've been through with Meg, after everything she's achieved in allowing herself to begin to trust you! Then you go and send her back to square one because you fancied a piss up. You knew she was nervous about people drinking, but all you could think about was yourself! You are not one of the kids, so stop behaving like one!'

'I had one night out, Jo, *one*! It's not been an easy time for me either. What do you expect me to do?'

'I expect you to be my partner and act like an adult and a father! You left Kayleigh to clean up your mess and deal with everything while you had your head down the bloody toilet. And you left me to deal with a deeply traumatised child who was experiencing an extremely dangerous flashback.

Don't you get it? You can't just offer to adopt someone and then carry on as nothing has happened to her.'

'Don't you dare!' Sean swung around to face his wife, trying hard to keep calm and not shout. 'You are the one who told me to keep my distance, give her time to trust me and not to jump in. I've been with you in this since day one when you've let me!'

'Where were you an hour ago? You certainly were not with me then.'

'Once! Once I wasn't there for ten minutes. Fine, I was vomiting. I got drunk last night; it did not cause a flashback. I am not responsible for what happened to her!'

'Your childish behaviour certainly played a part in what happened this morning! And cuddled up with Wes on the sofa! You looked ridiculous. You are a middle-aged man, not a teenager. You are also a father to Meg now! So, stop playing at it and stop making me the bad guy all the time and get involved.'

'I seriously do not understand you! I have done everything you have asked me to do. I have tried to be a parent, but it's not that easy when I have one bloody arm tied behind my back by you!'

'Oh, just grow up, Sean,' Jo retorted unreasonably. She knew he was right, but she refused to back down.

'I'm going to bed for a couple of hours before I say something I might regret!' Sean snapped and marched out of the room, irritated at the injustice of his wife's accusations. None of them could have possibly known that Meg would have a flashback, as they didn't know what caused it.

'Fine, go! Leave me to deal with the fallout as usual!' Jo shouted.

'Well, it's the way you want it,' he added sarcastically as he made his way up the stairs.

Still angry with her husband, Jo took several deep breaths and regained her composure before heading back up to Meg's room.

Kayleigh was sitting next to Meg on the bed with her arm around her. Meg's eyes were still glazed, but the shivering had calmed down. Kayleigh was talking gently about the trees outside and the colour of the sky, and how stunning it looked.

Jo watched, her heart filling with love and intense gratitude for her oldest daughter. 'Thank you, Kayleigh. You are amazing. Can we swap now? Will you go and take over downstairs?'

'Sure, Mum.' She stood and gave Jo a sudden hug.

'Let me know if I can help up here.'

Jo nodded and swapped places with Kayleigh. She pulled a bottle of essential oils from her pocket that she'd collected in the bathroom on her way back upstairs. She wafted it in front of Meg's nose.

'Peppermint and eucalyptus. It's a strong smell, so just take small sniffs. It'll help, trust me.'

Meg sniffed it several times and then moved away. Her eyes focussed on Jo. 'What happened?'

'You had a flashback, a terrible one. Are you able to tell me what you need right now? A lie-down? Bath? A cuddle?'

Meg stared unblinkingly into the air again. After a while, Jo began to think she was disassociating again.

'Meg...'

'Curry,' Meg said at the same time. 'Thhhhh...'

'It's okay. Take your time.'

'That place, the building... it always smelled of curry. Not nice and ready to eat, but kind of stale, and it was always there.'

Jo sat thoughtfully for a long time and subconsciously put her arm around Meg, who moved closer and put her arms around her too.

'Can I tell the police about this, please?'

'Why?'

'I'm not sure, but it may help. If there was a catering facility or restaurant nearby, for instance, then it might help them locate the building. You never know what will help.'

Meg nodded. 'Please don't make me go and talk to them. Not today.'

'Definitely not. The investigating officers want you to go to the station to look at some photos soon, but not today. This information may or may not be helpful. But there is no harm in letting the Inspector know.'

'Can I get into bed now?' Meg pleaded. 'I feel like I've been hit by a bus.'

'Emotionally, you have,' Jo said grimly. 'Get in. Can I stay with you until you're asleep?'

'Please,' whispered Meg.

Jo hugged Meg to sleep, stroking the girl's head absent-mindedly. She wondered about the flashback and the connection to the curry smell, hoping it would help the police find the elusive building.

Meg woke late afternoon to the wafts of something delicious coming from downstairs, which made her empty stomach rumble. She yawned and stretched, realising how stiff her body was from the earlier events. Feeling weak and shaky, she dressed and headed towards the gorgeous smell.

'Great timing!' Sean smiled warmly at Meg as she wandered into the kitchen. 'I'm doing spag bol. Fancy some?'

'Yeah, that would be great. It smells amazing.'

'My speciality dish,' he announced proudly. 'That, along with toast, crumpets, and, err, well, that's about it. Though

I'm also an expert at putting frozen food in the microwave and watching it heat up.'

'Where is everyone?'

'Scattered around the house somewhere, I imagine. Jo is in the lounge if you want to wait for dinner in there.'

'Thanks,' she slurred as a big yawn erupted from her mouth, and she went to find Jo.

'Hey,' Jo said, looking exhausted. 'How was your sleep?'

'Okay. No nightmares.'

'Excellent. Have you had a drink?'

Meg studied Jo for a second, then decided to take a risk. 'Has anyone told you that you're a bit obsessed with drinking?' she asked, grinning.

'Huh, the cheek!' Jo smiled. 'But yes, it may have been mentioned. Do you want to go and get some water, or would you like to sit down and I will give you a very long and comprehensive lesson on the benefits of hydration?'

'Meg.' She spun around and saw Jack behind her.

'For the sake of your sanity, just go and get a drink. Seriously, I had this conversation with Mum on many an occasion when I was your age. I sometimes think of it when I can't sleep, and it knocks me out in seconds.'

'You watch it too!' Jo grinned at her son.

'Food's up!' shouted Sean.

'Saved by the bell.' Jack laughed. 'Come on. Dad does an amazing spaghetti bolognese, but don't tell him more than once as he gets big-headed!'

Stamping of feet could be heard from all over the house as everyone headed for the feast laid out on the huge dining table.

'Tuck in before it goes cold,' Sean urged, glancing at his wife, who turned away, refusing to make eye contact.

Kayleigh took a large portion from the steaming pot on the table, plonked it on Meg's plate, and then did the same on her plate.

'Save some for the rest of us,' Cora said snidely.

'Oh, shut up, Cora. It's not like you ever eat anything. You push food around on your plate! It's wasted on you!'

'Kayleigh! Cora!' came Jo's exasperated voice. 'Can you please try to spend at least a minute in each other's company without arguing? It's boring and exhausting, and I would like one meal that does not result in indigestion!'

Meg looked around the table, everyone leaning over each other, grabbing spaghetti, garlic bread, and water. Cora and Kayleigh glared at each other. Meg also sensed something was going on between Jo and Sean as she witnessed the earlier exchange of looks. Despite that, it struck her that, even despite the disagreements, everyone seemed to just fit together. An altogether unfamiliar concept

259

to Meg, who had previously lived with people all just thrown in together. All angry, abandoned, or abused teenagers. She was used to eating with lots of people, but the meals were nearly always disrupted by someone losing their temper, fighting with the staff, or being restrained by them. At least twice a week, a chair was flung through the dining room window. Police were constantly in and out of the building. It wasn't uncommon for one of the kids to smash the fire alarm panel during a meal, as there was generally someone unhappy with the menu or simply bored and wanted to have some *fun*. So, the concept of indigestion wasn't an unfamiliar one to Meg; neither was suddenly having to escape and run for it during a meal when the staff called the police, who tended to grab whoever was closest and throw them into a cell for a few hours.

This, a life in which a family gathered together for meals, was as strange for Meg as a meal in a children's home would be for everyone who sat around her. The noise was at a similar level, but it wasn't incendiary; she didn't feel like someone was about to throw a chair through a window. However, she did wonder how long it would take for Kayleigh's explosive temper to erupt and land a bowl of spaghetti on Cora's head.

She observed Cora. Even though she had only known her for a few days, she really didn't like her. She was sullen, bad-tempered, and never had a good word to say about anyone.

Sensing that someone was staring at her, she suddenly looked up and caught Meg watching. 'What are you staring at?' she snapped.

'No idea. Trying to work it out,' Meg answered quickly, feeling some of her old spark rise up.

'Stop it, both of you!' Sean ordered, much to Meg's shock at being told off by him. 'You all heard Mum. Just let us have a meal without arguing for once.'

Jo glanced at her husband gratefully and gave him a small smile, which he returned.

'Wedding plans!' Tom announced. 'Including you lot, whom I suppose we have to invite,' he added with a grin. 'There will be 100 people at the ceremony and reception. Then we're expecting another 100 or so for the evening.'

'What's happening in the evening?'

'We are looking at hotels in town tomorrow. It would make sense if we can find somewhere that will host the reception and the evening party.'

'Sounds fantastic!' Kayleigh exclaimed excitedly. 'Sounds expensive.' Sean sighed dramatically.

'We have some savings...' Tom began.

'Dad is joking,' Jo intervened. 'We will be honoured to pay for your wedding.'

'Do you both want to come tomorrow and look at the venues with us?'

'One of us certainly will,' answered Jo. 'There is something one of us needs to do tomorrow, but either Dad or I will come.'

'Can I come too?' Kayleigh asked.

'Me too?' Jack asked keenly.

'Sure,' said Wes. 'It will be good to get a few opinions before we decide.'

'Great plan.' Jo smiled. 'Meg, either Sean or I need to go somewhere with you tomorrow. We will talk about it after dinner. Cora, seeing as you're the only one home, will you give the house a thorough pre-Christmas tidy and clean, please?'

'Why me?' she snapped.

'Because everyone else is busy,' asserted Sean. 'You can pull your weight instead of lounging in your pyjamas in front of the TV all day.'

'What? How can you say that? I haven't been able to get anywhere near the TV today due to everyone throwing up in the living room and those cleaners taking hours to get rid of the smell.'

'That's why it's good that you'll have the house to yourself tomorrow. No one will get in your way while you give it a good clean. We will help you when we get back if you haven't finished, but I expect to find at least two, if not three rooms, gleaming.'

Cora opened her mouth to argue but caught a look in her mother's eye that made her think better of it.

Apart from Meg, who was feeling apprehensive, and Cora, who was sulking, everyone else launched into an enthusiastic discussion. Everything from the various hotels in the city, to DJs, outfits, and even the colour of napkins was considered.

Jo and Sean disappeared upstairs after dinner, but not before instructing everyone to clean up. The six of them bustled around the kitchen, loading the dishwasher and scrubbing the hob.

'I love Dad's spag bol, but how does he manage to make so much mess?' Jack sighed, eyeing a splash of sauce on the ceiling.

'Stay there!' yelled Kayleigh, grabbing a cloth. She jumped onto Jack's back. 'Keep still.

I'm going to stand on your shoulders.'

'Seriously?'

'Shut up, you're making me wobble.' But her own talking made her wobble more. Her hands did a crawl along the ceiling, trying to find something to grasp onto as Jack attempted to move with her. Then, complete darkness fell upon the house.

'Ow!' moaned Kayleigh, as she landed on the floor with a thud, holding the light fitting. Next came the inevitable sound of heavy footsteps coming down the stairs and a police officer banging on the front door.

They all groaned; Jack and Tom hoisted Kayleigh roughly to her feet.

'Idiot!' Tom hissed. 'Don't you think there's been enough aggro in this house already today!'

Sean, Jo, and an armed police officer using a powerful torch barged into the kitchen to be confronted with five guilty-looking faces and one smug one.

'What's happened now?' sighed Jo.

'Kayleigh pulled the light fitting out!' said Cora happily.

'How on earth...' but Jo was interrupted as Kayleigh flung herself at her sister, knocking her to the ground, throwing fists and swear words. Tom, Wes, and Jack dived in to separate them, but the police officer moved his torch and guided Jo to the nearby fuse box, where she flicked the trip switch.

The light from the hall illuminated the kitchen. It provided a view of the three men in a tangled heap on the floor, and Kayleigh and Cora still rolling around, swearing at each other. Kayleigh had a bleeding lip, and Cora had the beginnings of what would be an impressive black eye.

Meg watched and grinned. Now it felt like she was back in the kids' home!

Chapter Fourteen

Go to your rooms, all of you!' Jo shouted, making Meg jump. 'I expect an electrician to come out, tonight, and the four of you can pay for it!'

'Five,' Wes said.

'Six!' Meg announced. 'Well, I haven't got any money, so I'll have to owe it...'

Kayleigh grinned at her, but immediately her grin turned to a thunderous expression as Cora said, 'FIVE! I'm not paying for something I didn't do. It wasn't my fau...'

'Cora, will you please just shut up!' seethed Sean. 'The lot of you are acting like teenagers again. Get upstairs, go online, find a bloody electrician, and pay for it. Go!'

Everyone scampered out of the room. Meg turned to go, but Jo put a hand on her shoulder. 'Not you. We need a chat.'

Meg looked up at her, worried. It hadn't exactly been calm since the others came home; maybe Jo and Sean thought it was her fault.

'Come on.' Jo guided her to the living room.

Sean joined a few seconds later, his face like thunder. 'They are really testing my patience. There is enough to deal with without them all acting like children. I am so close to banging Kayleigh and Cora's heads together.' He sighed, throwing himself into an armchair.

'I'm sorry,' Meg began. 'It's my fault that...'

'It is not your fault!' Sean insisted. 'It's not your job to stop them acting like a pack of feral animals. I feel sorry for the police officers. Twice now they've had to barge in, and the bloke who slipped in the vomit and crashed into Cora...' Sean couldn't finish his sentence and started to laugh, only to be joined by Jo, who gave an explosive snort.

'The look on his face,' she managed to squeak out through her laughter.

Meg looked confused. 'I don't remember that. I wish someone had filmed it.'

More laughter, and Jo bent over, holding her stomach as tears streamed from her eyes. 'Stop.' Sean also clutched his stomach. 'Or the police will be banging on the door again.'

He gave a huge roar of laughter, startling Meg, and continued to laugh hysterically.

Meg watched, feeling somewhat bemused as they both lost control.

'Have you two been drinking?' she asked in a bewildered tone. Which only resulted in more laughter from the pair.

'I might go to bed,' she added, thinking everyone had gone crazy.

'No. Sorry, Meg,' said Jo, taking a deep breath to calm herself. 'We need to have a chat. I think the last few days have finally hit us; we forget the utter chaos...'

'Or deliberately block it from our minds...' Sean sighed.

'Yes, that too, that the four of them bring whenever they are all under the same roof. They're worse now than when they were toddlers. And Kayleigh and Cora have got worse with each other over the years. But I've not seen them roll around on the floor fighting for a good while. They'll have to sort this out or find a compromise before Sean really does bang their heads together!'

Meg grinned, knowing Sean wouldn't do that, but it made for an amusing image in her head.

'Anyway,' began Sean, who had finally composed himself. 'Sorry to have to go into this now, but Jo rang Inspector Phillips earlier when you were asleep.'

Meg paled; all humour suddenly left her. 'Why?'

'I wanted to tell her about your flashback. Well, not the flashback, but the smell that initiated it. They have been desperately searching for the location of the, err, the place where...'

'Where those people took everyone,' finished Sean on behalf of his wife. 'They may have some leads, and the information about the smell makes them think there may be some kind of food production facility near to where you were held. This has led them to several possible locations. They want you to go tomorrow and look at these places and see if you can identify it. Apparently, they won't be allowed to comment when you're looking at places. They will just ask you to say yes or no.'

'Also,' Jo continued, 'after the last interview, you were asked to look at images of people on their computer; they would like you to do that as well. Will you?'

'And then what? What if I can't spot anyone?'

'A lot has been happening behind the scenes. Once you've identified the building and possible perpetrators, they will fill you in on their investigation. And if you can't identify anyone, then that's fine. They're just asking you to have a look. It may lead to more arrests, more evidence, or it may not. But the police have done a good job so far, and the evidence is mounting, so if, and only if, you feel able to do it, then they would like you to go tomorrow.'

Meg sat silently for a long time, thinking about what to do. She felt repulsed by the thought of returning to that building. The building in which she had been attacked and hurt so many times. The building in which she'd seen Jenny die.

She remembered the expression on the man's face as he cut Jenny's throat; it had been one of pure evil. Then he'd tossed her body aside as though it were a piece of meat. The feeling of hatred for him and the others made her stomach churn with anger and disgust. 'What if the, I mean, what if those people are there if I find the right building?'

'You won't be on your own. Armed officers will be there as well as those investigating. If you do find them, they'll be arrested or shot. Preferably the latter,' Sean stated, not bothering to hide his anger.

Meg waited for Jo to remonstrate with him, but much to Meg's surprise, she nodded in agreement.
'Okay. What time do we need to be there?' Meg asked Jo.

'Sean is going with you this time.' Jo replied gently.

'Why?'

'Because we are both your parents,' Sean said. 'Or want to be. Jo and I are a team, and we work together. Jo wants to go along and support you, but so do I. Jo accompanied you last time, so you have me tomorrow. Is that okay?'

Meg contemplated him, remembering everything he had done for her. She had never really had a dad, not a proper one, and she had never yearned for one either. She hated all the men her mother had brought home. But here was a kind, caring man who really wanted to be her dad. A man who'd sat up with her all night in the hospital, reading to her and playing films. A man who talked to her, had snowball fights with her, took her into his home, and cared about her.

'Sure, that's fine. What time do we have to be there?'

'Nine a.m.,' said Sean, his voice sounding weird to Meg, who nodded.

'I'll be ready for nine. Is it okay if I go to bed?'

'Of course,' Sean replied. 'Will you be okay, though? You can stay up for a little while and watch some TV to distract yourself. I don't want you going to bed with your head full of everything we've just talked about.'

'No, but thanks. Can I read for a bit when I'm in bed?'

'Sure. Read for as long as you like,' said Jo. 'And don't forget...'

'To take a glass of water, I know.' Meg grinned at Jo fondly. 'Goodnight.'

'Goodnight,' they both replied and watched as she headed to the dimly lit kitchen to get a glass of water.

As she reached the first floor, she quietly passed one of the bedrooms, in which she heard five sets of voices attempting to be quiet, all hissing over each other. She continued up to the attic, not wanting to get involved in any more dramas that night.

She snuggled under the duvet with her book and managed only two sentences before falling asleep.

In what felt like minutes, she heard a knock on her bedroom door. 'Breakfast's ready,' shouted Sean.

'Coming,' groaned Meg, feeling groggy and tired after a night of disturbing and vivid dreams.

She put on her dressing gown and stumbled downstairs, her stomach rumbling. The kitchen light was now miraculously working, and the fittings, all new and shiny, were in place.

Finding no one there, she wandered into the dining room; seven people were reaching across each other, grabbing slices of bacon or ladles of beans.

'Morning,' said Jo, and the others all grunted, their mouths full. 'Come and tuck in before it's all gone.'

Meg grabbed a plate and a glass of orange juice and sat there, still half asleep, feeling strangely uneasy. Suddenly, it hit her; she was going to the police station with Sean today. The acid fizzed around in her stomach; she pushed the orange juice away and began to feel sick as the smell of the food became overpowering.

'Just popping to the loo,' she mumbled, and left before anyone could respond.

She went to her room, and realising she was sweating, took a cold shower and dressed. She lay on the bed, trying to keep herself calm. The illusion of safety and a normal life, over the past few days especially, had helped her to bury some of her horrendous experiences. She couldn't forget; she knew she never would. But forcing them to the back of her mind was the only thing that helped her to get up in the morning and make her body go through the motions of the day.

She jumped at a knock on the door, and Jo opened it a crack. 'Can I come in?'

'Sure,' came the weak reply.

Jo sat on Meg's bed. 'I can't tell you that today won't be awful; we both know it will be. But it is another step towards the finish line. Once these animals are caught and behind bars, then you can slowly begin to look forward.'

'I don't think I'll ever be able to do that. How am I supposed to go to school or learn to do what normal kids do when this will always be in my head? And I don't know if I'll be able to go to school. Having to sit in a classroom and not be allowed out, I can't do it. I feel panicked about it already. I'll be trapped.'

'We're not going to throw you straight into a school environment, I promise. You will be seeing a therapist first.'

'*I am not*!'

'It is not up for discussion,' Jo added, refusing to react to Meg's shouting. 'And, when the time is right, we will arrange for some school work to be sent here, and you can do some lessons at home for a while. A catch-up, if you like. It will be handy to see what level you have reached in your education and what you need to do before going back to school.'

273

'I am not going back to school!'

'This is also not a discussion for today. You need to be as present as you can be. It's going to be exhausting, but I know you can do it.'

'Well, I don't!' came the sulky reply.

Jo saw the enormity of the girl's unadulterated terror and desperately wished she could go along with her.

'Sean will be with you every step of the way, and he will look after you. If it gets too much, he will bring you home. We all want these people to rot in a cage for the rest of their lives, but we want you to be safe, mentally as well as physically.'

'Will you come instead?' she asked beseechingly.

Jo hesitated. 'Sean is going with you. He wants to support you as much as I do. We're all in this together.'

Meg gave a bitter laugh.

'We are, Meg, and it's Sean's turn to be there with you. But I will be there in thought if not in person, I promise.'

'What are you doing instead? What are the others doing?'

'Still going to look at hotels for the wedding reception. It's the last thing I want to do, but Tom and Wes need support, in a polar opposite way to what you need, but it's important to them that one of us is there.'

'Is Cora going?'

'What do you think?'

'What is her problem?'

'I have an idea, but let's say, for now, that Cora is very unhappy. Don't worry about it. You have enough going on today. Whereas I, along with the happy couple, Kayleigh, and Jack, will spend hours looking at every hotel in the city.' She groaned. 'Anyway, it's time to go. Let's go and find Sean.'

They went down to the first floor and saw Sean's office door open. Meg had never been in his office before and tentatively followed Jo as she strode in.

'This bloody network is driving me up the wall,' he groaned to his wife. 'I've entered my password, my PIN and personal ID, and it is just saying "awaiting validation". Seriously, social care has the worst...' He looked up and was surprised to see Meg. 'Sorry, I didn't see you there.'

'Why are you working?' demanded Jo. 'You have to leave!'

'I know. I just wanted to update some notes on the system, a 30-second job normally. Forget it. I'll try tonight.' He stood up and put on his jacket and adjusted his tie, looking very smart.

'Why are you all dressed up?' Meg looked him up and down, the stress on her face deepening.

'Because people are elitists and treat you with more respect if you dress as they do, sadly.

'Anyway, this is just a work suit. I may have a top hat and tails somewhere if you prefer?'

'Shut up, Sean,' said Jo at her grinning husband, noting Meg's confusion. 'Just go!' She grabbed Meg and hugged her. 'Remember, you are in control. If it becomes too much for you, tell them to stop, or look at Sean, and he will bring you home. Got that?'

'Got it!' Meg answered, returning the hug tightly and not wanting to let go.

'Right, let's do this!' Sean told Meg.

Jo watched them leave, then went to the window in Sean's office and watched as they got into the car and drove away, her stomach churning with anxiety. She desperately hoped Sean would be able to handle it if Meg had a flashback or became angry or distraught.

'What are you doing?' came Cora's voice from the doorway. Jo turned from the window and saw her daughter looking around the room. 'Dad's office has changed since I was last home,' she mused.

'Yes, well, he can work from home more often now most things are computerised, which isn't always helpful as it means he struggles to take a break from work.'

'Have they gone? To see the police?'

'Yes!' Jo replied tightly, unsure why she felt so defensive. 'And have you changed your mind about today? Would you like to come and look at wedding reception venues with your brother?'

'No, I have not changed my mind!'

Jo left the room without another word. She really could not cope with Cora's attitude, today of all days.

Sean led the way into the police station and DS Murray was waiting for them in reception.

'Thank you for coming,' she said with a smile. 'I know it's hard and scary. Can we just step into this side room for a quick chat before we go upstairs?'

Meg nodded, and she and Sean followed the DS into a small room just near the reception desk.

'I just want to remind you, and I'm sorry to bring this up, but the only people who are aware of your location are Inspector Phillips, your social worker, and me. Also, please do not refer to Leon as Leon. He is locked up under Ewan's name. He is on the main database as Ewan, and the only people aware of his real identity are Inspector Phillips, DCI Leek, Jo, and the people in this room.'

'Why?' Meg asked, confused.

'Two reasons. Firstly, he is in solitary confinement; no other prisoners have seen him, so the gang may suspect he has been arrested, but they don't know for sure. They also may think that, because he failed his assignment, as you are very much alive, he may have gone underground for a while. They will not be as vigilant in suspecting their operation has been compromised.

'Secondly, there is a leak somewhere in the station. The sedative didn't get into the officer's sandwich by accident when they were watching your house. We need to take all the precautions we can. An anti-corruption team is investigating, but they're staying under the radar for the time being, doing deep background checks on everyone based here, from the cleaners upwards. Again, that is also confidential. Agreed?'

'Agreed!'

'Right then. We are meeting with DCI Leek, and we will show you some images on the computer. Inspector Phillips will join us, but only to testify that no partiality towards anyone in the photographs was deliberately or inadvertently indicated to you by verbal or non-verbal means.'

'What does that mean?'

'It means she's there so she can tell the court that no one tried to make you pick out a certain picture,' said Sean.

'Why didn't she just say that then?' mumbled Meg, irritated.

'Police talk,' whispered Sean, rolling his eyes, trying to lighten the intensity of the situation for Meg.

The trio entered a spacious room that held a large table in the centre; DCI Leek and Inspector Phillips stood and greeted Meg and Sean.

Once the formalities were over, Inspector Phillips sat at the end of the table while the DCI and DS sat behind Meg at the centre of the table and opened a laptop.

'Will you hold the mouse?' asked the DCI. 'Scroll down the images on the page. If you recognise any of the people in the photographs, just click on their image and keep scrolling. No discussion, just keep going. When you've finished, we will then print off any images and discuss them in the interview room, where it will be recorded. Do you understand?' Meg nodded.

'Sean, would you mind going to sit next to the Inspector, please?' Sean looked at Meg, who again nodded, and he anxiously walked over and sat next to Gina.

'Go ahead,' DCI Murray urged as the screen lit up. 'If you need to take a break, push your chair away from the table and look at Inspector Phillips, okay?'

'Okay.' Meg took a deep breath and placed her sweaty hand on the mouse.

As she scrolled, the tense atmosphere in the room became increasingly distracting. She closed her eyes for a second and took several deep breaths, mentally dismissed the anxiety she felt from the others, and refocused on the screen.

Four minutes passed as she desperately searched for a familiar face. It felt like four hours. It was then she saw him. Meg knew he would have to be in there, but looking at the arrogant face of her former care home worker filled her with such a rage that she wanted to put her fist through the screen and shatter his evil glare.

She reached for some water and took a long drink, hands shaking as she went back to the mouse and clicked on to his image. Next was Peter, the other care home worker, whose face was clicked with anger.

There was some movement by the officers next to her. Gina cleared her throat sternly and glared at them. They froze, but Meg ignored them and tried to clear her mind and body of the repulsion that was surging through her very core.

She continued, clicking on Javeed's wife, then Ewan. Then, the image of her nightmares appeared, right in front of her, in broad daylight. She physically recoiled and pushed her chair back so suddenly that everyone jumped.

'Do you need a break, Meg?' Gina addressed the girl, who was sweating profusely.

'Meg?' Sean said, a little louder.

She spun her head to see him, Gina, and the other two officers.

'Do you need a break?' repeated Gina kindly.

Meg shook her head and looked around the room. Remembering what Jo had taught her, she looked for five blue items, four red, three yellow, two white, and one black. It worked, and she became more grounded and reconnected with the space she was in. Fighting the urge to run, Meg moved back to the computer and clicked on the image of the man she'd witnessed murdering Jenny Evans.

She continued for ninety minutes; after seeing hundreds, if not thousands of faces, she had clicked on twenty-one of them before reaching the end.

'Done,' she croaked bleakly.

'Thank you,' said Inspector Phillips gravely. 'It will take a little while to get the images printed off and to collect the information of the people you have identified. Is there anything you wish to do before the interview?' she asked, looking at the DCI.

'Yes. There are some properties that we would like to visit with Meg. We have calculated the estimated speed she thinks she was travelling, national speed limits in suburban areas, and various noises Meg recalled. The information regarding the smell she remembered was also useful. We have five possible locations and would like to investigate if Meg is willing,' he finished and looked at her. Meg nodded.

'That's fine. Meg, Sean, and I will follow you in my car. This has to be done by the book.

'By every letter of the book. I don't want some defence barrister saying she was coerced.' The DCI nodded, as did DS Murray.

'Do you want a break or some fresh air before we go, or a chat?' Sean asked.

'No, thanks. I want to keep going before I bottle it.'

He agreed, but couldn't help but wonder what Jo would do. Would she insist on a break? Demand they left it for the day? He forced himself to stop second-guessing and agreed with Meg.

'Come on, then. Let's go.'

They all stood as one and made their way through the police station's empty corridors and into the yard, where they split up to get into their respective cars. Armed police piled into two separate mini-vans that had blacked-out windows.

The hunt was on.

'I'm going to record all conversation and movements while we're travelling, Meg,' explained Gina. 'This is all a search for evidence, and also an exercise to show that we have acted lawfully and diligently. Understand?'

'Yes,' Meg answered, wondering what *diligently* meant.

'Okay, time to move.'

Their first stop was alongside the canal; storage containers were dotted around the area, along with a row of battered-looking warehouses.

'Not here,' Meg said instinctively. 'It smells wrong. That canal stinks; I would have remembered that.'

'We need to look inside the warehouses either way,' commanded the DCI, nodding to the security guard, who began to open doors and roll up the shutters of the various buildings. 'If only to rule them out.'

'Fine.' Meg shrugged. 'But it's the wrong place.'

The armed police entered the buildings first and searched. When they shouted, "All clear," Meg and the entourage followed. They viewed all six warehouses. None of it was familiar.

'Sorry,' she said to the group. 'This is definitely not the place.'

'Are you happy, Ma'am?' asked the DS, looking at Gina, who simply nodded.

'All in!' DCI Leek commanded, and the armed guards ran to their vehicles, while the others followed at a more leisurely pace.

The next visit was to more warehouses closer to the city centre. Again, Meg knew it was the wrong place. The convoy circled back and drove past her old children's home, which was now boarded up. She quickly looked away from the foreboding building, remembering what had happened the last time she was there.

'Are you okay?' Sean asked, staring intently at the girl, who was sweating profusely. She nodded, too scared to open her mouth in case the rising, acidic bile coming from her stomach spewed out of her mouth.

The next place was also a dead-end. Meg began to feel guilty about wasting everyone's time as they set off for the next place. She wished the car would avoid pot-holes. They had plunged into three of them so far, and it made her sickness worse. She knew a particularly deep-one was coming up and was sure she'd be sick.

'*Stop*!' she screamed.

The car screeched to a halt; radios crackled as orders were given to the other vehicle to hang back.

'What is it?' Gina urged.

'There's another pot-hole coming up, in about ten seconds. A really deep one.'

'How do you...?' began Sean.

Gina understood. 'Are you sure you want to proceed?'

'Can I get out of the car? I need to be sick.' Meg said it calmly but was looking increasingly pale.

Gina nodded, and Meg began to vomit as soon as her feet hit the road. She made it to the surrounding grass verge and emptied her stomach contents all over it.

'Stay where you are, Sean,' Gina ordered firmly. 'And don't ask any questions. Not to me, and most definitely not to Meg.'

He looked at her serious face and felt his body shudder.

Meg got back into the car and gratefully accepted the water Sean passed to her. Gina got back onto the radio. 'Proceed with caution. Silent approach.'

The cars moved on, travelling slower than before and, just as Meg said, they bounced through a huge pot-hole just seconds later.

As they approached a desolate area that contained several warehouses, she began to smell curry through her open window. A battered sign outside one of the warehouses said, 'Harris Wholefoods.'

'We need to stop here,' Meg informed Gina. Again, radios crackled, and everyone stopped.

Gina looked at Meg expectantly. 'There are cars in front of one of the warehouses, next door to the food place. They might be in there.'

'How do you know it's the correct building?'

'I just know!'

Gina counted thirty vehicles outside the anonymous-looking warehouse. She radioed for more armed backup and police vehicles.

'On way, Ma'am. ETA, five minutes.'

285

'Silent approach! Out.'

'What do we do now?' asked Sean, who received a glare from Gina.

'Wait!' she said stiffly. 'As soon as the units are in place, I want you and Meg to go back to the station in a squad car.'

Meg felt a deep numbness fall over her, and a not unfamiliar sensation of floating above her own body and simply observing the scene with a disconnected curiosity. She jolted back into reality as almost a dozen vehicles screeched alongside them, and the occupants jumped out, carrying large guns.

The officers met in a huddle around one van. The road was cordoned off, and orders were given. She watched as a dozen armed officers disappeared around the back of the building, and another twenty, accompanied by uniformed officers who hung back slightly, approached the front.

The DCI was stood next to Meg's open window.

'Unit one in place,' came a static voice.

'Unit two in place,' came a second.

'All units, GO, GO, GO!' he ordered, before Gina could tell him to wait until Meg had been removed.

The air filled with the sounds of shouting, banging, and screaming; Meg felt as though her head was going to explode. Moving automatically, she jumped out of the car and ran towards the warehouse.

'Shit!' said Sean and Gina at the same time and jumped out to chase her, along with the DCI and three uniformed officers.

Meg was fast, even faster due to the adrenaline surging through her body, fuelled by anger and hatred. She felt no fear at that moment, just a desperate urge to get into that building, to save the people in it. Sean overtook Gina and the unfit police officers. He entered the building's broken-down door just seconds after Meg did.

'Stop!' Gina screamed to her officers, just as the sound of gunfire shook the ground.

CHAPTER FIFTEEN

Outside, Gina and the DCI were screaming into their radios, demanding a situation report. DS Murray caught up with them.

'What if they've shot her?' she gasped.

'Shut up!' shouted Gina harshly. 'Speculation is not helpful. We will know soon...' Gina's phone began to vibrate. Checking the caller ID, she saw it was Jo. She was desperate to send the call to her answer service, but she knew she owed her more. Jo's family was at risk. She had to tell her.

Gina left the group and answered; Jo immediately heard the gunfire.

'No, just head home, and I'll call you. This will be over in minutes,' Gina stated. Gina ended the call, and her radio crackled.

'All clear. Safe to enter.'

She ran inside the building, pushing the others out of the way, and entered a scene that would haunt her sleep for the rest of her days.

A large group of terrified young girls was huddled in one corner of the warehouse, many speaking frantically in a language Gina did not understand.

She looked around and saw video cameras pointed at filthy mattresses, many blood- stained. Gina then eyed a dark brown stain in the centre of the room; she followed the stain as it continued downwards towards a drain covered by a grid. She saw two armed officers, one obviously dead and one seriously injured; paramedics were doing all they could. She saw ten men dead, others severely injured, another twenty men forced face down, all handcuffed. Finally, she saw Sean face down on the floor behind a concrete slab with a small pool of fresh blood next to him.

'*Assistance*!' she shouted, running to him, followed by armed guards and paramedics. 'Sean!' She touched his body and felt some movement from him; she knelt and saw Meg underneath him, not moving.

The paramedics worked quickly, and they were both whisked away in an ambulance in seconds.

Shaking, Gina grabbed her phone. 'Jo, meet me at St Gemma's Hospital as soon as you can.' She listened for a second. 'I don't know,' she answered weakly. 'Just get down there.'

'I'll leave this in your hands,' she said to the DCI. 'Forensics are on their way. I want all of these girls in protective custody and those animals,' she nodded to the handcuffed men, 'locked up!'

'And the injured suspects?'

She looked at them in disgust, wishing she could order that they receive no medical assistance and endure a slow, painful death. 'Hospital, separate rooms, armed guard each. Take them to the city infirmary, not St Gemma's!'

'Ma'am,' he said as Gina ran out of the building.

Gina and Jo screeched to a halt in front of A&E within seconds of each other.

'What's happened?' Jo demanded. 'Have they been hurt?'

'I don't know. Let's...'

'*You don't know*?' screamed Jo. '*Why did you let them enter a building where guns were being fired?*'

People passing by were staring at the angry, middle-aged woman screaming at a slightly older police officer. Jo had a sudden memory of the day she and Meg went walking around the reservoir, and Meg had shouted, "What are you looking at?" to an elderly couple. She was just about to repeat the same thing when Gina strode through the automatic doors and over to A&E reception. Jo ran after her, and they were immediately directed to a corridor blocked by armed officers, who quickly moved to allow the Inspector and Jo access. They ran down the corridor toward a door that was guarded by more armed police. A doctor walked out of the room and jumped in shock to see two women running at him.

Gina and Jo both fired questions at him; he didn't understand what they were saying and struggled to make them stop.

Eventually, he silently pointed to the doorway he had just exited. The women fell silent.

'They are both in there.'

'Both?' Gina said. 'Are they dead?'

'Absolutely not! Go on. See for yourselves. We will talk later.'

Jo took a deep breath, and the officers opened the door for her. All the colour left her face, and she wobbled slightly. From behind, Gina steadied Jo and held on to her until she regained her balance.

'Hello,' came Sean's voice, strained but happy to see his wife. Jo saw her husband in bed with a bandage wrapped around his arm. Next to his bed was Meg's; she lay there, her eyes closed.

'Are you both okay?' Jo whispered, tears falling down her face. 'What happened?'

'Sorry,' Gina interrupted. 'There will be officers here in two minutes to take a written and recorded statement. You cannot ask about what happened during the raid until after that. I must admit, I'm also desperate to know what happened.'

'Fine!' Jo answered, 'but you are not preventing me from asking my family about their injuries! Is Meg unconscious?' Jo turned to her husband.

'No. She was knocked out, but she's been checked and has been awake. She's just asleep.

They said the painkillers may make her woozy.'

'And your arm?'

'Bullet wound,' he said rather casually. 'Hurts like hell, but they've cleaned it and given me pain relief.'

'Bullet wound? You were shot, Sean! How?'

'I can't tell you yet. I'm sorry. But we got lucky. It could have been so much worse.' He shuddered as Jo hugged him, just as two CID officers entered the room.

They introduced themselves and set up a video camera near Sean's bed.

'I'm afraid Meg and Sean have to be interviewed separately,' the detective told Jo. 'So Meg will have to be wheeled next door.'

'Go with her, Jo. Please?' begged Sean. 'We can talk about what happened after the interview.'

'Good luck, and I love you,' she said, kissing him on the cheek, then she followed Meg's bed, which carefully wheeled into the next room. The Inspector stayed with Sean.

Just as she did at home, Jo got onto the bed and put her arms around the child, who automatically moved closer to snuggle in whilst still asleep. Jo's anger at not knowing what had happened calmed slightly as Meg's arm reached around her waist. She was relieved Sean and Meg were relatively unscathed. Well, physically, anyway, she thought as she felt her eyes grow heavy.

They both jumped awake as a doctor entered the room; Jo glanced at the clock. She had fallen asleep hugging Meg two hours previously.

'Jo!' Meg exclaimed in surprise. 'Where are we? What happened? Where's Sean? What are you doing here?'

Jo gave a small smile. 'Talk to the doctor first, and then I'll answer what I can.'

The doctor walked over, giving Meg a big grin. 'I've met you twice now and, on both occasions, you've proved that your head is certainly one tough nut to crack!'

Meg and Jo both smiled back, remembering how diligent he and the other doctors were when Meg was admitted with severe injuries after her encounter with Ewan.

'Is she okay?' Jo asked.

'Yes. She received a blow to the head and regained consciousness in the ambulance. I'm under firm instructions not to talk about how the injury was sustained until after the police have interviewed Meg. I was informed for medical purposes only.'

'Yes, I can't ask you questions either, I'm afraid,' Jo said. 'But I'll tell you what I can when the doctor has examined you.'

He shone a light into Meg's eyes, tested her reflexes, asked her to follow his finger with her eyes and then stand up and walk in a straight line with her arms out and eyes closed.

'Are you taking the p....' Meg glanced at Jo. 'I mean, is this a joke? I feel like I'm pretending to be a zombie and that there are hidden cameras everywhere.'

He laughed. 'No, but if you end up here again with any kind of brain injury, then it's something I may consider. Got that?' he finished in a mock stern voice.

'Sure.' Meg smiled back and looked pale again.

'Back to bed. Doctor's orders. Quickly, or I'll set Jo onto you.' Meg slid back into bed and downed a cup of lukewarm water.

'Good. I will see you later. And don't worry, you'll be home before Santa.'

Meg rolled her eyes, but thanked the doctor as he left. She turned to Jo, who was now sitting on a chair beside the bed, and looked at her expectantly.

'Sean is fine. Don't worry about him. The police are interviewing him in the room next door. They will be interviewing you next, so you can't tell me much, as desperate as I am to know what happened. I will find out when you talk to the police.'

'Is Sean hurt?'

'Not seriously. He has a bandaged arm.'

'Why am I here? It's a bit blurry.'

'That's for the police to discuss with you.'

Meg fell silent and thought about what had happened. 'I have to go back to the police station and answer questions about the photos of the people I saw on the computer.'

'Given the circumstances, I'm sure that can wait until tomorrow.'

There was a knock on the door, and Inspector Phillips entered with two officers carrying filming equipment.

'Nice to see you awake. You gave us quite a scare!' the Inspector said sternly.

'Sorry,' Meg muttered.

'I'm more relieved that you're alive! Sean is asking about you. I said you could have your bed back next to his after the interview if you need to stay in. We need to film it. Jo and I will stay in the background. I'm an independent witness. Can I ask, have you told Jo about anything that happened?'

'No, she told me not to.'

'Can you confirm that, Jo?' asked Gina.

'My daughter is not a liar,' Jo replied through gritted teeth.

Meg felt her eyes prickle with tears. It was the first time Jo had ever referred to her as 'her daughter,' and it felt weird. Nice, but weird.

The camera was turned on, and the officers approached the bed. They asked questions about how Meg had identified the building. She repeated everything that had happened, from the potholes to the wholefoods warehouse.

'When the officers were in place and entered the building, can you tell us what happened next?'

Meg looked at Jo, feeling ashamed. 'Take your time,' the officer said. 'You are not in any trouble.'

'Iiiiii... Sorry, err, I jumped out of the car and ran towards the building. I don't understand why, but I had to. I could hear noises and thought I could save some of the others.'

'The others?'

'The other girls. I know now it was stupid; you lot practically had an army there, but... I don't know.'

'It's fine. Carry on.'

'I ran into the warehouse and got about two metres in, and I saw him!'

'Him?'

'Naz! The man Simone, a girl from the home, introduced me to. He would take me and her out in his car, and we'd go to McDonald's or hang out. It was just a laugh.

One day, he took me to that warehouse. Simone told me to relax. It was just somewhere to hang out. But it wasn't fun. When we got there, loads of men and girls were there. The girls looked scared and bruised.'

Meg stopped, her face going blank. Jo took a step forward but was blocked by the Inspector.

'Meg,' the other officer spoke gently. 'You are doing great. What happened next?'

'He said he had something for me in his office. Simone stayed behind, laughing and joking with the men. We got to his office, but it wasn't an office. It was a windowless room with just a mattress on the floor. I tried to leave, but he locked the door and threw me onto the mattress. He said... he said.' Meg took a deep breath, glancing at Jo, feeling ashamed and full of self-disgust. 'He said he always goes first with the "fresh meat".'

Meg grabbed the grey cardboard bowl on the bedside table and vomited into it.

'We need to stop this,' whispered Jo to Gina.

'No! If we do, she'll have to start again another day. Let her finish. At least then she won't have to repeat it.'

Meg took another drink of water, her hands shaking.

'What happened next?' asked the officer in the same gentle voice.

Meg turned away from Jo. 'He got on top of me and started ripping my clothes off. I bit him, and he punched me three times, once in the face and twice in the stomach. He pulled his trousers down, and he... you know...'

'You need to say it.'

'He raped me.'

'Can you explain what you mean by rape?' the officer persisted. Jo began to fidget, her face turning red with fury.

'Stop it,' hissed Gina, 'or you'll have to leave.'

'He... he… he put his ppppenis inside me.'

'Whereabouts inside you did he put his penis?'

'Where do you think!' spat Meg angrily.

'I'm so sorry, but you need to say it.'

'Inside my vagina,' Meg said in a voice that felt as though it didn't belong to her.

'And, afterwards, he stood up, did up his trousers, grinned and said, "it's always a pleasure to welcome the fresh meat." He left, and a few minutes later, two more men came in and dragged me into the main warehouse.'

'When you saw him in the warehouse today, what happened?'

'He stared at me. I mean, really stared at me. I stared back. He was standing in the exact place where he cut Jenny's throat.

He raised a gun and pointed it at me. It all seemed to happen in slow motion. I saw his finger move on the trigger, and I remember falling, really heavily. And that was it until I woke up in here.'

'Is there anything else you want to add at this time?'

Meg shook her head, and the video cameras were turned off. 'You were amazingly brave telling us that, Meg. Thank you.'

'Can you tell me what happened next?'

'When the gun pointed at you, the man did indeed fire. If he had fired even a split-second sooner, he would have hit you. Sean came in just behind you and flung himself on top of you, and you both hit the ground, landing behind a concrete slab. The fall made you bang your head, and you were knocked unconscious. The bullet grazed Sean's arm as he fell.'

'He was shot?' Meg croaked, with tears in her eyes.

'No. The bullet hit the place where you had been standing. Sean was falling too, when he threw himself on top of you, and the bullet grazed his arm. Painful, yes. Life-threatening, no. He showed amazing bravery.'

'What happened to the man? The one who tried to shoot Meg,' Jo demanded.

'He was shot dead by our officers less than a second after he opened fire.'

'Good!' Jo said fiercely.

'What else happened?' Meg asked.

'A unit of officers went round the back of the building; they encountered several men trying to escape, and there was a shoot-out. No officers were harmed. Ten men were killed outside, and another nine injured; an unknown amount escaped. There were also several fatalities inside the warehouse, mainly the perpetrators. Sadly, one of our officers was killed, and another is in a serious condition. A number of the gang were also injured and are in another hospital under armed guard.'

'I'm sorry,' Meg said. 'About the police officers. Why were people escaping from the back? Everyone was so quiet, and there are no windows in the building.'

Gina stepped forward. 'It appears they were tipped off,' her strangled voice muttered, 'and it could only have been someone from the station.'

Silence fell over the room while everyone tried to process the information.

'Did you tell Sean?' Jo asked coldly.

'I'm surprised you didn't hear his reaction!'

'He has every right to be angry, as do we. You have a child sexual exploitation gang of massive proportions! Child traffickers, murderers, and from what I've just heard, they have no problem getting their hands on as many guns as they like.

'They have continued to get away with it because a person or persons within the police force work for them. Is there anything I've said that's incorrect?'

Gina sat down heavily on the nearest chair and put her head in her hands.

'You have covered it very accurately, I'm afraid.'

'What are you going to do about it?' Jo demanded, hovering over the police woman.

'It is out of my hands. I have to return soon and wait in my office. An anti-corruption unit has sealed off the entire station. No one leaves until they have been questioned, and everything from our computers and phones to lockers will be searched. Two anti-corruption officers are waiting to take me back to the station.'

'They suspect you?' Jo, though angry, was shocked.

'Everyone from the cleaner all the way up through the ranks to myself is under suspicion. The Chief Constable was informed of a suspected leak after my officers were drugged when guarding your house. I asked DS Murray to call her after today's operation.'

'Who is this Chief Constable? I want some reassurances that Meg and my family are safe.'

'Chief Constable Danah Akhtar. She wants to come and visit you at home.'

'Why?'

'I assume to reassure you and ask if you spotted anything unusual when we have been working with you, which we no longer will be.'

'What! You're dropping the case?'

'Absolutely not! However, DS Murray, DCI Leek, whose team is also being investigated, and everyone else from my station has had to hand everything over to the Chief Constable. She is arranging a specialist team to continue to investigate this.'

'What about the photos?' Meg suddenly remembered. 'I was told to go back and be interviewed about the people I saw on the computer.'

'It's all been handed over. Someone else will interview you, but not today. The new team will need to catch up on what we've done so far and examine the evidence. They also will be the ones to question everyone found at the warehouse, the victims, and those involved. There is one more problem, however...'

'Only one more?' Jo was practically foaming at the mouth.

'Someone tipped the press off; the station entrance is crawling with them.'

302

'Do they know about Meg?'

'Probably, but they are gunning for the police. They won't try to apprehend the victims.'

'Can you guarantee that?'

The Inspector stayed silent.

'I'll take that as a no then! And surely this means everything Meg has done could be in dispute if you have bent officers running the show?'

'We don't know the extent of the damage yet.'

'Will you stop talking in riddles and tell me what the hell is happening!'

'The anti-corruption team will be examining the case with a fine tooth-comb. They'll check if all the evidence is where it should be, or if anything has disappeared. Every single action we have taken, everything Meg has told us, will be investigated. I am sorry, Meg,' Gina said, looking at her. 'We have let you down. We have let a lot of innocent young girls down. I have to go, and I doubt you will see me again, but please believe that I did everything I could to find out who was responsible for this. I failed, and I'm so sorry. Your bravery has astounded me. Please don't let this stop you from giving evidence and putting these monsters behind bars.'

'Why won't we see you again?'

'I oversaw the investigation. The officers answered to me. The press want heads to roll. I'll be submitting my resignation after I've been investigated. The Chief Constable will be sure to request it.'

'I'm sorry,' Meg said sadly.

'So am I,' Jo added. 'I know we've had our differences, but I do respect your integrity and absolutely do not believe that you would allow corrupt officers to roam free.'

'Thank you. Thank you both,' Gina said. 'I have to go now. Take care and stay strong.'

Meg nodded, lost for words, as she watched Gina put her shoulders back and stride out of the room to go and meet the people who would be the beginning of the end of her career.

'Come on,' said Jo. 'Let's see if you and Sean are fit to be discharged and go home.'

The three of them were taken home by even more armed police. Looking at their guns made Jo feel queasy. She hated guns, and now they were a part of their everyday life. A firearm had almost killed Sean and Meg only hours before. She wondered if she could trust the officers guarding them.

'Who guards the guards?' she mumbled.

'What?' asked Sean.

'Nothing. I just want to go home.' She sighed.

They passed another man with a gun on their doorstep and entered the house to find everyone glued to the television.

'Turn it off...' Jo said, but was interrupted by Meg.

'Please leave it on.' She turned to the screen, and the news reporter was speculating why the entire station was locked down. However, Meg realised it was more than speculation; he was extremely accurate about what had occurred. Too accurate. If she doubted there was a leak before, then she was sure now.

'What happened?' Kayleigh demanded.

'We found the place,' Meg said. 'The place where the men would take us. I ran inside and nearly got your dad killed. He got shot saving me. I'm sorry.'

'Dad?' Jack looked at Sean, confused and scared.

'A bullet meant for Meg hit my arm. I'm fine. Don't worry.'

'*A bullet*!' Kayleigh gasped. 'And what's this about?' She pointed to the TV. 'They're saying that all the coppers in there are bent.'

'Not all,' Jo added sadly, thinking of Gina, 'but some, certainly. This is a well-organised gang who seem to have eyes and ears everywhere.'

'Are we even safe?' Cora demanded, glaring at Meg, clearly blaming her for everything.

'I'm going to my room,' Meg said. 'Will you tell them everything?'

Jo and Sean nodded.

'Do you want me to come with you?' Jo asked. But Meg had already left, and if she heard, she ignored it.

CHAPTER SIXTEEN

Meg went upstairs, an idea forming in her head and growing stronger. She reached her room, picked up her iPad, and began to write. Her fingers flew across the keyboard as she recalled every single thing that happened to her since arriving at Crookshaws Children's Home. Meg described how she had been introduced to the evil gang and lured into their trap; she named as many girls as possible and wrote how she'd met Jo and, later, Sean. Meg wrote in detail about Ewan abducting and nearly killing her. She stated how amazing Inspector Phillips was, and added that she would send a copy of her story to the press if the Inspector was forced to resign. She detailed every piece of evidence she had given, verbal and filmed, and demanded to know if the police still had it.

Meg wrote for two hours. When satisfied, she Googled the number of the Chief Constable's office and dialled.

She got through to an arrogant receptionist who patronisingly informed her that the Chief Constable was a very busy woman and had no time for school kids ringing her.

'I'm recording this call,' Meg snarled; she gave her name and number. 'If the Chief Constable does not ring me within the next thirty minutes, then this recording, along with the email I wish to send to her private address, will go to the press!' Meg ended the conversation and waited.

Her phone rang precisely two minutes later.

'Meg, this is Chief Constable Akhtar. Call me Danah. I apologise for my receptionist. She...'

'She did not take me seriously because I am a child!' stated Meg assertively. 'Have you ever thought about why you have a problem? You only listen to politicians and other police officers. I have something I wish to email to you. Some of your coppers are bent; I'm not emailing this to an address where anyone can read it. I know you will have an email address that the public is not aware of. Can I have it, please?'

'I know you're angry, and I was hoping to come and see you...'

'Not until you have read my email, and not until after Christmas. It's Christmas Eve in two days. The people I live with need a break. Read my email. Please only reply to acknowledge it, and I will meet you the day after Boxing Day.'

'We need to interview you before then.'

'Tough! I've given many interviews. I've written down everything I have said in them in my email to you. I want to know if any of them have gone missing. My email provides a lot of information. Enough to keep you busy until the 27th of December.'

There was a long silence; the Chief Constable realised she had no option other than to follow the girl's demands. Hearing her determined voice and recalling her secretary repeating the threat to go to the press, she reluctantly agreed and gave Meg her private police email address. 'Emails to this address come directly to me. No one has access to them.'

'Good. I will send it now. Remember, all I want is a reply to say that you've received it, and then you are to leave us alone until the 27th.'

'As you wish,' came the stifled reply of someone who was not used to taking orders, especially from a child.

'Good. I have just pressed send. Goodbye!' Meg pressed the button to end the call with more force than necessary and realised she was sweating and shaking.

'May I ask who on earth you were speaking to?' came a stern voice that made her jump. Meg saw Jo standing in the doorway, arms folded.

'The Chief Constable,' Meg replied defiantly. 'I've emailed her and blind copied you and Sean into it. I'm not hiding anything.'

'You didn't tell me what you were going to do. Why?'

'Because you wouldn't have allowed it.'

'So, you went behind my back?'

'Yes. I'm not going to apologise, because I'm not sorry. You and Sean need a break; you need to spend some time with your family. The police will not be back until the day after Boxing Day. I want you all to enjoy Christmas.'

Jo stared at Meg for so long that she began to feel uncertain; her confidence wavered slightly.

'Our,' Jo blurted.

'What?'

'Our,' she repeated. 'You said Sean and I need to spend time with our family. You're right, but that includes you. It means all of us, together. And thank you. A break is what we all need. Though blackmailing the Chief Constable is...' Jo put her head down, and her shoulders began to shake. Meg thought she was crying and ran over to her, but she was amazed to see Jo wasn't crying. Well, she was, but it was tears of laughter falling down her face.

'What's going on?' came Sean's voice, and he entered the room, looking at his wife in surprise.

'Meg has just...' Jo began, and then broke off into peals of laughter. Sean looked alarmed.

'Has just done what?' he demanded, glaring at them both.

Jo held her stomach, which was in agony from laughing. She squealed something inaudible to Sean and burst out laughing again. Meg smiled at her and then laughed herself, finding she also couldn't stop. The overwhelming stress of the past few weeks needed to be released, and now she and Jo were almost on the floor, laughing.

'Will someone tell me what the bloody hell has happened now!' Sean snapped.

This started them both off laughing again, tears streaming down their faces; even glancing at each other or at the red-faced Sean resulted in more and more peals of laughter.

Sean sat on Meg's bed, annoyed. His phone pinged. With nothing better to do other than to watch Jo and Meg roll about, making no sense, he took his phone out of his pocket. He was surprised to see an email from Meg to the Chief Constable that he'd been blind copied into. He read it through, skipping over parts that were too painful to read. He reached the last paragraph, and his jaw dropped. It read:

"If Inspector Gina Phillips is forced to resign, and if you do not have a comprehensive answer to my questions when we meet, then I will send this email and the recorded phone conversation to the press. You will come to the house on the 27th of December at 3 p.m. I do not want anyone from the police to contact us before then. If they do, then the only interview I will be giving will be to a journalist."

'You blackmailed the police Chief Constable!' Sean stated. 'Blackmailed her, threatened her with the press. Are you serious?'

'Deadly!' she squealed.

Jo was now sitting on the floor, recovering from her outburst and holding her stomach, too scared to look at Sean's face in case his baffled expression set off more laughter. Meg slumped on the floor beside her.

'Are you still angry?'

'What do you think?' Jo answered breathlessly.

'You blackmailed...'

'We know, Sean. I wish you would have heard the phone conversation. Meg put the Chief Constable well in her place. So, stop repeating yourself and let's try to have some sort of Christmas!'

'Okay,' he said, bewildered. 'I'm ordering pizza. I'm starving, and, I've got to say, I have received very little sympathy considering I was shot today!'

'It's a scratch, Sean! Try giving birth to four babies and then come and tell me about pain.'

'Huh,' he said, trying to hide a grin. 'Come on. Pizza and a film; a sloppy, unrealistic Christmas one.'

'Perfect!' Jo announced, and they went downstairs to try to have a normal evening.

Meg found the evening unsettling. It started off fine; she found herself on one of the sofas, squashed between Tom and Wes, with Sean on the end. Jack sprawled on the floor, while Jo and the other girls sat on the other sofa. They all reached over each other, grabbing different slices of pizza, and Cora put on *Love Actually*.

'Perfect Christmas film,' Jo announced. 'But I'll never forgive Alan Rickman for giving that necklace to *that* woman and cheating on Emma Thompson!'

'It's not real, Mum, and you say this every year! He didn't sleep with her.'

'He might have done. It may not have been shown. Anyway, it's still adultery. If your father...'

Sean groaned. 'Every year I get accused of committing imaginary adultery. I've never given anyone a necklace but you, as I've told you every year! This conversation is as predictable as day turning into night!'

'You gave me one on my eighteenth,' Kayleigh said with a grin. 'Oh, shut up. You know what I mean!'

It was then that Cora, who had been giving Meg smug, knowing smiles for the last two hours, made an announcement.

'Funny you should mention that,' she began. 'Dad gave me one for my eighteenth as well, and I didn't take it to uni. I've searched everywhere today, but I can't find it.'

313

'It'll turn up,' Jo said, not really paying attention.

'Hmmmm, strange, though,' continued Cora maliciously.

Jo stopped, and this time, she did pay attention. She looked at her daughter suspiciously; the girl was up to something. Kayleigh noticed as well.

'What are you getting at?' she asked her sister, narrowing her eyes.

'Nothing. I'm stating a fact. The necklace was in my bedroom, and now it's not. It has to be somewhere, and it's not as though we've had lots of people in and out of the house since September when I last saw it.' She turned and glared at Meg.

'Are you accusing me?' Meg asked in disbelief.

'I'm not accusing anyone. I don't believe in coincidences. You appear, and my necklace disappears.'

'Shut up, Cora,' said Kayleigh. 'Stop being such a cow.'

'Well, I would like it back! *My* dad gave it to me!'

'Sounds like someone is jealous about sharing Daddy,' came Jack's voice from the floor. 'I wouldn't put out anything past you, Cora. You've been a miserable, malicious pain in the arse ever since we got home. I'm fed up with you. If it wasn't Christmas, I would have gone back to my uni digs to escape you.'

'*Me*! What about everything else? Police on the doorstep, Dad getting shot, Wes vomiting on me and *her*…' she pointed at Meg, '… putting us all in danger. You know she's got a criminal record...' Cora stopped talking and went red. 'What I mean is that she's probably got a criminal record; people from those homes always do. I want her room searched!'

'Room searched, you say?' Jo said in a dangerously calm voice. 'Cora, Sean, Meg, follow me.'

'You think I took a necklace?' Meg said, sounding hurt. 'Why would I do that?'

'Ooooh, let's think,' Cora announced dramatically. 'To sell to one of your scummy mates, so they can buy drugs!'

'You are well out of order, Cora,' Kayleigh said. 'I can't believe...'

'Keep out of it, Kayleigh!' Jo ordered. 'I'm not going to have you two fighting   again!

Come on, upstairs!' She got up and looked at Cora, Sean, and Meg.

'No! If you think I would steal from you after everything you've done for me, then you can get lost. And to think I was going to say yes to be adopted by you when that idiot social worker interviewed me!' Meg got up and stormed to the front door.

Jo ran after her and whispered, 'Trust me on this, please. No one thinks you've stolen anything. Please, I am begging you, just trust me. I've got a good idea about what's going on.' Meg's red face and tearful eyes glared up at the woman she thought loved her.

'Go to hell!' she spat. 'I can't believe I let myself trust you. I'm going.'

'You are not!'

'You can't stop me. I will do want I want!'

'I can stop you, and so can the police officer on the door. I know we will find the necklace in your room...'

'*Well, if that's what you think, then...*'

'Stop!' shouted Jo, raising her hand. Meg ducked.

'I wasn't going to hit you,' Jo said, shocked, looking close to tears. 'I'm sorry, it's just a gesture. Please believe me, and please believe that I know you didn't steal anything. I know Cora inside out. Please, just play along.'

'Why should I? I'm sick of these games, and I have had enough of Cora; she's twisted. I've met plenty like her before. They always win.'

'Not this time,' Jo stated firmly. 'Please, do as I ask and don't speak. Please trust me.'

Meg nodded, but turned and hit the wall in anger while Jo went back to the lounge to get Sean and Cora.

'Running away is a sure sign of guilt,' Cora declared. Kayleigh had her fists clenched in fury. Sean and the rest of the family were looking at her in utter disbelief.

'Cora, Sean. Come on.'

'Mum, you don't seriously believe...'

'Leave it to us, Tom!' she replied firmly and left the room, followed by Sean and Cora.

They made their way up to Meg's room; Jo observed a delighted-looking Cora very closely.

'Where should we begin?' Jo asked Sean, keeping one eye on Cora. She noted her daughter glance at a vase on the window-ledge.

'Sean, go and turn that vase upside down.' Bewildered, he did as his wife asked, and sure enough, the necklace fell out.

'How did you...?' Sean began, but fell silent when he saw Jo's expression.

'Well, there you have it,' Cora said with delight. 'If that isn't evidence, then I don't know what is.'

Jo placed a firm hand on Meg's shoulder. She could see the girl was about to explode. 'We haven't finished the search yet,' Jo said, gripping Meg's shoulder slightly harder. 'Good idea, Mum. There could be all sorts of stuff in here.'

'I imagine there is, but I didn't mean search this room. Next, we will search your room.'

'*Mine! Why?*'

But Cora received no reply as Jo was already making her way down to the next floor. Cora tried to get down the narrow stairs first, but Sean ushered Meg after Jo, and he followed, leaving Cora stuck behind his bulky frame. Cora burst into her bedroom last.

'You've no right to search my room, Mum! It's private. Besides, what are you looking for?'

Jo gave the impression that she was looking around the room but kept Cora in her peripheral vision and saw her daughter take a split-second glance at her bed.

'Sean, would you mind lifting Cora's mattress, please?'

'What? *No!*' shouted Cora, and ran to her bed and sat on it.

'I'll lift it with or without you sitting there,' Sean said grimly. 'Move or be moved!'

Like her mum, her dad's voice was very calm. Too calm, but she could detect something underneath the calmness, and it scared her. She stood up and moved away from the bed. Her Mum was blocking the doorway, and Meg stood silently, bewildered.

Sean lifted the mattress and found a sheaf of papers. He pulled them out and began to look through them, his face going redder and redder. Cora had turned pale and looked terrified.

'What is it, Sean?' Jo asked knowingly.

'It's Meg's partial social care file and notes, including the record of juvenile cautions.' He checked the user ID on the top of the page. 'Apparently, I printed these out this morning at... 10.04 a.m. I wasn't here at 10.04 a.m.'

'No one was apart from Cora. We all left just before ten to look at hotels. Remember this morning when you logged into your work system, and it froze, and then you needed to leave? Who else was in the room? Who was left in the house alone? And why did Cora announce downstairs that Meg had a criminal record?'

'Meg must have done it,' Cora said in desperation. 'It's clever, setting me up like this, printing her own records and...'

'Shut up!' Jo's voice was like a whiplash. 'Where is everything else?'

'Everything else?'

'You know what I mean. Or do we have to turn your room upside down? We will do.'

Cora knew the game was up; she had underestimated her mother yet again.

'Bottom of the blanket box,' she said in a strangled tone.

Sean opened the blanket box and pulled out the sheets, towels, and duvet covers until he reached the bottom. He gave a loud intake of breath.

'My credit card! I wondered where that had gone. It disappeared after the cleaners came on, erm, the day we all vomited.'

'Take everything out, please,' Jo said.

Sean removed his credit card, two twenty-pound notes, another necklace, and a pair of gold cufflinks given to Tom on his 21st birthday.

Cora's parents glared at her; Meg looked confused.

'Ever since Cora arrived home, and we told her that we wanted to adopt you, things have started to go missing. I noticed my necklace went first,' Jo said, nodding to the one on the floor. 'It was my mother's; it means a lot to me, as you know, Cora.

'Next, Sean's credit card went, but I asked him to keep it quiet. I didn't know about Tom's cufflinks, but I did notice two twenty-pound notes had disappeared from my purse. Yesterday, when we all left, I got to the end of the street and had to turn around as I'd forgotten my phone. I heard a printer working upstairs. I assumed it was that one,' she added, nodding to Cora's printer. 'But obviously, it was yours, Sean. You were still logged in, and Cora accessed Meg's records. After all of her sneaking about, she must have thought Christmas had come early when she saw the juvenile cautions, especially the one for shoplifting.'

Sean was shaking with anger. 'I'm going for a walk,' he announced, his voice sounding strange.

'I'll come with you,' Jo said. 'Meg, I'll take you to the lounge to stay with the others. Cora, do not leave this room. That is an order!'

Cora threw herself onto her bed again and began to cry. Jo looked at her coldly and left the room.

'Sean, go and tell the others what has happened, please, and give Tom his cuff links. Meg, come into the kitchen with me,' Jo instructed.

Meg mutely followed, still confused and angry.

'I know you're not a thief,' Jo began.

'I am, though. I got arrested for shoplifting.'

'I don't care what happened in the past; you were living with a gang of teenagers with little adult supervision. I read the police reports about your arrests; Gina showed me. The arresting officer stated that he believed you were coerced into stealing that bottle of vodka. There never any reports of you being drunk or even drinking alcohol.'

'I hate alcohol!' Meg retorted.

'I know; it was obvious you weren't stealing it for yourself. Also, I know you would never steal from Sean or me.'

'How?'

'I just know. I saw Cora's jealousy from the first day she arrived home. She has many issues that need to be worked through. Sean and I have tried so hard to help, but she thinks everyone else is the problem. We tried to take her to see a therapist when she was even younger than you, but she wouldn't get out of the car, and then when she was around your age, Cora had to spend some time away from home to get some help.'

'With what?'

Jo appeared unsure. 'I need to talk to Cora before answering that. It's her information.'

'*So what*?' Meg shouted. 'She's just stolen my information!'

'I know, but doing the same as Cora won't make things right.'

'Why does she hate me so much?'

'I don't believe she hates you. I think she dislikes herself, and that inevitably presents as hatred towards others. She doesn't know you, but she is jealous of you.'

'Jealous of me!' Meg said in disbelief. 'She has had a great life. Parents who love her, a family, safety...'

'I know, I know,' Jo offered soothingly. 'It's not your fault, and I'm sorry for her behaviour. Please trust that Sean and I will handle it. Now, I am going for a walk with Sean before he explodes. He's told the kids what happened, but don't be scared. They will support you and look out for you until we return. Sean and I need to discuss what to do about Cora and her bullying!'

Meg stiffened at the word "bullying", and her eyes flashed. Jo was looking for her bag and luckily missed the gesture. She deliberately relaxed her body and looked at Jo.

'I'm, erm, I'm ssssorry for...' Meg looked away.

'Telling me to "go to hell" or for shouting at me?' Jo asked sternly. 'All of those.'

Jo hugged Meg. 'Apology accepted! I trust you, and I love you, and one day, you *will* believe that. Go on,' she said, ending the hug. 'Go and join the chaos.'

'Can I just have some time here, on my own, for a few minutes?'

'If you need some time, that's fine,' said Jo, looking at her curiously. 'Are you sure you're okay?'

'Fine. Just need some peace and quiet.'

'I'll see you later, then. I'm going for a walk with Sean. Go and join the others when you're ready.'

'Will do,' Meg replied with mock cheerfulness. 'See you soon.'

'Sure. Bye then...'

'Yep, bye.'

Bullying! Meg thought. As soon as Jo said the word, Meg knew what to do. She'd been in many kids' homes.

There was only one way to stop a bully. From the second you walked through the door at any new home, the other kids would be watching and working out if you were strong or weak. The weak ones never stood a chance; the only way to survive was to go in hard and fast and never show fear, and certainly never be a victim.

She crept past the living room door, though there were many angry voices, and she doubted she would have been heard. Nonetheless, she still crept up the stairs. Reaching Cora's door, she took a breath and let the adrenaline and anger surge.

She knocked on the door.

'Go away!' demanded Cora.

Meg knocked again, louder this time. Heavy footsteps headed towards the entrance. Cora flung the door open.

'I said go...! What the hell do you want? You can definitely go away,' she hissed at Meg and made to close the door.

Meg put her weight onto her back foot and used her other leg to kick the closing door with such force that Cora was flung backwards and landed with a heavy thump onto the floor.

'Who the hell do you think you are! Wait until I tell...'

But she didn't finish her sentence; Meg lunged at her and grabbed Cora's shirt, pulling her to her feet, surprised at how little she weighed despite her height advantage.

'I'm not someone you can lie about and bully, you evil, spoilt cow!' With that, Meg landed a stunning right hook directly into Cora's face; she then followed with her left hand. Cora doubled over, and Meg kneed her in the stomach with all the force she could muster. Gasping, Cora fell to the floor again and screamed.

'You shouldn't kick people when they're down,' Meg stated in a dangerously calm voice. 'Not in a fair fight, anyway. But you don't play fair. You lie. You're sneaky. You don't deserve anything you have. You are a waste of space.' With that, Meg swung her leg and kicked Cora in the kidneys.

'*Get up, you coward*!' she shouted.

Meg swung her leg back for a second kick and found herself suddenly pulled backwards.

'Get off me!' she screamed and landed an elbow into the stomach of whoever was holding her. She heard a grunt and was free. She dived on top of Cora and grabbed her by the neck, but this time, two people yanked her off and threw her onto Cora's bed.

The red mist settled, and Meg saw Tom, Wes, Kayleigh, and Jack in the room; Jack rubbed his stomach. 'Good elbow you've got there,' he said, grimacing.

Meg stood up, barged out of the room, headed upstairs, and violently began to throw clothes into a bag.

'What are you doing?' came Kayleigh's voice.

'Leaving! Jo and Sean will throw me out after this, and I don't care. I'd rather be in a kids' home. They are crap, but at least you know where you stand. You either fight or shut up. Sneaky little cows like Cora wouldn't last two minutes in one of those places.'

'Mum and Dad won't throw you out. Come back downstairs. We all need to work this out before they get home.'

'No!' Meg threw random items into a bag.

'You won't get past the copper on the door, stupid! How the hell are you going to run away?'

Meg stopped; she hadn't thought of that in her blind rage. She just knew it was better to leave rather than be thrown out.

'Get downstairs! Quickly. No one is against you. We will work out how to cover for you.'

'Why?'

'Because you haven't done anything that we all haven't wanted to do this Christmas.

Come on. I'm serious. Mum and Dad could be home any second.'

Meg reluctantly went back to Cora's room with Kayleigh. Cora was sitting on a chair in the middle of the room. The others surrounded her and seemed to have a lot to say, but they all fell silent when Kayleigh and Meg entered.

'Keep her away from me!' Cora wailed hysterically.

'Shut your mouth!' Jack fumed.

'Jack, I'm sorry I elbowed you. I didn't know who it was; I was caught up in the fight.'

'It's fine,' Jack replied and, to Meg's shock, smiled.

'Right,' Tom began, 'this is what's going to happen. Cora, you have a split lip and will have a black eye tomorrow. Another one! You will be in bed by the time Mum and Dad get home, with your light off. Do not move if they come in! Tomorrow, at breakfast, you will tell them that you flung your door open in a temper and whacked yourself in the face.'

'Why on earth would I do that? I'm going to tell them exactly *what she* did!' She pointed to Meg.

'No, you're not, as we are all going to say that Meg was with us all the time they were out and that you probably did that to your own face to get Meg into trouble. Who do you think they'll believe? You? A thieving little sneak who has been taking our belongings and hiding them to try to get Meg kicked out, or all of us? You're in it deep enough already.

327

After the way you've treated Meg and made this holiday miserable for us all, as usual, no one will back you, and you deserved exactly what you got. Just be grateful we stopped it when we did!'

Cora glared at her brother in shock. 'You are going to take some criminal kid's side over mine?'

Meg took a step forward, and Kayleigh pulled her back as Cora looked at her fearfully.

'Anymore talk like that, and we won't stop her next time. Now, you come to breakfast tomorrow, no attitude, no looks at Meg, no hints. You say exactly what I told you to say. Repeat it!'

Cora remained silent.

'*Repeat it*!' roared Tom, making everyone in the room jump.

'Fine! I was in a temper and flung my door open and smashed myself in the face!'

'Good, and not a word more. We will be watching you. Now go to bed. Everyone else, downstairs.'

They all left the room apart from Tom, who ensured his sister got into bed. 'And stay there!' he said firmly, snapping off the light and closing the door.

Downstairs in the living room, everyone sat quietly.

'Put a film on. Any film. Make it look natural,' Tom urged.

'Meg, no one at all blames you for what you did, but Dad is close to losing it, so we have to pretend it never happened. When they get back, say you're going to bed. Maybe Kayleigh and Jack could go at the same time just in case Cora says you jumped her on the way up. Got it?'

Everyone nodded. Tom looked at his watch. 'They've been gone forty minutes. Fast- forward the film so it's thirty minutes in. Everyone, stop sitting up straight. Just act normal, lounge about like you normally do...'

They heard a key in the door lock. 'Press play, quickly,' he hissed, 'and pretend we've been watching it the whole time!'

Jo and Sean entered the living room seconds after Jack hit the play button, and then he paused it as his parents came in.

'Everyone okay?' asked Jo.

'Yeah, just watching a film.' Kayleigh yawned. 'Are you guys okay?'

'Just needed some air,' said Sean. 'Has Cora been down?'

'No,' answered Wes truthfully.

'Good!'

Kayleigh yawned again. 'I think I'll go to bed. I'm knackered.'

'Me too,' Meg added, giving a slightly exaggerated yawn.

'Yep, this film is knocking me to sleep,' said Jack. 'I think I'll go too.'

'Oh, okay,' said Jo, looking surprised. 'Meg, do you want me to come up with you?

Maybe chat about today? It's been... eventful!'

'No, but thanks. I just need to sleep.' She gave Jo a brief hug on the way out of the room, and the others followed.

'Night all,' Sean said and threw himself down on the sofa. 'Stick the rest of the film on, Tom. I could do with some easy watching before bed. Come on, Jo.' He patted the seat next to him, and she gratefully sat down and stared at the TV, but couldn't shake off the feeling that something had happened while they were out.

CHAPTER SEVENTEEN

What on earth has happened to your face?' Jo asked, shocked, as Cora entered the dining room and sat down for breakfast. Everyone else was already at the table, hungrily tucking into their food.

'Nothing,' Cora answered.

'Enough lies.' Sean sighed. 'What happened?'

Cora flinched as Kayleigh kicked her from under the table. 'Fine! I was in a temper last night. The door stuck a little like it always does, so I flung it open, and it smacked me in the face. It caught my lip and side of my face.'

'You must have done it with a hell of a lot of force; you've got a black eye. That's two black eyes now. You look like a panda,' Kayleigh said calmly.

'I did open it with a lot of force. Can we leave it?'

Everyone continued eating. 'Meg, can you pass me the orange juice, please?' asked Jo.

'Sure.' And she passed it over.

Those who had finished took their plates and went to wash up.

'Not you, Cora,' Sean said as Cora stood with her plate. 'We're going out.'

'Where?' she muttered sullenly.

'Out! Get your coat. Do not push me today!'

Cora scuttled off, and everyone set about their day. Wes and Tom were going for a shower and planned on doing some last-minute Christmas shopping. Jack was going for a run when his breakfast had settled, and Kayleigh said that she had no intention of moving from in front of the TV all day.

Meg stood to leave after finishing her last piece of toast.

'Sit down,' Jo said quietly.

'But I've finished.'

'Sit down!'

Meg nervously returned to her seat.

'Hold your hands out flat on top of the table.'

'Why?'

'Just do it.'

Meg reluctantly put her bruised hands on the tabletop.

'Where are the bruises from?'

Meg didn't answer.

'Meg, why are your knuckles bruised?'

Meg looked down, again refusing to answer.

Jo sighed. 'Fine, go to your room. It's too busy for us to talk down here. Move!'

Meg stood quickly and headed to the door, and Jo followed. Meg reached her room first and mutinously stretched out on her bed.

Jo entered and picked up a chair. Glancing at the half-packed bag of clothes, she placed the chair facing the bed and turned to Meg.

'Sit up!'

Meg quickly sat up and perched nervously on the edge of her bed.

'I had a feeling something wasn't quite right last night when you asked to stay in the kitchen. Also, when Sean and I got home, something felt unsettling. When I saw Cora this morning, I had a better idea. That's why I asked you to pass me the juice; I wanted to check out your hand. So, let's have it. What exactly happened last night?'

'I went up to Cora's room when you left. She tried to shut the door on me. I kicked it open and punched her in the face, twice. I kneed her in the stomach when she was bent over and kicked her when she was on the floor.'

'Did you go to her room intent on being violent?'

'Yep! I will not let her bully me. I didn't see it as her bullying me until you said it. I've lived in too many places. If you let someone bully you, then it never stops and gets worse and worse. You have to fight, or your life is a misery.'

'Who else was involved?'

'What do you mean?'

'Well, you obviously decided to run away afterwards as there's a bag on the floor with some of your clothes hanging out. It wasn't there yesterday. Again, who else was involved?'

'I'm the one who hit Cora. I knew you'd throw me out afterwards, so I started packing.'

'Why did you stop?'

'The police officer standing on the doorstep with a gun. The coppers in cars watching the building. They would have stopped me.'

'And in a blind rage of throwing all of your things into a bag, you suddenly remembered this? Then you stopped packing, went downstairs, and watched a film?'

'I did go downstairs and see some of a film,' Meg replied, choosing her words carefully.

'What was the film called?'

'Erm, I can't remember.'

'Understandable. It had been one hell of a day. What happened in the part that you watched?'

'I wasn't really looking. You said it yourself, it had been a hell of a day.'

'So, back to my earlier question. Who else was involved?'

Meg looked out through the window and at the now sparse tree.

'Meg...'

'I've told you what I did. I expect you to throw me out, and I have nothing else to say.' Meg folded her arms stubbornly, scowling at Jo.

'Ooh, you have a great deal more to say! Also, no one is throwing you out! I have said this over and over. You are a member of this family. Families, decent families, do not throw their children out. So, I repeat, who else was involved?'

'You can keep asking that, but I'm not going to answer!'

'I was!' came a voice from the doorway, and Kayleigh entered. 'I told Meg to stop packing and get downstairs.'

'Come in, please,' said Jo. 'I do not appreciate you listening at the door. Sit next to Meg!'

'Kayleigh, are you saying you were the only other person involved in this?'

'I'm saying I was involved, Mum.'

'Kayleigh didn't know I was going to front up to Cora!' Meg said, defending her.

Jo sighed. 'I've had enough, seriously. I really am at the end of my tether, as is your father. Kayleigh, you know the three of us will stay here all day until I have the answers, so just get it over and done with.'

'I heard a bang and shouting and went upstairs and saw Meg in Cora's room. Meg left not long afterwards and came up here and started packing. I followed and told her that the police were everywhere and she wouldn't be able to run away.'

'Who else was involved? Who was in Cora's room while you were up here? I do not doubt for a minute that Cora would have rung me if left on her own.'

'We were,' came three male voices from the doorway.

'Seriously!' Jo said incredulously. 'Do you all just hang about in doorways listening? Come in, sit on the bed, and talk!'

'It was my idea,' Tom began and proceeded to tell his mum about what happened the night before.

'Right,' Jo said sharply. 'The truth at last. Get out, all of you. Go and do what you had planned.'

They all stood. 'Not you, Meg,' Jo said, and she watched the others leave. 'For your sakes, do not listen at the door. Shut it on your way out and go downstairs!'

Jo turned her attention back to Meg, who was surprised she had butterflies in her stomach.

'This wasn't a fight in the heat of the moment, Meg. You planned it.'

'I was looking out for myself...'

'I am speaking! So, will you please listen? I told you I would deal with it...'

Meg jumped off the bed. '*You have dealt with nothing; she's been a cow ever since...*'

'Sit down!' Jo thundered. 'I knew exactly what was happening from day one! But I do not barge into situations without thinking about how to deal with them. I had to make sure Cora was caught red-handed so there was no suspicion on you. I did deal with it, and Sean is dealing with Cora as we speak. But how dare you behave in such a way? I trusted you to behave yourself. I am more than aware of how stressful yesterday was. How stressful everything has been, but to resort to violence is pure cowardice, and I am ashamed of you. Not only did I think you had more intelligence, but I thought you had more respect for me!'

'I do have respect for...'

'You, all of you, have lied to me about this.'

'I did not lie. No one did!'

'You didn't tell the truth when I asked you. That is the same as lying.'

'I'm not a grass!'

'No, you are a child, and you are in my care, so remember that. You are not in charge of this household. You do not take matters into your own hands, and you certainly do not hit people!'

'Oh, so it's fine for Cora and Kayleigh to have a punch up right in front of you in the kitchen because of the stupid electricity, but I'm not allowed to do the same.'

'That was not the same, and you know it. And no, Kayleigh and Cora's fighting was not fine either.'

'Okay, I'm sorry. Can I just go back to bed now?'

'Nope! Firstly, that was not a proper apology, and secondly, you are not getting away with this. When the time is right today, you will apologise to Cora in front of me! This afternoon, we are finally putting the decorations up. A nice family afternoon. No arguments, no bitterness, no fighting! In the meantime, the Christmas decorations are in the back of the garage, which is full of rubbish. You will take as many bin bags as you need and fill them with all the rubbish from the garage. You will sweep up, find the Christmas decorations, bring them in, and untangle them all. It is at least a full day's job. You have until 12:30; now move!'

Meg jumped up, her legs still shaking a little.

'Jo...' she began as she reached the door.

'Save it. Get to work!' Jo replied sighing.

Meg put on her coat, grabbed some bin bags, and hunted around for the key for the garage.

'Cupboard under the stairs on the hook.' Jo's voice appeared from nowhere, and she was also putting her coat on.

'Where you going, Mum?' asked Kayleigh, appearing in the doorway.

'Food shopping,' Jo answered grimly. 'Christmas food shopping! Want to come and help?'

'Errrrm, if you really want me to, then I suppose...'

Jo grinned. 'Joking! Taking you to a supermarket at the best of times is asking for trouble, but just before Christmas? No, thank you.'

'Thanks.' Kayleigh grinned in relief and rushed off just in case her mum changed her mind.

Meg reappeared with the key and went outside. After a lot of fiddling and twisting and turning, she managed to open the door and immediately swore under her breath.

'What was that?' asked Jo who, unknown to Meg, was watching.

'Nothing!' Meg answered quickly.

'Good,' Jo answered, hiding a slight grin. 'I'm going now. I'll be back by 12:30. One p.m. at the latest, so get to work.'

Jo got into her car and pulled off the driveway as Meg turned back to the garage and was faced with a wall of cardboard boxes. She had no idea about the amount of rubbish behind them. She jumped as she heard a hissing noise. Meg took a step backwards, trying to work out if she'd heard a snake in there.

'Oy, idiot!' came a voice, still being hissed. She looked around, and Kayleigh was leaning out of the bathroom window.

'What!' Meg snapped, still shaky from thinking there was a snake.

339

'Has Mum gone?'

'Why are you hissing?'

'*I'm being quiet!*' Kayleigh shouted.

'Yeah, she's gone.'

Kayleigh disappeared from the window and appeared outside with the boys.

'Right! We'll help you for an hour; any longer, and we risk Mum or Dad coming back and catching us.'

'Err, thanks,' said Meg.

They knocked down the cardboard barricade in seconds and squashed it all down.

'It's full of rubbish,' groaned Meg.

'Jack, can you climb to the back and dig out the Christmas decorations?' Kayleigh asked. 'One of us can start untangling them in the house while the rest of us plough through.'

'No problem.' Jack grinned and leapt over the rubbish, old bikes, and skateboards. Other than an encounter with a giant spider's web, he returned several minutes later with two massive garden sacks containing tinsel and a part of a plastic Christmas tree sticking out.

'I'll go and sort those,' Wes announced, grabbing the bags. 'I'm dressed for shopping, not climbing around old rubbish!'

The rest worked quickly, throwing rubbish into bin bags, and putting the gardening equipment, bicycles, and things to keep on the driveway.

'Hour is up!' Kayleigh announced, sweating. 'Meg, give the garage a brush, leave this stuff outside, and start putting it back when Mum or Dad get back. I'm going for a shower and then I'm putting my pyjamas on and throwing myself in front of the TV. Tom and Wes are going into town, and Jack is going for a run. Remember, we did not help!'

'Why did you help?' Meg asked.

'Because that's what families do, you numpty! Now go finish sorting the Christmas decorations, lay them out on the dining table, and listen out for Mum or Dad. As soon as they get back, go and start putting stuff back in the garage.'

'Why in that order?'

'Listen, we've had hundreds of punishments from them. We know what we're doing!'

'Okay. Thanks, everyone.' Meg looked at them all shyly as they moved off to do their own things.

Wes had completely untangled all the decorations and the Christmas lights. 'You just need to give them a dust now,' he said. 'And make sure you get some dirt on your hands and face!'

'Cheers, Wes.' Meg grabbed a cloth, cleaned up the decorations, and then went up to her room to look out of her window. She had a perfect view of the street in both directions and sat on the window seat with a book and read while she waited comfortably for over an hour, glancing up every time she heard a car engine.

When she saw Jo's car turn into the road, Meg raced downstairs, reached the driveway, and picked up a bike just before Jo's car pulled up.

For several minutes, Jo sat in her car, watching as Meg continued to put the bikes and gardening equipment back into the neat and tidy garage.

'That was quick,' Jo said, finally getting out and nodding at all the full bags of rubbish.

'Can I help you with the shopping?' Meg mumbled, desperate to avoid any questions about whether she had received any help.

'Please.' Jo opened the boot to what appeared to be half a supermarket bagged up.

'Wow! That's a lot,' Meg said in surprise. She grabbed two bags in each hand and hurried off to the kitchen before going out for the next lot.

Jo was standing in the garage, looking around. 'Where are the Christmas decorations?'

'On the dining table. They needed untangling and dusting. I wasn't sure where to put them after that.'

'Dining table is fine. You have done a good job in here. A thorough and amazingly quick job,' Jo said, narrowing her eyes and looking at the dishevelled and dirty child in front of her.

'Should I get more bags from the car?' Meg asked.

'No, go for a shower. I'll hoist Kayleigh from the sofa. I assume that's where she's been all day?'

'She was last time I saw her,' Meg answered evasively and rushed off for a shower, keen to get out of Jo's sight.

Twenty minutes later, returning downstairs with dripping hair, Meg was irritated to see Cora in the kitchen.

'Dry your hair!' Jo said, passing Meg a towel. Sighing, she took it and scrubbed her hair vigorously.

'Is everyone in?' Sean enquired.

'Jack is in the shower, Kayleigh is putting snacks out, and Tom and Wes texted to say they're ten minutes away.'

'Excellent, then it will finally be Christmas!'

'One final thing,' Jo added, looking at Meg. 'I believe you have something to say to Cora?'

Meg flushed with anger and then embarrassment. Hesitating, she cleared her throat. 'Cora?'

Cora and turned and looked at her. Noting the black eyes and cut lip, Meg was surprised to realise she felt genuine remorse as Cora looked so pale and distressed.

She walked over to Cora. 'Your mum said I had to apologise and I would have just said "sorry" because she told me to. But I really do want to say that I'm sorry, and not because your mum said so. I'm so sorry. I have always lived in places where if someone did something to you and you didn't fight them, then everyone else would have a go because they'd see you as soft. Please believe I'm sorry.'

Cora looked at Meg for a long time; having someone stare at her like that made Meg nervous. She was about to walk away when Cora finally spoke.

'Our mum.'

'What?' asked Meg.

'*Our* mum told you to apologise, not just my mum. I'm sorry too. I've been a total cow. I'm ashamed of what I've done to you. It's not an excuse, but I've got some other stuff going on and, well, I don't know how to deal with it.'

'Stuff about me being here, you mean?' Meg asked without anger.

'No. Well, yes, but not just you.' Cora looked down, wringing her hands.

'Okay...' Meg said. 'I'm confused.'

'I know this will sound stupid, especially to you with all the places you've had to live and not having a proper family but...' Cora took a breath and sat down at the breakfast bar. Her parents joined her, and slowly, Meg took a seat.

Cora suddenly looked up as Kayleigh walked into the kitchen on the hunt for food.

'Do you want me to leave?' Kayleigh asked, sensing the atmosphere.

'No, you might as well hear this too.' Cora sighed. 'But don't interrupt!' Kayleigh took a seat at the breakfast bar and Cora continued.

'Tom, Kayleigh, and Jack are clever. They all got A* in their A-levels, got their first uni choice. They are athletic, confident, and anything I try to do, well, they've already done it. I was always so scared of failing, and I did. I didn't do well at school, struggled with my exams, and only just scraped a place at uni.

'I missed quite a lot of school, when I was about your age...' Cora looked at her dad, who smiled gently at her. 'I had some problems with food. Big problems. It felt like the only thing I had any control over. I thought I was fat, and that's why I wasn't like the others when it came to sport. But it got out of control. All I wanted was to be as thin as possible, and I was terrified of putting weight on. Mum and Dad noticed and made me get help. I had to go away for a while to a centre. Three months to be exact...'

'Hang on!' Kayleigh said. 'Was that when Mum said you'd gone to France as an exchange student?'

Cora nodded and even managed a tiny smile.

'Didn't you find it strange that no one came and stayed here to exchange with me?'

'Moving on...' Jo urged.

'It was difficult when I came home. Everyone had moved on. I went back to school and my friends had moved on as well. It was lonely, and I took it out on everyone. I still saw a therapist once a week, but she would ask questions about my eating, which had got a little better.'

'I'm sorry,' Meg said quietly. 'It sounds rough. But what has that got to do with you hating me?'

'The one thing I had left was my mum and dad. When Jack went to uni, I was the only one left at home for a year. It felt like I had some attention finally. No one interrupting or barging in. But then I come home for Christmas and find you, and then I'm the invisible one again. When we went for that meal and Dad said that he had two new kids, you and Wes, I'd had enough. I know Wes and Tom will be living in London, but I hated you being here. I thought you were taking the little bit of love from my parents that was mine.

'I know now that it wasn't about you. All my life, I've been jealous and resentful, especially of Kayleigh and the way she's so free and open and can talk to anyone. I thought uni would help me find myself, but the loneliness and anxiety got worse. My eating is becoming disordered again and I'm not in a good place. I've been a total cow to you. To you all. I...'

Cora stopped as tears poured heavily down her face, and she let out shuddering sobs. Jo and Sean made to move towards their daughter, but to their surprise, Kayleigh got there first and hugged her little sister.

'I'm sorry, Cora. I didn't know any of that. I'm sorry for always giving you a hard time. I wish I could take it back.' Cora returned Kayleigh's hug, and both sisters began to cry.

Meg looked at Jo, bewildered at everything that had just been said. Jo smiled sadly at Meg and then joined her other girls for a hug.

'We'll sort this out,' she assured Cora. 'We are here for you, always. I'm sorry I didn't see how bad things had become for you again.'

'I understand, Mum.' Cora looked at Meg, but without malice or anger. 'You've had a lot happening. I failed all of my assignments in the first term. I wanted to tell you, alone, but there's been no time. I'm sorry.'

'Don't be sorry, Cora. I'm the one who's sorry…'

'Me too,' added Sean. 'We've let you down. Mum is right. We'll work it out, together.'

They all sat in an easy silence for a while, each thinking about what had been talked about until Jack came in, irritated.

'Are we doing the decorations or not?' He paused. 'What's going on?'

347

'Nothing you need to know about today,' Sean answered. 'Right, let's go and start on the decorations. Is that okay?' he asked Cora.

'Yes, come on. Otherwise Christmas will be over at this rate.' Cora smiled, her voice still weak.

Sean messed about with the CD player and pressed play on *Fairy Tale of New York.*

'You know they call this song homophobic now, don't you, Dad?' Kayleigh laughed, knowing she'd get a rise out of him.

'Who does?' demanded Sean, looking around.

'We definitely don't, Dad. Don't worry,' Tom said, laughing. 'In fact, there's a certain line in the song that the whole pub screams out in town.'

'What line? What pub?' Sean asked, looking more and more bewildered.

'I believe they're referring to the bar in which you did a striptease. On stage. With a drag queen,' Jo stated succinctly.

'Everyone shut up and get the decorations sorted,' Sean ordered, his face now beetroot.

Much to everyone's surprise, it was a great afternoon and evening. The family went mad with the decorations, ate never-ending snacks, and even Cora smiled on occasion. It was a raucous time; everyone was happy, even Meg, who felt at ease for the first time in years.

Finally, Sean dimmed the lights, and they all flopped in front of an old Christmas film, the lounge lit only by the TV and lights that shone gently and rhythmically from the Christmas tree.

'Come on, sleepyhead,' came Jo's voice, and Meg roused just as George Bailey was proclaiming that it indeed was a wonderful life, 'you fell asleep.'

Meg yawned and wished everyone goodnight, then sleepily walked up the stairs with Jo behind her, carrying water.

Pyjamas on, Meg jumped into bed, and Jo sat beside her. 'I really am proud of you for the way you apologised to Cora and showed real remorse.'

'I saw her and felt shi... err, awful. I really am sorry. It will never happen again, I promise. I'm sad that she's been going through so much.'

'Me too, and I know you won't behave like that again,' Jo said kindly. 'And the garage, it looks remarkable.'

Meg went red with shame. 'Jo, about the garage, I… err...'

'Meg, I wasn't born yesterday. I know the others helped you; I knew they would.'

'You did? Am I in more trouble?'

'No. You accepted what I said and did as I asked without complaining. Of course, I knew the others would

349

help you out. They're good kids. Well, adults, I suppose.' She sighed wistfully.

'They were great, even though I thought there was a snake when Kayleigh hissed at me.'

'Best not to tell me,' Jo added with a grin. 'Do you need to talk about anything? I know it's been a crazy time.'

'No, not until after Christmas. I'm scared I'll get a flashback and ruin the day for you all.'

'If you do, then you do. We'll support you. Please, and I know this sounds easy when it certainly isn't, but please don't sit there and wait for one or expect one. Just do what you're doing and try to enjoy yourself. Actually, don't try to enjoy yourself. *Do* enjoy yourself; that's an order.' Jo grinned.

Meg smiled tiredly. 'I will.'

'Good. Now lie down and sleep.' Meg snuggled under the duvet, and Jo kissed her on the forehead. Meg was asleep almost instantly.

Jo crept out and met Cora on the landing on the floor below.

'Bedtime for you too?' She looked sadly at her daughter.

Cora nodded, lingering on the landing, then headed for her room.

'Night, Mum,' she said quietly.

'Can I come in?' Jo asked.

Surprised, Cora nodded, and Jo followed her and waited while Cora got into bed.

'Are you too old for a cuddle now?' asked Jo cautiously.

Cora didn't answer, but neither did she refuse.

'Budge up.' Jo got under Cora's duvet and put her arm around her daughter.

'I'm always here for you. I'll always be your mum, and I will never, ever stop loving you. Do you know that?'

Cora nodded and let out a sniffle. 'I'm sorry about everything I've done since I've been home. I've been horrible.'

'Not horrible. Confused, jealous, and yes, seriously out of order on occasion, but I don't love you any less. I've made mistakes too. I've missed things and not been there for you enough. I'm so sorry. I have missed you and would love some time alone soon. Would you like that?'

'That'll be amazing,' Cora said, surprised at her own excitement. She returned her mum's hug and also fell asleep. Jo sat watching her sleeping daughter for a long time. Feeling how disturbingly thin she was when hugging her, Jo felt ashamed she hadn't realised Cora's deep-rooted issues with food and anxiety had once again come crashing down on her.

Sighing and vowing to talk to Sean about Cora the next day, she gently stood, crept out of the room, and went to her own bed, truly and utterly exhausted from the past few weeks.

Chapter Eighteen

I*t's Christmas*!' shouted Kayleigh excitedly, jumping on Meg's bed as she lay sound asleep a couple of days later.

'Kayleigh!' Meg jumped in fright. 'You scared the cr...'

'Kayleigh! I told you to wake Meg up, not scare the life out of her,' said Jo, appearing in her dressing gown. 'Your dad is still recovering. Go and jump on the boys' beds; I don't see why they should miss out!'

'Happy Christmas!' Kayleigh grinned, giving Meg a hug. She ran out of the room before Meg could reply.

'Are you okay?' Jo asked, closing the door to block out Kayleigh's screams and a lot of swearing from Tom.

'Yeah,' she groaned sleepily.

'What time is it?'

'Six-thirty a.m.! Kayleigh gets a little over-excited on Christmas Day, and that's putting it nicely. She almost bounced Sean out of bed. Anyway, Merry Christmas!' Jo gave Meg a hug. 'I didn't see much of you yesterday. Everything okay?'

'Fine, honestly. I needed to do something in here. Nothing bad, I promise.'

'Okay.' Jo looked at Meg, narrowing her eyes slightly. 'We usually have wine or champagne with Christmas dinner, or for breakfast if you're Kayleigh! How would you feel about people drinking?'

'It's fine. It really is.'

Jo nodded. 'Come on, downstairs to the carnage.'

'I'll meet you down there in two minutes. Need the loo.'

'No problem. I'll go and make sure Kayleigh hasn't jumped on Cora's head. But they do seem to be getting along better since our talk, so there is hope yet.'

Meg jumped out of bed as soon as Jo left, and lifting her mattress, she collected a bundle of envelopes, each addressed to a family member. Putting on her dressing gown and slipping them into her pocket, she went downstairs, following the noise that was blasting from the living room.

'Finally!' Kayleigh said as Meg walked in. 'Do you want a Bucks Fizz?'

'A what?'

'No, she doesn't!' Sean answered for her grumpily, hugging a cup of coffee. 'And you can wait too. It's not even seven a.m. yet!'

'Presents?'

'Fine!' Sean agreed, still recovering from being woken by Kayleigh bouncing on his bed. 'Go for it.'

Everyone except Meg jumped up and searched the piles around the tree for their names, and within seconds, wrapping paper was being thrown around the room.

'Meg?' Jo looked at the girl, who was agitated and had a sheen of sweat covering her face. 'Are you not going to open yours?'

Meg didn't move from the sofa, instead lifting her legs and curling her arms around them in an attempt to shield herself from the embarrassment and upset that she felt. She couldn't bring herself to move or join in the scene. She didn't want presents, and she knew she didn't deserve them. It felt so alien to her that she wanted to run away.

'Wait!' Jo warned as she saw Meg glance at the door. 'If you won't go to the presents, they shall come to you.' Along with Sean, Jo got up and put a pile of presents on the sofa. 'Open them!' Jo urged kindly.

Meg put her head down to hide the tears that were welling up. Jo sat next to her and gave her a present.

'Come on.' she said quietly. 'I'll help you unwrap the first one.' She grabbed Meg's clenched hand, and they unwrapped it together.

'I never thought I'd have one of those things in the house!' Sean stated with mock anger. Meg glanced at him, confused. Seeing his grin, she continued and pulled out a red Manchester United shirt.

'Wow!' she said loudly and looked embarrassed again. 'I mean, ttthank you.'

'It's our pleasure.' Jo looked at Sean.

'It really is,' he added. 'Though there is still time to convert you to a decent team who...'

'Sean, please shut up!' Jo ordered and gestured towards the rest of Meg's gifts. 'You   can do the rest!'

Her insides cringing with embarrassment, Meg opened her other presents, including a Man United hat.

'For our next snowball fight!' Sean laughed, looking up from opening his own presents. Meg received new trainers, books, games, a lot of clothes, and best of all, a new laptop computer.

Meg sat around her presents, slightly stunned at the amount she'd received. 'You'll need the computer for your homework,' said Jo in a mock stern voice. 'So no excuses not to do it.'

'Thank you,' Meg whispered. 'The iPad would have worked just as well. You shouldn't have...'

'Yes, we should!'

They both turned to watch the others squeal in pleasure and laugh at some of their joke gifts. Tom, Wes, Kayleigh, and Jack all gave presents to each other, Meg, and their parents, while Cora hovered in the background.

Sean groaned as he saw Kayleigh's gift to him was a fake bullet-proof jacket. 'You are not funny!'

Meg opened more gifts and was again close to tears at how thoughtful everyone had been. She nervously put her hand in her dressing gown pocket and gave everyone an envelope.

'Sorry, it's not much,' she said nervously. 'I will buy you all something when I can.'

They all stopped and looked at their envelopes, intrigued. Jo and Sean exchanged a look, both cursing themselves for not thinking of giving Meg pocket money.

They opened their envelopes and pulled out a sheet of paper, and slowly, each person began to laugh. Meg had spent the previous day writing a limerick about each one of them.

'Huh, the cheek!' exclaimed Jo, but laughing all the same. 'And I don't have an obsession with hats, scarves, and hot chocolate!'

However, seven other voices overruled her loudly. Sean snorted loudly when reading his. 'It was a bullet wound, not a scratch!'

Everyone carried on reading their own limericks and then swapped them around. Meg had managed to exaggerate and rhyme everyone's characteristics except Cora's; hers was more generic. Meg certainly didn't want to elaborate on

Cora, so she wrote a funny limerick instead, much to Cora's and her parents' relief.

'They are brilliant. Thank you so much.' The pride in Jo's eyes was obvious, and everyone joined in with their praise, to the extent that Meg wished she could crawl under the sofa.

'Sorry, there's nothing from me,' Cora said. 'I was going to go shopping but couldn't face it. The crowds...'

'Don't worry, Cora,' Kayleigh told her sister, her eyes soft. 'I definitely want an extra- large birthday present, though!'

'No problem,' Cora replied, relieved.

'Bin bags!' Jo announced. 'Come on, everyone. Put the wrapping paper away. Dinner is at one p.m. Meg, you are peeling carrots, Tom is on potatoes, the rest of you are on chopping and laying the table, and Sean is...'

'On his backside, having some peace. But I'll do the washing up.'

'Deal,' Jo said as everyone put their wrapping paper in bin bags and began to collect their presents to take to their rooms.

'What should I wear? After my shower, I mean?' Meg asked Jo. 'Do you all wear smart clothes?'

'I think you should definitely wear your Man United shirt!' Jo said. 'It will be fun to watch Sean's face when you appear in it.'

Meg laughed. 'Thank you so much. I didn't expect you to...'

'I know,' interrupted Jo. 'You should expect. It will get easier, I promise. Now go shower and dress; I've got a turkey to burn!' She kissed the girl on the forehead and went off to the kitchen.

It was ten a.m., and everyone was showered, dressed, and in the living room playing games or trying to watch TV. Kayleigh had finally persuaded her dad it was time for Bucks Fizz, which Meg discovered was a mixture of champagne and orange juice. She was pretty tempted to have a try when Kayleigh offered her a sip, but Jo's stern glare was enough to stop her.

They all stopped and looked at each other curiously when there was suddenly a knock on the door.

'Are we expecting anyone?' Jo asked Sean.

'No!' He got up to answer the door. He was gone for at least five minutes, and everyone, Meg especially, shuffled uncomfortably. Logically, she knew it couldn't be anyone terrible. The armed officer certainly would have stopped them, but she still felt slightly sick with nerves.

'We have a visitor!' Sean announced, striding back into the room. Meg's jaw dropped when she saw he was being followed by Inspector Phillips. It took her brain a few seconds to recognise the Inspector, as she was dressed in regular clothes and not a police uniform.

'Not on official business,' Gina said quickly to Jo, whom she could see was flushed with sudden annoyance. 'I wanted to stop by to give you this, Meg.' She handed the girl a beautifully wrapped gift. 'It's to say Happy Christmas, of course, but also to say thank you.'

'Thank you for what?'

'Sit down, Gina,' Jo said, moving up.

'Thanks. It's to say thank you for saving my job. I heard about your conversation with the Chief Inspector, and thank you. She sent me a copy of your email. I have to say that blackmail is a criminal offence, and also that it was amazing! I've never seen Chief Constable Akhtar so angry. She's terrified of bad publicity. You played a blinder, and I've not laughed so much in years.'

'Yes, Jo and Meg were in a bizarre state of hysterics too,' added Sean, looking bewildered again as the Inspector began to giggle.

'Do you want a Bucks Fizz?' Kayleigh asked Gina suddenly.

The Inspector hesitated. 'I don't want to invade your Christmas. I came to thank Meg and drop a gift off.'

'Please stay and have a drink with us,' Jo offered kindly. 'You are very welcome.'

'Well, okay then. Thank you. But more orange than champagne as I'm driving.'

'Sure.' Kayleigh jumped up, grinning. 'Can't have a drunken copper behind the wheel; even Meg wouldn't be able to fix that one.'

'Kayleigh!' Jo exclaimed, shocked, but Gina burst out laughing.

'No. I think she'd love to find something on me, but she won't dare while Meg has her exactly where she wants her. You should join the police when you're older, Meg. You certainly know enough about how we work.'

'I think I've had enough of police,' Meg said. 'Not you,' she added hastily. 'Anyway, I'm joining the army when I'm sixteen.'

'You most certainly are not!' came Jo's forceful voice, the tone shocking Meg.

'So, what are your plans for today, Gina?' Sean jumped in quickly before Meg could respond.

'Not working. My first Christmas Day off in years and, as I'm not on-call either, there is a bottle of whisky at home with my name on it, and an afternoon of Christmas TV.'

'Are you married? Divorced? Kids?' Sean asked nosily.

'None of the above. I've realised that I'm married to my job. My former partner told me that over a decade ago when I had to leave during Christmas dinner as I was on-call. To be honest, I was glad to go to work. When we were at her parents' house, the dullest people on the planet, I almost kissed my mobile when it rang.'

'Knew you were a lesbian.' Kayleigh handed Gina a drink. 'I've got a better gaydar than my gay brother and his boyfriend put together.'

'Fiancé!' Tom said.

'Kayleigh!' Jo groaned, putting her head in her hands.

Gina laughed loudly; Meg watched the Inspector, noticing how normal she appeared, sitting there laughing, holding a drink. She felt a sudden surge of affection for the woman.

Meg made eye contact with Jo and nodded to Gina. Understanding the non-verbal exchange, Jo nodded in complete agreement.

'Stay for dinner, Gina. Please? It will be lovely for us all, and you never know, the kids might actually not fight if you're here.'

'I couldn't possibly...'

'Why not?' asked Sean. 'We've spent so much time together recently. As Jo said, it would be great to get to know you better. After all, you were there when I got shot!'

'Scratch,' coughed Kayleigh, Tom, and Wes at the same time.

'Shut up!' Sean growled. 'How about it, Gina?'

'Well, if you'd like me to, I would be delighted. Thank you.'

'Excellent, and if the kids start fighting, please don't hesitate to arrest them and have them thrown in a cell for the day.'

'No problem.' Gina grinned.

They all sat at the table to a fantastic dinner; the noise was incredible. Everyone talked over each other while wearing paper hats from the Christmas crackers. The jokes got worse as the champagne flowed more freely. Kayleigh was right, Meg mused, as she realised Sean was drunk. He wasn't aggressive or mean; his jokes did become worse. His face reddened, and he did look ridiculous in his massive Christmas jumper and lop-sided paper hat.

After dinner, Sean and Gina washed up, and they all sleepily collapsed in front of the TV, too full to move.

'How are you doing?' whispered Gina, who was sitting next to Meg, noting they were the only people in the room who hadn't nodded off.

'I'm okay, I think. Well, I've not had a lot of time to think. I'm always waiting for the next thing to happen. Like that Chief Constable of yours coming in a couple of days. What's she like?'

'Career police officer.' Gina snorted disapprovingly.

'You don't like her?'

'She's not what I'd call a police officer, more of a politician in a uniform. Your case and everything you have helped us discover is what normal coppers do, but she's more afraid of the press than ensuring the correct people are caught. She wants quick arrests, not long investigations, but she is under a lot of pressure from above, to be fair. When I joined the police force, it was a living nightmare. I'm a woman, I'm black, and also an out lesbian. I didn't have an easy time of it, and that was just from my colleagues. But I'm still old school, started on the beat. I've been spat at, beaten up, threatened with knives and guns. I don't like taking orders from people I don't respect, especially someone fast-tracked to the top without putting the work in.'

'How do you think I should handle her?'

Gina smiled. 'You know exactly how to handle her. Keep doing what you're doing. You are the victim here. However, you have done a remarkable job in taking back some control. Make sure you keep hold of it. Don't let her railroad you.'

Meg nodded thoughtfully and was about to ask another question when she saw the news on the TV begin. The headline appeared in large writing across the screen. She dived for the remote control, which was on Jo's knee, startling her awake in the process.

'What's going on?' Jo demanded.

Meg turned the TV volume up and watched in astonishment as the headline stated *Christmas Chaos at Dover*. The newsreader announced that all shipping containers arriving at Dover on Christmas Eve had been searched, causing a massive backlog. She stated that there were rumours that a container filled with child refugees had been discovered, but, as yet, the reports were unsubstantiated.

'Refugees!' Meg spat. 'Prisoners, more like. I'm going to ring the press.'

'You are not,' Jo said. 'Because of you, the police have found these girls, and they are safe. The press does not need to know.'

'They certainly do not,' Gina added. 'It could jeopardise the whole operation. Thanks to you, these girls have been saved from unimaginable horrors; the press will be informed in time. Hopefully, after the girls have been safely returned home.'

Meg looked at Jo, tears in her eyes. Jo smiled and moved to sit next to the girl and hugged her while they, and the whole family, watched the rest of the news piece, which reported rumours of several arrests. 'I'm proud of you,' whispered Jo. And, for once, Meg sat in silence instead of batting back the compliment.

The news gave everyone a burst of restless energy. 'Coats on, everyone,' Jo told the family. 'Let's go for a walk before it goes dark and walk that dinner off, and then I suggest a game or two.'

'*Twister*!' screamed Kayleigh, almost bursting Gina's eardrum and receiving a stern glare from the Inspector that actually rendered the unstoppable Kayleigh McGloughlin into silence.

'Wow!' Sean exclaimed to Gina. 'Please teach me that. I've not been able to shut Kayleigh up for almost twenty-one years!'

'It takes decades of training, I'm afraid,' Gina said, looking at Kayleigh thoughtfully.

They all marched outside into the late foggy Christmas afternoon; Gina walked at the back, chatting with Kayleigh, while armed officers walked alongside in silent observation.

'I'll be glad when I don't have to see another gun.' Jo sighed to Meg and Sean.

'I'm sorry...' Meg began.

'Don't apologise! It is not your fault. I don't like guns.'

'Or the army?' Meg quizzed.

'No!'

'Why?'

Sean glanced at Jo cautiously. 'Jo's brother, Simon, was killed in Iraq in 2003.'

'Simon was five years younger than me,' Jo explained. 'Completely army barmy all his life. He joined at sixteen. My parents had to give permission as he was under eighteen, and he went to an army training college.

'Simon was at the college when the World Trade Centre in New York was attacked. It was then I begged him to leave as I knew there would be war, but he refused. He graduated top of his class from the college and joined the parachute regiment. I'd never seen him so happy; he loved the paras and was desperate to go to Iraq. He was sent out days after his eighteenth birthday. He died there in May 2003. I still don't know the full details; a lot of the information remains classified. We were informed that he was killed in action during an explosion. There was no body to bring home,' Jo finished sadly.

'I'm so sorry,' Meg said and held Jo's hand.

'It was a long time ago, but I miss him. War and fighting are such a waste of life. I never want any of my children to join the armed forces, and if you think for one second that I would sign the consent forms at sixteen, then forget it.'

Meg dropped the subject and carried on walking in silence. Kayleigh and Gina appeared to be having an intense yet quiet conversation behind them. Wes and Tom were holding hands and discussing their honeymoon, and Jack was talking to Cora about his girlfriend.

They were all happy to arrive home, where they played a raucous game of Twister, in which there was a lot of kicking of legs and arms. Then they all indulged in even more food as Sean and Tom laid a huge buffet on the table.

Meg was exhausted and quite relieved when Jo sent her to bed at ten p.m. after saying goodbye to Gina, who went home in a taxi.

Jo went up with Meg and gave her a hug when she got into bed. 'How was your Christmas?' she asked.

'It was the best one I've ever had.' Meg yawned. 'Is that what everyone does on Christmas Day? Well, in proper families, I mean.'

'Everyone is different, but I imagine ours is fairly usual for people who have children. It is a difficult time of year for many people. Some have had big arguments and don't meet up, or they reluctantly get together and argue and fight. Christmas is also harder for those who have lost loved ones; traditional family occasions do that.'

'I'm sorry about your brother, and I'm sorry for talking about the army, especially today.'

'You weren't to know,' Jo said kindly, stroking Meg's hair gently. 'He was a lot like you in many ways. Brave, outspoken, and he had a wild side.' She rolled her eyes comically. 'And I'm sorry too. You have your life to live, and I will support you as much as I can. If you want to join the army at eighteen, I can't legally stop you.'

'Not sixteen?'

'Not a chance! There's no rush to decide what to do when you grow up. I want you to have time to experience a proper childhood, and you will soon enough, I promise.'

Meg nodded sleepily, her eyes beginning to close.

Jo slipped out of bed, covered her up, and kissed her on the forehead.

'Love you,' she whispered.

'Love you too,' Meg muttered practically in her sleep. Jo's eyes prickled, happy and amazed at Meg's words. Resisting the irrational urge to wake her up and ask her to repeat them, she crept out of the room and went downstairs to join those still awake.

'Everything okay?' Sean asked with concern, looking at his wife.

'Everything is great.' She smiled. 'The best Christmas ever.'

Chapter Nineteen

Meg was introduced to the Boxing Day McGloughlin Games the next day over breakfast. They all explained that every year they took turns to decide what to do. The year before had been Jack's turn. He'd set up a mini-Olympic tournament in the park, which included the hundred-metre race, the long jump, as well as a hurdles event with hurdles that he had secretly *borrowed* from uni for Christmas. Obviously, he was crowned champion and was the current holder of the unique family trophy they had all made when they were children.

'So, what's it to be this year?' Jo asked. 'And, more importantly, whose turn is it to choose?'

'As the current champion,' Jack announced pompously, and was bombarded by pieces of flying food and booing, 'I announce that this year Meg will decide what the McGloughlin Games will be!'

Meg looked around the table at everyone. 'Only if you want to, that is,' Jack said.

'I do,' Meg replied with a grin. 'I'm just counting how many of us there are.'

'Do we all have to...' began Cora.

'Yes!' replied her dad, not allowing her to finish.

'Football!' Meg announced. 'Four-a-side, at the park. One team, my team, wears red. The other, white t-shirts maybe?'

'And who are the team captains?' asked Jo.

'Well, Jack is last year's champion, so he can be the white team captain, and I'll be the red team captain.'

'You are going down!' Jack laughed.

'I'll choose my first player first, and then you choose yours, and we will take it in turns.

Sound fair?' Meg asked Jack, ignoring his jibe.

'Whatever,' he said lazily. 'You can have them all if you like. I'll still win on my own.'

'So cocky.' Jo sighed. 'Go on, Meg. Pick your first player.'

'Tom!' she said, without hesitation.

'Dad!' Jack came back immediately. 'Kayleigh.'

'Wes.'

'Jo!' Meg said quickly, grinning as Jack was left with an angry-looking Cora.

'Cora,' Jack said, annoyed, but nowhere near as annoyed as Cora, who detested sport.

'Excellent,' Sean said. 'But remember, this is fun. No dirty play, no nasty tackles, no fighting. Got it?'

They all nodded, each one of them planning to ignore him.

'Good. Let's get changed and slaughter the red team!'

'Sean!' Jo said sternly. 'What did you just say about it being fun?'

'Don't be a sore loser before we've even started,' he challenged his wife, whose eyes flashed.

'We will see about that!' she said, striding out to change.

Taking jumpers for goalposts, the family arrived at the park, the grass crispy with frost and the sun covered by cloud, emitting a slight drizzle. They all shivered as Jack, who had brought along a tape measure, arranged the goals and marked the centre of the pitch with spray chalk.

'Where did he get that from?' Meg asked, confused.

'Jack takes sport very seriously; he has everything you need for any possible game,' Jo said as Jack threw a pair of goalkeepers' gloves over to them and huddled with his own players, finally giving their gloves to Cora.

'Anyone good in goal?' Meg asked.

'Me!' said Tom, firmly taking his gloves.

'Cool, let's get them!' Meg announced, fondly adjusting her new Manchester United shirt. 'I'll mark Jack. Kayleigh, you stay on Wes, and Jo, will you stick to Sean?'

'Certainly will,' she replied, her eyes still gleaming.

371

'Great,' Meg said. 'But keep pushing forward. Make them the ones who need to mark!'

Meg and Jo kicked off and passed back to Kayleigh. Jack sprinted forward and took the ball from his sister. He turned to shoot just as Meg came in with a sliding tackle that not only passed the ball to Kayleigh, who ran up the field, but also took Jack's legs from underneath him. He lay sprawled face down on the ground as Meg got up.

'Still think you would've won on your own?' she said, grinning, and sprinted off to join Kayleigh, who was approaching Cora in goal. Sean was trying to run to defend, but Jo was behind him, arms around his waist and literally digging her heels into the ground. As big and strong as he was, his wife refused to budge, and Kayleigh passed the ball to Meg, who blasted it past Cora. She screamed and ducked as the ball came flying towards her.

Jack stormed up the field, shouting about illegal tackles, his father and Cora being pathetic, and Wes, who was stroking a passing Golden Retriever and chatting to the dog's owners, being useless.

After dragging Wes back to the game, they played for an hour until the light rain became torrential. The score was 9-2 to the red team. Jack, usually so laid back, was red in the face with anger at losing.

'It wasn't a fair match,' he grumbled. 'Flying tackles, holding people by the waist, poking me in the eye.' He glared at Kayleigh. 'I want a rematch tomorrow!'

'It was an accident. Get over yourself... loser.' Kayleigh teased and then ran as Jack lunged towards her, and they both disappeared up the street.

'Will Kayleigh be okay when Jack catches her?' Meg asked, worried.

'I'm more worried about what will happen to Jack if he does catch her,' Sean replied, wiping mud from his eyelid. 'That was a good choice; I really would have enjoyed it if a certain person had let me play!'

'Sean, you never learn, do you?' said his wife. 'Goad me at your peril!'

They got back to the house, and Jack, yet again, was face down on the floor. Kayleigh was on his back and had his arm twisted up it.

'Say *Jack is a loser*!' Kayleigh demanded.

The armed police officer looked uncertain; Jack's head was practically on his boot.

'Sorry, I wasn't sure if I should intervene,' he said to Jo and Sean, grateful they had arrived.

'Leave them,' Sean said. 'They'll come in when they're bored.' 'Sorry, sir, but the security risks...'

'Up now!' Jo said to Kayleigh. 'And you, Jack!'

'I'm trying to!' Jack panted, irritated that his mum was having a go at him. 'Kayleigh is on my back!'

'Yes, but you chased her, so you're both to blame. Up!'

They both irritably got up and attempted to enter the house simultaneously, getting jammed in the doorway. Jack forced his way through, elbowing Kayleigh out of the way.

'Loser!' she hissed, grinning.

'Jack,' Jo said sternly. 'You know what to do. Go on...'

Taking his shoes off and leaving them in the hall, Jack miserably trudged upstairs while everyone made their way to the kitchen to drink gallons of water.

Jack reappeared, his bad mood gone, much to Meg's surprise, and looking calm and happy again.

'Jack doesn't stay angry for more than a few minutes and never holds grudges,' whispered Kayleigh. 'He's very competitive but soon gets over it.'

Jack cleared his throat loudly. 'Ladies and gentleman,' he announced dramatically. 'It is my honour to award this year's McGloughlin Boxing Day Cup to Meg. Please come and take your prize.'

Meg stepped forward and was handed a weird-looking object. 'It was a papier mache shaped F.A Cup years ago,' Jack whispered. 'Now it's a wonky thing, but still the McGloughlin Cup!'

'Thank you,' Meg said, copying Jack's formal tone. 'I'd like to thank my teammates and, of course, our opponents for making it so easy,' she finished, laughing.

They all laughed and wandered off to clean up before lunch.

'Don't worry, it will wash,' said Jo, who was watching as Meg examined her dirty Man United shirt. 'Just bring it down after your shower; it'll be dry in a couple of hours.'

'Are you sure? It looks a bit battered.'

'I'm sure. Go shower, and then lunch and a lazy afternoon, and I want you to have an early night. Tomorrow will be a long day. Only Sean and I will be here. The rest are going into town for some sales shopping and the cinema.'

Meg nodded; her rosy cheeks lost their colour, and she angrily left the room. Meg had certainly not forgotten, but the last couple of days had been fantastic. She was dreading revisiting her memories and giving what she suspected would be the most in-depth and painful interview she'd endured so far.

The following day, at precisely three p.m., there was a knock on the door. Chief Constable Danah Akhtar stood there; behind her appeared to be an entourage of people.

'Mr McGloughlin?' she asked Sean, who nodded, instantly disliking the arrogant-looking woman. 'I believe you are expecting us.'

'We were expecting you, not your mob,' he replied.

'We are here to interview Miss Walsh. The detectives will be assisting with the interview, and the others will be setting up the recording equipment. May we come in?'

Sean reluctantly moved from the doorway, allowing them to enter. Meg was in the dining room with Jo, and they were both equally surprised to see how many people had arrived.

'Megan,' said the Chief Constable. 'I'm Danah Akhtar.' She reached out and shook the girl's hand.

'I prefer Meg to Megan.'

'Of course. Meg it is.' She smiled and introduced herself to Jo.

'Are all these people necessary?' Jo asked.

'Apparently so.' Sean said from the doorway.

'May I introduce Chief Inspector John Obuya. He is the head of our central human trafficking department. Inspector Alice Stephenson heads the central Child Sexual Exploitation teams, and Chief Inspector David Matthews oversees the Murder Investigation teams. The others are here to set up the voice and visual recording equipment for the interview,' the Chief Constable explained.

'Why is everyone of such a high rank?' asked Jo, looking concerned.

'This is a high-profile case. We suspect a leak within the station where Meg provided her statements. We have decided to use high-ranking officers from headquarters and run through the whole story again.'

'Wait!' Jo said. 'Meg has provided numerous statements. One on the night I found her, one from her hospital bed, and others from the police station. Why does she have to repeat them?'

Danah Akhtar looked slightly less arrogant, even a little unsure. 'You've lost the evidence, haven't you?' Sean said, sounding more resigned than angry.

'Not all of it,' she replied carefully. 'Parts of the hospital video have been distorted, along with the interview with DCI Leek and DS Murray that was undertaken at the station. The video filmed on the evening Jo brought Meg in is still intact. Also, the video interviews you both gave after the warehouse raid are in our possession and fully intact...'

'But?' Sean asked sarcastically.

'The accompanying paperwork authorising the initial interviews has, erm… disappeared. Both hard and digital copies cannot be found. So, though the video is still present, it can't be used in court because there is no paperwork. It would be deemed inadmissible. A judge would throw it out immediately as there is nothing to say that we interviewed a minor procedurally.

'I'm sorry, Meg. We are doing all we can to find out who is working with this gang, but whoever the person or persons are know what they are doing. But we *will* find them!'

'Are you saying Meg has to restart from the night I found her and go through everything all over again?' Jo asked with disgust.

'I'm afraid so, but that will be it until the trial, I promise.'

'The trial?' Meg asked.

'Yes. We need your statement again. We have numerous people in custody and a great deal of evidence, such as DNA, fingerprints, and statements from the survivors of the warehouse raid. We also have statements from most of the other girls, who we managed to move to locations around the country. But yours is the main one. Once everything is together, we will await a date for the trial.'

'Do I need to go to court?'

'Not necessarily; there are a lot of special measures in circumstances such as this. You could appear by video link, be behind a screen, the judge and barristers would remove their wigs. There are lots of options, but that can be discussed later. Are you ready to begin?'

'I want Jo and Sean to stay in the room,' Meg demanded.

'That's fine,' answered the Chief Constable, who had already anticipated the question. 'They need to remain off-camera. Still, you'll be able to see them. Sean's interview from the hospital is in our care and not been tampered with, and Jo's written statement from the night she found you is secure. So, yes, they can stay, but they cannot speak. Is everyone in agreement?'

Jo and Sean nodded solemnly and moved away from Meg, both giving her a kiss on the head as they passed her, and went to stand behind the camera.

'Okay, I shall begin with the questions,' said Inspector Stephenson, 'and the others will add theirs where appropriate. I'm sorry, but I will need to ask for some details that will be distressing and push you on the answers if I need to do so. But please remember that I am on your side, and I believe you completely. We all want to convict these people. Please give as much detail as you can. I can't be seen to lead you.'

Meg glanced at Jo and then back to the Inspector.

'Let's get this over with.

The cameras were set to record, and Inspector Stephenson introduced herself, the other two interviewing officers, and Meg. She also stated that Joanne and Sean McGloughlin were in the room.

'Meg,' she began, 'can I ask why you happened to be at Crookshaws Children's Home alone when the rest of the home's residents were away on a short holiday?'

Her fingers tapping on the table, Meg repeated the story of why she wasn't allowed to go on holiday, and then fidgeted in the chair as she had to repeat what happened on the awful night that she ran away.

'For the purpose of the video,' Inspector Stephenson stated, 'I am now showing Megan Walsh an image. Can you tell me who this man is?'

'Yes. It's Javeed.'

'Thank you.'

The Inspector pressed Meg for more specific details of Javeed's behaviour during the time Meg had known him. Intimate details, words she didn't want to say, and thoughts she didn't want to think made Meg sweat profusely.

Jo whispered something to the Chief Constable, who quickly scribbled on a piece of paper and passed it to Inspector Stephenson.

'Do you need a break, Meg?' the Inspector asked, making the girl jump.

'No!'

Before the evening you ran away,' continued the Inspector, 'did you witness Javeed or anyone else behave inappropriately with the other girls?'

'He, Javeed, and another staff member, Peter, would go to Simone's room a lot when they were on the sleep-in shift. Hers was the room next to mine, and I'd hear them.'

'Hear them doing what?'

'Having sex, I imagine, but I never saw them. But Simone would brag about it and tell everyone Javeed and Peter were her boyfriends. She would go out mostly with Jjjj...'

'Take your time.'

Taking several deep breaths, Meg attempted to speak again. 'Javeed's brother, Naz, would come to the home a lot when Javeed worked on his own or with Peter, and sometimes other men came to visit.'

'Do you remember any names or descriptions?'

'There was Danny. He was tall, didn't speak a lot. Ed, he hung around too, fairly short, shaved head.'

'Ethnicity?'

'Eh?'

'Danny and Ed. What colour was their skin and what language did they speak?'

'Oh, white and English. I think their accents were local. They would take different girls out with Simone; they'd nearly always come back drunk or stoned. I kept out of the way when they were there and stayed in my bedroom. They never came around when other staff apart from Javeed or Peter were working.'

The Inspector nodded and continued to ask Meg more of the questions that she had previously answered. The Inspector wanted every intricate, intimate detail, and every possible description, Meg looked around the room anxiously, her hair now soaked in sweat, hands trembling. Then she made eye-contact with Jo.

'Time for a break!' Jo announced firmly and walked over to Meg, took her hand, and led her from the room.

CHAPTER TWENTY

Jo took Meg up to her bedroom and got some fresh clothes, as Meg had completely sweated through every item she was wearing and began to shiver as the sweat cooled.

'How long have we got?' Meg asked Jo quietly.

'As long as you need,' Jo answered firmly and sent Meg to the en-suite to change. Sean appeared with hot drinks and jam doughnuts; he looked furious.

'I'm sorry,' Meg began as she came out of the bathroom in fresh clothes. 'You don't need to be in that room. Or I can go to the police station and do it there.'

'Over my dead body you will,' Sean growled. 'They are staying exactly where I can see them. Useless bunch of t...'

'Sean, leave it, please,' Jo said, looking towards Meg. 'Your anger won't help. And Meg, do not apologise. You've done nothing wrong. Now, drink and eat a doughnut. You need the sugar!'

Meg ate and drank quietly.

'One thing to remember,' Sean added in a much calmer voice. 'They will ask you about the hitchhiking and kidnapping soon. Whatever you do, stick to Ewan. Don't refer to him as Leon at all. We don't know what this new lot of coppers know and don't know. I don't imagine they're dodgy, but it is best to stick with the "don't trust anyone" motto for now.'

Meg nodded. 'There's more I'll have to say about the children's home that I haven't told you.'

'That's fine,' Jo said gently.

'But you will both hate me and think I'm disgusting and...'

'And nothing!' Jo declared. 'The only people we think are disgusting, and hate, are those animals who preyed on children such as you. You are not to blame, and I will say it over and over until you believe it.'

'Can we go back down?' Meg asked quickly, 'I need to finish this, and Jo, please don't ask for any more breaks. I want it over with.'

'I can't promise you, Meg, but I won't do it unless I'm seriously concerned for you.'

'No! I said...'

'I know what you said, but I disagree. The police want answers. I want you to be safe, and that's what I will do.'

Meg didn't answer. She marched down the stairs and back into the dining room.

Throwing herself into the chair, she looked at the police officers. 'Let's get on with it!' The camera began to record again, and more and more questions were fired at Meg. 'How often were you taken to the warehouse?'

'I don't know,' Meg answered truthfully. 'There was no pattern. Sometimes every day, sometimes not for a week. Other times we'd go there, and they would give us dresses or school uniforms and take us to posh houses where people held sick parties. If you didn't turn up or disappeared, you'd have the shit kicked out of you, or their favourite was holding a hot iron to people's backs while the other men held them. I can still smell the skin burning,' Meg finished, looking so clammy and pale that Jo became seriously concerned Meg would pass out.

Meg described the houses in which the so-called parties were held in and gave as much description as possible about the men who were there and what they did to the girls in the different bedrooms. Even Chief Constable Akhtar's inscrutable face began to show shock and stress as the scale of the operation and enormity of the police cover-up hit her. She scribbled on a piece of paper again and passed it to the Inspector, who looked shocked.

'Meg,' she began, looking at the paper again. 'Were any police officers at these parties?'

'How would I know? It's not like they would come in their uniforms!'

Another piece of paper was passed to the Inspector, who nodded grimly. 'Meg, I am going to show you staff images of high-ranking officers on the county's police website. Before I do, can I ask if you have ever looked at this website before?' She showed her the page on the screen.

'No,' Meg said with certainty.

'As I said, these are very high-ranking officers within the force, so you would not have seen them during your visits to the police station. Can I ask if you rec...'

'*Him*!' Meg shouted, making everyone jump. 'And him!'

'For the video, Meg has identified Deputy Chief Constable Ian Jones, and Assistant Chief Constable Derek Akpan. Will you please continue to scroll down the site and see if you recognise anyone else?' the Inspector asked.

Meg did so, but no one looked familiar. She was about to push the laptop away when something caught her eye.

'What's this?' she asked, pointing to a column on the right-hand side of the screen that was scrolling by itself, showing small writing and the occasional photo.

'It's our Twitter feed. Why, did you notice something?'

'Can you go into it?'

The Inspector redirected the site to Twitter, and Meg scrolled down the page frantically; she had seen someone, she was sure of it. '*Him*!' she said finally.

The Inspector looked closely and enlarged the photograph. It was a newspaper report and photo of Deputy Chief Constable Ian Jones, two city councillors, and the member of Parliament for the area outside the official opening of the youth centre.

In the background of the enlarged image, Jo and the centre's manager were both clearly visible. The paper praised the work of the police along with the local councillors and the member of Parliament for raising money and awareness for the need for a youth centre.

It also had a quote from Jo, who stated she hoped the centre would make a huge difference to young people in the area. Meg read the article twice and then pointed to the member of Parliament and one of the city councillors.

'All of those men were at the sick parties, along with your copper!' she snarled and glared at Jo. 'It looks

like they worked together to get a place to find "fresh meat!"'

'Interview paused,' said the Inspector, who'd received a tap on the shoulder from her boss.

'I need to make some phone calls,' the Chief Constable said. 'No one in this room is to leave or to use any radios or mobile phones, and no one is to speak to another person. Anyone who does will be arrested!'

She walked out of the room, leaving behind a deathly silence. Meg glared at Jo with blazing fury in her eyes; she didn't understand. Did Jo know? Was she involved?

Jo knew precisely what Meg was thinking and looked shaken to her core. She attempted to give the girl reassuring looks, but they were batted back by the waves of anger flying from Meg's whole body.

They all sat in absolute, agonising silence for half an hour until the Chief Constable finally returned.

'Press record on the video!' she ordered and joined the interview table, then questioned Meg about the senior police officers and politicians she had identified. Meg told her everything she knew and how she had either witnessed or been subjected to sexual assault by them. The Chief Constable pushed Meg to go into excruciating detail about exactly who had done what to her. She asked her to give the other girls' names who had been attacked at these parties.

The Inspector confirmed that the girls they had removed and relocated to safe spaces, away from the city's children's homes, had not been asked to look at images of police officers or politicians. But they would be re-interviewed. When Chief Constable Akhtar finished, she instructed her Inspector to continue.

The Inspector, clearly shaken at what had been disclosed, riffled through her notes.

'Ah, yes, Javeed. You ran away from Crookshaws Children's home on the evening he raped you. Had he attacked you previously?'

'Twice before,' Meg said in a dead voice, 'but only after his brother told him it was okay.'

'Final question from me,' the Inspector said. 'Why did you run away then and not before?'

'I couldn't stand it any longer. I went to the train station. I was going to jump in front of a train and kill myself, but there weren't any running. The indoor shelter was locked, so I wandered around all night, slept in a few places, and carried on wandering around the next day. I still wanted to die, but I found somewhere to sit down and stayed there. Everything in my head stopped being real; I felt like I wasn't in my own body. I just sat there, and that was when I... that was when Jo found me.'

'Thank you,' said the Inspector and opened her mouth to say more but couldn't find the words. 'I'll hand you over to Inspector Obuya, who is head of the Human Trafficking Unit.'

'Can we take a break first?' Jo interjected.

'No!' Meg snapped and looked at the man who had taken over from Inspector Stephenson.

'Thank you, Meg,' he said, his deep voice resonating around the room. 'I'd like to talk to you about Mr Ewan

Hunt. I believe you ran away from these premises earlier this month. Is that correct?'

'Yes.'

'You made it to the motorway entrance, and Mr Hunt picked you up. Can you tell me anything about what happened next?'

'I told him I was going to Wales, and he said he'd drop me as far as Manchester. We travelled in silence for a while, and Ewan said he was running out of petrol. So, we stopped at a service station, and he said he was hungry, so we got something to eat in there. Then the car tyre was ripped to shreds when we left the service station, that's when he booked us into the hotel and... and tried to kill me. You have the full story in writing. I sent it to the Chief Constable and I gave video evidence. I'll sign whatever you want to say it's true.'

'Thank you. The information you gave on the Christmas Eve arrival at Dover was accurate, as you may have seen on the news. What you won't know is that we found 500 girls squashed into three different storage containers. Some were barely alive, but they are receiving medical attention and care, and are slowly recovering. Gina Phillips really came through for you there; she disobeyed orders from Detective Chief Constable Ian Jones and organised a massive search at

Dover on Christmas Eve. This was only possible because you prevented Chief Constable Akhtar from suspending her.'

'Stop right there, Inspector!' the Chief Constable ordered. 'I was working on the information given to me by Ian, who raised suspicions about Gina Phillips. I hope you are not implying anything to the contrary!'

'Actually, Ma'am, I'm not,' Inspector Obuya said. 'I don't think you are implicated. I'm simply stating that Meg's loyalty to Gina saved five hundred lives, and many more now that we know how they operate abroad, and more importantly, who!'

The Chief Constable nodded stiffly and gestured to the final officer present, who took over the line of questioning.

'Hi, Meg. I am Chief Inspector David Matthews, head of all the county's Murder Investigation departments. I know you must be exhausted, and luckily, this one won't take long. I have the written and signed statement about the murder of Jenny Evans. One that wasn't interfered with!' he added angrily. 'I just need you to confirm the events and have one question. Okay?'

Meg nodded and picked up the piece of paper her statement was written on, "*There were around twenty children present during the murder…*"

Meg reread her own words about Jenny's death, the words on the paper coming in and out of focus as Meg began to feel dizzy. Eventually, she looked up at the Chief Inspector.

'Is that all correct?' he asked.

'Yes,' Meg said, tears in her eyes.

'Thank you.' He put a photograph in front of Meg. 'Is this the man whom you witnessed murder Jenny Evans?'

'Yes.'

'And what name do you know him by?'

'Naz,' Meg said, barely loud enough to be heard.

'Thank you. You have done an amazing job today. With the evidence we have and the new leads you have given us, the prisons will be hosting rather a lot of new inmates shortly.'

'What about the warehouse next door?' Sean asked, 'the food place, were they involved?'

'No, not at all.' Answered the Chief Inspector. 'They mass produce school dinners everything from shepherd's pie, lasagne and the meal that provided the vital clue, curry, which has the strongest smell of them all. The owner had no idea as to what was going on next door, he was horrified. They were investigated of course, but totally innocent.'

'Thanks.' Sean muttered quietly.

Everyone stood. Wires were unplugged, cameras packed away, and finally, goodbyes were said.

'I'll be in touch shortly, and thank you for your cooperation,' said Chief Constable Akhtar to Meg.

'I hope you'll be in touch soon to tell me you have located and arrested your corrupt officers.' Meg answered coldly.

Danah Akhtar simply nodded in agreement, yet again lost for words at being told what to do by a child.

'Can I talk to you?' asked Jo tentatively to Meg when she heard the door close and the last of the day's visitors had left.

'What exactly do you want to say?' Meg said, her bright blue eyes blazing with anger. 'You set up a centre where kids could be picked up by that gang? You carefully trained the staff to turn a blind eye? You invited paedo politicians and coppers to come and take their pick? You praised those bastards in the newspaper? Everyone is talking about bent coppers leaking information; maybe they should look at who was in charge of setting that place up!' Meg spat. 'Is that how you found me? Or should I say, is that *why* you found me? Are you in on this and been playing me all along? You make me sick! You...'

'*Shut up Meg*!' roared Sean from the doorway, as his wife stood frozen, mouth agape, all colour gone from her face. 'Go to your room. Now!'

Meg flung around and glared at him, ready to hurl accusations at him.

'I suggest you keep your mouth shut and get to your room,' Sean said, his voice now deadly calm, which scared Meg more than the shouting. She stormed out of the room, slamming the door, just as Kayleigh, Tom, and the others entered the house.

'What the hell is going on?' Kayleigh asked, shocked.

'Ask *your* mother!' Meg snapped and barged past them, storming up the stairs and slamming her bedroom door with so much force that the wardrobe rocked. She flung herself onto the bed and punched her pillow over and over. Meg shouted every swear word she could conjure until she finally burst into tears, feeling betrayed and heartbroken.

Kayleigh knocked on Meg's door two hours later and walked in without waiting for an answer.

'Want to tell me what's going on?' she asked Meg.

'No.'

'Okay... anyway, it's dinner time. Dad told me to come to get you.'

'Not hungry.'

'Sorry, kid, but he said either come down on your own, or he'll come and carry you down.'

'He wouldn't dare! And I'm not a kid!'

'Don't push him, Meg. Honestly. I don't know what's happened, but he's fuming, and believe me, he will come and get you.'

Meg swore and punched her pillow again.

'Stop being dramatic! I'm going down now. You will end up downstairs either way, so you might as well come in with me. It'll be easier.'

'Fine.' Meg reluctantly headed to the dining room with Kayleigh.

Chapter Twenty-One

It was a familiar scene; Tom, Wes, Cora, and Jack talked over each other. Only Jo and Sean appeared to be quieter than usual. Kayleigh gave her parents and Meg an anxious look; she knew the police had spent the day at the house. Meg appeared angry at her mum and dad, but gobby as Kayleigh was, this was one occasion where it was definitely better to keep her mouth shut.

Meg sat, refusing to meet anyone's eye, ate a tiny amount, and pushed the rest around her plate until everyone finished. She robotically took her plate into the kitchen and watched until no one was looking, then sneaked back upstairs to her room. Closing the door and locking it, she turned to the bed and jumped as she realised she wasn't alone.

'You can't hide from me forever,' Jo said calmly as she patted the spot next to her on Meg's bed. 'Come and sit down.'

'No!' Meg said and turned towards the door.

'We either have this conversation here, privately, or I will follow you, and I certainly don't want it to turn into a huge family argument. Do you?'

Meg stood at the door for a while, refusing to answer, and finally walked over to the chair and sat down.

'Do you honestly believe I would be involved in the sexual abuse of children?' Jo began. 'I am not asking for an argument. I want the answer to that one question.'

Though she didn't show it, Meg was startled by Jo's tone of voice; it was distant, cold, almost professional.

Meg looked at her feet, her head spinning. The images of those men outside the youth club where she and Jo first met and built the foundations of their relationship swam in front of her eyes. Jo's image and quote in the newspaper praising those people. Those monsters of her dreams, who came alive during her flashbacks, made her feel physically sick.

'Why were you with those men? Why did you tell the newspaper how great they were?' she muttered, still looking at her feet and refusing to make eye contact.

'A member of parliament, city councillors, and a senior police officer who all worked to obtain funding for the youth centre is who I was praising. How on earth was I to know or even suspect their true motives? How could I possibly have known what disgusting people they are? I was as shocked as you when you saw the newspaper and identified them, and I'm horrified and disgusted I worked with them.'

'You worked with them?'

'Yes. I'm Head of Youth Services; we were trying to secure funding for a youth centre.

'They helped to raise the money, and I set the centre up.'

'For a place for girls to be picked up and mauled by those perverts.'

Jo remained silent. If Meg didn't believe her or lost trust in her, she knew their relationship was over no matter what she said or did.

Meg stood up and looked out of the window. She thought back to the awful night when she'd climbed out of it and been picked up by Leon or Ewan or whoever he was. She recalled learning that Jo had spent five days and nights at her bedside in the hospital.

Was it to shut me up in case I talked when I woke up? Meg thought. And when Jo had taken her home the night she first found her, was it so that she could tell the gang where she was? Then Meg remembered the hugs, the times they'd laughed, Jo getting into bed next to her and stroking her hair. Supporting her through the horrendous abortion and standing up for her the way she had against those evil surgeons and nurse who had treated her like she was a nobody.

Why would Jo have taken her on walks so they could talk? Supported her when having flashbacks? Cared if she ate or drank? Jo could have easily handed her over to the gang at any point. Instead, she'd kept her safe and made her feel loved.

Meg turned and looked at Jo.

'No,' she said.

'No, what?'

'No, I do not believe you had anything to do with those men. I'm wrong. I was angry, confused, tired, and when your name came up, it terrified me. I'm sorry for what I said, I really am.'

'Okay,' said Jo.

'Okay?'

'Okay. Come and sit down. We need to talk.'

Meg walked to the bed and sat next to Jo. 'The more I've thought about this,' Jo began, 'especially since seeing the newspaper article, the more I also believe it's not only the police who have a leak.

'We know some local councillors are involved, an MP. Who else? And where is all of the information coming from? It can't possibly be just a couple of bent police officers.'

'I think so too, but about what I said....'

'What do you want me to say, Meg? It hurt me a lot. I was accused of horrific crimes by someone I love dearly. Of course I was upset, but it doesn't mean I don't understand why you jumped to such a conclusion. Obviously, it devastated you, seeing me with those animals. You've worked so hard to lower your defences and trust me, and I imagine it's probably one of the hardest things you've done, trusting Sean and me. However, you did it, as scary as it was, and still is, I suspect.'

'A bit,' Meg said. 'I trust you both, but yes, it still scares me sometimes.'

'Of course it does. Trust doesn't happen quickly. I'm aware that you didn't mean what you said. You'd had yet another terrible day talking about everyone who has hurt and abused you. Then suddenly, I pop up, in the middle of the most powerful of the lot of them. Obviously, it shook your world. It shook mine, and I'm not the victim of those crimes. I was horrified and devastated and have been questioning myself for hours. Was there anything I missed? Did I do anything to enable them? Why didn't I realise that such a large amount of money for such a project is something very scarce indeed? Of course I've been blaming myself, so why on earth wouldn't you, who has been abused or abandoned by so many adults, doubt me? It is pretty damming evidence. In your position, I would have thought the same. I'm sorry Sean shouted at you, though. I wasn't happy with him.'

'He was looking out for you. Anyway, I deserved it. I was out of order. Has he calmed down now? I didn't look at him at dinner. Would he really have carried me downstairs?'

'What? No! Why do you ask?'

'Kayleigh said if I didn't come down, he'd carry me down.'

'We asked her to persuade you any way she could, but no. Sean didn't threaten anything. That girl...'

'How come you ended up in the newspaper photo?' Meg asked suddenly, changing the subject.

'Maybe I was caught by accident in the background, but it feels unsettling. It could be a huge coincidence. Too much of a coincidence.'

'Do you think you were set up?'

'Possibly. I didn't know you at that point, so it couldn't have been about you. Sean is the Director of Children's Services; I am the Head of Youth Services. If those committing these crimes wanted some type of contingency plan, if the victims talked, then we may have been suspects. That's only one theory, but no one expected you to come and live with us and tell us about what happened. So, you coming to us either would have thwarted their plan or helped it. I have no idea, but something is not right, and I intend to find out what.'

'We!'

'What?'

'We will find out.'

'Deal,' said Jo.

'Don't suppose any hugs are going?'

Jo looked at Meg with an unfathomable expression.

'I mean, only if you want to,' Meg began. 'I'm sorry about what I said. I didn't mean it. If you don't want me anymore, I understand. I wouldn't want someone who accused me of being...'

Jo held her hand up to silence Meg, whose words were tumbling out and falling over themselves. 'That's the first time you have ever asked for a hug,' Jo said, smiling.

'Oh, I'm sorry. I...'

'Meg, shut up!' said Jo, putting her arms around the girl and squeezing her for dear life. There was a knock at the door, and Sean came in, happy the pair were hugging.

'I'm sorry, Sean,' Meg said. 'I was shocked. It took me back to those people who got me to trust them and then used me... It scared me. I'm sorry.'

'I understand,' Sean replied. 'I shouldn't have shouted at you.'

'Yes, you should. I deserved it.'

He sat on the bed next to Jo and Meg, put his head into his hands, and sighed. 'This is huge. Police, politicians, international child trafficking, people planted in kids' homes and who knows where else. I'm not surprised you don't trust anyone, Meg. I don't think I do anymore.'

'Me neither,' Jo replied. 'I'm not even sure if I want to go back to my job. Who knows how big this web is?'

'I suggest we go away, the three of us. Somewhere hot and calm when the others have gone back to university. Let's not make any decisions until then. We all need a break,' Sean announced, and Jo nodded in agreement.

They all jumped at another knock on the door. 'Come in,' Sean said.

Kayleigh entered, followed by Gina Phillips. 'I'm not here on official business, Meg. Don't worry. Jo called me earlier and told me, in the strictest confidence, about your interview. No wonder they wanted to get rid of me; they were scared I was building a relationship with you and gaining your trust. They would have been terrified you would identify top police officers such as the Assistant Chief Constable.'

'I can't believe I didn't recognise the MP,' Meg said. 'I watch the news and follow politics.'

'It isn't your fault! Anyway, he was arrested an hour ago,' Gina said. 'The newspapers will be full of it tomorrow. Actually, the news at ten may have gotten there in time.'

'How did they find out?' Meg asked. Gina looked at Kayleigh, who grinned.

'Kayleigh!' Jo said threateningly.

'Just following orders,' Kayleigh said.

'Following orders? Whose orders? What do you mean?' Jo asked, sounding tired and confused.

'Probably not the best time to tell you, but, Gina, sorry, the Inspector and I have talked quite a lot, and I'm going to police training college when I graduate.'

'*What*!' Sean shouted. 'You almost got shot when you arrived home and called them a bunch of fascists with small...'

'Well, things change, Dad. I had no idea what to do after my degree, and Gina said...'

'I said Kayleigh is an ideal candidate to join the force. Brave, independent, fearless, but also kind and compassionate. Don't worry; now my job is secure, I'll ensure that she's posted to wherever I am. I'll keep a close eye on her.' Gina finished, looking at Jo.

'I'm confused,' Jo said. 'How does this involve the newspapers?'

'Gina and I had a chat too, Mum. Seeing as these guys love being in the press so much, we didn't see any harm in upping their coverage. A few calls from an unregistered mobile on a withheld number to news desks all over the country will certainly have done the trick.'

Jo shook her head in bewilderment. 'I've got one child blackmailing the Chief Constable and another tipping off the press. Any idea what the others are up to?' she asked Sean.

'No idea, and I don't want to know.' He checked his watch. 'Shall we go and check the news?'

Kayleigh's calls had worked; the top story on the ten o'clock news was: *MP ARRESTED IN CHILD ABUSE SCANDAL*. The newsreader went on to announce that a member of parliament, two city councillors, and several senior police officers had been arrested and detained for questioning in their role in an alleged child sexual exploitation gang.

The images showed the MP being taken out of his home in handcuffs. No attempt had been made to shield him from the cameras. Then the cameras swung around to Chief Constable Danah Akhtar, much to the surprise of everyone in the room. She gave a passionate statement about no one being above the law and stated that they were following a legitimate line of enquiry.

'She's good. Doesn't miss a trick,' Gina said grimly. 'Making herself the face of the investigation. No doubt she'll come out of this smelling of roses.'

Meg glared at the repulsive politician on TV, his hair slicked back and his fat cheeks bright red in front of the glare of the cameras. Meg recalled the foul smell of whisky on his breath and his fat, hairy body.

'What's next?' she asked, shaking herself quickly out of the memory she was sinking into. 'I mean, what do I have to do next?'

'Nothing until the trial; it'll be sometime next year,' said Gina.

'There is one thing,' Sean said. 'Your meeting with Steph about us adopting you is in a few days; New Year's Eve, in fact. Nothing to worry about. She'll ask you what you want and sort out the paperwork and court documents.'

Meg said nothing. 'Everything okay?' Jo asked, concerned.

'Yeah. I don't like that Steph. But I've never liked any of my social workers. I don't trust them.'

'Well, you're wrong this time,' Sean said. 'Steph is dedicated and loyal and makes my job a lot easier. It's one meeting, so go along with it. Nothing formal. No video cameras, no recordings, just the two of you chatting about being adopted.'

'Fine. Still don't like her,' Meg muttered under her breath so only Gina heard.

'Where will the meeting be, Sean?' Gina enquired.

'Here, at the house. We'll make sure only Steph and Meg will be in. The rest of us will make ourselves scarce until we get a call to say they've finished.'

Gina nodded. 'Well, I hope it goes well, Meg. I'd better go. I'll see you all soon, and Kayleigh, best not to call any more of your future colleagues fascists!'

'Yes, Ma'am!' she said with a grin. 'Come on. I'll show you out.'

The next few days were relatively calm in comparison to the past few months. Meg played football with Jack at the park, and he was impressed with her skills and promised to ask his parents to look up a local team for her. The family all hung out together, mainly peacefully. Watching films, eating, playing board games, going for walks, and simply being with each other.

Meg could see Jo and Sean were in their element and was happy they'd become slightly more relaxed. She knew the past month had been incredibly hard for them too, and she felt sad and guilty at what she had put them through. Meg attempted to discuss it with them and was firmly told she was not the guilty party. Jo said if she re-lived the evening and found Meg in the car park again, she would do precisely the same thing.

Sean agreed. 'And you also achieved what I thought was impossible.' 'What?' Meg asked, puzzled.

'Ensured that things are crazier around here than they normally are when everyone is home!' He grinned and received a dig in the ribs from his wife.

There was a lot of wedding talk as Wes and Tom planned their big day. Tom asked Kayleigh to be his best woman, and she was delighted to accept and had already begun to plan the stag do and her speech, both of which worried her parents.

Jo was going to give Tom away, and Sean was doing the honours with Wes. Cora even agreed to be a groomsmaid.

Meg noticed Cora still looked pale and anxious. Despite the way Cora had treated her initially, Meg understood and felt sorry for her. Cora was so different to her siblings and parents in every way, apart from looks.

Meg looked around at the rest of her soon-to-be new family, one she'd always craved, and now she had one, it definitely wasn't what she'd expected.

Meg had always wanted a mum who wanted her, loved and cared about her. But she had never considered having a father. She remembered how terrified she was when she first met Sean. A great hulk of a man who turned out to be so gentle and kind to her, and yet highly protective. She doubted Ewan would ever forget him, she thought with a satisfied grin.

Meg glanced at Kayleigh, who a true force of nature. She wondered if Kayleigh would manage being bossed around in the police force. She was so outspoken, fierce, and courageous. However, Meg hoped no one gave her a gun.

Tom and Wes were content; happiness radiated from them. Meg had never been to a wedding and was looking forward to the big day.

Jack was spread on the floor, as usual; he was, as his mum said that day on the beach, a quiet man who didn't give a lot away, quite the opposite of his big sister, but Meg adored him. They were all crazy, she thought. She remembered the fighting, Kayleigh placing the house into darkness, the vomit-fest, as it was now referred to. She would be sad when they all went back to university.

'Are you okay, Meg?' asked Jo, who had been observing the girl as she examined the family.

Meg smiled. 'I will be, especially after I've being dragged to that therapist you keep nagging me about.'

Jo returned Meg's smile and put her arm around her.

'Thank you,' Jo whispered.

'New Year's Eve!' Sean said suddenly. 'Let's make it a good one. Meg's adoption interview will be complete. Kayleigh will be joining the police next year, God help them! My son is getting married and will no doubt spend every last penny we have, so I think we should have a party while we can still afford it!'

'Will the police allow visitors?' Jo queried, ignoring her husband's attempt at humour.

'Can't see why not. We'll compile a guest list and give it to them. All agreed?'

'It's a bit short notice, Dad. New Year's Eve is tomorrow,' Kayleigh said. 'We could go to the pub.'

'I think the armed guards might be a bit of a dampener down the local.' Jack laughed.

'Fair point,' said Jo, picking up a notepad and pen. 'Let's get some names together, ring around in the morning, and give the guest list to the police by lunchtime.'

'Put Steph on the list, will you, Jo? She's really come through for us and been so helpful to Meg, despite being thrown in at the deep-end with a kid she didn't know a thing about. I want to express our thanks.'

Jo scribbled Steph's name down and began to add others that were thrown at her.

Cora sat up with a start and opened her mouth to speak before closing it again. She looked around the room frantically, her eyes finally settling on Kayleigh.

'Are you okay, Cora?' her sister asked.

'Yes. Feeling a bit restless. Fancy a walk?'

'Now! It's freezing.'

Cora looked into Kayleigh's eyes desperately, as though trying to communicate something silently.

'Okay, yes. Let's go for a walk,' Kayleigh answered curiously.

Both of them said a hurried goodbye and left the room. Jo and Sean swapped confused looks but let the two of them go for their walk uninterrupted.

Meg sneaked out of the room, unnoticed over the noise of random guest names being shouted at their mum and then arguing about each other's choices. She knew there would be a big argument. Still, not a nasty one or anything scary. It would probably be amusing, but she was shattered and slowly took herself to her room. She looked at herself in the bathroom mirror, which confirmed that she was exhausted. It had been yet another long and painful week. The day of the interview had been horrendous, and the horror of seeing Jo with those men still lingered. Meg felt incredibly guilty about accusing Jo. But the scene in the newspaper scared her nearly as much as all the horrendous things that had happened to her over the past six months.

She lay on her bed fully clothed and tried to block out the memories that were threatening to surface. She counted every crack in the ceiling, listened carefully to the sounds the wind caused, and finally allowed her heavy eyes to close.

CHAPTER TWENTY-TWO

Meg woke early on New Year's Eve. The sun shone through her curtains; she opened them to a bright and frosty morning. Despite the time, she could hear movement downstairs and went to investigate.

'What's going on?' she asked sleepily, entering the kitchen.

'Mother, Queen of Shopping Lists, is on the rampage,' said Kayleigh. 'She's already ripped Dad's drinks list up and is wandering around somewhere talking manically to herself about mini sausage rolls; she's obsessed.'

As if to prove Kayleigh's point, Sean roared: 'I swear to God, Jo, if you say mini sausage roll one more time...'

'Oh, shut up, Sean! Go and clean the house!'

Kayleigh switched on the kitchen radio, and Meg grinned; at one time, hearing them argue and shout would have terrified her. Now, it was just funny.

Jo came storming into the kitchen, glaring at her list, and walked straight into Kayleigh, bouncing her from the doorway.

'*Mum*!'

'Why would you stand in the doorway? Go dress. We are all going shopping soon!'

'Morning,' Jo said to Meg without pausing for breath. 'Have you had breakfast?'

'Yep. Had a few mini sausage rolls,' Meg said, grinning.

'Don't you start!' ordered Sean, marching into the room. 'Who even eats mini sausage rolls nowadays?'

'I'm not coming shopping, Mum,' Kayleigh said. 'I told you earlier, but you kept on talking about mini sausage rolls!'

'Next person to say mini sausage roll is not coming to the party!' Sean declared.

'You are coming, Kayleigh,' Jo said. 'The house needs to be empty while Meg and Steph have their interview.'

'Yes, and as I explained earlier, when you were ranting about... the food that can no longer be mentioned, I am meeting Gina.'

'Gina? The Inspector? Why? She's coming to the party tonight!'

'Mum, sit down!' Kayleigh ordered and quickly snatched the list from her frazzled mother. 'Firstly, I know you're stressed about Meg's interview, so stop talking about 1970s finger-food. Secondly, I explained earlier, I'm meeting Gina to discuss the police force. She's offered to give me some practical advice. So, will you please have a cup of tea, decaf! And chill out. It is seven a.m., and you are driving everyone mad!'

Kayleigh put the kettle on, leaving her gobsmacked mother to process her words.

'Wow, like mother, like daughter,' Sean said. 'Kayleigh, will you teach me how you did that before going back to uni?'

'Don't you start either, Dad,' Kayleigh said menacingly. 'Sit down and have a drink!'

The four of them sat at the breakfast bar, the atmosphere calming as silence fell.

'Morning,' came Cora's sleepy voice as she stumbled into the kitchen. 'Why is everyone shouting about sausages?'

'Don't ask,' Kayleigh replied. 'Mum has gone mad!'

'How do you feel about today's meeting, Meg?' Jo asked, ignoring Kayleigh.

'Not as nervous as you, I don't think. You seem to be a bit, er...'

'Manic?' Sean offered.

'I'm nervous for you,' Jo conceded. 'I wish I could stay. Not in the room, just be in the house. I don't understand why we all have to go out.'

'Procedure.' Sean said. 'Normally it would be done at the office. But here is easier, given the circumstances. But I'd also rather stay here than face a supermarket on New Year's Eve with my wife!'

Jo ignored him and continued to worry.

'There's nothing to stress about, Mum,' Kayleigh said confidently. 'Everything will be fine.'

Jo nodded, but remained distracted. There was something, a fleeting memory that came and left so quickly she couldn't remember it.

'Which room are you meeting this woman in?' Kayleigh asked. 'I'll go give it a quick tidy so that Mum doesn't stress.'

'Dining room, I think.'

'I'll go sort it,' Kayleigh said, jumping up.

'I'll give you a hand,' Cora offered, moving towards the door.

'Great, and Meg, make sure those two behave!' Kayleigh instructed, nodding to her parents.

Meg laughed. 'I'm going to miss her when she goes back to university,' she said to Jo and Sean.

'Life will certainly be quieter,' Sean added, sighing. 'And I can't believe Cora and Kayleigh are tidying up together, happily!'

Meg had her breakfast while Jo completed her shopping list more calmly, and everyone got ready for the big shop. Kayleigh left at nine-thirty, wishing Meg luck with her interview with Steph, as did Jack, who announced that under no circumstances would he join his family in a supermarket and instead was going for a long run. 'I've got my mobile. Just text when all is clear,' he said and left before his mum could stop him.

'I'm going for a walk, Mum,' Cora said. 'I can't cope with the crowds in the supermarket. Do you mind?'

'Of course not.' Jo looked at her anxiously. 'Please call me if you need me.'

'I will, now go!'

Sean herded Tom and Wes into his car and left just before ten, and Jo sat in the dining room with Meg, waiting.

'Maybe a little late now,' Jo began, 'but do you definitely want this? Want us? It is forever, you know?'

'I know, and I do,' Meg stated with absolute certainty. 'Do you still want me?' A slight quiver came into her voice.

'More than anything. Don't ever forget that I love you, got it?'

'Got it!' answered Meg as they heard a knock on the dining-room door, and Steph entered.

'Good morning,' she chirped, and sat down opposite Meg.

'Right, I'll leave you to it,' said Jo, standing and giving Meg a kiss on the head. 'Just call when you're finished.'

'Will do,' Steph replied, smiling.

'Jo!' Meg said as the woman was leaving. '

Yes?'

'I love you too. See you later.'

Jo smiled and hurried out of the room. She felt jumpy and on edge and couldn't work out why. This was the easy part, so why did it feel wrong? She reluctantly left the house, checking the armed guards were still in place, and drove off in her own car to meet Sean.

'How are you, Meg?' Steph asked.

'Good, thanks.'

'Good? You've been through so much over the last six months. Are you sure adoption is what you want? It's hard for children to settle into a family home after they've been in care, and especially when they have suffered such things as you have.'

'I'm fine,' Meg said shortly. 'I've agreed to see a therapist, and those men will be on trial soon and hopefully go to prison for a long time.'

'About the trial. You know you will be called as a witness, don't you?'

'Yep. Someone, I can't remember who, told me about special measures like taking wigs off and stuff; it sounded a bit weird. I don't want to do it by video link or behind a curtain; I want to see them and tell my story. I'm not hiding anymore.'

'That's very brave, but coming face-to-face with your abusers, rapists… even Leon will be there. Will you be able to face the man who kidnapped and almost killed you?'

Meg's insides froze; luckily, years of practice had taught her not to show fear, and her face kept the same expression.

'I'm not looking forward to it,' she replied, keeping the same easy tone of voice, though her every instinct was screaming at her to run. Steph had not been told her kidnapper was called Leon, and there was no way she could possibly know his name unless...

'Of course, it might not go to trial,' Steph said.

'Why?' asked Meg, trying to remain casual.

'Witnesses change their minds all the time. Sometimes the details become too foggy; other times, they can't face it and change their mind at the last minute. Do you think you will change your mind?'

'I hope not,' Meg replied, staring directly into Steph's eyes. 'They are evil and deserve locking up, and so does anyone who has helped them.'

Jo and Sean were at the busy supermarket entrance. They all had a trolley each. Jo had planned the trip in meticulous detail, giving them a list and an aisle each. It was planned with military precision. 'Get in, get what we want, and get out!' Jo ordered. 'No messing about and *do not* buy anything that is not on the list!'

'Seriously, Mum...' Tom began, and was quickly silenced by his mother's *death glare,* as they all secretly called it.

'Right, go!' Jo said, and everyone dived into the store with their trolleys and dispersed in different directions. Walking past the newspaper stand, Jo saw the photographs taken for the local newspaper were now in every single national publication.

Jo hesitated and looked at the headlines. "*Institutionalised Corruption?*" screamed one. "*Parliament to Prison?*" another asked. Finally, "*Cop a load of this!*" another newspaper, which Jo had never read in her life, stated. Again, it showed a photograph of the member of Parliament in handcuffs being led out of his house. A sub-headline said, "*More exclusive images inside!*" Jo picked the paper up and opened it; she recoiled as she saw herself in the photograph outside the youth centre that Meg had spotted during her interview.

She thought about that day. She'd been so proud they had finally managed to raise funds and open the centre. The opening day was deemed a huge success; it was called an achievement for the city by the local press. There were other photos from the opening day, ones Jo had not previously seen. She glared with anger at the MP talking to the now-suspended Deputy Chief Constable Ian Jones, along with...

419

Jo froze and looked closer at the image. She took out her phone and rang Sean.

'I'm going as fast as I can!' he answered.

'Come to the newspaper stand, *now*!' she shouted, scaring passers-by, and ended the call.

Back at home, Meg knew something was very wrong, and she also knew that there was no way out, not without a fight. The armed officers were at the front door; she doubted they would hear her if she shouted, and what would she shout? She began to doubt herself; maybe Sean had told Steph Ewan's real name.

'Some men escaped during the warehouse raid,' Steph said. 'Even after the trial, you may not be safe, or worse, you may put Jo and Sean in danger. They may threaten to kill them to shut you up, and you won't have armed guards forever. Are you sure you want to put Jo and Sean in that position? They will be looking over their shoulders for the rest of their lives. At least if you go back to a kids' home, there will be no one there you love. No one who can be threatened to get at you.'

'Why are you so keen for me to go back into care?' Meg asked, still attempting to remain casual.

'I'm here to work out what's best for you, Meg. I think the best thing for you, and Jo and Sean, is to go back to a children's home and forget about giving evidence. There is no need to have it dragging over everyone, is there?'

'Dragging over everyone?'

'Questions will be asked in court, Meg. Who requested the funds for the youth centre? Jo, that's who. Who appeared behind the men accused in the newspaper? Jo! More importantly, whose name was on the invitations that were sent to those men?'

'Let me guess,' said Meg. 'Jo's.'

'Wrong! The invitations were sent by the Director of Children's Services, so the court will see Sean invited them along.

'Well, I did, using his email address, but who can prove it? Bit of a coincidence? That's why you should come with me today and never see Jo, Sean, or the rest of the family again. We'll move you to another part of the country; you can start afresh.'

It was the smile that did it. The slimy, two-faced smirk of Steph's she'd always hated, which now appeared at the end of her despicable speech that made Meg stop the pretence.

'No doubt I'll be involved in an "accident" while moving to another part of the country and not survive if I go with you. I've never trusted you. Social workers are not my favourite people, but you are a smarmy, evil, two-faced cow. You've set Sean and Jo up nicely, I'll give you that.'

Steph sat back in her chair and looked at Meg; her eyes had no emotion whatsoever, but her smile was manic. 'Your poker face is not as good as you think it is, Meg. I spotted how you reacted when I said *Leon* instead of *Ewan.'*

'You've been a part of this all along, haven't you?'

'Sean is incapable of doing his job,' Steph continued, ignoring Meg. 'He was always quick to take up offers of assistance. Did you never wonder why you didn't get a new social worker when yours went off to have a baby? I saw to that, though Sean will be landed with the blame, of course. Further evidence against him.

'When you ran away from Crookshaws, I put myself on the duty rota. A few drops of something nasty in someone's cup of tea is enough to make them think they have food poisoning. Then the call came. I must admit, it threw a slight spanner in the works when Sean's wife found you. She almost recognised me at the police station as I was at the youth centre's opening, but we turned it to our advantage.

'When I told the gang where you were living and you were under police surveillance, well, it was easy. Our friend, Liz, gave the night shift their special sedative sandwiches, and all Leon had to do was wait until the officers passed out. He certainly got a shock when you climbed through the bedroom window. I've got to admire how quick-thinking he was,' Steph continued; it appeared as though she was thinking out loud and not talking to Meg.

'Shame, he was seconds from killing you. So close. Sadly for Gina Phillips, she started to become a little too close for comfort. How did you stop her from getting the sack? I always wondered. We set her up perfectly, and Liz destroyed the evidence of your interviews. Come on, what did you do?'

Meg said nothing and stared with disgust at the woman in front of her. 'How could you do that? To young girls?'

'Money, of course,' she said, as though it was the most obvious thing ever. '£3000 per new girl. All I had to do was look through the files, go to the kids' home on a compliance visit, and then hand the information over. Yours was easy. We already had Javeed and Peter in place, but I still got a nice payday.

'So, what with Sean not aware that his department had anything to do with the youth centre and Jo being married to him, it was perfect that you did end up with them. We have laid an evidence trail that will implicate them into setting up the youth centre as a trap to provide "fresh meat" to our friends.

'It will also be easy to prove they were the ringleaders and forced you to give false statements. We will be using that evidence, and they will go to prison, but isn't it better than a knife to the neck one cold, winter's evening, just like poor little Jenny Evans?'

'*You evil bitch*!' Meg shouted. 'There is no way a few invitations and Jo asking for a youth centre will prove they were involved.'

'As I said, we've made evidence trails. Fake evidence, but it will work. Chief Constable Akhtar will want a quick result, and we've nicely laid everything out for her. She isn't someone who likes to think outside the box; she likes quick results, not prolonged investigations. Anyway, that is not your problem; if you refuse to leave with me right now, then you will be leaving in a body bag.' Steph pulled a long hunting knife out of her bag and slammed it onto the dining table. The metallic sound of the blade echoed around the room.

'You'll be caught,' Meg said, her eyes not leaving the knife.

'My cover will be blown, but I will simply kill you, leave, and go to the safe house where my colleagues are waiting; the ones who escaped. So, what's it to be? Die here and have Jo and Sean find your body, or die away from here? You are not getting out of this alive.'

'What's the matter?' Sean asked his wife impatiently as he reached the newspaper stand. 'I'm sticking to the list!'

Jo showed him the newspaper. 'Why was Steph at the youth centre?' he asked, puzzled.

'You tell me. It was your office that sent the invitations.'

'We didn't. I was told the councillors were doing it.'

'Who told you that?'

'Steph!' Sean replied, looking ashen.

'We need to leave. Get in my car. Ring your office, tell IT to look into who emailed the invitations and tell HR to email Steph's details, everything down to her application form.'

'Where are we going?'

'Home, move!'

They both ran from the supermarket. '*Tom*!' Sean bellowed to his son and then threw his car keys at him, '*Got to go*!'

Sean got on the phone as he and his wife sprinted across the car park. Jo spun out of her parking space, causing many horns to blare at them and several cars to swerve. Jo got onto the main road and put her foot down.

'Thanks,' Sean said. 'Put me through to HR immediately.'

'What is it?' Jo asked.

'My email address sent out the invitations,' he said anxiously to Jo, just as an HR worker picked the phone up.

He issued his demands. 'I want the file within five minutes,' he snapped and ended the call.

'Jo, what the hell is going on now?'

She didn't answer and concentrated on the road, her face fraught with fear.

'Have you decided?' Steph sneered at Meg and wrapped her hand around the handle of the knife. 'Where do you want to die?'

'Nowhere, thank you. I kicked Leon's arse quite nicely. I reckon I could take you out even easier.'

'So be it.' She sighed, standing up and approaching Meg. Steph hesitated slightly when Meg did not move a muscle. 'You are making this too easy for me.' She raised the knife above her head and plunged it down towards Meg's wrist.

Meg moved swiftly. The knife wedged into the table, exactly in the place her wrist had been a split-second earlier. She jumped to her feet, took her chair in her hands, and swung it full force into Steph's head; the woman went flying and landed with an enormous crash.

The dining room door flew open and armed officers came in, pointing their guns at Steph, screaming at her not to move. They were followed by Gina and, most surprisingly, Kayleigh and Cora.

'What the hell...' Meg began, but was interrupted.

'Thank God you're here,' Steph wailed. 'This child is insane. All I did was try to see if she wanted to be adopted, and she attacked me with a chair.'

'Oh dear,' Gina said. 'Did it hurt?'

'Well, of course!'

'Good! Shame she didn't hit you harder.'

'What! This child attacked me; I want her arrested immediately!'

'Self-defence is not a crime,' Gina said. 'Especially when someone has threatened to murder you with a knife. Don't bother denying it; we have cameras all over this room. Oh, and speaking of friends, thank you for telling us about Liz, the former PC Everett, who has now been arrested.'

'None of the video footage can be used,' spat Steph. 'Your position is compromised, so you're not allowed to authorise it.'

'No, but I am,' said Chief Constable Akhtar, entering the room. 'And I did. Gina came to me and told me there were concerns about you and your trustworthiness.

I did a bit of digging, and well, you have been working hard, haven't you? Ever since the days when you were a secretary for a city councillor, who went on to become a certain member of parliament; it's nice you stayed in touch. Gina, would you like to do the honours?'

'Certainly, Ma'am.' Gina said, and formally arrested Steph, taking great pleasure in handcuffing her wrists tightly. 'Now, take this thing out of here!' she said to her officers, who dragged the woman out of the building kicking and screaming, just as Jo and Sean came sprinting in.

'What took you so long?' Kayleigh said.

Chapter Twenty-Three

Gina and Danah Akhtar remained behind for a debrief with Sean, Jo, Kayleigh, Cora, and Meg.

'I'm very impressed with your daughters, Mr and Mrs McGloughlin; talk about cool under fire,' said the Chief Constable.

'Will someone tell us what the hell has happened?' Sean snapped. 'By the way, Steph...'

'Is a member of the paedophile ring. She used her position to find girls for those animals,' Kayleigh snarled. 'Also, she tried to set you and Mum up to take the blame if the police found out. She also used to be the secretary of our Right Honourable perverted member of parliament. Oh, and PC Everett, Liz, was the leak at the police station.'

'And Steph tried to kill me, but I smacked her with a chair,' Meg added.

'Yes, but we were watching from the surveillance van the whole time, and as soon as she moved with the knife, we were in here within seconds. Meg managed to strike first,' added Gina.

'Please start from the beginning,' pleaded Jo, slumping into a chair.

'I think Cora and Kayleigh should tell the story. Do you agree, Ma'am?' asked Gina. 'I most certainly do.'

Cora took a deep breath, and Kayleigh smiled at her encouragingly. 'When I printed off some of Meg's notes,' Cora began, turning red with embarrassment, 'I read through them all. When you were all talking about the adoption meeting the other night, I remembered seeing Steph's name on some documents from Crookshaws. I wondered why Dad said that Steph knew nothing about Meg before stepping in as Meg's new social worker when we were doing the New Year's Eve guest list. That's when I asked Kayleigh to come out for a walk with me.'

'When Cora told me,' Kayleigh began, 'it bothered me that Steph never mentioned she'd met Meg before, or even knew anything about her. Steph is the compliance officer and checks all the files and visits all the homes, so it's possible she would have remembered Meg's name if she had checked her file, and why didn't she say she had been to Crookshaws?

'Also, it got me thinking, why would a 9-5 compliance worker be so keen to go back to anti-social hours and do the on-call rota? After Cora and I talked, we rang Gina.

She was suspicious also, but there was no evidence. Later that evening, when you had all gone to bed, we logged into Dad's work computer...'

'You did what!'

'Come on, Dad. Your password is Arsenal, and your PIN is Mum's date of birth; hardly rocket science. We checked Meg's file and the records for Crookshaws. Steph visited Crookshaws six times this year and signed the official log to mark the home as compliant. She also checked Meg's file twice and initialled it. The last date initialled was the day before Meg said Naz appeared, and he and Simone took her out.

'This is the main social care file. The daily note files from the kids' home are being collected right now. I imagine they'll have Steph's fingerprints all over them. With this in mind, Gina and I requested to see the Chief Constable. Would you like to continue?' Kayleigh asked Danah, who nodded.

'Thank you, Kayleigh. Though nothing was conclusive, something smelled, and I was concerned about Meg being alone in the house with Steph. So, I authorised video surveillance, with only Gina, Kayleigh, and Cora being aware. Before you left this morning, Kayleigh and Cora set up the cameras in the dining room...'

'I thought it was odd you both offering to tidy up,' Jo said.

'Anyway,' continued the Chief Constable, 'as soon as you all left and Steph was in the building, the surveillance van pulled up across the street. I also ordered a team of armed officers to come to the house immediately to be on standby. I'll let Meg tell you the details in time. But Steph was planning on either taking Meg away and killing her, which was her preferred plan or, if Meg refused to leave, which she did, her orders were to kill Meg right here, stroll out as though nothing had happened, and go to the safe house, where the men who escaped from the warehouse raid are hiding.'

'Where is this safe house?' Sean growled.

'We will find out soon; she won't hold up under questioning, and then we think we will have every single surviving member.'

'Think?' asked Jo.

'Yes, but if there are any remaining, they will be running for the hills. We've got them, and we have Steph's recording, basically giving everyone up. The rest will remain in custody until trial, which I will do my utmost to expedite.'

'Can I ask why no one thought to tell Sean or me about this plan?'

'That was down to me, Mum,' Kayleigh said. 'Cora and Gina wanted to tell you, but I knew you wouldn't allow it. If Steph had been legit, all would have been fine, but Meg didn't like her and I listened to her. She's met enough arseholes to be able to spot one a mile away. I'm sorry, but Dad just went on about how great Steph was, and you listened to him. I'm not blaming either of you, I promise, but if I'd told you, then you would have stopped the meeting and Meg, along with both of you, would have still been in danger.'

Kayleigh finished her sentence and sat back and waited for one of her parents to explode; to her surprise, neither did.

'I'm sorry,' Sean said unexpectedly. 'Meg, if I had any inkling at all that she was a sly, duplicitous, evil person, you know I would have done something, don't you?'

Meg nodded but glanced at Jo; her reaction was the one she was most afraid of, but if she did shout at Kayleigh, then Meg would jump to her soon-to-be sister's defence.

Jo felt Meg's eyes on her and met them. Meg had an unnerving sense Jo knew exactly what she was thinking.

'You should have entered as soon as you saw the knife,' Jo finally said to Gina. 'Meg was placed in danger, and you could have prevented that. What if Steph hadn't stabbed the table and plunged the knife straight into Meg? You wouldn't have got to her in time.'

'No, we wouldn't,' Gina replied. 'I ordered the *go* as soon as Steph approached Meg, and everyone charged in. Meg got her first, actually, but we would have had her. I've been doing this for a very long time. I know what I'm doing.'

Just then, something similar to the sound of horse's hooves came trampling through the hallway.

'Where the hell did you go?' demanded Wes, glaring at Sean and Jo, not seeing Gina, Danah, Cora, or Kayleigh behind the door. 'I got to the checkout, and no one was there; Tom had to pay on his emergency credit card, which you said he couldn't use. Tom said you'd run off and thrown your car keys to him. We were bricking it driving home. He's not insured to drive your car, and we nearly hit a...'

Sean jumped up and opened the door fully. 'Chief Constable Danah Akhtar and Inspector Phillips are here,' he said pointedly.

'Sorry,' Wes said. 'Now I think about it, maybe Tom is insured...'

'Let's just say Gina and I are suffering from temporary deafness, shall we?' said the Chief Constable, shocking everyone.

'Sure,' Wes replied sheepishly, as Tom prodded him from behind. 'Er, we don't have enough for the party.'

'No party!' announced Jo. 'Family only. Go and ring everyone now and cancel. There's a list in the kitchen and phone numbers.'

'Mum!' began Tom.

'Do it now!' replied his mother in a dangerously calm voice that had them scurrying to the kitchen.

'Do you believe you've got everyone involved?' Jo asked Gina and Danah. 'This group of people has connections in high places. What if more politicians or police officers are involved?'

'We don't know,' the Chief Constable answered honestly. 'But we do have a lot of people in custody, and we will be asking those questions. Hopefully, someone will break and tell us if others are involved. The offer of a shorter sentence in return for names may be an appealing prospect. Speaking of which, I'd better go. Lots to do! I promise to keep you informed.'

'Yes, me also, I'm afraid,' Gina added. 'There are many interviews to do and even more paperwork to get through. I doubt I'll be seeing my bed for several days.'

'Travel with me, will you, Gina?' asked the Chief Constable. 'I've got an idea for you that's right up your street. Obviously, it will need to come with a promotion, if you'd like to discuss it?'

'Yes, Ma'am. Sounds intriguing,' replied Gina, looking flustered but pleased.

'Happy New Year, everyone,' she said, turning to hug Jo, Sean, Meg, Cora, and then Kayleigh. Then, to everyone's surprise, the Chief Constable did the same before looking at Kayleigh straight in the eye.

'I'll be watching your progress at the police college with interest, Kayleigh McGloughlin; show them what you're made of! You'll get a place, as Gina and I are both providing references for you. So, do not let us down, understand?'

'Yes, Ma'am,' said Kayleigh to her future boss.

'Very good. Almost got you trained already,' Danah replied with a grin on her way out.

'I got her wrong, the Chief Constable.' Meg said, surprised.

'We all did,' Jo said. 'Can we have a chat later?'

'Am I in trouble?'

'Of course not. But let's grab some time when we can, okay?'

'Sure.'

'Good. Sean, will you deal with the kids and whatever they want? I'm just going upstairs for a while.'

'Are you okay, Mum?' Kayleigh asked, concerned.

'I need a bit of time alone. I'll be back shortly.'

Sean went and dealt with Tom and Wes in the kitchen, along with Jack, who had returned from his run. All were in uproar about the party being cancelled. He told them what had happened while they were out, which soon silenced them.

'University is sure going to be dull after this holiday,' Jack said.

'I'm not sure about you,' Sean replied wearily, 'but I'm desperate for dullness, believe me!'

They all worked together and prepared some food; Meg also went to her room to have some quiet time to herself. She needed to think about the day and the fact someone had tried to kill her, again. She had made herself appear much stronger and almost carefree when downstairs, but now, alone, she let herself go. Lying on her bed, she allowed the shock to hit her; she was shaky and felt afraid. The armed guards were still in place, but she doubted they'd be there for much longer. She got up, staggered towards the bathroom, rinsed her face in cold water, and headed down, determined to make it through the evening.

'Come in, Meg,' Jo said as Meg wandered into the kitchen to find Jo and Sean talking quietly with Kayleigh and Cora. 'We were talking about earlier, as you may have guessed. I was saying I couldn't believe Kayleigh and Cora didn't tell Sean or me what was happening, but...'

'They saved my life, Jo. They saved a lot of lives. You can't have a go at them. It's not fair!'

'But,' continued Jo, 'we also said how proud of them we are and how brave they were in protecting you and the whole family.'

'Oh,' Meg said, feeling foolish.

'Oh, indeed,' added Sean tearfully. 'I'm sorry. My mistakes caused part of this. You three are the bravest daughters anyone could wish for. I am so incredibly proud of you all.'

Cora, Kayleigh, and Meg moved towards him and gave him a hug. 'You were manipulated, Dad,' Kayleigh said. 'By a clever, evil gang. You did not make mistakes. They set out to implicate you.'

'Thank you,' Sean answered, impressed and surprised by Kayleigh's mature speech.

'And,' continued Kayleigh, 'if I ever see Steph again, I'm going to beat the living daylights out of her!'

Sean laughed. 'That's more like it. Come on. Let's do something with the evening. We will have plenty of time to talk about what happened. I certainly need to process everything!'

It was a much calmer evening than planned. Everyone was still shocked at what had happened in their dining room hours earlier and kept thinking how much worse it could have been. They watched TV and hugged and wished each other a Happy New Year as Big Ben chimed; everyone then scattered to get drinks and food. Meg was finding the house claustrophobic, so she slipped out of the back door and sat on the step, taking deep breaths of the cold air.

She jumped as the door opened, and Jo stepped outside, carrying a coat and a hat. Despite herself, Meg couldn't help grinning at the hat and put it on without complaint. Jo sat on the step next to Meg and put her arm around the girl.

'I know you're not doing well; you don't have to hide it.'

'Just for tonight, I do. Everyone else has had a rough time too. You especially. Also, I remembered I didn't actually get adopted today. Obviously, I didn't expect the social worker to try to stab me, but she could have filled in the forms first!'

'Please don't joke, Meg. I know it's a self-defence mechanism, but this is too big. Also, I don't care about a piece of paper. It'll be done next week and will be approved, and a judge needs to sign it off. Don't worry.'

'Do you want me to call you Mum?' Meg asked nervously.

'What do you want?'

'Can I stick with Jo? The word "mum" doesn't have nice memories for me. You do, and I don't want to lose them.'

'Of course. You're my daughter, whatever you call me.'

'Thanks.'

They sat in silence for a while, looking at the stars shining brightly onto the cold New Year.

'About the court case, the trial...' Meg began.

'You're going to stand in court, aren't you? No video link. No screen.'

'Only if you give permission.'

'Can I ask why?'

'A few reasons. I've been reading the newspapers on my iPad. Some are being incredibly racist and using me to do it. Men and women of all different colours and backgrounds did this and not one particular race or ethnicity. I don't want them to use me as a weapon to write horrible things. Some blame the political party of the sick MP. It's not about political parties. It's a perverted man, not an entire party. Also, I really want other children who are going through hell to know there is a chance they will be listened to and can hope for justice. But mainly, I want to look at those... can I swear?'

'Just this once.'

'I want to look those bastards in the eye and show them I am not scared of them. I want them to see I beat them.'

'The press still won't be allowed to name you, even if you do it without special measures.'

'I don't care; they will report I stood in court and spoke out. It doesn't stop me from feeling ashamed or from blaming myself, but I need to do it for me.'

'If you need to do that, then I'll give you permission. I don't like it, but I understand. As for feeling ashamed, you have nothing to be ashamed about. But you need time and help to realise that, and you will. One day your paradigm moment will hit you.'

'What moment?'

'Paradigm. It's an emotional "ah-ha" moment that changes the way you see things. Your emotional operating system, if you like, will upgrade and you will understand things in a new light. The therapy and the therapist will help you find that new light, and you *will* find it, Meg. But please don't believe this is all over. Next year, sorry, this year now, won't be easy. You've got a lot to get through; the trial is just one of those things. You have a long, hard road ahead of you. Emotionally and practically, but I'll do what I can and be with you.'

'What about work?'

'I've had enough. I emailed today and officially retired. I have done over thirty years, so I'm entitled to retirement. I want to enjoy the next thirty years or so. I want to be there for you while you grow up, and Cora needs a lot of support at present, so I want to be there for her too. But I want to dedicate my time to those I love from now on. You've helped me to see that more clearly.'

Meg sighed and put her arms around Jo. 'This year, everything you said will be hard, will I be able to do it, do you think? Get through it?'

'Yes, you will get through it, but I need you to promise to tell Sean or me if you feel overwhelmed. The therapy won't be easy either; it will take a long time. All the things you have been through won't go away when those people hopefully go to prison. It's going to be eventful, hard, deeply traumatic at times, but we will also find fun and laughter. We always do.'

'So, what's next?'

Jo sighed and stared up and the stars, their brightness feeling inappropriate and wrong.

She knew what lay ahead for Meg and how hard it was going to be.

'Next,' she said, kissing Meg on the head, 'we buckle up, hold on tight, and fight our way through it together, as a family.'

The End

AFTERWORD

This book is a work of fiction; however, Child Sexual Exploitation is not. It is happening every single day in the UK and throughout the world.

Historically, some public figures have been brave enough to stand up and take a stand against this and have been vilified, even to this day there are politicians and city councils who would rather turn a blind eye than admit that there is a problem.

The children, raped, abused and left with life-long trauma need brave people to have their backs and demand for enquiries within local authorities and ensure that the Police take all measures to support the victims of these heinous crimes whether current or historical.

There are social workers, care home workers, charity workers, therapists, police officers and many, many others who do an outstanding job at protecting the young people in their care. These people who act with integrity, honesty and go above and beyond are the true heroes of our society and recognition for their work is often over-shadowed by the occasional 'bad-apple' who undermine the good people and destroy the young people.

Very few young people find their Jo and Sean and they are left within a system that is underfunded and over-capacity. In this book, Meg received what all children and young people deserve, a loving family, an escape from abuse and justice. Sadly, this is unlikely to happen in real life.

Please see the end of the book for useful links.

ACKNOWLEDGEMENTS

Upon completion of this book, the scariest element was asking people I know to read it and give feedback. However,

I am eternally grateful to those who did and provided some invaluable advice.

My wife Beryl was the first to read the book. Not only did she make notes, point out any errors, but she lovingly ensured that drinks and food would magically appear in front of me while I was engrossed in writing.

Thank you to my children Jade and Nathan, who provided a great deal of feedback. One question by Jade changed the whole story for one character. Thank you.

Also, special thanks to Toni Nel for giving such in-depth and helpful feedback and for being an all-round fabulous person. Jane Fish, who wanted it noted that she completed the book whilst standing as her phone charger wasn't very long. Julia Hinchliffe, who did the first round of corrections and edits. Ruth Alborough for her compassionate feedback for Meg.

Further, thanks to Judith Giles, my youngest child's first-ever teacher, for her enthusiasm for the book and also

Paradigm

for being one of those unforgettable, inspirational teachers. My daughter's journey through life will be significantly enhanced due to those early lessons from Judith.

Also, thanks to Sarah Wheatley and Alison Bainbridge for their time and feedback.

Huge thanks to my very patient and humorous editor, Karen Sanders of Karen Sanders Editing at https://karensandersediting. wordpress.com/

And finally... thank you to an excellent author Nicky Bond, who I have known for nearly forty years, since the age of four! For her advice, answers to the weirdest of questions and being so willing to help. Her latest, fabulous book, Assembling the Wingpeople, has just been released, and you can catch up with her and all of her work at www.nickybondramblings.blogspot.com

USEFUL LINKS

If you, or anyone you know, <u>have been aff</u>ected by any issues in this book then here are some links that may help:

- The Children's Society https://www. childrenssociety.org.uk/what-we-do/our-work/ preventing-child-sexual-exploitation

- NHS: How to spot CSE https://www.nhs.uk/live-well/ healthy-body/how-to-spot-child-sexual-exploitation/

- CSE Police and Prevention https://www. csepoliceandprevention.org.uk

- PACE Parents against child exploitation https://paceuk.info/

- NSPCC https://www.nspcc.org.uk/what-is-child-abuse/ types-of-abuse/child-sexual-abuse/

- Childline https://www.childline.org.uk

Lightning Source UK Ltd.
Milton Keynes UK
UKHW021813181122
412440UK00009B/331